AFTERBURN

AFTERBURN

S. L. VIEHL

A ROC BOOK

ROC
Published by New American Library, a division of
Penguin Group (USA) Inc., 375 Hudson Street,
New York, New York 10014, USA
Penguin Group (Canada), 90 Eglinton Avenue East, Suite 700, Toronto,
Ontario M4P 2Y3, Canada (a division of Pearson Penguin Canada Inc.)
Penguin Books Ltd., 80 Strand, London WC2R 0RL, England
Penguin Ireland, 25 St. Stephen's Green, Dublin 2,
Ireland (a division of Penguin Books Ltd.)
Penguin Group (Australia), 250 Camberwell Road, Camberwell, Victoria 3124,
Australia (a division of Pearson Australia Group Pty. Ltd.)
Penguin Books India Pvt. Ltd., 11 Community Centre, Panchsheel Park,
New Delhi - 110 017, India
Penguin Group (NZ), cnr Airborne and Rosedale Roads, Albany,
Auckland 1310, New Zealand (a division of Pearson New Zealand Ltd.)
Penguin Books (South Africa) (Pty.) Ltd., 24 Sturdee Avenue,
Rosebank, Johannesburg 2196, South Africa

Penguin Books Ltd., Registered Offices: 80 Strand, London WC2R 0RL, England

Published by Roc, an imprint of New American Library, a division of Penguin Group (USA) Inc.

First Printing, August 2005
10 9 8 7 6 5 4 3 2 1

Ｒｏｃ REGISTERED TRADEMARK—MARCA REGISTRADA

LIBRARY OF CONGRESS CATALOGING-IN-PUBLICATION DATA:

Viehl, S. L.
    Afterburn / S.L. Viehl.
        p.   cm.
    ISBN 0-451-46029-4 (hardcover : alk. paper)
    1. Life on other planets—Fiction.   2. Peacekeeping forces—Fiction.   3. Rescue work—Fiction.
I. Title.

PS3622.I45A69   2005
813'.6—dc22   2004030164

Set in Adobe Garamond
Designed by Elke Sigal

Printed in the United States of America

PUBLISHER'S NOTE
This is a work of fiction. Names, characters, places, and incidents either are the product of the author's
imagination or are used fictitiously, and any resemblance to actual persons, living or dead, business estab-
lishments, events, or locales is entirely coincidental.
    The publisher does not have any control over and does not assume any responsibility for author or third-
party Web sites or their content.

There is a real Emily Kim,
and like her counterpart
she is a funny, patient, compassionate,
and very dear friend.

Emily, this book is for you.

AFTERBURN

CHAPTER 1

*B*urn knew he'd be dead in minutes.

No one would believe it had happened this way. Not to Sublieu-tenant Byorn mu Znora, the best gunner in the Pmoc Quadrant Planetary Militia and, quite possibly, the entire Allied League of Worlds. Not while he flew one of the fastest attack strafers ever built by the League's military engineers. Not when he had the most advanced weaponry known to humanoid kind at his fin tips. Not after all the tactical flight training hours he'd logged over the last eight months while working to attain his qualifiers.

Not that any of that mattered now.

Burn's first solo mission as a fighter pilot was about to end in complete disaster, and there was nothing he could do except sit back and wait. It wouldn't be long. The raiders surrounding his ship were Hskt-skt, a reptilian slaver species currently at war with the League. The cold-blooded Hsktskt refused to take military prisoners and immediately executed anything wearing a League uniform. They also used displacer weaponry, which, unlike the League's penetrating pulse-energy ordnance, would use matter-pulverizing energy waves to vaporize Burn and his ship. All very quick and efficient; zero chance for survival.

But I'm not ready to die yet.

If Burn had been in the water, he might have had a chance. Under the waves he could have caught a strong current or darted into a labyrinthine recess of the seamount reef. He was much faster in the water now, too; hardly anyone in his natal pod could keep pace with him anymore.

However, this was not home. This was airless, frigid, unfriendly space. He'd always thought it exciting—the star-pocked blackness had the same lure as the dark water of the dangerous outer currents—but it had no mercy. No, once those blighted, unfeeling Hsktskt lizards blew him up, space would open its endless maw and swallow the explosion, and whatever particles of Burn and the strafer it left behind.

"*Suns* if I'll go like this," he muttered.

Burn's muscles knotted as the ends of his articulated fins hammered his console, searching for options that didn't exist. Adrenaline made him unconsciously strain against the harness specially adapted to fit and secure his alterformed aquatic body within the liquid-filled interior of his ship. He didn't have to see the reflection of his features on the vid screen to know his dark hide had blackened and all of his sharp teeth glittered, white and wholly exposed. Any other 'Zangian catching sight of him like this would have given him a wide berth, and herded everyone else away from him, too. 'Zangian males in a killing rage, rare as those were, became a danger to anything that moved.

Burn felt he had the right to be furious. It wasn't fair. Against one raider, he might have had a chance. With a little luck, he could have dodged two or three.

The array of glittering blips that had appeared out of nowhere pulsed on his display. He counted them again, but none had winked out. Three had converged upon him in one coordinated attack, with twelve more streaming in right behind them.

What would Dair say at this moment? *Fifteen Hsktskt raiders . . . kiss your ass good-bye.*

Burn didn't have an ass, at least not in the humanoid sense, and he'd never kissed anything—'Zangians only used their mouths to feed and fight—but it was a phrase his cousin Jadaira mu T'resa had often used when referring to something completely hopeless. It seemed particularly apt at this moment. At least he had enough time left to alert the ground crew, which had been sending him signals he hadn't answered since encountering the raiders.

"Flight Control, this is the *SeaDance*," Burn transmitted over the secure relay channel, along with his current scanner readings. "Multiple gstek-class raiders have closed on my AO from all sides. I'm cut off."

He could well imagine his controller's reaction; the Hsktskt weren't supposed to be in the patrol squadron's area of operations. Burn's squadron and other League militia forces had chased the reptilian slavers from the Pmoc Quadrant three revolutions ago. Aside from a few stray renegades, and small scouting missions nosing around now and then, the Hsktskt had never returned.

Until today, and wasn't that bloody damn tragic.

"Acknowledged, *SeaDance*," a crisp female 'Zangian voice said over his headgear. His cousin Jadaira, who was also his commander and best friend, had taken over Flight Control from someone Burn wished he could bite hard. "I show you presently at vector eight-six degrees, one-sixteen east, fourteen solar. Confirm track and position."

He checked his alidade panel. "That's my blip."

"Patrol has been dispatched to intercept, which you would know if you'd bothered to answer a signal." Her voice crackled, but with cold anger, not relay interference. "Stop stream and initiate evasive maneuvers. Stand by for patrol ETA."

As she spoke Burn imagined the twenty attack strafers being launched from the surface of his homeworld, Kevarzangia Two. All forty occupants of the strafers were, like him, native 'Zangian aquatics who had also undergone surgical enhancement/alterforming to become League pilots and gunners. Forty SEALs, however, couldn't save his tail, no matter how fast they flew. For all her superior tactical flight experience, neither could Jadaira.

No one could.

"Unable to comply, commander." His scanners showed power spikes coming from five of the raiders' weapons arrays. If he didn't move now, he never would.

"Say again, *SeaDance*."

"They're already flashing teeth, Dair." Not like 'Zangians did, as a warning, but like mogshrikes closing in to fight over a fresh kill. The Hsktskt didn't show what they wouldn't use. Had he been in the water facing actual 'shrikes, the only way Burn could have avoided a messy death was to transform himself into a parasite-eating *mvrey* and attach himself to one of their bellies.

Which, when he thought about it, wasn't such a terrible idea.

Weaponry and propulsion core systems on gstek raiders were located in a heavily shielded section at the back of the underside of the ships. If he replotted his course and slid up from beneath them . . . he began calculating and punching in adjustment vectors.

"Initiate evasive maneuvers at once, Sublieutenant," Dairs ordered.

Burn wouldn't be evading anything, and his cousin knew it. He thought of Dair pacing around the Flight Control deck, her rounded belly undulating with the subtle movements of the unborn child growing inside. His dam had never given him a sibling, but Dair had more than made up for that.

If Burn was going to die, he knew he would miss his little cousin, and the chance to be present at her whelping. He had been fairly convinced that Dair had intended to pick him to be her pup's watchout. But she had her mate, Onkar, now, to watch over her and their podling.

He should say something, though; even under these circumstances a proper farewell to kin was a matter of form. Also, Dair had once been in this position, and he would emulate the dignity she'd shown at the time. "Keep that pup of yours in clear water, Jadaira."

"I'm receiving clutter on your channel," she responded.

His heart swelled. His cousin was giving him the chance to change his mind and not disobey her command. She was also relating what she thought of his plan, which she had probably figured out by now. He'd always been as easy for Dair to read as a star chart.

"No, you're not," he told the panel.

"Sublieutenant, transmit your heading." When he didn't respond, she transmitted a far more irate, "Abort, repeat, abort."

"One spin and I'll haul fin," he lied.

"Blast you, Burn, I gave you a direct—"

He terminated the relay and finished banking the strafer, which had him facing his attackers. Looking death square in the eye was his second-favorite thing to do.

Powering up the weapons array and switching the firing controls to the flight panel dispelled the last of Burn's tension. Saree, the wing leader and one of the few 'Zangians who preferred to fly without a gunner, had taught him a few of her special tricks. And he wasn't dead yet, so he could spend his last minutes of existence doing his first and most favorite thing.

"All right, you big, ugly, uninvited scum eaters." Burn overrode all the ship's control safeties before he engaged targeting and throttled up on the primary engine. A transparent bubble sealed itself around him and glowed faintly red as the targeting/firing sphere began tracking and displaying the raiders' movements. "Here I come."

He pushed the throttle through the stop ring, which forced the engines past their safety limits to produce maximum thrust. The *SeaDance* responded to the hazardous surge of power by shooting directly into the center of the fifteen ships.

Because they had expected him to flee, not to fly directly at them, the Hsktskt were completely unprepared. Their power spikes fluctuated as they compensated for his change of position, but not fast enough to avoid the rapid pulse fire roaring out of his nose cannons.

As Burn fired at three ships, he decided that he liked the targeting/firing sphere. Nicknamed StarFire by its unimaginative but decidedly smug creators from Quadrant Engineering, it was a system the League had hoped to eventually supply for all of its single pilot/gunners like Burn and Saree. For now, StarFire remained in the prelim testing stage. Burn had originally been selected and trained to operate the prototype because he had more experience on weapon systems—as well as confirmed kills—than any gunner in the quadrant.

On his first pass, three raiders' propulsion and weapons systems imploded, taking out two ships and severely crippling the third, which fired back and took out one of Burn's backup engines before its power cells died.

"Bite my flukes," he muttered, bringing the *SeaDance* about for another pass.

It was a genuine shame that this would be the only time Burn would be able to put StarFire through its paces. The prototype responded beautifully, instantly tracking and obeying the eye movements he used to control it, locking without error on multiple targets, and coordinating cannon fire effortlessly. Before the Hsktskt killed him, Burn thought he really should mention to Dair how well the weaponry system operated. The only problem was that if he enabled his transponder, she'd just scream some silly order to retreat at him and he'd spend his last moments of existence arguing with her.

No, Burn had better things to do. Like die, and take a whole clutch of the bastard reptilian slavers with him.

One of the gsteks had an excellent gunner on board; he walloped Burn dead on early in his second pass, rolling through return fire as if it were rain. That destroyed Burn's primary engines. In turn he shunted over to the secondary engines, making the strafer shudder violently, and used the rest of the pass to blow up another four ships.

As the last of the Hsktskt raiders scattered, Burn made the strumming sound that was 'Zangian laughter. "Not the rotflesh you thought I was, am I?"

Burn flipped the strafer around to face the remaining eight ships. Hull stress from debris impacts and other, less accurate, displacer hits began to take its toll, but Burn ignored it, put the flight controls on programmed autoevasive and released his harness, allowing him to free spin inside StarFire's sphere.

Neuroclamp transmitters, designed to relay the slightest twitch of his muscles to the sphere's central processor, shot out to encircle his waist, upper torso, and flukes. The largest n-trans attached itself at the base of his skull and snaked hairlike leads to curl around the outside of his haffets. The leads picked up the synaptic pulses along the nerve pathways of his brain. Through the n-trans web he was linked body and mind to StarFire.

This was the part of prototype testing Dair had ordered him not to perform. *You're absolutely not to hardwire yourself to that blaster master* had been her exact words when he'd argued with her about it. *I don't care how much more control it will give you, either. No one knows what that kind of hookup will do to a 'Zangian brain; even one as tiny as yours.*

Whatever size his brain was, it felt fine. Dair worried too much.

StarFire's console lit up and the sphere rolled wildly as Burn quickly tested the n-trans links. Autocontrol guided the strafer as it barreled back into the cluster of ships. One good shot would disintegrate the *SeaDance* around Burn, but for some reason the Hsktskt held their fire.

"What are you, playing hard to get now?" he muttered as he whirled within the sphere, sending out a barrage of multidirectional pulse fire.

A quick glance at his console revealed why the Hsktskt were being so coy: most of his engine's coolant, regulant, and fuel lines had ruptured. The fuel wouldn't ignite in airless space, and while the coolant might contaminate his liquid atmosphere, it had no effect on him. Without regulant, however, the stardrive would go critical within minutes. The stardrive's core didn't need oxygen to vaporize him, the strafer, and anything within ten kim of them.

"So that's why you don't think I'm pretty anymore." He retracted the sphere, dropped into his harness, and watched the raiders' stardrives activating as they prepared to jump to light speed. StarFire controlled his complement of smartorps, but reprogramming their trajectory protocols took a few precious seconds. "Ah-ah-ah. Too late to swim back to your dams."

Before he fired the smartorps, Burn took a last look at the twin suns that provided light and heat for K-2. The binary amber giants, spinning together, forever caught in each other's magnetic fields, glowed benignly back at him.

They approved. He had fought well, and he would drag his enemies into the black with him. That was all that mattered. And Dair would remember him with admiration for this, his supreme sacrifice.

"*Duo*, deep with you." He hit the firing panel.

The smartorps launched on invisible waves of pulse propellant, lazily heading for and then missing the raiders as they returned to the strafer. Just before they struck the reinforced cowling protecting the *SeaDance*'s stardrive, Burn released a pulse of victory.

A blinding blue light filled his eyes.

"End Program Pilot Trainer Solo Flight Nine-Seven," a polite drone voice announced over the audio panel.

The raiders, the *SeaDance*, the suns, the stars, and space itself disappeared from Burn's blue-dazzled vision field. They were replaced by the strafer sim's walls and, beyond that, the yellow mesh of the dimensional simulator's projection grid. Purge valves opened, and the liquid atmosphere inside the narrow confines of the pilot trainer unit began to drain away.

Burn stretched his cramped limbs before he disengaged StarFire. Because he had been breathing water for the training session, it took a moment to transition from using his gills to inflating his lungs. Spitting out the water made him cough a little, but breathing oxygen was no longer the chore it used to be. His SEAL physical augmentations allowed him to stay out of the water far longer than any unaltered 'Zangian male his size.

SEAL biotech, however, did nothing to prevent him from being sucked out of the trainer by an emergency evac purge, which spilled him out to flop like a beached *clafaereas* on the yellow mesh floor of the simulation grid.

Burn hated being dumped almost as much as he despised breathing air. As soon as he finished clearing his gills, he let Control know it. "I wasn't in any danger!"

"I think you are now, Sublieutenant," someone said over the audio.

K-2's ship simulators had been designed by League Flight Academy instructors for two reasons. One was to allow pilots to practice tactical flight operations and procedures without risking valuable vessels in space. The other was to accommodate the unusual physiologies of the native 'Zangians, who, even with SEAL modifications, could only survive a maximum of forty-eight stanhours away from their native aquatic environment.

Keeping K-2's patrol fleet and its future pilots safe allowed quadrant to send its more mobile troops to defend the outer borders and serve at the front.

The strafer sim was a useful piece of equipment, and felt so real that Burn could never tell the difference between flying real and sim, but he resented the way Control had terminated the training sequence. Until he saw the twenty other strafer pilots, all dripping wet and standing in a semicircle around his sim. They had stepped out of trainer units identical to his, and none of them looked in the least bit happy.

Burn rolled a recessed eye toward Saree, Dairs' wing lead pilot and presently second-in-command. "Land's end, why are you all in here? I thought it was a solo mission."

Saree walked up, kicked him in the side, and then made an about-face and marched out of the envirodome.

Once Burn caught the breath she'd knocked out of his lungs, he pushed himself up and separated his flukes to stand. By that time most of the other SEALs had followed Saree off the grid.

"What happened?" Burn demanded of the two 'Zangian males left. "Why is everyone so angry?"

"It may be because you blew up our ships and killed us," Curonal told him. "*All* of us."

"I did not." Burn felt highly indignant as he scanned the angry faces around him. "I killed all the damn lizards."

"We *were* the lizards, perceptive one." Loknoth looked ready to take a bite out of him. "We had them cut off from the rear, until you went 'shrike-fest with the blasters."

"But all I saw were . . ." Burn stopped and groaned. New hull technology allowed fighter strafers to change their profile in space and appear as any other vessel, from an indolent cargo freighter to an enemy scout ship. "*You* came in copycat on the second wave?"

Loknoth looked at Curonal. "*You* can have him as *your* gunner."

"Do I truly appear that dim-witted to you?" Curonal asked Loknoth.

Two other SEALs entered the simulator. The first, Onkar, was a heavily scarred former rogue male almost as large as Burn. Onkar had undergone recent augmentations to repair severe injuries sustained during a battle with Hsktskt raiders, and was still adjusting to them, but he was rapidly regaining his formidable strength and speed. Onkar wore his new subcommander's rank on the collar of his dark blue flightsuit, but the glitter of his new promotion only enhanced the grimness of his expression.

Onkar wasn't happy. Which meant . . .

Burn glanced at the smaller, more radically alterformed 'Zangian female accompanying the subcommander. Onkar's mate and Burn's cousin, Jadaira mu T'Resa, had been born a full-white 'Zangian, but had required transplants of human tissue and organs to repair plague-induced birth defects. Like her mate Onkar, Dair had recently suffered grievous injuries during her battle to save the war-displaced, cultish Skartesh species, only no one quite knew how or why she had recovered.

Burn didn't care what had saved his cousin's life. That Dair was still alive was all that mattered to him.

Whatever had happened to Dair had done more than snatch her back from death. It had physically transformed her all-white body, melding the DNA from her 'Zangian and Terran body parts. No one was really sure what she had become. Her now-silvery hide looked ghostly against her modified commander's dark gray dress uniform, while her body was an eerie, graceful blend of half-humanoid, half-aquatic parts.

Dair also looked mad enough to bite him. Several times.

"Greetings, cousin." Burn couldn't fathom why anger darkened her almost-human face. It was just a simulation. "Why did you dump me out like that?"

Dair strode up to him and, although he was twice her size and three times her weight, slapped him smartly on the snout. "Idiot. What were you thinking, targeting your own stardrive and blowing yourself to bits like that?"

"Jadaira," Onkar said. "Calm yourself."

A former rogue who had spent most of his life alone in K-2's dangerous outer currents, Onkar never spoke much. When he did, he commanded immediate attention and respect.

From everyone but his mate. "I'll calm when he explains," she said before turning to poke one of her modified fins' strange new "fingers" into the lower vault of Burn's chest. "Well? Why did you ignore my orders?"

"It was useless to try to escape." He gave her a reproachful glance. "You might have warned me that the pod was playing Hsktskt."

"So the lizards could turn around and obliterate them? I think not. You were supposed to play bleeding bait."

Burn scowled. "That would never have worked."

"Oh?" Her eyes glittered, all ghostly silver fire. "And precisely *when* did you become an expert on flight maneuvers and tactical engagements, you sludge-headed, bottom-feeding, worthless hunk of 'shrike bait?"

"A half-blind pup could see the holes in that strategy." Guilt made him glance at Onkar, who had lost an eye during a real skirmish with the Hsktskt. The doctors had replaced it with an Ylydii transplant. "Ah, no offense, Subcommander."

Onkar only shook his head and looked at the upper vault of the envirodome.

"Don't try to get him on your side." Dair jabbed Burn again to draw his attention back to her. "*I'm* your commander. You answer to *me*."

Burn assumed a resentful, slightly hump-backed posture, one that would have been far more impressive in the water. "All right, I shouldn't have disobeyed the order. But if the pod had been real Hsktskt, which is what they looked like, then my actions were correct."

"They weren't. Yours weren't."

"I couldn't tell, and fifteen raiders would have obliterated a good chunk of the colony. I had to act on the threat." He couldn't resist rubbing the stinging spot on his face with one fin end. Dair smacked *hard*. "Anyway, I took out the three that were real and saved the day."

"By killing yourself and the pod, and turning twenty-one very expensive ships into a cloud of dust particles?"

"Simulated dust particles." He gave her a gentle, reassuring bump. "Now, why don't you thank me for killing those ugly podling-eaters and assign me to fly Rescue Three?"

Onkar made a sound suspiciously like a smothered groan.

"Thank you? Give you a real ship? You're lucky I don't suspend you from duty!" Dair's voice changed from irate to tympanic-membrane piercing. "If you think for one nanosecond that I'm going to let you pilot any ship for Bio Rescue when you insist on acting like a scar-hungry adolescent wrill-brained—"

"Jadaira." Her mate put one of his fins on her sloped shoulder. "Burn did react to a threat, as would anyone unaware of the copycat maneuver. We shall have to rethink that strategy."

The older male's defense surprised Burn. They had never been friends, and Burn's closeness to Dair had created a certain amount of tension between them. Since Onkar had mated with Dair, however, he had changed. He was still as possessive of her as ever, but now he seemed quieter and more thoughtful.

"You're supporting what he did?" Dair regarded her mate with narrow eyes. "Yes, I can see why you would, too. You'd have done the same stupid thing."

"In the same position, with the same readings? Yes."

"You, I let catch me and father my child. What was I thinking?" Dair turned and stomped out of the chamber.

Burn waited until the door panel closed before he sighed. "You know, she used to be a lot more fun before she was saved from death by that omnipotent, miraculous force."

"She used to be on patrol, with you as her gunner," Onkar reminded him. "Waiting for the pup, being grounded, and training you to pilot has not been easy for her."

"Easy?" Burn snorted air, making a rude sound through his gillets. "She's put me in this trainer so often I should leave it filled and regard it as my second home."

"She is concerned for you." Onkar reset the trainer's controls and powered down the flight module array. "She knows, better than anyone, the risks you will encounter as a Bio Rescue pilot."

"I won't encounter any if she doesn't let me fly a real ship." Which he coveted more than testing StarFire. "When is she going to quit acting like my dam and let me have one?"

"When you earn the privilege." Onkar gestured toward the door panel. "Come, it's past shift end."

It was only a short distance from the Main Transport building to the departure station, where specially adapted glidebuses waited to transport the aquatic 'Zangians back and forth between the sea and the land-dwellers' colony. As he accompanied Burn, Onkar signaled his mate several times via his wristcom.

Jadaira didn't respond once.

She was likely more upset than she had appeared. Onkar had noticed how increasingly volatile her temper had become, and it was not only due to their pending whelping and the endless medical testing Jadaira had to endure. Too much was changing too fast, on the land and under the water, and as usual his mate was trying to keep a balance between both sides.

Burn noticed Onkar's fruitless attempts to contact Dair. "Blocking your relays, is she? She truly has her tail in a twist."

"Likely she does."

"So what can I do to chase her away from mine?"

"Byorn . . ." Onkar hesitated as he tried to choose his words carefully. He was still not accustomed to casually conversing with other 'Zangians, or making observations about their emotions. The years he had spent swimming rogue had been silent, lonely ones. "Jadaira worries about you."

"I already have a dam to do that. I don't need two." The younger 'Zangian scratched at the side of his face. "What I really need is to get wet."

Despite the skin shielding worn under the 'Zangians' uniforms, which allowed a thin layer of water to circulate over their sensitive hides, itching and flaking while out of the water was a common problem. While their skin cells sloughed off ten times faster than those of land-dwelling humanoids, Onkar suspected that Burn's discomfort came more from his desire to avoid another rebuke. Particularly from the one male in the coastal pod who could still be considered his physical equal in the water.

"What fuels Jadaira's anger is her deep affection for you. You are more like a sibling than a cousin." Onkar narrowed his recessed, bicolored eyes against the sunslight, which K-2's atmosphere filtered to become a vibrant green. "I envy the closeness you share."

That seemed to startle Burn. He stared at Onkar for a moment before he finned regret. "I'm not trying to aggravate her, you know. Not deliberately. She doesn't understand what it's like. What it feels like."

Onkar knew that Jadaira didn't, and the problem was growing almost as fast as her young cousin. Colony doctors had discovered that SEAL technology accelerated the maturation process for some 'Zangian males. Burn was unusually large and aggressive for a male to begin with, and the onset of his adult hormones wasn't helping.

"You and I can no longer see the whole of ourselves in the water," he said, reminding the younger 'Zangian of their size and power. "We males also have drives that Jadaira will never fathom or possess."

"Explain that to her. *Duo* knows, I've tried."

"It is something she can never know." Onkar was glad of that. Some of the more aggressive needs he shared with Burn would have frightened his mate out of her wits. "Being the biggest and strongest among a kind does not entitle us to employ those advantages. More often than not, we must refrain from using them."

Burn grunted. "I do."

"Not as often as you could. When you fly, you must think as well as react."

"I do." He ducked his head. "All right, thinking isn't as easy as reacting. But honestly, Onkar—"

He made the fin gesture for silence. "You have been a soldier for some years now. Firing on another vessel kills hundreds, sometimes thousands of other beings, but it is remote and unseen. Someday you will have to watch others die at your hand, and it will change you. Be prepared for it."

"I am. I mean, I will be."

"I do not mean your physical training. You have a fine mind, Byorn. Try using it instead of relying solely on your strength and aggression." Onkar saw another 'Zangian approaching them and glanced at his wristcom. Still no return signal. This was worse than Dair's usual sulk. "It seems I must go and retrieve my mate. I will discuss your training with her, but think on what I have said."

The subcommander limped back in the direction of Main Transport. Behind him, he heard another, smaller pod male speaking to Burn.

"Heard you went nova in the trainer today."

"Took half the pod with me." Burn strummed a laugh. "Have you checked out the StarFire yet?"

Onkar's patience strained to the snapping point, but he kept going. *Byorn is still young. Time and experience will temper his recklessness.*

He managed to regain control over his own, and after a brief search found Jadaira by herself in one of the vessel hangars. She was performing an unscheduled preflight check on Rescue Three; work being her method of relaxing tension on land. Judging by the way she rammed down one engine cowling, it wasn't working.

"Why are you here?" she asked without looking at him.

He kept his tone mild. "You didn't answer my signals. I was concerned."

She snorted. "You should be. If he *ever* does that again, I'll rip out his gillets."

"I think you will not."

Now she looked at him. "Watch me."

The hangar was deserted, and there was an emergency immersion tank sitting on one side of the modified gstek. Onkar checked it to make sure it was filled before he went to his mate and picked her up in his arms.

"Onkar!" She shoved at him, but not enough to make him drop her. "What are you doing?"

"Getting you wet."

He stripped off her uniform, and then his own. She had not worn a skin seal again. Thanks to the integration of her human and aquatic DNA, Dair no longer required the close-fitted shield that kept her hide wet, unless she meant to stay on land for longer than a day. What Onkar most feared about Dair's mysterious transformation was that it would allow her to survive on land indefinitely.

That would allow her to leave their homeworld, and him.

Something of his fear must have shown in his eyes, for Dair's tone changed. "I shouldn't have snapped at you the way I did. Sometimes Burn makes me so mad I can't swim straight."

Mindful of her condition, Onkar eased them both into the tank. *I felt the same about you not very long ago.*

I was never as reckless as Burn is. She rolled over and swam beneath him, rubbing her rounded belly against his flat one. Speaking in their native baelaena allowed her to use body language and tone to relay a subtle blend of hint of mischief with her next words. *Well, almost never.*

What about the missions when you were nearly blown up by a stardrive gone critical, or sucked out into space through a ruptured hull panel, or boarded by Hsktskt, or attacked by that orbital minefield—

She glided around him and nuzzled the broad, flat expanse of his neck. *You forgot about the time I nearly toasted myself in the suns' corona.*

Onkar released a stream of bubbles through his gill vents. *I will never forget that.* He still had nightmares about the moment when he had lifted her dying body out of her wrecked ship, and taken her to die in the nameless place. *The central problem with Byorn is not atypical. His growth spurt and the new adult hormones he is experiencing for the first time are changing him. Remember, Jadaira, until this season he was still an adolescent.*

Are you telling me that now I'm supposed to treat him like an adult male? Her arms churned the water. *His behavior is more outrageous than it was when we were podlings.*

He will soon find a young female upon whom to focus his attention, Onkar predicted. *Then most of the aggression he displays will be in the breeding caverns, where it belongs.*

Duo, *don't tell me that. I can't imagine Burn having pups. He's barely six years old.* Her silvery eyes glittered as she touched her abdomen. *We're older, and I still have difficulty thinking of you and me as parents.*

Did she regret their mating? Or did she fear, as he sometimes did, that her transformation had somehow also affected their child? Or was it, so soon after her brush with death, all too much for her? *Jadaira, I want our pup as much as I want to breathe, but if this pregnancy has put too much strain on you—*

Stop. She bumped into him, refusing to allow him to finish the thought. *Your worries are unnecessary. I will be fine, and so will our little one.*

Onkar felt immediate, if somewhat guilt-tinged, relief. He could not imagine Jadaira dying, not when she had survived being burned so horribly. He had held her until she had drifted within moments of death, and then witnessed her astonishing recovery. In the nameless, sacred cave where the 'Zangians went to die, there had been a flash of light, sound and motion that had snatched Jadaira back from death and transformed her body. The miracle confounded everyone, so much so that hardly anyone spoke of it. Surely the whelping would not hurt her. Teresa would have indicated something by now. Of course, the Terran marine biologist was still furious with him for mating with Jadaira and making her pregnant. To Teresa, her stepdaughter was yet a child, and given her way Jadaira would still be in an observation tank.

Onkar knew his mate was far more mature than her Terran step-mother could ever know. He also knew that without Jadaira, there would be no life left for him. With a quick turn he faced her and cradled her against his chest. *Do you want to stay here the night?*

There isn't enough room for what I want to do. Jadaira gave him a sharp nip on the jaw. *Are you feeling up to a run in the caverns?*

Breeding 'Zangian females were usually complacent and uninterested in sex after becoming pregnant. Not so with Jadaira, whose human DNA had radically altered her sexual behavior, much to Onkar's distress and pleasure.

Do you still wish me to chase you? Another of Onkar's fears was that she would seek out the company of another male. While 'Zangians were polygamous in nature, breeding couples generally remained monogamous until after their whelping. Yet nothing about Jadaira could be deemed conventional, and Onkar refused to take anything for granted.

Oh, Onkar. The ghostly color of her eyes softened. *I wish for you. Only you, now and forever.*

Eternity might just be long enough for him, Onkar thought as he tucked his head over hers. *Then let us go home, Jadaira. Home to the sea.*

CHAPTER 2

*M*ajor Shon Valtas removed his mask and breathing gear as he waded out of the surf, just in time to see two 'Zangians dive into the depths from the cliffs overhead. One of the native aquatics was a large, dark-hided male; the other a small, silvery female. The twin suns outlined them with a halo of amber-orange light before they made graceful arcs of their streamlined bodies and plummeted down toward the churning waves.

That could be me up there, diving with her.

Jadaira and Onkar were too engrossed with each other, Shon saw, to notice him or the paw he had lifted in greeting. He didn't mind. Shon's interference in Dair's life had nearly killed her more than once, and she deserved the happiness she had found with her mate. Shon was grateful that she still considered him a friend, although that was all, as she had once kindly informed him, that she would ever feel for him.

Most days Shon didn't resent Dair's choosing Onkar over him to be her life mate. Most days.

Unlike the 'Zangians, Shon was not at home in the water. He had to wear a breathing rig whenever he swam, and he could not dive deeper than one hundred feet without risking injury or death due to the immense pressure of the ocean depths. Shon's homeworld was not K-2, but oKia, an icy-cold world of tundra and thick forests, where his people had evolved from the fiercest and most successful of lupine predators. The oKiaf's element was snow; rugged cliffs and dark valleys their natural territory.

Perhaps that was why Shon found the sea so fascinating. Like Dair it was beautiful, unpredictable, and filled with life and, for him, just as unattainable.

Water streamed from his long black mane and ran over his sleek shoulders, the dark hair partially covering the two parallel golden marks on his chest pelt. The thick brown and black hair that covered the rest of Shon's body began to dry in the breeze, turning faintly white from residual salt. He wore only a pair of abbreviated trousers and the flipper-shaped footgear that allowed him to move underwater more efficiently, but were awkward on land. Walking in them always made him understand why the aquatic 'Zangians disliked being above the surface so much. He could kick off his footgear, but they were permanently stuck with their flukes.

I wouldn't mind having that problem.

It was hard to remember that only a few months ago he had feared and hated the water. Now he hated being away from it for longer than a day or two, and had entertained the idea of applying for a permanent transfer to K-2 so he wouldn't have to leave the sea.

Or her.

Shon looked out at the horizon, where a group of dark dorsal fins cut through the waves above the seamount ridge. The coastal pod coming out to greet Dair and Onkar, as they did to anyone who entered their territory. Oddly, it made him feel lonely, to watch the 'Zangians mass. He had never felt alone until he had come to this world, and been exposed to the 'Zangians' friendly, communal way of life.

Where is my place? Where are the family and friends waiting for my return?

There were none on oKia; that much Shon knew. He had done the unthinkable by disobeying his father's wishes and leaving his homeworld, and then the unforgivable by joining the military and undergoing SEAL alterforming. His manhood notches on the family totem had been chopped out of the wood by now; his name rubbed from all the hunting story hides. He would never be mentioned, or welcomed, or wanted among his tribe and, looking as he did, no other would have him.

He no longer had a home or a people.

"Major Valtas." A colonial security officer stumbled a little as he made his way down a sand dune toward him. "Sorry to disturb you, sir, but you're needed back at colony." He held out a towel.

Shon might not have had a home, but he certainly had a job. "I'll get changed and report in twenty minutes."

"Not an option, sir." The officer, a placid-looking Psyoran, made a flutter of regret with his rainbow-colored frills. "I was ordered to personally transport you to Chief Norash's office."

"Any particular reason?" Shon asked. "Besides the chief's perennial impatience with waiting?"

The officer's colors shifted, a sign of increased emotion among the Psyoran. "I can't say for absolute sure, sir, but I think it might have to do with the twenty or so Skartesh that have been waiting outside your office all morning."

Of course it was the Skartesh. It was always the Skartesh, ever since Shon had been surgically altered and enhanced to become a stand-in for their dead Messiah.

Shon quickly toweled off most of the moisture remaining on his pelt before he pulled on a tunic and picked up the last of his land gear. "Let's go."

The security officer's glidecar waited at the edge of the cliff, and from there he drove Shon back to the colony. As they passed the new construction and restoration projects, Shon absently scanned faces and assigned species. More new transfers were coming in by the week, many from planets in other quadrants. One peculiarity caught his eye; a one-legged Omorr male having a spoken conversation with a tall, slim Terran female.

His driver followed Shon's gaze. "Now that's something you don't see every day. What's that Omorr doing, fraternizing with that Terran?"

Shon didn't comment. With a few exceptions like Dair's step-mother, Shon didn't care much for Terrans, who were mainly ignorant, obnoxious xenophobes and tended to create trouble wherever they transferred. He was interested in the Omorr, however, whose formal and occasionally inflexible manner didn't detract from their universally respected intellect, or their other, more mysterious talents.

The glidecar slowed as the officer at the controls gawked at the unusual couple. "She isn't spraying some sort of body fluid around him, is she? I've never actually met a Terran, but my brother told me that's one of their defense mechanisms."

Shon suppressed a sigh. "Terrans spit a little saliva on someone to show contempt or disgust."

"*On* people?" The Psyoran shuddered. "Is it poisonous? Should we stop and warn him?"

Shon glanced back at the unlikely pair. The Omorr seemed perplexed, but the female had a benign look about her. "The skin on the front of their heads usually turns red or purple first. She's not changing color. Keep going."

"I should have been watching where I was walking," Emily Kim said as she bent to pick up the last of the alien's cases. "I do apologize for bumping into you."

The alien, a male judging by the cut of his tunic, regarded her with round, dark eyes. "That is not necessary. Had I been attending to my path, I should have been able to anticipate yours and keep myself out of it."

He was not speaking in Terran, but the tympanic insert she had been issued at Main Transport allowed her to understand him perfectly. Still, this was not the sort of encounter she had long imagined having. She had hoped to freely discuss environmental and cultural differences with her first alien contact, not collide blindly with him and end up sprawled over his luggage.

"Should we keep blaming ourselves and making apologies to each other, or may we exchange names?" Some species, Emily had been told, required more formal or ceremonial introductions, while others reserved the use of personal names for family or species members. In any case, it was always wise to inquire first.

"An exchange seems suitable, under the circumstances. I am Hkyrim, of Omorr." He scanned her from head to footgear. "Please do not interpret this as an insult if I am incorrect in my preliminary identification of your species, but you are Terran?"

"I am. My name is Emily Kim." She made the polite palm-up gesture the attendant on the jaunt from Terra had taught her. "I just arrived on colony this morning."

"So, too, have I." Hkyrim made the same gesture with one of his three arms. He didn't have fingers, but the delicate membranes that webbed the ends of his spade-shaped hands seemed to serve the same purpose. "I will be working at the colonial medical facility. What, if I may ask, is your assignment?"

Goodness, he was a polite one. "I'm slotted to serve as a personal assistant in Administration." She had been disappointed to discover she had been assigned to work with another Terran, but surely one who had spent twenty years on K-2 couldn't be the usual sort. "It's not as exciting as medical, but I enjoy the work." And she was good at it; her employer back on Terra had tried everything to keep her there, including an offer to double her salary.

"My own position is one that keeps me secluded in a laboratory most of the time."

"I could stop by sometime and take you out for a meal interval," she blurted out.

"You probably will not wish to visit me at the FreeClinic, Emily Kim."

The FreeClinic—that was the medical facility on-planet. "I don't mind visiting hospitals."

"I am assigned to process pathologic and forensic specimens for the medical examiner." His gildrells made what appeared to be agitated movements. "This sometimes requires my participation in and performance of autopsies."

"Oh." Emily blinked. "You'll be working in the hospital morgue."

"Yes."

She tried to think of how to comment on that with some sort of enthusiasm. "Your work must be very . . . interesting."

"I never hear complaints from my patients." The Omorr looked as if he might say more, and then his expression became shuttered and polite again. "Do you require any further assistance?"

"No, thank you." She had chattered on too much; he was obviously bored. Or maybe he was worried about her spitting on him. She really couldn't tell. *If only Terrans didn't have such a rotten reputation off-world.* "It was very kind of you to help me up." As well as interesting to discover how strong he was—he had lifted her without effort, using only one arm.

"As I knocked you down there, I could do no less." The Omorr bent over from the waist, and it took a moment for Emily to register that he was actually *bowing* to her. "I must now report for my newcomer orientation, and then find the colonial archives. I wish you well, Emily Kim."

She murmured an appropriate good-bye and watched Hkyrim hop away. His species only had one leg, so he bounced more than walked. It didn't seem to bother him, however.

Did I stare too long at him? That marvelous fringe of prehensile tendrils covering the lower half of his face had mesmerized her; she had thought it a beard until she looked closer and saw what appeared like a nest of white snakes, or three-foot-long fingers. She had wanted to ask what their function was, but that was the sort of thing that offended another life-form, or so she had been told.

The great many things she had been told about aliens were part of the reason she had come to this world.

Emily checked her wristcom. Her own orientation did not begin for another hour, so she still had ample time. Her living quarters, while a little small, were adequate for her needs. She had dumped all her cases there so she could do some exploring.

The sight of so many exotic alien beings walking about—so freely and openly—had entranced her. Being spellbound, not Hkyrim, had been the actual cause of their collision. But how could anyone who had spent her entire life among her own kind not be plunged into a daze by the gorgeous variety of life here?

Not everyone on colony seemed equally delighted at the sight of Emily. More than one alien had made rather obvious efforts not to come in close proximity to her. Others stared with what seemed like angry expressions, but at times it was difficult for her to tell. Alien countenances were completely new to her, so she might have been mistaken in her interpretation of them.

He liked me, though. I think.

Hkyrim hadn't smiled, and his voice had come through her TI with something of a cool tone, but that might have been his natural manner. She wished she knew more about the Omorr so she could tell. He appeared to be a very pleasant person. That, and she was dying to know what he used that beard of tendrils for.

A short walk down one winding path led to a glidebus station and a bank of public access terminals, the latter of which were all occupied. Emily stepped behind one immense, gray-furred being and waited for her turn.

A red eye—the alien only possessed one—turned on her. A narrow slit appeared in the fur below it and growling sounds emerged. Her TI translated the rough voice as saying, "What do you want, Terran?"

She made the palm-up gesture again. "I would like to use the terminal, when you are finished." If he took too long she would simply board a glidebus and take it to orientation.

"Relocate another meter back," it growled. "I won't concentrate with you standing so close. And retain your body fluids."

An eight-legged, black-and-green arachnid female using the terminal next to the red-eyed furry alien turned and made a low, hissing sound that didn't translate.

The furred alien seemed to understand it, for its red eye shifted to meet the arachnid's black eye clusters. "You know they're as miserable as the Skartesh."

"Not alwayz. Leave her alone. Zhe izn't threatening you." The three-foot-high spider female turned and lifted two of her legs toward Emily. "I am finizhed here, Terran, if you wizh uze of thiz terminal."

"Thank you." Emily stepped up to the terminal and engaged the locator system. She was approximately five minutes from Colonial Administration. While she studied the most direct route to get there, a message flashed on the screen indicating she had a priority signal waiting to be opened.

Please, don't let it be orders to return home. Emily opened the relay.

The image of a purple-skinned, masculine-looking humanoid appeared. It wore such a fierce expression that Emily took an involuntary step back from the unit.

"Welcome to Kevarzangia Two, Miss Kim," the alien male said. It sounded the same way someone would issue a death threat. "I am Carsa, the administrative assistant whom you will be replacing. By now my transport has left K-2 so that I may attend to a family emergency on my homeworld, so there is no need to reply to this relay."

"I wouldn't dare," Emily murmured, and then bit her lip. Next to her, the gray-furred being made a nasty sound that was probably a laugh.

"I am extremely reluctant to leave K-2 at this time," Carsa continued, "but I feel confident that with your qualifications you can serve Administrator Hansen as adequately as I have."

Or he would come back and beat her senseless? That was what his narrowed eyes seemed to imply.

"I have left a detailed disk of ongoing projects and negotiations in my console storage unit for your review. You will wish to pay close attention to those items that concern the Peace Summit. Delegates from the Ninrana, Skartesh, Ylydii, and 'Zangian species will be meeting in orbit above K-2, hopefully to settle their differences and address the immediate planetary needs of this system."

Emily had read a little about the recent, aborted coup on Ninra, but the Terran news agencies reporting it had given it their customary contemptuous spin, even suggesting that the Ninrana's looming extinction was deserved.

Emily wondered if the colonial archives would provide a more enlightened view of the conflict. She could go and check them after her own orientation, and perhaps see Hkyrim again while she was there.

"As for Administrator Hansen," Carsa said, "I can personally attest to her kindness and infinite capacity for patience, and I believe you will find her a fair and understanding supervisor. However, if you wish to win her confidence, it would be best to display some initiative. Review the data I have left for you and learn the organization systems. The administrator finds strong emotions trying, as she has empathic talent, so keep calm. I would advise you bring her coffee, frequently, during the early-morning hours of your shifts. She seems to need the artificial stimulation it provides most at that time. Ah, and if a silver-haired Terran male named William Mayer pays a visit to the administrator, I advise you not disturb them. During such times, I usually leave to take a break or a meal interval."

Emily smiled at the image. Carsa might look like a killer, but he was all heart.

"My family matter bars my return to K-2, but I have embedded my personal relay code in your desk terminal. Please use it should you have any questions. Fare well, Miss Kim."

A shadow passed over the terminal, and Emily glanced over her shoulder to see the passage of a nine-foot-tall being as it trudged toward a restricted-use glidebus. It seemed to be a cross between a humanoid and a killer whale—minus the white spots—and it wore a pilot's flight-suit.

It was also wearing the kind of ferocious scowl that made Carsa seem, in comparison, as dangerous as a soft, fluffy kitten.

Maybe I'll walk to orientation.

Burn was always the first back to the water after a duty shift ended. Always.

"Running a little late today, eh, Lieutenant?" the transport driver said as Burn boarded the empty glidebus.

"I had some reports to file." He flicked his collar insignia. "And it's Sublieutenant now."

"Not for long," Burn thought he heard the driver mutter as the transport pulled away from the curb.

Burn's natal pod dwelled in the warm waters off the coast, some fifteen kim from the outskirts of the colony. The short trip gave him time to hook up his lines to the bus's storage tank of seawater—carried exclusively for the 'Zangians' use—and think over what he was going to say to the others.

What is there to say? Based on the data I was given, I made the only logical choice. I was dead anyway.

He knew Saree and the other pilots would likely resent him for the unhappy end result of their training session, but that wasn't his fault. Dair had deliberately kept him in the dark as to the copycat maneuver. If he didn't hold that against her, then the pilots' pod should be just as forgiving toward him.

And if they aren't, then they can eat my wake.

Burn watched as the terrain gradually sloped upward from the relatively flat land-dwellers' territory to become a wall of rocky cliffs. A familiar tingle of excitement sizzled along his nerve endings as the air grew moister and saltier. He had his flightsuit unfastened before he climbed down the glidebus's exit ramp, and dragged it off his body by the time he reached the edge of the cliff's uppermost plateau.

Before him stretched out the largest of K-2's oceans, what the land-dwellers called the Western Sea. Four thousand kim wide and twice as long, it contained so many major reef formations that they were visible from orbit, and was thought by the land-dwellers to be populated by nearly all the aquatic species found on the planet.

To Burn, the endless, rolling, whitecapped waves and blue-green depths were simply home.

He dropped his uniform and skin seal on the rock and looked down. The tide had rolled in, deepening the water of the diving inlet to a dark blue. He breathed out, flattening his lungs, and then leapt off the edge of the cliff, somersaulting head over flukes before straightening out at the last possible moment to enter the water like a dark gray bolt of lightning.

Cool blue enveloped him, flooding his gill vents and driving the last bit of air from his lungs. Burn dragged in as much water as he could expel before touching off the bottom silt with a kick and swimming out for the seamount ridge. Although he had barely disturbed the surface with his dive, and swam silently, dark figures were already gathering in the distance and heading his way.

'Zangians were capable of communicating with others in three different forms of language: clik, fin, and balaenea. Clik, a collection of tonal sounds and pulses, relayed brief, necessary communication to any member of the pod within a kim. Fin, made of wordless, soundless body gestures and movements, was used and understood by most intelligent aquatic species. The 'Zangians' most evolved language, balaenea, used elements of clik and fin along with subtler, more sophisticated sounds and gestures to relay the most complex and lengthy interactions.

No one was using clik or balaenea today, however.

Most of the pod turned and left at the sight of him, while the few 'Zangians who bothered to acknowledge his presence treated him to a few stiff fin gestures of distant greeting or simple recognition. The reception didn't qualify as an outright insult, but only just.

Burn refused to allow it to bother him. He might have violated protocol and upset everyone, but that was the price to be paid for creative thinking. Whatever his friends or Dair thought, destroying the raiders had been his primary mission, and he had carried it through to a successful completion.

Burn. Madura, one of the few pilots who had not been assigned to the training exercise, swam up to greet him. *It's about time you returned.* She turned slightly to look back at the retreating pod. *Why is everyone calling you Pod Killer?*

Because I killed them in a simulation. He swam past her and saw a large figure heading directly for him. *Land's end, did they have to tell my mother?*

The young female released a strum of mirth. *Oh, Burn, they'll tell everyone.*

Znora mu V'ndema, one of the largest and oldest matriarchs of the coastal pod, swam up and circled around Burn in an agitated fashion. *Are you injured? Curonal said how that leech-hided runt caused you to be thrown from that wretched contraption she forces you to endure.*

I am not injured, Mother. Burn felt impatient with Znora's nuzzling and glided past her. *Dair is not white anymore, either. You will have to think up a new name to call her.*

Byorn, wait. Where are you going? Znora caught up to him and gave him a wounded look. *May I not even greet my son properly now?*

He faced her. *I do not need you chasing after me as if I were a wayward podling.*

Perhaps when you cease behaving like one, I will not. His mother swam closer. *What is the matter with you? You are hungry, of course.* She nudged him. *Come, let us go and feed.*

Burn's stomach was empty, but he had no desire to trail after his dam to the feeding grounds. *I'm not feeding now. I'll be back later.*

Byorn, wait—

He didn't wait. He shot off into a nearby lateral current, using the energy to boost his speed. By the time Znora could turn to follow, he was almost out of her sight, and he kept swimming fast until he hit the colder waters above the black rock labyrinth of the northern reefs, where the coastal pod seldom came.

His mother would never follow him here. Cold water gave her joints trouble, and she disliked being separated from the pod. Then again, so had Burn, at least until recently. He had started coming here about the same time he grew so long that he couldn't see his flukes in the water anymore.

He was larger and stronger than Dair, than his mother—than anyone—so why did the pod insist on treating him as if he were still shedding his belly spots? Would his mother never stop acting as if he were still taking milk from her mammary glands? *Duo,* didn't she ever look at him properly? He was a meter longer than she now, an adult. Large enough to mate, if he desired a female, or to brave some of the outer currents.

Tiny bubbles turned the current around him milky as a large wrill bloom encompassed the reef. The miniature crustaceans were too small to chew and provide a proper meal, and Burn disliked the taste of the bigger ones, but he moved through the cloud and ate them until his gullet was full and his belly stopped cramping.

A fat, indolent *gnaldrof* slithered out of its cramped hole in the reef to investigate the unusual feeding activity. Its bulging eyes inspected Burn the same way it would its nemesis, the *doowtasquid.*

See what I'm reduced to? Eating garbage food. He cast a resentful glance back in the direction of his home waters. *I wager they didn't turn their back fins like that on Dair.*

Unimpressed, the *gnaldrof* made a flatulent sound and returned to its den. It didn't bother to lace its wake with the mild venom in its posterior ducts.

Burn should have been glad that the eel considered him beneath its notice. *Gnaldrof* venom never caused permanent damage, but it smelled like rotflesh and made anything thin-hided itch unbearably for hours. Yet even the eel's indifference infuriated him.

Would it have killed it to hiss and acknowledge my presence?

All Burn truly wanted was to be a pilot. It had been his ambition ever since he had followed Dair into the military. Well, perhaps not always—when he was younger he had been distracted by all the lovely weaponry and armament the League had given him to play with—but surely he was old enough now to be trusted with more important duty. And there was nothing finer than taking command of a ship and facing off with the enemy, flying into battle with engines screaming, outwitting the lizards and anything else fool enough to put itself in his path.

Frustration made him flip in the water, dispersing the wrill bloom and clearing a path to the outer edge of the reef. Beyond the ragged curve of the rock-builders' abandoned carapaces lay darker, colder water where no 'Zangian swam. Burn darted forward and then halted as if he had bumped into an unseen wall.

He had never crossed into the outer currents.

Like space, the region of the sea beyond the warm coastal waters was vast and empty; far too dangerous to support anything but the most mindless, uncivilized life-forms. Mogshrikes, the 'Zangians' only natural predator, spent their lives stalking the freezing currents for migrating masses and wandering rogues.

I could survive out there. Burn had grown large enough to present a danger to smaller, younger 'shrikes, and he could certainly outswim the older, more dangerous ones. *Onkar did, for years.*

The only reason 'Zangians entered the outer currents, however, was because they had been outcast from their natal pod. Burn might have made fools of the other SEALs during their training session, but they wouldn't drive him out for doing that. They wouldn't dare.

The pulsing anger inside him faded as he looked back at his home territory. *Would they?*

Burn didn't waste any time debating the matter with the *gnaldrof*, or himself. It wasn't fear that made him turn away from the column of dark water, or put a little extra speed into the swim back to warmer, brighter currents. He would simply sort things out with the other SEALs and put this matter behind them.

The same way he did the outer currents, as fast and as far as he could swim away from them.

Liana swam quickly away from the threat. Behind her lay something shapeless, dark, and menacing, but ahead there was brilliant light and the promise of haven. Colors glowed around her and, as she moved closer, delicious trills from fresh, eager food vibrated against her hide. She was so hungry; she could not remember the last time she had fed. The petite veils of her lateral fins ached to be released, to spread their multihued webbing and lure something tasty into their barbs.

Not yet. Make sure it is safe for the others.

Liana ignored the pleasures and temptations around her. Slowing and listening carefully were imperative, if she were to send a summons. This place might offer permanent refuge, something she felt the Ylydii needed desperately right now, but she would not be careless and risk others' lives.

So many depended on her that she could not call them by name or even count them anymore.

Part of her hated that—she had never wished to rise this far—but she had been born of the green. With the green came terrible responsibilities, especially toward the one who mattered most. The one who had sent her here, the one who had forced her to keep silent and keep moving. The one she had left back in the cold darkness.

The one she would not think about, ever, until this was done.

Liana slowly swam through the light. She could not yet see the great schools of *rextab* and *brevlisgre*, but she felt their massing and movements. The water tasted clean, almost sweet on her tongue. No threat came to confront her, nothing disturbed the currents but that which could warm empty bellies.

When Liana felt sure of the place, she pulsed out reassurance to the lead females of her synchrony. *No danger here. Secure. Food.*

Now she could, at last, relax and enjoy her surroundings. Had she ever swum waters this soft and warm? In the quiet cove where she had been born, perhaps, or while exploring the shallows above the sunken cities. She saw no sign of her grandmothers or the time-worn ruins; only green and purple columns of light streaming down from the star-dappled surface. Wherever she was, Liana felt completely at ease and wholly protected. Her sisters within the synchrony would soon join her, and call to their sequestered males, and they, too, would revel in this place.

They would come. Any moment now.

Liana thought about releasing her veils, but decided to wait for the other hunters. Luring worked better when there were many webs to link together, and of course the males would need to be fed first or they would whine and screech like infants.

An odd taste filled her mouth. It was only the slightest trace of something strange on the current, but she couldn't identify it. Whatever it was, it made the ridge that ran the length of her long dorsal fin stiffen. Her veils remained furled and cool, but their fluttering tips tingled as the sensory organs there, too, sampled the current. Something about this place had changed, and that was of deep concern to her. She had summoned the others; she had to find the source of the odd taste before they arrived or risk their lives as well as her own. She would send her bodyguards. . . .

Liana turned and saw no one behind her or flanking her. Her guards were gone. *What happened to my escort?*

Liana had never been alone, not since she had slipped from her mother's birth canal and all the whelping throng had immediately seen the green monarch's ring within her eyes. Born of the green, she carried the rarest, royal affliction, so highly prized among her kind, and she had been pampered because of it from that day forth.

The grandmothers and aunts and cousins had done their best for Liana, and had kept close until she had enough strength to make her own kills. But feeding was not meant to be done alone, and neither was exploring, not even for one meant to rule.

Liana had never been alone, could not be left alone. The waters closed in around her, squeezing on all sides. Had she fallen into an abyss? Been caught in some narrow cave? Her mother would be frantic.

Her mother—the one—

A streak of yellow-white flashed before her eyes, and the sound of a guttural male voice rang in her brow.

Here she is. Wedged herself into this conduit somehow. Grab her flukes.

Liana was pulled from the tight restriction and out. The water was still around her, but it was dark and too cold. She could see nothing, not even the smallest glimmer of light. She heard no sound but the harsh voice snapping out words she did not understand. Something jabbed her in the side and she released a pulse crying for help.

Mother. Mother where are you mother mother—

Here. A heavy body bumped against her own. *Be silent.*

Liana's sore, bruised hide told her what her eyes could not. Someone had wrapped her body in cords. Another, much wider cord covered her eyes. Her veils strained at the confinement, but the cords were too thick and made of something that cut into her hide when she twisted.

It took a moment to understand that the place she had been before had only been a dream. *What has happened?*

It was not her mother who answered her, but Nerala, the female captain of her mother's transport. *We have been boarded by mercenaries, my lady,* she told Liana. *They have taken over control of the ship.*

The strange taste was still strong on Liana's tongue, but she knew what it was now: Ylydii blood. It made her want to retch, but she clamped her throat shut and held it so until the surge passed.

What do they want with us? she asked Nerala when she could safely speak.

The female captain began to answer, and then cried out. The blood in the water grew stronger, and a limp, heavy weight struck her side.

Please, Liana thought as she pressed her body to the captain's bleeding, still form. *Please, please let them kill us quickly.*

CHAPTER 3

*A*na Hansen was already awake when she felt the sleeping platform depress and reshape itself on the empty side, but she kept her eyes closed and her body still. She could feel the exhaustion weighing down her lover's body, dulling the sharp edges of his highly analytical mind. She also knew why he felt the way he did.

Fifteen hours on shift. Five more in surgery. Something went wrong.

It was times like these that she was glad she could sense other people's emotions, mental states, and often their thoughts. She would wait until he fell asleep, and then she would slip out of bed and dress for her work shift.

"I don't have to be empathic to know you're awake," he said, his voice a weary rasp.

Ana rolled over and looked into William Mayer's face. Morning sunlight wasn't kind to his weathered face or thinning silver hair. Luckily, she didn't adore him for his outward appearance. "You ruined my plan."

"You make plans at"—he glanced at the room panel—"oh-four-twenty-eight in the morning?"

She had already taken four signals from her colleagues on the pending Peace Summit, but she only nodded and snuggled up beside him. "I was going to attack you as soon as you fell asleep."

"Don't be gentle." He moved her onto his chest and dropped his head back against the pillows. "Whatever pain you inflict, I probably deserve it."

Defeat came through the waves of fatigue. "Bad night?"

"I fully intended to be here in time to take you to whatever reception we had scheduled," he said, and released a sigh. "Right before the relief cutter reported for duty, my nurse brought back a neck injury. Turned out to be a reconstruct who had tried to refit his cranial case mounts and cut four inches into his own brain stem. When I walked out of surgery, it was daylight."

Ana's medical knowledge was basic, but she knew reconstructs only had a brain and a short length of spinal tissue. The remainder of their bodies were constructed, mechanized alloy chassis that provided physical support for the organic parts. "Were you able to save him?"

"No, I lost him three hours in. There was simply too much wound area to repair, and the damaged cells were dying faster than we could regenerate them." His dark eyes filled with self-disgust. "I should have—"

"Shhh." She pressed her fingertips against his mouth. "You did what you could. You always do." She stroked his brow. "Go to sleep."

His arms tightened around her. "Stay with me until I do?"

Ana's first meeting that day was scheduled to begin in ten minutes. She knew it would take her three to dress and five more to drive to her office. Then there were the briefs to read over, a thousand more details to coordinate for the Peace Summit, and signals to send and receive. She should have left for work thirty minutes ago.

Instead, she nodded and stayed where she was, her cheek pressed over Liam's heart, and listened as the strong, heavy beat slowed. Only when his breathing became deep and regular and his grip loosened did she ease out of his arms and slip from the bed, touching the form control on her side so that it mimicked the shape of her body.

She hated leaving him like this, as much as she hated coming home to an empty dwelling. Yet when her shift was over, he likely would be back at the hospital, operating on someone else.

It won't have to be this way forever. As Ana put on her makeup, she calculated the remainder of her tenure on the Colonial Council. In another cycle someone else would be elected to take her place, and then she would have more time for herself. Once the surgeons quadrant had recruited transferred in, Liam would have fewer professional demands. That would be the time to really start talking about what direction to take with their future . . .

What future? Why was she kidding herself?

Ana jerked her tunic over her head. She had to be realistic. From the beginning of their relationship, they had been forced to make appointments simply to see each other. Thinking to give them more personal time, Liam had agreed to move into her quarters, but their shifts seldom coincided so they were hardly ever home at the same time. Simply sharing a meal or a conversation proved a daily challenge.

Ana loved Liam, but she was under no illusions about where she stood in his life. First there was preserving the health and welfare of everyone else on colony, then came time with her. She couldn't even blame him for it, as her attitude toward her own responsibilities was the same. Colony business always came first, her personal relationships second. Their mutual attitudes were realistic, direct, and perhaps even admirable.

What their attitudes cost them as a couple made Ana often wish she could slam her head into a wall panel.

Ana signaled her office to tell her assistant that she was going to be late, but there was no answer. Carsa, a Triburrin who had recently undergone transgendering to become a male, had never been late before. Naturally he would be today, the one day she needed him at the console to juggle the endless stream of signals and data coming in about the Peace Summit.

Maybe Carsa decided to linger in bed with his new mate. Ana smiled to herself, picked up her data case, and quietly let herself out the front door panel.

As she drove to Colonial Administration, Ana considered what life would have been like for her if her first love, Elars, had not been killed. They had been so young when they mated, and Elars had had very definite ideas about their future.

"I know Terran females are much more independent than those of my species, but I would like my mate to devote herself to being our family caregiver," Elars had said. "Does that make me a terrible prospect as a husband?"

At the time Ana had been happy to throw herself into the traditional role of a Venyaran mate: caring for their home, preparing their meals, and looking forward to bearing their young and raising them.

Elars had died before he could give her children, however, and in her grief the only solace Ana had was in finding a job on a newly established multispecies colony, far from the world she and Elars had loved.

When Ana arrived on K-2, she had thrown herself into her work, allowing it to fill her every waking hour. Now it had become her life, and it was forcing the man she loved as much as Elars to take second place to it.

He understands. He understands, and he will still love me even when I'm not there.

Ana saw that she was more than a quarter hour late by the time she reached her office, and as a result rushed to get to her console. "I don't have time for coffee this morning, Carsa," she said as she hurried by the front desk.

"I'm not Carsa."

Ana came to a complete halt and stared at the being sitting behind her assistant's desk. "You're not." She hesitated and peered through the shadows. Whoever it was, it was humanoid, and possibly female. "*Were* you Carsa?"

"No."

"Lights." Ana felt her heart sink as the overhead emitters illuminated the unsmiling face of a young female. A very young, attractive female.

A very young, attractive, undeniably *Terran* female.

"I'm not actually scheduled to begin until tomorrow, but I thought I would stop in on my way to orientation," the young woman said in a mellow, pleasant voice. She offered her hand. "You must be Administrator Hansen."

Ana shook her hand and was vaguely startled to realize that here was one of the rare humans from whom she could pick up no emotions or thoughts whatsoever. "Come into my office." When they were inside, she gestured to the chair in front of her desk. "Let's see, where to start . . ."

What was Jurek-sa thinking, replacing Ana's extremely personable assistant with this child from her unpleasant homeworld? Surely he remembered how horrible most Terrans were. With the Peace Summit only a few rotations away, the last thing Ana needed now was a new office assistant.

"Perhaps I should give you a quick overview of your duties." Maybe that would scare the girl enough to send her running for the next transport back to their homeworld.

"That won't be necessary. According to the slot profile, I will be acting as your personal assistant, coordinating your schedule, communications, and data flow," the new assistant stated. "My other duties include processing pertinent information relating to new transfers, existing residents and, for the next interim, Colonial Council business. I have been cleared with a T-5 security rating." She folded her hands neatly in her lap. "Are there any additional duties of which I have not been made aware?"

"We're about to conduct a multispecies, interplanetary Peace Summit. In orbit." Ana watched her expression, but it proved as unreadable as her thoughts. "Perhaps you haven't realized this, but you've transferred to a planet populated and frequented mainly by aliens."

"Yes."

"That would be two hundred *thousand* aliens, originating from four or five hundred *different* worlds."

The younger woman didn't bat an eyelash. "I knew K-2's colony was a multispecies settlement prior to making my transfer application."

"You *are* Terran, aren't you?" Sometimes crossbreeds deliberately hid their alien characteristics so they could pass better as purebloods, although generally that practice was only so they could maintain permanent residence on the homeworld. With the exception of a few species that preferred to keep their gene pools unsullied, nobody off Terra much cared what mixture of DNA anyone else had.

Light brown eyebrows arched. "Born and raised on Terra; certified 100 percent pure human-blooded via DNA scans, which I was given every year since gradetech. I can provide data verification, of course, if you'd like to review my disks."

"I don't mean to imply—I mean, no, thank you. Why did you choose to transfer here?"

"It seemed a desirable destination. Administrator, if my being human presents any difficulty for this office, please feel free to request my transfer to another department." The new assistant made a graceful gesture. "I will not be offended."

Now that was a nice way to turn this whole thing around so that it was Ana's personal problem. She felt a grudging respect for the polite yet straightforward way she had done it, too.

"Since you're being frank, I'll do the same. We have only seventeen Terrans residing on K-2, and with the exception of you, me, Dr. Mayer from the FreeClinic, and Dr. Selmar from the Underwater Research Dome, none of them were raised on the homeworld." Ana smiled to take some of the unhappy emphasis off the last word. "Most of us have or have had alien mates."

The younger woman merely nodded as if absorbing the information.

Ana was beginning to admire her unshakable demeanor. It was truly a shame the girl was a Terran; she had the makings of an excellent diplomat. "You may see yourself as having the type of intrepid or pioneering spirit capable of handling so much alien interaction, but . . . may I be frank?"

"Please."

Ana tried to think of something a Terran would consider horrific. "I can't have an assistant who screams the first time a slime-coated Rilken slides a sticky tendril up her skirt to see what she has under it."

"Should I find myself in such circumstances, I would gently discourage the Rilken," her new assistant told her. "I never scream." She tilted her head. "Do you dislike other Terrans, Administrator?"

"No. My best friend is a Terran. So is my lover." She sighed. "They are the exceptions. It's true that I don't think much of homeworld Terrans. Or their prejudices."

"Most Terrans assume any member of our species who mates with an alien is a sexual deviant who should not be allowed near small Terran children." Mild eyes moved to inspect the wedding photoscan on Ana's desk. "Should I make that assumption about you, based solely on what I've been told?"

"Absolutely not."

"Then perhaps you will extend the same courtesy to me." She rose. "It is near time for me to report for new transfer orientation. Please feel free to contact Administrator Jurek-sa and request another assistant, if you so desire." She gave Ana a polite smile and slipped quietly out of the room.

Ana was tempted to call after her, but instead prepared for her meeting over at security. She couldn't run a background check on the young Terran woman, much less request Jurek-sa give her a reassignment.

She had no idea what her new assistant's name was.

Chief Norash's small, shrewd eyes narrowed as Shon walked into the briefing room. "You're wet."

"I was picked up at the beach after I'd been diving," he told the chief of K-2's colonial security forces. "If you'd like me to report dry and in uniform, try having your officers pick me up when I'm actually on duty."

Norash idly used his extended nasal appendage to scratch a spot on his thick yellow-and-brown-streaked hide. "What I meant was, to be more precise, that I thought you were hydrophobic, Major."

"I was." A few months ago Shon's fear of the water didn't allow him within a hundred yards of an ocean. "I got over it."

"Maybe you'd care to share your secret." Norash nodded toward the Trytinorn compound on the outskirts of the colony. "My mate can't convince our son to bathe more than twice a week."

"Is he an adolescent?" At the chief's nod, Shon suggested, "Try bribery. Some with a great deal of sucrose or some other tooth-decaying substance he's not permitted to have very often."

"May I never have to repair the teeth of your children." Norash's floor groaned slightly as he shifted position, coming around his console and inspecting the data displayed on his terminal. "You've heard about the Skartesh?"

"Some."

"Administration tells me that they've decided they won't speak to—or through—anyone but you." Norash checked the time. "Ana Hansen was supposed to join us for this briefing, but she's late. Blasted civilians never can keep to a proper schedule."

Shon wasn't fooled by the Trytinorn's attempt at camaraderie. "Whatever you or Admin have in mind, the answer is no."

Norash eased his hindquarters into a special harness that allowed him to remove some of the weight from his legs—the Trytinorn equivalent of a chair—and gave Shon a mild look. "That's a fairly adamant statement, considering what you were willing to do before the cult was disarmed."

"My assignment to impersonate Rushan Amariah was over as soon as the invasion of Ninra was defeated," Shon reminded him. "While my SEAL augmentations cannot be reversed, and I will resemble a Skartesh for the remainder of my life, I have no valid reason or motive to continue playing a role for the cult." He looked up as a fair-haired Terran female entered the office. "Administrator Hansen."

"I do apologize for being late. This has been one of those mornings." Ana handed each a disk. "Copies of the Skartesh Elders' latest communication. Text only, I'm afraid; the compound has disabled their audio and video." She gracefully arranged herself on the edge of one of the chief's oversized chairs. "To give you the short version, the cult has decided to maintain their position on the separatism issue. They've also elected you, Major, as their species representative and colonial liaison, effective immediately."

"I respectfully decline, Administrator."

She gave him a sympathetic look. "I was hoping you'd accept the position, at least on a temporary basis. You were the main reason our mental health counselors were so successful in helping to deprogram and reeducate the cult after the invasion. It was also your idea to have the Skartesh make amends to the Hlagg."

Since a Skartesh riot accidentally released thousands of different Hlagg insect life-forms from their sealed embassy into K-2's biosphere, the Hlagg and the Skartesh had been working together to track and contain as many of the insects as possible. The Hlagg's unique symbiotic relationship with their insects enabled them to control the tiny creatures through vocal intonation, but on their homeworld they had never been obliged to hunt them.

Shon had been the one to suggest to the dismayed Hlagg ambassador and the embarrassed cult Elders that the Skartesh, with their highly developed senses of smell and hearing, might serve as excellent scouts. Over the last several weeks, the cult's best hunters had been out tracking for the Hlagg, and many thousands of the escaped insects had been successfully recovered.

"These people meant enough for you to risk your life, several times, to save their species," Norash put in. "Surely those feelings haven't changed."

"That was an *assignment*." Shon gritted his teeth. "I may look Skartesh, but I am oKiaf. The cult is not my responsibility, and I am hardly qualified to act as their leader in anything."

"We'd be willing to give you all the support you need, Major," Ana said. "The final decisions would not be left in your hands."

Which meant more deliberate manipulation of the cult by K-2's well-intentioned governing body; something Shon violently opposed. "I am not Skartesh. I can't represent them."

"There is no specific rule that a rep/liaison must be a native of the species they represent," Ana told him. "Nor is there any requirement on service duration."

He glared at her. "Is there a rule about how much harassment an undercover intelligence officer has to take from bureaucrats wishing to control a group of traumatized refugees?"

"All of us appreciate how complicated your former assignment made things for you here," Chief Norash said. "That does not negate the fact that we still harbor over seventy thousand Skartesh on this planet. Seventy thousand beings who tried to commit mass suicide only a short time ago, and who still largely consider you their preferential Messiah."

"I have—very patiently, and with great detail—explained what I did, and why, to the Elders of the cult." Shon turned to Ana Hansen. "I don't know what they've convinced themselves of now, but at the time they understood that I am not a member of their species and that

I was never 'chosen' to do anything but act a part in order to protect the cult, and to keep them from attacking the occupied worlds in this system."

"Religious beliefs are ever-evolving," Ana Hansen suggested. "When Rushan Amariah's parents were executed for their actions against the Skartesh, and you were revealed as an undercover operative, the cult lost all its leadership. I can't say for sure, Major, but I believe they are desperate to find new focus. Because of your efforts on their behalf, in the past and the present, they believe that you were sent to save them."

"By Pmoc Quadrant Intelligence," Shon said. "Not their Gods."

"It doesn't matter where you came from to them. They want to consult with you on matters of vital importance to the future of the Skartesh. They refuse to have anything to do with anyone else, except the Hlagg." Ana's wristcom chirped, and she frowned. "It appears I have an emergency situation I have to attend to." She rose and smiled at Norash and then Shon. "Please reconsider, if you would, Major. You could be a tremendous help to a very frightened species. Chief, I'll signal you later. Excuse me."

Once the administrator had departed, Norash secured the door panel and put the room panel controls on maximum security.

"Shouting at me isn't going to compel me to change my mind," Shon told him.

"That's not why I'm sealing up the room." Norash pulled up an assignment file and turned his viddisplay so that Shon could read it. "I received three inquiries from PQMI yesterday as to your current assignment status, workload dispersement, and location."

Quadrant Intelligence knew exactly where Shon was, and what he was doing. "I'm scheduled to begin flying medevac with the Bio Rescue program."

"Your orders read that this pilot duty was a voluntary and temporary assignment," Chief Norash said.

Tension was beginning to knot the muscles in Shon's neck. "They shouldn't. I put in for a permanent transfer to K-2's planetary patrol squadron as soon as the deprogramming of the cult was completed."

"Your application must have been misplaced, then. PQMI is basically asking when they should date your orders for your transfer back to oKia."

"oKia." Shon blinked. "I was never stationed on my homeworld, and it's never been under any threat of invasion." Had that changed? Were his parents in danger?

"Let me make one thing utterly transparent." Norash removed a disk from his terminal and handed it to Shon. "You did not receive this data from me, Major."

Shon examined the disk. It was unmarked and the recording terminal ID tag had been deliberately erased. *Bootlegged.* "Understood."

"On that disk you'll find details about a recent attack on the oKiaf planetary patrol. The mercenaries were repelled and destroyed. This is all public knowledge. What isn't generally known is that one of the Faction's assassins was able to slip through the security grid during the firefight and land on-planet. He went directly to Central Intelligence during a shift with minimal night staffing, infiltrated the building, and blew it, along with himself, into orbit. Forty officers were killed, including Horvon Jala."

"Jala." Shon had to put down the disk before it snapped in his paw.

Horvon Jala had been Shon's superior officer in Intelligence from the beginning. It had been Jala's idea to alterform the young oKiaf officer to double for Rushan Amariah. He had trained Shon, and then personally supervised the Skartesh infiltration operation from oKia. Aside from Shon's own father, Jala had been the most influential male in his life.

It was not the loss of a fine officer that hurt. The pain of knowing how the old man had been murdered cut deep, like an Omorr blade in a skilled hand.

Horvon had always wished to die in battle, and instead he had been murdered while sleeping peacefully in his bed.

Shon took a moment to stow his outrage. "Why wasn't I informed of this?"

"There has been a system-wide shutdown to control the flow of information, so the enemy does not know just how successful their assassin was. Quadrant will likely send a signal as soon as they reorganize oKia Intelligence and cut your orders."

"They're restaffing."

Norash nodded. "As rapidly as possible, and they're looking for a replacement for Jala. My sources tell me that your name is on top of the list." His expression darkened. "Apparently you have more experience than is listed on your service records. Along with undercover infiltration, Jala was in charge of all quadrant prisoner special interrogations."

"Jala and my father served in the prisons; I never did." Shon thought of his sire, and how his brief military experience had scarred him. "I enlisted as an undercover field agent, not an interrogator. I would not follow in my father's tracks."

"There are rumors about your species. Nothing concrete, you understand, but word cycles around. Prisoners talk about secret chambers, and tell stories about hearing important captives being beaten to death one night only to reappear with no wounds the next morning."

Shon shrugged to cover his shock at the chief's illicit knowledge. "Prisons are rife with that sort of waste."

The Trytinorn regarded him steadily. "If you are what I think you are, then your reassignment will not come through as a request. Intelligence will yank you out of here faster than you can say 'Messiah.'"

"What is your position on this matter?" Shon asked, still wary.

"Had I the sort of talent for Jala's kind of work, I likely would have joined an all-male cloister in the most remote portion of the rainforest on Trytin," the chief said. "Or, perhaps, ended it before someone could force me into doing something I personally found revolting. If that were possible."

"Possible, but extremely difficult." Shon turned the disk in his hands. "I need time, Chief. Time to think."

"I'll run interference for you for as long as I can. But make no mistake, Major. I'm in charge of security for one colony. The people who will be coming for you are responsible for thousands of worlds. If it comes to a shoving match, I will lose, and you will go."

"I won't let it come to that, Chief." Shon stood and began to salute before he dropped his arm. "This has nothing to do with military business. For this, I now consider you a friend."

"The friend of an oKia warrior need never go hungry, or hunt alone, or sleep without an eye to watch his back," Norash said. "Isn't that how it goes?"

"We also share our females," Shon informed him, "but given the differences in our sizes, that would likely not go well for them, or us."

"My mate would find it novel. I would be too busy trying not to step on any woman of yours." Norash uttered an amused sound before his expression sobered. "Valtas, you have my eyes at your back. Keep yours there as well. They will be coming for you."

Shon nodded. "I'll be prepared."

"We're prepared to return to the surface, Dr. Selmar," the blubheaded humanoid said. "You wanted to speak to me about some problem before we left?"

Teresa Selmar wanted to yell at the reconstruction site manager, Pridsan, but she settled for another visual survey of the Underwater Research Dome's upper deck. The damages to K-2's first subaqua science facility didn't trouble her as much as what had caused them, or how they were being repaired.

The wall of transparent plas, which admitted half of their natural light, was an important feature of the URD. Land-dwelling scientists from K-2's colony had never had an opportunity to dwell among the 'Zangians in their element, and they expected to learn a great deal more about the aquatics via observation through the dome's walls.

The specially reinforced plas also kept water and native life-forms out, and Teresa and her staff from drowning.

"It's these panels that your crew installed in my upper level," she told him. "They'll have to go."

Pridsan, a squat Farradonan whose shape resembled that of a Terran who had been compressed into the form of a block, gave her a belligerent look. "Doctor, these panels are identical to the ones that were originally installed."

Teresa tapped her short fingernails against the new plas. "Those would be the panels that cracked and threatened to collapse in on us after the three mogshrike attacked the dome."

"It was one mogshrike, according to the reports I reviewed," the blocky humanoid told her. "The other two were attacking the natives. Besides, I find it very hard to believe that three 'shrikes would attack the URD simultaneously. I've worked on this planet for thirty revolutions, and we know those monsters always swim rogue. They'd probably devour each other before they'd hunt cooperatively."

Most of the colonists believed the same thing, because that was how it had always been with 'shrikes. Up until the day Teresa had opened the URD.

"I was here when it happened, Pridsan, and I can count. Trust me, we had three of them." Teresa recalled the terror she had felt, standing helpless on the inside of the dome as one of the 'shrikes slammed its massive head into the viewer panels. The mental image of that gaping maw, lined with all those jagged teeth, still made her stomach clench. "We're expecting members of the Peace Summit to pay a visit to the URD. I'm not going to have substandard materials cause an interplanetary incident."

"Whatever drew the 'shrike to attack was an aberration, and there's nothing I can do about that. Maybe you should call off the visitation." Pridsan scowled at one of the staff researchers, who stood talking to a pair of his workers. From their gestures, it was obvious that they, too, were discussing the integrity of the viewer panels. "Maybe you should tell these diplomats to stay on their ship."

"That should contribute mightily to the peace process," Teresa said. "How should I phrase it? 'Welcome to K-2, stay the hell out of our sea?'"

"If you think that will work." Pridsan expelled some air. "Look, Doctor, my people and I are slotted to break ground on the new outpatient facility over at the FreeClinic tomorrow. This site hasn't been allocated any more time or alternate materials, so we're done here. There's nothing more I can do for you."

"Then how do I get better panels?" Teresa demanded.

The Farradonan shifted his I beam-shaped shoulders. "Make your case with the construction code office, or petition the council."

"That will take weeks, maybe months." Teresa thought for a minute. "What about the Department of Colonial Construction? Wouldn't they have something to say about the safety issue?"

Pridsan regarded the plas wall. "OCS approved your original design as safe. They gave us the schematics they had on database so that we could rebuild according to them. They won't red-flag this site as unsafe. It will have to be the facility manager here."

"*I'm* the facility manager."

"Then you decide whether to shut it down or continue on until you can have better replacement materials approved. I do wish you luck with it." Pridsan went over to his workers and exchanged a few words with them before escorting them out to the air lock. The researcher gave Teresa an exasperated look before returning to her station.

"I know just how you feel," she muttered before striding into her office to start composing her council petition.

Half an hour into justifying the expenditure for safer, multilayered, reinforced panels, Teresa took a break to make a server of coffee. As she swallowed some analgesics to treat a budding tension headache, her door panel chimed. "Come in."

A towering being with multijointed limbs ducked over to pass beneath the too-short threshold of the door panel. Although the N-jui were classified as humanoid, T'Kafanitana strongly resembled an eight-foot-tall, maroon-colored version of a Terran praying mantis. A talented chemist and researcher, T'Kaf worked as Teresa's lab manager and general assistant.

The N-jui straightened and regarded Teresa with four sparkling dark eyes. "Doctor, forgive the interruption. I have the results on those water temperature samples that you requested." When Teresa indicated the server in her hand, T'Kaf shook her head. "Thank you, but no. That beverage makes my diaphragm spasm all night."

Teresa grinned. "More for me. What did you find out from the temp data?"

"Nothing abnormal." T'Kaf went over and loaded the lab results into the main console terminal. "Samples taken from a two-hundred-kim section of the Western Sea coast match temperatures measured in the same region over the last two decades. The water is not growing any colder."

"There goes my main theory right down the drain." Teresa studied the numbers. "So if the coastal waters aren't cooling off enough to attract the 'shrike, then what is?"

The N-jui made a cautious gesture. "It could be a shift in the migratory patterns of their primary food sources. Or, perhaps, their breeding habits are changing."

"Have they been interbreeding?" a male Terran voice asked.

Both women looked up at the man standing in the doorway. His short black hair, cool blue eyes, and smooth features were unmistakably Terran. The brown uniform and double-bar insignia on his collar indicated he was a League captain.

Teresa could react, or she could play it cool. Since they had an audience, she chose the latter. "May I help you?"

"That's my question." He walked in and sized up the room and the N-jui before doing the same to Teresa. "Captain Noel Argate, Pmoc Quadrant Marine Research Division."

Captain *Noel Argate. How far the mighty have fallen.* "I was under the impression that MRD have their base ops on a water world two systems from here." A planet filled with aquatic life-forms too primitive to protest whatever atrocities the League committed in their waters, and what the *hell* was Professor Emeritus Noel Argate doing in a damn uniform?

"We are. I'm a marine biologist, temporarily assigned to K-2 to observe your native population." Argate offered Teresa his ID and assignment disks. "Quadrant occasionally has skirmishes on worlds with populated marine territories, so some of what I learn here could possibly help the civilians caught in the war."

Help civilians. Maybe if he were repeatedly prodded by a high-energy discharge device, Teresa thought. Otherwise, the Noel Argate she had known wouldn't have wasted the effort it took to flick nasal discharge in the general direction of anyone who couldn't pay him, advance him, or kiss his perfectly toned, world-renowned ass.

"Hold that thought, Captain." Teresa inserted the disks and verified Argate's claims with Colonial Administration. Either he had a forger with first-class skills, or he was on K-2 on legitimate business for the League.

Which was impossible. Noel would never have left Terra, and he certainly wouldn't have taken the massive compensation cut it would have cost him to join the military.

Teresa pulled a copy of his orders from Transport and compared them to the one he had presented to her. "All right, Captain, let's assume you're not lying through your teeth." She handed the disks back to him. "What do you want from me?"

The old Argate would have given her a suggestive look. This one merely offered up a polite smile. "I'd like the opportunity to work at the URD and provide whatever assistance I can. Of course, you're in charge here, Doctor. If you feel my presence would be a hindrance, I can set up quarters back at the surface colony. If space permits, however, I would be delighted to stay here and possibly help with your mogshrike problem."

Teresa blinked. The man was on some sort of psychosis-inducing substance. That was the only possible answer.

"Excuse me, but I must go and check on an experiment I was conducting in the lab." T'Kaf rose and collected the lab results. "I will speak to you later, Dr. Selmar." She spared Argate a glance and inclined her head. "Captain."

Teresa could secure the door panel after the chemist left and have it out with Noel Argate, the architect of her ruin back on Terra. That was what he was expecting, though, and she had no intention of playing up to his ego. She took shelter in a calm silence and what she hoped was an indifferent stare.

"Your lab chief doesn't care for Terrans, I take it?" Argate asked.

"Her species tends to be somewhat reserved." Teresa had picked up on T'Kaf's instant dislike of the League captain, too, but the N-jui might have simply resented the man's intrusion, or sensed Teresa's silent but violent internal reaction. "T'Kaf is not accustomed to working with males."

"I'd heard that N-jui don't permit males to leave their homeworld." A little contempt edged his tone. "Rather like Ylydii females in their attitude, aren't they?"

That's right, throw out that casual reminder of how well educated you are. Teresa felt a little better, now that she was seeing the man's true persona emerge. *You just don't realize that you're on my turf now.*

"Ylydii females are dominant, and keep their males like pampered domesticates," she informed him. "One class of N-jui males are essentially mindless, walking semen vessels who are devoured after mating."

"Ah." The captain nodded. "I will remember the distinction, particularly if I am ever propositioned by your lab chief."

The sense of humor was new, too. "T'Kaf is not a breeder. Like their males, there are at least six different subgender classifications of N-jui females, but only the breeders mate and kill." Teresa's gaze went to a large, dark shadow passing outside the viewing panel. "I'll have to discuss this with you another time; my mate is waiting for me."

Argate followed her gaze. "You married a 'Zangian."

"The natives here are polygamous, seasonal breeders, so there is no such institution." She showed him some of her teeth in a display that would have seriously upset an aquatic. "However, Dairatha and I have scandalized the pod by remaining exclusive to each other."

"That provokes a thousand more impertinent questions, but I won't keep you." The captain offered a data chip. "This is my relay code. If you decide you have the time and space for me here at the URD, please let me know."

Teresa knew quadrant wouldn't have sent Argate to K-2 simply to serve as an observer or researcher. Nor was he here to be her new best friend—not with the unpleasant history between them. If he really had joined the military, then the League wouldn't have wasted him on K-2. They had better things to do with their enlisted scientists, such as having them design and build more death machines for the war.

If that's why he's here, I'd better keep him where I can watch him. If it's not, I'd better keep him here anyway.

"There's an empty office at the end of the midlevel corridor, on the small side, but the adjoining quarters are rather comfortable," she said. "As long as you don't disrupt my staff's routine, then you can occupy that for the duration of your assignment." She could also monitor his transmissions and activities, as her own office was directly next to it.

"Thank you, Dr. Selmar. I'll see that you won't regret your generosity." He inclined his head and then left the office.

I let the devil steal my dance shoes, Teresa thought, *and now I ask him to waltz.*

A bump on the viewer panel made Teresa swivel around to look into her mate's recessed eyes. One of the oldest males in the pod, Dairatha mu J'Kane's bulk now stretched out almost three meters in length and weighed close to half a ton.

The sight of Dairatha made Teresa forget about Noel and filled her instead with strong, conflicting emotions. Despite their differences, the 'Zangian was the only male she had ever loved, would ever love. Yet because of their differences, that love was ultimately doomed. His size now made all but the mildest love play physically dangerous for Teresa, and soon it would no longer be possible for him to leave the water. In time the only manner in which they could be together would be with Teresa in a breathing rig, or like this, staring at each other from opposite sides of a wall.

Dairatha, who, like all 'Zangians lived in the now, never worried about such things. *Come-out, come-out,* he finned, turning in a long, slow circle to show her his entire length. Such a display was usually only made to capture the interest of an unmated female, but he still used it with her to show that his affection and desire remained constant and unchanged.

Teresa swallowed against the tightness in her throat and pressed one hand to the plas. "I'll be right there, my love."

CHAPTER 4

"One of the controllers over at Flight said we were going to love this," Loknoth told Burn as they entered the briefing room. "So I assume the commander is having you incarcerated for the remaining duration of the war."

"Why let him go when the war ends?" Saree asked. "I say keep him locked up until he is too old and toothless to do more than chase softshell *sterbol* around the silt."

Burn ignored the acid-tinged teasing and took his place among the other trainee pilots. The pod was still angry with him, but Dair wouldn't reassign him now. Not with the Peace Summit about to take place. If anything, she would give him a strafer to fly and let him take his place among the patrol. She needed all the pilots she could get up into space.

The more Burn thought about it, the more sense it made. Dair had had enough time to think over his maneuver; she'd have seen the merits of his actions by now. She'd also taken the time to cool off and avoid any more unpleasant interactions—she'd certainly spent enough time avoiding him in the water yesterday. *Maybe she's come to her senses and will let me have Rescue Three.*

The briefing was short and to the point, and was given by Onkar, not Dair.

"We have diplomatic ships from Ylyd and Ninra converging on the planet, as well as a ship of Skartesh launching from K-2. Patrol shifts will provide escort and cover for all of the delegates. Any unauthorized vessels will be reported at once to Flight Control, and ground command will then decide if and how they are to be engaged." He looked out at the other 'Zangians. "These people who are coming here are not only dignitaries, but important leaders on their worlds. You will remember that in your dealings with them and act according to the appropriate protocols."

Burn had been too young to meet the last Ylydii delegation, which had traveled to K-2 when he was a pup for a brief cultural exchange with the colonists and the natives. The meeting between the two species had been held in space, and while some of the other young members of the coastal pod had been permitted a short visit to the Ylydii ship, his mother had refused to let him go.

It had frustrated him at the time, to be kept back like a newling. Hearing how strange the alien aquatics had seemed from other podlings had only made him feel worse—he'd really wanted a look at them himself—but Znora had been flatly adamant.

You're too young, Byorn.

Now he wasn't. *Maybe this time I'll get to meet one of them.* Their females were said to be smaller but very exotic-looking, and very strong-willed.

Burn waited as position assignments were called. Saree was slotted as wing leader, as always, but that didn't worry him. Neither did it bother him when he wasn't called to join the body of the patrol. Dair had decided in his favor, obviously, and he would be flying Rescue Three, at the very front of the patrol.

Then the briefing was over, and the pilots filed out to the flight line to board their assigned ships, and Burn was left behind, with no assignment at all.

Onkar waited until the last of the pod had left before addressing him. "She's still very angry with you, Byorn."

"Which means?"

The other male didn't mince words this time. "You're grounded from flight duty and will report for remedial trainer sessions until further notice."

Burn looked up at the controller's view panel, and saw his cousin standing and talking to some of the tower crew. "We'll just see about that."

Onkar didn't try to stop him, but he did accompany him as far as the lift to the control level. "Remember that while Dair is my mate, she is still in command of this unit. I cannot thwart her orders."

"Did you try?" At Onkar's nod, Burn released a rude burst of air through his gillets. "Fine. If she wishes to punish me, then she can do it to my face, in person."

Dair didn't appear surprised to see Burn, but she barely gave him a glance. "Your training session initiates in three minutes, Sublieutenant. You'd better haul tail over to the simulator."

"I've flown all those sessions a minimum of three times each, Commander. I can perform the flight patterns in my sleep."

"I've altered some of the scenarios so that you can concentrate more on strategic flying." She waved him off. "Get to it."

"No." He waited until he had her full attention. "You're drowning me with this training waste, Dair. I'm trained. Use me. Watch me fly."

Her silver eyes flashed. "I have better things to do than witness the moment you vaporize yourself in orbit."

Verrig, the chief of flight engineering, stepped up behind Dair. "If you younglings can't play nicely, I will relieve both of you from duty."

"You can't do that to me," Dair snapped.

"On the contrary." The chief gave her a mild look. "I most certainly can, if I feel you are physically unfit for duty. One of the perks of being in charge of the hardware around here." He gestured toward a console. "Shall I consult with Subcommander Onkar on the matter?"

Burn bit back a strum of mirth. "I think he has you by the tail, cousin."

Dair gave him a lethal glance. "Shut up, Burn."

"Trainer pilots relieved from duty generally end up scrubbing out engine vents for me," Verrig advised him. "A month of that might curb your amusement."

"If you're looking for someone to take on your gunner, Jadaira, I could use one."

The 'Zangians and Verrig turned to see Shon Valtas standing nearby, shamelessly listening in on their conversation.

Dair eyed him. "I thought you were through with trying to commit suicide, Major."

"You won't regret it, Shon." Burn gave the oKiaf a slap on the shoulder. "I'm checked out on the StarFire now; have they installed the sphere in your strafer yet?"

"We're still waiting for authorization," Verrig put in. "There have been some problems finding pilots who can let the control array take over. They end up resisting it, which sends the array into auto-shutdown."

"The StarFire array will *not* be installed in *any* of the patrol vessels," Dair stated flatly. "Even if quadrant approves it, it's too dangerous for anyone to use until we do more testing on our people."

Burn tapped the side of his head. "I had no problem with it."

"Anyone with *functional* brains," Dair amended. "In the event you've forgotten, our mission now is search and rescue, not search and destroy. Standard weapons systems are more than adequate for any mission needs."

Burn couldn't believe it was his cousin talking like this. "Having a pup really has turned you into a paranoid old dam, Dair."

She looked ready to smack him again. "Be happy I'm willing to allow you to serve as Major Valtas's gunner, and he's crazy enough to put up with you."

"You can't keep putting me off, you know," Burn told her. "Eventually you'll have to put me in the pilot's seat, and then I'm going to outfly everyone in the pod. Even you, Dair. Is that why you've kept me grounded? Because you don't want me to take your place?"

Verrig caught Dair's arm. "No hitting or biting. My crew doesn't need to be cleaning blood out of these consoles."

Shon clapped a hand on Burn's shoulder. "Okay, my friend, you've had your say. Time to fly."

"Just a minute." The anger faded from Dair's eyes and was replaced by that blank frostiness she used when dealing with unpleasant mouthbreathers. "This is not personal between you and me anymore, Sublieutenant. This is the military, and I am your commander. You will follow the orders I give you."

"Or?"

"Or you will be permanently relieved of duty. Naturally you can apply for review and reassignment. I believe there are some openings in Engineering and Flight Control or, if that might prove to be too much of an intellectual challenge, the Facility Maintenance Crew."

The insult made Burn's hide darken, and he turned to Shon. "I'll run the preflight, Major. Subcommander." He didn't trust himself to speak to Dair, so he walked out to the corridor and headed for the Flight Line.

Dair had wrestled with the aftereffects of her transformation for weeks. The integration of human DNA into her own had not only permanently changed the color and structure of her body, but had given it some new, strange, and often disturbing functions. Like the heated, crawling sensation she felt over her hide whenever she was thwarted. At the moment her face felt as hot as if she were back on Ninra, baking under the merciless sunlight there.

There were the new emotions, too. Such as the one she was feeling now, which made her want to chase after her cousin and beat him senseless. Didn't he understand that she was only trying to keep him from killing himself in some male-hormone-laden idiocy?

She had no answers, so she looked at Shon. "Would you explain to me why males feel compelled to behave like that?"

"I believe Byorn's finally growing up." Shon seemed amused.

"Perhaps his body has, but his mind and his mouth are growing more infantile by the day." A wave of nausea made Dair grope for a handhold, and then Shon was there, his arm supporting her. "Sorry. Teresa tells me this gastric distress is common for breeding Terran females. Just my luck, I get to experience it as well." She began the full, slow breathing exercises Teresa had taught her.

"I've never seen you so at odds with your gunner before," Shon said. "What is wrong between the two of you?"

Dair debated whether to talk about it or not—pod business was a private thing—but it might help to get Shon's perspective. "Burn's dam, Znora, cornered me when he began his pilot training."

"I remember her. She does not like you."

"More like she's hated me ever since I was born," Dair corrected him wryly. "I thought she would attack me physically when she discovered that Burn had signed up to follow me into the military. Over time I think she realized that I would protect Burn while he served as my gunner. Now she's terrified that he's going to get himself blasted into space dust, and I won't be there to save him."

"And you're afraid that she's right?"

Dair pressed her hand over the curve in her abdomen. "I know a lot more about the maternal instinct now, Shon. At least, I know how I'd feel if it were my pup sliding into a flight harness."

"Jadaira, you have put enough pressure on yourself, flying watchout for this Peace Summit and keeping Bio Rescue operational," Shon told her. "You can't also keep Burn grounded forever. He's performed beyond expectations in the simulators."

"You checked his logs?"

"His achievement scores in the trainer are better than mine were. In some cases, better than yours."

"I know." She closed her eyes against the uncomfortable stinging sensation coming from the new holes in her eye rims that Teresa had said were new tear ducts. "I know I should let him go. But, Shon, if anything happens to him, and I'm not there to prevent it, I'll also know that I'll never forgive myself. Is that some sort of bizarre human emotion?"

"No," the oKiaf assured her. "It's love."

She uttered the burping sound that Teresa had assured her was human laughter. "Then I guess I do really love that 'shrike-sized idiot." Her stomach rolled, and she breathed in deeply until the sensation eased. "Considering how pleasant this pregnancy-associated nausea feels, I rather wonder why her species isn't extinct by now."

"Perversity. Terrans aren't happy unless they regularly purge their gullets." Shon helped her over to one of the flight control terminals and eased her into the seat. "Jadaira, this is likely not the best time to talk about what happened to you after you were pushed through the suns' corona, but I feel responsible. If I hadn't—"

"Don't." She rested her hand against his mouth to stop his words.

"You must stop blaming yourself for my injuries. *I* decided to chase the Skartesh and keep them from flying their ships into the suns. *You* were unconscious on one of those ships at the time, remember? How could you have prevented any of it?"

"That was what I was thinking, after, when Onkar brought you to the dying place." He seemed to be struggling for words. "Jadaira, I am responsible for more than you know."

"Let's not nip each other over the details. We saved the Skartesh— that was the important thing. My stepmother tells me these changes may contribute to the evolution of my species." She grimaced. "I don't think I'm going to tell the other females about morning sickness, though. They may decide to stop having pups altogether, and that will be the end of our species."

"This transformation wouldn't have happened if I hadn't interfered in your life," Shon said. "I couldn't let things take their normal course."

"Of course you couldn't." *Duo* knew the only reason the Hsktskt weren't occupying K-2 and all the other worlds in their system was thanks to Shon's impersonation of the Skartesh's dead Messiah.

"But I am to blame—"

Moving as silently as ever, Onkar joined them. "I will take my share of the blame, too, Major."

Dair watched the two males face each other and held her breath. In the recent past, Onkar's jealousy over her friendship with Shon had been obsessive; he had nearly killed Shon twice out of possessive rage. She only released her breath when her mate extended his arm and clasped one end of his fin to Shon's paw in friendship.

"Your mate should be on medical leave," Shon said, ignoring her subsequent hiss of outrage. "I worry that the stress of safeguarding this Peace Summit will cause harm to her and your child."

"I have been doing my best to convince her of that, but my mate feels otherwise," Onkar said. "Unfortunately, she still outranks me as well."

"Don't talk about me like I'm not here," Dair demanded. "Shon, report to the Flight Line before my cousin hijacks a strafer. Keep him strapped to the weapons array until after this Peace Summit is over."

"Will you allow him to pilot after the summit is concluded?" Shon asked.

"If he's still in one piece, yes."

Teresa had made no headway in finding out Noel Argate's real reasons for coming to K-2. As Noel was about as sentimental and affectionate as a tapeworm, she suspected it had nothing to with her personally. Yet everyone she spoke to, from Colonial Admin to Argate's commander, insisted the captain had told her the truth. The truth from a man who had built his entire academic standing on Terra by climbing the bony pile of the many careers he had methodically ruined.

Teresa should know, since her own had been the first sacrifice on the altar of Noel Argate's ambition.

She pushed aside thoughts of the captain and surveyed her staff as they gathered for the meeting she had called. Like her, the URD residential staff had been working around the clock to clean up and repair what was needed to reopen the facility. Instead of the excitement and anticipation that had been present on the day the 'shrikes attacked, there was now an air of weary pride among the workers.

This wasn't just a research facility to them anymore. It was their territory, and they'd fought and bled for it.

There were also more than a few troubled looks directed toward their view of the waters outside, which was why Teresa had decided to bring them together.

"Good morning. As you know, repairs to the URD are now officially complete, as of yesterday. As of today, I am raising hell with the council to acquire some additional reinforcement for the view panels. I expect to get them by the time the URD is decommissioned and declared obsolete." Teresa acknowledged the tired chuckles with one of her own. "The bureaucrats and data pushers don't know how dedicated we are, but they'll catch on. In the meantime, I thank all of you for a job well done."

A few people applauded, and there were various other sounds of approval and gratitude from those who didn't know the Terran custom of slapping two appendages together.

"Elders of the coastal pod are taking their own measures to safeguard their people and us by sending out pairs of males to patrol their borders." Teresa displayed a photoscan on the wall vid of two big males swimming in the defensive, parallel position. "Those of you who are going out diving for botanical samples, keep these patrols in sight at all times. If there is any sign of trouble, return to the URD at once."

Teresa prepared to introduce the next topic when she saw Noel slip into the back of the room. He nodded toward her before moving to an empty seat.

We're best friends now, are we? The side of her mouth curled. "You may have noticed that we have a visitor from Quadrant Marine Division. His name is Captain Noel Argate, and he's a marine biologist specializing in Terran aquatics. He may even be able to help us with our 'shrike problem."

"Are there a great many 'shrikes on Terra?" someone asked in a deliberately innocent tone.

"Not the last time I was there, but maybe things have changed. Captain Argate?" Teresa gestured for him come to the front, and happily yielded her place at the platform to him.

Now, she thought, *let's see how you ooze your way out of this one.*

Argate scanned the faces around the room before he spoke. "I'm not quite up to speed yet, but I have looked over some of the data on the recent changes in mogshrike behavior. Dr. Selmar indicated that the native sentients have stepped up their safeguards, so my first question would be, what are *you* doing to protect this facility?"

"We've set up a security sensor grid along the seamount ridge, and are monitoring whatever comes in from the outer currents," Teresa told him. "The problem with monitoring is that the mogshrikes move too fast to give us enough time to evacuate. We can't avoid an attack; we can only respond to one."

Argate nodded. "Has any effort been made to identify why the 'shrikes are moving into the warmer waters? It was my understanding that the temperatures here are too high for them to tolerate."

For someone who just arrived on planet yesterday, he's amazingly up-to-date on things. Out loud, Teresa said, "That was true, up until the day we opened for business. The current theories are in two camps. The mogshrikes may be in the process of changing the way they hunt. They've always lived as rogues, so we're not sure why they would now choose to organize into pack hunters. There has also been a marked increase in the number of smaller 'shrikes being detected by our deep-sea probes, which could indicate an overpopulation problem. There is no explanation for the recent birth rate explosion, either, except for the fact that 'shrikes have no natural predators except for themselves."

"It would help if we could locate the 'shrikes' breeding grounds," one staffer put in. "We could monitor the activity there; get some sort of idea of what they're doing differently."

"The reason we've never discovered a 'shrike breeding ground is because I don't believe they exist," Teresa said. "These are free-roaming animals that cover enormous territories in pursuit of migratory shoals."

"When they desire a mate, they likely hunt one," Noel said. "The way they would food."

You'd know. "That would keep the 'shrikes from having to break with their traditional, solitary behavior to rendezvous at a particular spot," she agreed, "but it doesn't explain the increase in population. Let me access the archived readings." Teresa went over and displayed a spreadsheet on the wall vid. "According to these probe recordings, 'shrike births have more than doubled this cycle alone."

"They must be communicating with each other," Argate said, and then frowned as laughter erupted around him. "I'm sorry, but that's the only explanation. How else would they find each other over such great distances?"

Teresa took another moment to savor the gaffe before she clued him in. "The 'shrikes have no vocal cords, no language, and no reason to develop either. The most primitive language among the aquatics, modal action patterns, or what the 'Zangians call 'fin,' is nonverbal body language understood by many species. We've never observed the 'shrikes using or responding to fin."

"Seeing as they occupy waters not inhabited by the 'Zangians, they may not speak the local dialect," Argate said. "Have you considered that?"

Teresa considered asking the captain to go and jump in the moon pool without a breathing rig, but then decided it was a good idea to inform him—and remind everyone else—precisely with what they were dealing.

"Mogshrikes are a cold-blooded species at the peak of their evolution," she stated flatly. "They've existed on K-2 for at least forty million years. They feed on anything that moves: wrill, teleosts, copepods, balaeneans and, if hungry enough, each other. These creatures are incredibly ancient, and have had ample time to evolve into the perfect killing machines. Which is what they are."

"So have the 'Zangians, and according to the data I've studied— mostly written by you, Doctor—their brains are as complex and developed as any advanced humanoid's," Argate said, his tone implying her conclusions might be at least questionable. "So why automatically classify the 'shrikes, who have existed at least as long as the 'Zangians, as mindless monsters?"

She wondered how snide and superior Noel would be if she brought him face-to-face with a 'shrike and let him collect a little data.

Now there is an idea. "Ballie, would you go down and pull the probe vids we have in the storage room?"

"*IceBlade*, you are cleared for launch."

Burn shifted in his harness, chafing at the uncomfortable and wholly new sensation of breathing air while seated inside a strafer. "Major, why didn't you remind me that you're a mouth-breather before I agreed to be your gunner?"

"Probably because I breathe through my nose." Shon used maneuvering thrusters to clear the launch pad before turning the strafer nose-up to engage the primary engines. "You've flown before without liquid atmosphere, in Rescue One with Jadaira."

"Yeah." Burn groaned as the g-forces slapped him back and kept him pinned. "I hated that, too."

The green skies around them quickly turned a star-pocked black as the *IceBlade* escaped the stratosphere and K-2's gravitational fields. Once in orbit, Shon righted the strafer and flew to where the remainder of the planetary patrol had assembled.

"About time you got here, Major," Saree transmitted. "Take position at the left rear, behind Loknoth in the *CoveSong*. We'll be flying standard patrol formation around the planet. Stay toothy; these delegate ships are slotted to arrive on our watch."

"Just what we need," Burn muttered. "More civilians to herd."

"Our orders are to escort only." Shon moved the strafer behind Loknoth's *CoveSong*. "Keep the portside sensors on continuous sweep and let me know if you pick up any energy signatures."

Burn checked their coordinates. "Portside is where the moon ring is. I don't think they're holding their whine session there."

"Merc ships use asteroids and natural satellites as cover. If anything comes out of there, it won't be to provide a welcome." Shon adjusted their course to match Loknoth's and remain in the double-bow formation. "What are we carrying?"

Burn checked his panels. "Pulse cannons, fully charged, smartorps tubed and ready, a clutch of signal jammers, drill probes, and cell shunts. Plenty of extra shielding." He thought of the StarFire prototype and felt even more annoyed. "Want me to dust things while I'm sitting back here?"

Shon chuckled. "No, but if you see anything move that shouldn't, you can dust that."

Burn felt a little better as the patrol completed its first orbit of the planet. Serving as Shon's gunner wasn't as important as having a command and flying his own ship, but he could observe and ask questions, maybe pick up a few tricks.

"Where did you get your wings, Major? The Academy?"

"oKia. I used to joc freighters before I enlisted." Shon followed Loknoth's lead and bypassed a cluster of asteroids. "First time they put me in the seat of a fighter, I nearly crashed into a Transport hangar. Big difference in control response."

"Dair's been making me fly everything in the trainer, from mini-launches to ore haulers." Burn checked a signal light on the companel but found it too weak to register more than static. *Probably an echo from the planet.* "I don't know how those spider miners can stand piloting those monsters. Takes forever to get them off the pad."

"Aksellans are far more patient than most species. Stand by, I'm getting some wave clutter." Shon fell silent for a moment. "Are you reading that? It's patterned."

"I thought it was an echo. Can't pull more than fuzz off the transponder, but I'll see if I can trace the source." Burn narrowed the companel's range finder and watched the numbers scroll onto his screen. "Point of origin is close by, maybe within a thousand kim. Whoever's transmitting must not have any power behind it; it's still barely registering on my com."

"Patrol leader, this is *IceBlade*," Shon transmitted to Saree. "We've detected a repeating signal, low wave, unable to read. Could be a distress call."

"I'll see if I can boost it," Saree responded. "Downrelay to Rescue One."

"It's not a voice trans," Burn said as he studied the data scroll. "It's binary, position code maybe. No ID, but the frequency is Ylydii."

"The only ship with a flight plan filed for this sector is the Ylydii ambassador's ship," Saree replied. "We'd better call this one in to Flight."

"Stand by, Wing Leader." Shon shut down the intership relay. "Burn, if I turn the ship into the wave, can you amplify it through the hull?"

It wasn't standard op to use the strafer's shock-absorbing alloy skin in that manner, but Burn tapped some keys and redirected the transponder. "Acknowledged. Receiving more of it, Major." He watched the numbers again. "That's definitely position and bearing. Ship is not flying to K-2, though—it's headed out of the system."

"The Ylydii make many jaunts out of here?" Shon asked.

"No. They contract offworlders to do their transport. Ylydii ships aren't built for intersystem travel." Burn widened his sensor sweep, encompassing the position of the transmitting vessel. "They've got another ship with them. Appears that they're docked."

"Wing Leader, recommend we do a flyby and see what's going on out there," Shon transmitted to Saree. "Something is not right with that vessel or its heading."

"Attempting to signal the Ylydii ship," Saree responded. After a short period of silence, a sharp sound came over the open channel. "Their transponder array is down or they're not responding; my relay is just bouncing back. Patrol, initiate flight pattern star-delta. Major, if you would, take point."

Shon eased out of formation and moved to the front of the other strafers as they realigned into the scout pattern. "Wing Leader, recommend we power down weapons until we have a visual or contact."

"Acknowledged and agreed. Patrol, put all weapons on standby."

Burn felt a new wave of frustration as he made the changes to his firing control panel. "Major, if something's wrong, shouldn't we fly in prepared to engage?"

"We can't approach a com-disabled diplomatic ship with our power cells flaring, Sublieutenant. The Ylydii crew would read the spikes and interpret our advance as a coordinated attack. So would any mercs that have taken over control of the ship."

"Right, so we fly by and fin hi," Burn grumbled. "What happens if the other ship *is* a merc and attacks us?"

"Then we find out just how good a gunner you are, Sublieutenant."

The flight to rendezvous with the Ylydii ship took only a few minutes, and Burn's attention strayed from his sensor panels only when the enormous vessel appeared outside the starboard view panels. "Suns, that's big."

As all life-forms did, the Ylydii brought their native environment into space with them. Unlike the compact strafers, their vessel had obviously been designed for maximum space and comfort for the aquatic crew and passengers. A central control module served as the hub for two orbiting wheels of gigantic, transparent immersion tanks. Each tank stretched out the length of ten strafers and boasted enough liquid to comfortably accommodate a dozen or more occupants, while interconnecting conduits provided easy access to other tanks and areas of the ship.

"Looks like no one's home." Burn scanned the emitter stations, which were positioned to illuminate the tank environments but remained dark and cold. "Power relays are functioning at minimum levels." In fact, the entire ship looked dead, and that made Burn's neck itch. "Major, permission to engage weapons array."

"Not yet." Shon made a pass under the ship, where a small cargo carrier vessel sat docked to the command hub. "They may have suffered some collision damage."

"With no debris field? I don't think so." Burn scanned the carrier and the resulting spikes on his panel made his heart pound. "Major, that docked hauler is outfitted to the teeth, weapon cells powered, ready to fire."

"What about the repeating signal? Where is the point of origin?"

Burn switched over to the companel. "Inside the ambassador's ship. Correction, there are two signals. One is too faint to read. The other originates from the docked carrier."

"Why didn't we pick up that one?"

"It's being focus-transmitted, sir. Directly back toward planet Ylyd."

Onkar's harsh voice came over Burn's headgear. "We have you on monitor and have contacted Ylyd. The second signal is a distress call. They're asking the Ylydii fleet to rendezvous with them to repel an attack."

"No one's attacking them." Burn rechecked his readings. "It's a decoy, Subcommander. The mercs probably have other ships concealed or waiting just out of sensor range."

"That's my feeling," Shon added.

"You can't attack the ambassador's ship," Onkar told them. "If the signal is, by a far stretch, legitimate, then it will cause an interplanetary incident and disrupt the peace talks before they begin."

Burn thought the peace talks might have a better chance if there were people still alive to attend them. "Major, we have to board the ship. I can take the transpod over and relay what's actually happening in there."

"We'll need a diversion," Shon said. "I show a clutter region within fifty kim; that's where I'd stash the ambush ships. If we fly over and begin shooting our way through it, it should draw them out, and create enough interference to let the transpod slip in undetected."

"It's risky. Byorn—"

"I'll be armed and ready. They'll be distracted and unprepared."

"Very well. Major, I'm launching Rescue Three to handle casualties. Byorn, protect the ambassador and her people, no matter what the cost."

Burn saw a power spike on his board. "Major, carrier preparing to fire."

"Patrol, initiate evasive maneuvers," Shon transmitted to the rest of the pod just before the carrier detached from the Ylydii ship. The smaller vessel darted out and fired a wide spread of pulse energy at the *IceBlade*. "Gunner, engage weapons array and return fire."

Burn already had his panels up and his systems ready by the time Shon gave the order. "Firing wing cannons, launching torps." He sequenced his vollies to Shon's rolling flight pattern as the major evaded the worst of the attack spread. Shudders vibrated through the strafer as the pulses he couldn't dodge glanced off the hull.

To keep from firing on their own ships, Burn monitored the winding flight paths of the other strafers. New power signatures peppered his sensor panel. "Reading six new contacts," he told Shon and gave him the bearings. "They're coming out of the clutter."

Shon avoided a side-volley from the carrier and flew in and under the diplomatic vessel. "Think you can handle a midflight transfer?"

Burn looked up at the open dock port the carrier had left unguarded. "As long as you can fly and fire at the same time."

"Transfer weapons control and prepare for emergency transpod dock," Shon said. "Flood the pod with liquid atmosphere."

A midflight dock was one of the most complicated and dangerous of pilot maneuvers. Burn engaged the panels that separated him from Shon before opening the strafer's rear flood valves and filling his own pod with liquid synthetically treated to closely match the composition of 'Zangian seawater. Once he was breathing liquid again, he transferred weaponry control to Shon and enabled the severance system.

"Transpod ready for detachment," Burn signaled from the pod's transponder.

"Coming up on Ylydii ship dock portal," Shon's voice said over Burn's headgear. "Prepare to release at my green."

Burn powered up the small positioning thrusters that would give him approximately twenty seconds to dock with the larger ship. "Ready, Major."

"Release point in five, four, three, two, one, *green*."

The transpod ejected out of the body of the strafer and flew directly up. Burn guided the direction of the positioning thrusters, matching his hatch collar with that of the Ylydii ship. Despite his care, he went in hard and hot, and the two portals met with a violent jolt before unification clamps on both sides engaged.

"Transpod in dock." Burn wasted no time as he ripped off his harness and darted up to manually seal the hatch atmosphere collars and scan what was on the other side of the Ylydii's atmosphere lock. The display showed positive pressure on the interior liquid atmosphere. "Portal entryway filled and clear. I'm in."

"Release transpod and seal portal hatch once you've boarded," Shon advised him.

That meant the patrol was going to attempt to dock other strafers' transpods with the Ylydii. It would help to have some backup, but for the immediate present, Burn had to go in alone.

He strapped on his abdominal weapon harness and secured it before opening both hatches and swimming up into the Ylydii ship. Never had he been more conscious of his size than when his pectoral muscles brushed the portal's wide collar rim.

Duo, watch my tail, because I can't anymore.

CHAPTER 5

While Teresa was waiting for Ballie to return with the files she had requested, she thought she might fill in a few more of the gaps in Captain Argate's xenobiologically challenged education.

"The mogshrike and 'Zangian species have existed a thousand times longer than any known humanoid civilization, but they went in completely opposite directions on the evolutionary scale," she said. "Unlike the 'Zangians, 'shrikes have no language."

"That you know of," Noel tagged on.

"We're pretty positive that they're dumb as bricks, Captain." It was better than comparing the 'shrikes' mentality to Argate's, although she could see certain parallels that almost begged to be drawn. "Evidently no part of their evolution or environment has ever required them to develop vocal structures or communication skills. Because of their advanced social structure and cerebral development, the 'Zangians were obliged to do the opposite. They easily comprehend abstract concepts like mathematics, art, and philosophy. 'Shrikes do not, nor do they show a response to anything but the availability of prey." Teresa smiled at Noel. "You might recognize that sort of behavior from your observations of Terran sharks."

Noel inclined his head, acknowledging the point.

"We think they may have come to a competitive stage in their evolution," one researcher said, oblivious to the undercurrents. "After all, the only natural predator the 'Zangians have is the 'shrikes."

"If that were true, then the 'shrikes should wipe them out in short order," Argate said. "They are the larger and more successful of the two species."

"Not necessarily." Teresa curled her hands into fists. "For one thing, 'Zangians fear their enemy, but they don't run from them. They confront and fight." Which was precisely how she would handle Noel from this point forward.

The captain produced a slightly puzzled frown. "I thought staying in warmer water was the 'Zangian way of hiding from them."

Argate was a master of the implication, as he had always been. However, Teresa wasn't a seventeen-year-old with more hormones than brains anymore, and this world was *her* oyster, not his.

"'Zangians can tolerate colder temperatures, and sometimes do travel through the outer currents," she told him. "But wherever you go in the sea, you'll find few places to hide. Until now we feel the 'Zangians have been trying to coexist by staying out of the 'shrikes' way, but even they admit that time may be at an end."

"With the change in feeding and hunting behavior? I'd say you can count on that, Doctor," Argate said. "If nothing is done to aid the 'Zangians, and a thermal barrier no longer exists, then what happens in the next revolution could very well determine the survival of one species or the other."

"The 'Zangians are more intelligent, and we can help them," Teresa said, her voice turning flinty. "They'll survive."

Ballie returned with the vid disks, and Teresa loaded them into the wall terminal.

"These were taken by deep-sea drone probes," she told Argate. "We programmed several to monitor 'shrike activity, and this is what they've transmitted over the last four years."

The first clip clearly showed a 'shrike cruising along a wide, powerful current.

"This is an average-sized adult male mogshrike, approximately thirty meters long and weighing one hundred and sixty tons. To our knowledge, 'shrikes are the largest aquatics on the planet." Teresa felt her stomach knot as the monster swam directly in front of the probe, which focused its lens to pick up fine details of the creature's dark, spiny hide. "Their hides are identical in color to the ocean floor, which they use as camouflage, and are further protected by a thick layer of barbed denticles. The 'shrike also have eight plated fins, barbed on the edges and tips, and multiple rows of very large, sharp, serrated teeth."

Argate seemed mesmerized by the vid and said nothing as he continued to watch.

The vid changed angle, and showed a 'shrike from the underside. "The two segmented, dangling objects you see extruding from the perianal area are claspers. They're filled with a paralyzing toxin, which is released when the clasper comes in contact with anything. 'Shrikes use these appendages to whip through large shoals and stun several hundred fish at the same time."

The captain leaned forward to squint at the slightly blurred portion of the image. "There appear to be more than two."

"The others are cleaner fish called *mvrey*. 'Shrikes usually carry hundreds attached to their bellies; the symbiotes use them for transport, and keep their hides clean of debris and parasites. You'll note that the *mvrey* stay at least a meter away from the 'shrike's mouth—this is for purposes of self-preservation. Anything that stimulates the electroreceptors lining the outer mouth rim . . ." Knowing what was on the vid made Teresa pause and then tell the wall panel, "Slow replay to one-third normal speed."

A *doowtasquid*, its deep yellow gullet sacs pulsing with neurotoxin, crossed the path of the 'shrike. It saw the shadow of the creature and whirled in slow motion to jet away, but one of its tentacles brushed the 'shrike's mouth.

Even with the sluggishness of the replay, the 'shrike moved like a flash of light, darting forward, opening its cavernous maw, and swallowing the squid whole.

At the moment of the strike, everyone in the room, including Noel, visibly flinched, as if they had been caught between the 'shrike's massive jaws.

"That is a conventional electroreceptor response," Teresa said quietly as everyone watched the 'shrike's mouth work and clouds of poison stain the water. "Actual time of strike, about one-tenth of a second."

Argate sat back and wiped away the beads of perspiration that had popped out over his upper lip. "It's chewing it. The poison . . ."

"Has no effect on the 'shrike. Neither do venom, spines, barbs, or other defenses used by anything else it eats." She watched the next segment, which showed a 'shrike whipping its claspers through a shoal of *tawsnavet* trying desperately to burrow into the silt. Hundreds of the fat, flat-headed bottom-feeders were left stunned and floated up toward the surface, where they were scooped up by the 'shrike. "Unhappily, nothing is immune to 'shrike toxin except another 'shrike."

The last sequence showed two mogshrikes battling. The lashing, humping movements of their bodies did not match the menace of their crushing jaws and the wounds inflicted by their razor-sharp teeth. When the smaller 'shrike's thrashing body grew limp, the larger charged it head-on and swerved at the last moment, snapping off a third of its head during the pass. The victim's small brain popped out of its cracked cranium and free-floated until the victor came on a second pass to snap it up.

This time the occupants of the room jerked in their seats.

Teresa shut off the vid and watched two of her newer researchers exit the room rather quickly. "We have developed strong ties with the 'Zangians, and have done our best to integrate them into our society. They are not merely sentients, they are our friends now. Do you understand the difference, Captain, and why when it comes to taking sides, we're going to choose to help and defend the 'Zangians?"

What Teresa didn't say was what she would do to Noel if he tried to interfere. That, she felt sure, didn't need to be stated.

Argate was quiet for a moment, and then asked, "What have you planned to do to stop the 'shrikes?"

"Stop them? I really can't say. Do you have any suggestions?" she returned, her tone sugary.

"You could organize efforts to hunt and kill them," he suggested. "It would be difficult, but that would insure the outcome you desire."

Ah, yes, Noel was all about insurance. "That would be the military's response to attacks by an enemy, not ours."

One of the younger chemists gave the captain an uncertain look. "But, Dr. Selmar, if it saves the 'Zangians . . ."

"We are scientists, not hunters." Teresa gritted her teeth. "We don't kill aquatics here. *Any* of the aquatics."

Argate's mouth quirked. "Very well. The 'Zangians are already in an evolutionary shift that will eventually force them to live above the surface. That could be hastened along, as you've done with your SEAL experiments, could it not? You might save both species that way."

Even if the Elders approved such a scheme—which they wouldn't, having already prohibited any future SEAL experiments on their species—Dairatha and the older 'Zangians could not make that kind of transition. Their size made permanent land-transition impossible, and trying to alterform them for better tolerance at such an advanced age would likely kill them.

Teresa shook her head. "Even if we could convince the 'Zangians to leave the water, the SEAL process wouldn't work for the older natives. We'd split the population, and seriously endanger those who can no longer leave the sea."

"You're talking about giving them a choice." Noel made this sound like the act of an unbalanced person.

"They're recognized sentients, Captain. We can do no less." Teresa spread out her hands.

"Then you're back to killing the 'shrikes."

"That would reduce aquatic biodiversity, which would be of no benefit to the 'Zangians or this planet's marine biosphere." As much as she wanted to see them dead, Teresa knew she couldn't execute the mogshrikes. "As part of the food chain, the 'shrikes keep many nuisance species in check. For example, the *doowtasquid* have no other natural predator, and they're extremely prolific. Exterminate the 'shrikes and in twenty years you'll be able to walk across the Western Sea by stepping on squid backs."

"You've only recovered 'shrike carcasses so far during your studies here, is that correct?" Argate asked.

"Parts of them. The sea doesn't give up many intact bodies to the sand." Teresa looked over at one of the young male divers. "Ojon here found about one-sixth of a 'shrike carcass a few weeks ago, floating topside."

"It was mostly shredded tissue, but we were able to salvage some of the endoskeleton," the diver said. "No bones, but a dense network made of the same cartilaginous material as their fins and spines."

Noel seemed intrigued by this. "Why don't you capture a live specimen, so you can answer some of these annoying questions?"

More laughter erupted around the room, but this time it was quick and brittle, while expressions changed from tolerant to horror-struck.

"Captain, maybe I wasn't clear about the dimensions of the adult mogshrike," Teresa said, enjoying the moment. "Let me give you a visual. We're talking about an animal that is the same size as a standard launch shuttle."

"So are blue whales, and we've successfully captured many of those on Terra." Noel made it sound as if he'd done so, personally, and only while using a large butterfly net.

"Whales are benign mammals who are friendly toward humans. Terra has plenty of the equipment necessary for deep-sea expeditions and nonharmful captures." All of which Argate had probably appropriated for himself. "Attempting to capture an alien creature on a planet where none of that exists might be done, with a great deal of difficulty, if the specimen were noncombative. Throw in the 'shrikes' natural defenses, lack of empathy, and general viciousness and you go from very difficult to impossible."

"Most 'shrikes in the deep sea never come within sight of land," Ballie put in. "We'd have to go out there and hunt them."

"The 'shrike eat anything that comes near them, too," another staffer explained. "We've lost at least fifteen DS probes that strayed too close, and those weren't even organic. No telling what one or more of them would do to our expedition vessels."

"Of which we only have two," someone else said.

Noel rested his chin against his hand and made a show of thinking. It was a studied pose—one he had used with great effect since his own student days. "We could use one of the natural bays. Provide some lure, reel it in, and then block off sea access with electrified nets."

"You're not serious." Ballie paled. "Captain, the only thing that lures 'shrike is blood in the water, and that makes the 'Zangians go berserk."

Argate frowned. "We'll explain to them why we're putting out the bait."

Teresa had to smother her own appalled reaction. "Captain, we appreciate your . . . enthusiasm, but even if you did capture and secure a specimen in such a fashion, we could never get near enough to it to examine it in any scientific fashion."

"We could experiment with neuroparalyzers and sedatives," Argate suggested. "See what could be used to keep it docile."

Teresa knew MRD did such things—she herself had experimented on the 'Zangians—but she had to uphold the Elders' rulings now. She also wouldn't trust Noel with so much as a wrill hatchling. "We are currently prohibited from experimenting on any native life-form."

"Let me understand you correctly," the captain said, looking clearly puzzled. "You are willing to kill these creatures if they threaten your installations or your native friends, but you refuse to capture and study them, which would be the only manner in which you can identify the cause of their recently changed behavior. Given your sentiments, Dr. Selmar, you may as well shut down this facility and go back on land. You have no hope of controlling the mogshrike invasion."

Teresa blinked. "This isn't an invasion."

"Isn't it?" Argate lifted his shoulders. "However you wish to label the situation, Doctor, these mogshrikes present a threat on several levels. Genuine threats can be studied, resolved, or eliminated, but they can't be ignored or wished away."

Teresa looked out through the viewer panel at a pair of 'Zangian males swimming by on patrol. She had known both since the day they were born, and they were now typically happy, friendly adolescents, just on the verge of adulthood. This particular pair had been too young to join the SEALs before the 'Zangian Elders put an end to the experiment, but they were just as important to her as any of the pilots she had alterformed.

The patrol seemed casual, but the males took it very seriously. Young as they were, they both carried battle scars from practice bouts skirmishing with older males in preparation. Now, if a 'shrike attacked, they knew how to fight it. If more than one attacked, they would both die fighting.

She couldn't allow that to happen.

Maybe I can use Noel for a change. "All right, Captain. Let's talk about how we'd go about capturing a mogshrike."

Liana had been held captive for an unknown length of time. She and the ship's captain remained blind and bound, and had been segregated to one small corner. Their captor had sealed one end of the tank and stood guard at the other. Nothing else happened, and the waiting without knowing was maddening.

When Nerala's bleeding increased, Liana dared to swim forward until she tasted the guard's sweat. *The female with me is badly wounded,* she said. *She requires medical aid.*

Does she. Too bad your medics are dead. Something shoved Liana and jabbed her. *Get back there and stay.*

Liana returned to the corner where they had been penned. She had already checked Nerala by touch, using the end of her snout to locate the source of the blood: a great slash in the captain's chest. Left untreated, Nerala would soon die. Struggling against the web of cords wrapping her body had proved useless; Liana could not free a single veil to stop the flow.

If only she were brave enough to charge the guard blind. But Liana feared the weapon the male carried, and had no way to see it or the male's exact location. All she could do was huddle close to the injured Nerala, warming her as best she could with her own body heat, and wait for what would happen next.

Kill us, she thought over and over. *Kill us, shoot us, end it now.*

Liana might have taken her own life. The manner in which she had been bound had been brutal, and with some flexing she could work the cord tighter around her chest and gillets, essentially strangling herself. She certainly would have surrendered to death willingly. But she had no idea where her mother was, or what was being done to her.

She had to live, if only to know.

At times there was movement in the tank. The guard muttered some things in his clipped language to another who entered and exited at irregular intervals. Whenever the other male paid a visit, the sound of air bubbles preceded a slight shift of weight in the water.

Liana understood the reason for the movement, sounds, and infrequent visits. The intruders who had taken over the ship were using breathing equipment. That meant they were land-dwellers and not aquatics. This was an advantage, for most land-dwellers were weak, bony creatures who swam like cripples. Their breathing equipment was equally fragile, and had hoses to bite through and regulators to smash.

But who had brought them to the ship? Why were they here? What did they intend to do? If only she knew the answer to one of those questions.

Nerala gradually regained consciousness, but did not move very much. *My lady, have they harmed you?*

She asked her question in the old language, which only another Ylydii could gather into their head bones and sort out into words.

Liana saw the wisdom of using it and answered in kind. *I am bound and my eyes are blindfolded, but I am not hurt anywhere.* She forced herself to remain as still as possible, as the cords seemed to be shrinking and cutting deeper into her hide. *I asked for aid for you but they would not provide it.*

Do not concern yourself with me. Nerala seemed truly indifferent to her own imminent demise. *Where is your mother?*

Liana felt her throat tighten. *I don't know.* If she began losing control now, she would end up harming herself and finishing off Nerala. *How was the ship taken? Did they capture the entire crew?*

I do not know how they boarded us, but our people put up a brave fight, my lady. Like all Ylydii, Nerala avoided the direct mention of death. *I barricaded myself in the command center and tried to signal for assistance, but our transponder was the first thing they destroyed.*

Liana could taste the stink of the male guard as he swam over to them. A device squawked, and then his voice was translated into understandable language. *What are you slots humming about?*

Slots. As if all they had of value was that. Liana felt her blood heat.

His translator cannot reveal our sounds as words, Nerala muttered quickly before answering the guard in spoken Ylydii with, *We sing to give comfort to each other.*

Liana felt the disturbance of the water as the guard slashed the end of his weapon in front of their faces. *Keep it down.*

Of course. Liana kept her tone polite, even as she imagined using her teeth to fashion a slot in his face.

She and Nerala remained silent for a long time, and then carefully began singing to each other again.

How can we summon help? Liana asked.

I have already enabled the only other transmitter on the ship, my lady, Nerala said.

Liana hated being reminded of the locator device the medicals had inserted in her spine. Carada had insisted on it, however, and had forbidden her to make any protest. *Surely such a signal could not be heard out here.* They were thousands of miles from Ylyd and any hope of rescue, and the implant was designed to work underwater, not in space.

Sounds travel, Nerala said. *It may be very weak, but it could be recognized by a sharp ear.*

Liana thought of the 'Zangian aquatics, some of whom were said to patrol space around their world in fighter vessels. At the same time, they did not know if all the intruders were land-dwellers. *We must do something else.*

I am of no use to you now, my lady. I can feel gouts passing through my vents. Nerala listened to the water for a moment. *This one is armed but he is alone, and the other will not bring him new air for another quarter hour.*

What should I do?

This one cannot cry out or raise an alarm if he cannot breathe from that device strapped to his back. She paused and forced air through her vents. *Use my passing to draw him closer. Sever his lines.*

I do not want you to die. It was a childish, stupid wish. Liana didn't care, and then something gathered inside her. Her mother had raised her with dignity; she would expect her to behave like an adult. *Forgive me, Captain. I will assure that all of our sisters hear your name, and come to know what you did to protect us. You will never be forgotten.*

I am honored. Nerala's song grew faint. *I must leave you now, my lady. Live in the light.*

She could barely voice the appropriate farewell, and then she said as she wanted, not as she should. *Go with love.*

Happiness warmed Nerala's final words. *I do. I . . .*

Liana felt the last gush of clotted, bloody water ease from Nerala's gill vents, and heard the final beat of her great heart. Uncaring of her shrinking bonds or what the guard might do, she threw back her head and released a pulse of sorrow.

Darkness shrouded the interior of the Ylydii ship, with only emergency exit lights casting a red glow in the water. Everything had been flooded with the dark, slightly briny liquid—taken directly from Ylydii oceans, Burn guessed—but the temperature of it was far too cold to be comfortable.

A wall panel showed that the ship's main computers remained offline, and only minimal power was being used to keep the hub tanks turning and their liquid atmosphere from freezing. There were no signs of equipment failure or accidental destruction. He wasn't sure what had happened until he turned a corner and saw two figures floating serenely toward him.

Both were aquatics, but not alive. From their wounds, both had been shot through the skull at close range by pulse fire.

Burn kept his weapon harness on as he swam slowly, watching for movement, listening for any sound. The silence was so complete that his heart seemed to pound in his brow.

Don't shoot anything. He was reasonably sure any survivors would have been imprisoned where they couldn't cause any trouble, but the mercenaries might not have captured everyone. *Wait. Stay alert.*

He caught sight of a humanoid male in a breathing rig, treading water and holding a weapon ready. He was positioned before an open hatch leading from the cargo hold to the access corridors. He was not Ylydii, or even aquatic. His garments were minimal and crisscrossed by straps to which more weapons and blades were attached.

Burn kept out of sight and considered how to make this first contact. If the guard was a crew member working for Ylydii, then it would be criminal to attack him. If he was a mercenary, he would have knowledge Burn needed. His general inclination was to believe that the other male was a mercenary. Surely no crew member serving in a liquid atmosphere could work well while being hampered by such an awkward breathing rig.

The only way to know is to approach and speak to him.

A limp black body with multicolored, veil-like fins floating listlessly in the water drifted out of an open hatchway. It was a dead crew member. The guard lifted his weapon and fired at it, knocking it back from where it came.

Or not.

Burn shot forward and slammed the guard into the nearest solid object. With his fin hook he sliced through the supply lines at the mercenary's tanks and jerked the rig down so that the straps pinned his upper limbs. The guard's rifle sank to the bottom of the compartment.

It gave Burn mild pleasure to see the panic on the other man's countenance as he circled around and pressed his hook to the soft flesh of his throat. He recognized the aquatic translation device the mercenary wore, which would allow him to understand Burn. *How many others?*

The humanoid gaped, and then convulsed as water flooded his mask. His bulging eyes darted to the portside access way.

Burn followed the glance. *Is that where the rest of them are? Tell me and I'll let you go.*

The merc nodded frantically, twisting as he tried to raise his arms, as if to point. Then he slashed out, and the bright glitter of a blade flashed in Burn's face.

Burn jerked to avoid being stabbed in the eye, taking a glancing blow on the side of his face. He slashed his hook across the other male's soft neck flesh, opening the thick veins there. *You should have told me.* He waited until the merc went limp and swam into the starboard access way.

Signaling Shon was vital, but Burn didn't dare engage his transponder until he knew how many hostiles were present. The proximity scanner in his headgear showed him that the passages ahead were clear, and identified a power source. He swam quickly and silently to the blip, which turned out to be a console in the ship's communication room.

They left this unguarded?

Someone had blasted through the hatch to get inside, but once there they hadn't given the equipment much attention. Two of the three consoles had sustained minor damage from rifle blasts, while a third appeared inert and nonoperational.

Evidently the mercenaries were complete morons.

Burn rebooted the third console. A cracked vid screen flickered on, displaying the status of a destroyed transponder. Tapping a few keys, he used the ship's intercom system to pick up a weak signal coming from the portside. Being inside allowed him to make out the code, which was a standard body locator beacon.

There they are.

He used the computer to access a schematic of the ship's layout. The mercs would be in command and guarding the prisoners, so he found a path to go around them and into the portside through the guest quarters reserved for air breathers. Once he had worked out how he would go in, he plotted an escape route.

There he ran into the first of many problems. Alone he could get to the prisoners, but he'd have to disable all the guards or risk being captured on the way out. Then there was the problem of getting the Ylydii off the ship. The transpod would only hold three at the most. He'd have to get to their launch bay and take one of their space-to-surface shuttles, providing that it had intact liquid atmosphere.

He pulled up a monitor screen that showed the interior of the launch bay, and swore. The pad was empty and the launch lock had been left open after they jettisoned the launches.

Burn knew that, unlike the 'Zangians, the Ylydii could not survive outside their liquid environment for more than a few minutes. He might be able to get to the captives and free them, but no one was leaving the ship. He'd have to regain control of the helm and find a pilot.

If there was no pilot . . .

He pulled up the ship's flight, engine, and navigational protocols. The Ylydii had conglomerated the best of several standard League ship designs, but they had used circular and spherical adaptations and configurations that were totally unfamiliar to him.

Burn plugged his transponder into the communication array and used the ship's power relays to boost and shield the signal he sent to Shon. *Major, the ship is under mercenary control. I'm in communications, and ready to go after the survivors on the portside.*

We've got fifteen merc support ships out here with more on the way. A burst of pulse fire temporarily disrupted the relay. *Burn, get those people out of there.*

It could help if you'd send over a pilot who knows how to fly this spinner.

I already have, Sublieutenant, the oKiaf transmitted back. *Enjoy your first solo flight.*

"The one who got away."

Teresa turned to see Noel Argate watching her from the edge of the moon pool deck.

She already knew what she would say before she removed her regulator and mask, but she took her time doing so. "The one who said he didn't need an alien-lover girlfriend wrecking his career."

"Teresa. You remembered. I'm touched."

"It isn't every day you find yourself dumped by your lover and expelled from your master's program for cheating on a test you studied six months to pass." She stayed in the water. "That program you planted on my computer was inspired, by the way. Everyone thought I had used it to hack into the university's database and get those test answers. No BioTech on the planet would even glance at my enrollment application after you railroaded me."

He held up one finger. "Don't forget, I drove you off the planet as well."

"That, too." How like Noel to admit it so baldly, and right to the face of his former victim.

"Fortunately for me, you're not a vindictive person."

"You have always pegged me so well." She removed the long blade from her shoulder harness and let the light gleam along its honed edge before replacing it. "Feel like going for a swim?"

"Maybe later, when there isn't any steam pouring out of your ear canals." Noel chuckled and dropped down to sit on the deck step, seemingly indifferent to the fact that seawater instantly soaked his immaculate trousers to the knees. "Your prediction was dead on, you know. I wrecked my career quite adequately on my own."

She arched her brows. "Really. What brought you down? Sleeping with the wrong professor's wife, or pissing on the wrong colleague?"

"Terran marine biology has become choked with the young and the restless these past few years." Mild annoyance made faint lines appear across his forehead. "A promising experiment went bad, and someone with slightly more ambition than me took advantage of it."

"Exposed you before you could clean up the mess and cover your ass, did he?" She let her grin spread wide. "Lord, Noel, as justice goes, that's almost poetic."

He looked down at the rippling surface of the pool. "It ruined my marriage and my career."

Finding out he'd married someone else sent a small shock wave through her. "It obviously did nothing to block your dive into the exciting field of intergalactic military science."

"I wasn't thinking when I enlisted. I just had to get away from it; get off Terra and start over." He tugged at the front seam of his shirt. "The uniform takes some getting used to, but the rest of it isn't much different than teaching at BioTech was. I travel more. My colleagues aren't Terran, of course, but one gets used to that off-planet."

"How enormously courageous of you." She swam to the edge of the pool. "Do go on. I should start weeping, oh, any year now."

"I think you've cried enough over me." He reached out to help her out.

"I hate to deflate your self-opinion, Noel, but it was only that one time, when I found all my belongings in the yard in front of our apartment." Teresa ignored his hand and climbed out of the pool. "Mostly it was for the clothes. The rain and mud had ruined half of them, and I couldn't afford to replace them."

"The housekeeping drone wasn't programmed to do that. I guess it got its wires crossed." He rubbed a hand over his face. "God, you really must hate my guts."

"Long time ago." She began peeling off her wetsuit, and hesitated. It had been decades since she had lived on Terra, where public nudity was only one of the many social taboos. "I'm naked under this. If that's a problem for you and your delicate homeworld sensibilities, best turn your back."

He shrugged. "Seeing you naked was always a pleasure, but I don't want you to feel uncomfortable."

"I haven't been a pretty young coed for twenty years, Noel," she said wryly as she continued to strip. "These days my body fights gravity, and gravity is starting to win."

"Nonsense. Mature women have their own appeal." He studied her. "You've grown up beautifully, Terri."

"Thank you. I think I can die happy now." She stowed her suit and rig in her locker and pulled on a dry tunic and trousers. *Get this over with, now.* She faced him. "What are you doing here, Noel, and what do you want?"

He stroked his chin. "Friendship being out of the question, I suppose."

"I'd rather tongue-kiss a man-of-war."

He didn't seem offended by that. "All right, then, all the cards on the table. I want a mogshrike, Terri. What I can learn from it may help our troops when we move through aquatic territory."

"And that's all?"

"That's all." He smiled. "You don't have to be afraid of me anymore. You have the greater advantage here. These are your people, your facility, your research. No one is loyal to me; no one even cares who I am. Half of them only see the uniform anyway."

"The military hasn't done much to endear itself to us since they commandeered the data we collected during the SEAL program." Teresa knew they were using it for intelligence work, too, as evidenced by Shon Valtas's alterforming into a double of Rushan Amariah.

Noel shrugged. "Look, Terri, I'm going back to the war in a month or two. Why not get a little of your own back this time? Use me and what I can requisition while I'm here. You've certainly earned the right, and you need me."

"Do you really think we can cage one of these monsters?" She shook her head before he could answer. "I must be out of my mind to be seriously considering it." Seawater ran into one of her eyes, and she knuckled it.

"I can assure you that I've personally managed creatures equal in size on Terra. Quadrant's brought in even bigger, nastier ones on other worlds. It won't be a problem for MRD. Here." He pressed a clean towel against her stinging eye. "What we need is your direction, and permission to do it."

If only it were that simple. "Tranqing a 'shrike might actually be easier than getting permission to do it. The colony has a council that loves to veto things like this. Also, the 'Zangians have a deep and abiding hatred for 'shrikes, and for good reason. We couldn't bring it anywhere near them; they'd kill it immediately."

"I've scouted a small bay about thirty kim to the north. It's not inhabited by anything but smaller fish and some reef feeders, and the submerged rock formations are perfect for what we need. I can have a team of engineers on-planet and building the containment barriers within twenty-four hours."

Suspicion rose hot and fast in her again. "Had it all planned out, did you?"

"I was hoping, that's all." He didn't avoid her gaze. "We've tried this on other worlds, without much success. The military is very interested in seeing how species like these can be subdued."

"You mean, butchered."

"We're at war, Terri." He gestured toward the URD's dome. "What you're dealing with here could be what we encounter if we have to enter marine territory populated by similarly hostile aquatics. What I learn here could be invaluable to preserving the lives of our troops."

"Then I have to question your choice of specimen." She tossed the towel into a nearby bin and slipped on her footgear. "You know there isn't anything like mogshrikes on any water world in this quadrant. I know, I've checked."

"There is one species, as yet unidentified."

"The only thing that comes close is . . ." She trailed off and stared at him.

There *was* one species. Like the creature believed for so many centuries to be living in Loch Ness on Terra, the only creature comparable to a mogshrike had never been proven to exist. It was called the ultimate nightmare, feared by even the most fearsome.

"The rogur." She wanted to laugh. "Oh, that's priceless."

"Catching one would be."

"The rogur are a myth. Probably dreamed up by some traders that the Faction stiffed or enslaved."

"It exists, Terri."

"The Faction would be very interested to hear that," she said, "seeing as they've been trying to find the rogur for years. They even published the results of the orbital surveys they conducted, so that competitive species would stop trying to land illegal probes in their oceans. In three centuries of searching, no one has ever found a rogur. No live ones, no bones, not so much as a fossilized rogur tooth has ever been uncovered."

"But the Hsktskt still fear the rogur, and they have to be stopped," he said.

He actually believed it. "For God's sake, Noel, the rogur isn't real. It's a boogeyman story, invented to scare little Hsktskt into being good killers. That's all." A thought occurred to her. "Why all the interest in a fairy tale?"

"The war is progressing slowly but surely into Faction space. We know there is something living on their homeworld, something that makes mogshrike look like guppies."

"How do you know? Where's your proof?"

He seemed to struggle with an answer before he said, "We've heard some rumors. Satellite recon shows the coastal cities on the Faction homeworld have been abandoned. The only things that would make them do that are the rogur."

Finally Teresa understood. "You're planning to invade the Hsktskt homeworld. Good God. When?"

"Eventually." There was no remorse in his eyes, no hint of regret or shame in his voice. Noel had always been able to sleep very well at night, Teresa remembered. Even after he had done some fairly unforgivable things. "As you say, Terri, here is the bottom line: I don't trust you any more than you trust me. I can't use you the way I did when we were both young and stupid, and you can't make my situation any worse than it is. Just consider what will happen if I leave and quadrant sends someone else in. Someone who will take over the URD and do exactly what he wants, whether you like it or not. And if it comes to that, who do you think will get quadrant's blessing?"

Right now the only thing Teresa was sure of was that he meant what he said. He would find a way to use her adopted planet, or if denied, someone else would come and take what they wanted by force.

She could use him to save the 'Zangians, or she could take her chances with a stranger. "All right. I'll go and speak to the Elders. Look at me, Noel."

He looked.

Teresa placed her hand on the center of his chest and pushed. He went over the edge and into the moon pool with an enormous splash before he resurfaced, sputtering.

"Why did you do that?"

"Whoever told you I wasn't a vindictive person?" She smiled gently down at him. "Lied."

CHAPTER 6

*B*urn met no other mercenaries on his way to the portside tank where the surviving Ylydii were being held. Part of him was glad; the small wound inflicted by the male he had killed had already stopped bleeding, but the rawness of it inflamed the rage inside him. He focused on making his way through the ship and cooling his blood by working out the Ylydii's helm controls in his mind. Within a few minutes he was in the corridor leading to the occupied tank.

The taste of death fouled the water, adding to his fury, but with it came something else—something coiled and tense and alive.

Burn needed to make the survivors aware of his presence, and narrow their point of location, but releasing a full pulse might alarm those guarding them. Instead, he uttered a soft wave of wordless sound, low enough to be mistaken for the normal noises made by the ship. Almost at once the wave bounced back to him and gave him all he needed to know about the occupants beyond the tank's single open hatch.

One male wearing equipment to breathe; a mercenary. A second form, motionless with death. And the third, almost as still as the second, but breathing.

Duo. He released a second, more focused pulse.

The low vibrations that returned this time painted a vivid portrait of the third. She was female, long and beautifully shaped. The graceful echo of her form absorbed him, sending small shocks of pleasure down his spine, until he realized why she was hardly moving. Something tightly wrapped around her form.

Restrained.

The pleasure of feeling her through the water faded. She was in trouble, perhaps wounded. Her companion was dead, and the water was rank with blood. At least here on the ship the smell and taste of it wouldn't attract predators, as it would if they were on K-2.

Burn wanted nothing more than to charge the tank, but he forced himself to think as a soldier, not an outraged male. *Have to protect her. Disable the mercenary first.*

There was one way in or out; he could see signs that the other hatch leading into the tank had been welded shut. He couldn't risk firing a weapon blindly into the interior; the charge might hit the survivor and kill her. That left subterfuge, something at which he had never particularly excelled. He swam back and forth, keeping his movements as minimal as possible so as not to disturb the water too much.

A low-pulsed hum—not 'Zangian—enveloped him. He went still and shuddered as it caressed his hide. The music of it sank through his flesh and seemed to warm the center of his bones. Only when a second wave washed over him did he pick up the subtle difference in intensity from the first. The eerie song was not being directed at him; she was singing it to the guard.

She was also moving closer to the hatch.

Quit that wailing, a harsh humanoid voice said, *or I'll blast you a new blowhole.*

Burn repositioned himself just outside the tank. He waited until he felt the singer in the center, and felt the disturbance in the water as the guard lifted his weapon. Then he kicked off a wall panel and shot into the tank, making himself into a missile and slamming into the guard's legs.

Bubbles and pulse fire sprayed through the water as the guard was upended into an uncontrolled spin. Burn disarmed him with a single flip of his flukes and grabbed the pulse rifle before using the stock wedge to crush the flow valve at the top of the guard's air tanks.

I'm Militia, he called out. *You're safe now.*

A shadow darted beneath him, a patch of quick-moving black. Adrenaline surged in his veins as he flipped over and darted down, slamming into the small form and pinning it to the bottom of the tank.

The pulse released from the creature was frightened, capitulating, and not at all like the sound that had come from the survivor. Keeping one fin hook pressed to the soft flesh beneath it, Burn flipped on the light of his headgear.

She was Ylydii, and she was blindfolded. Cord-netting covered her body from neck to flukes.

He tore the cloth from her head. That revealed large black eyes, rimmed with gold, which blinked and then widened to stare into his. The soft black of her eyes matched the hide covering her trunk and fins. It was so dense it reflected none of the dim light, but instead seemed to absorb it. She might have been a very dark 'Zangian female, except for her fins, which, even as tightly furled as they were, stretched three times the length of Burn's.

Who are you? he demanded.

A . . . member of Ambassador Carada's staff.

Burn clenched his teeth. Catching her like this was making him feel things completely inappropriate to the situation, so he focused on releasing her from her bonds. *Why were you trying to escape?*

She worked one pectoral forelimb free and began helping him strip away the net. *I thought you were one of them.*

I identified myself when I disabled the guard.

They said they were Militia, too, when they came for me. Fear colored the soft pitch of her voice. *Is anyone left alive?*

I don't know. Burn eased the last of the net from her flukes and saw that she still held her fins in tight furls. *It's all right, I'm not going to hurt you. I was sent to help. Where is the ambassador?*

She made a fin gesture for helplessness. *I don't know.*

He felt a change in the water. *Are you injured?*

No. Her great dark eyes narrowed. *But you are.*

It's nothing. There were no currents into which he could drop to increase his speed, so Burn tore off his flightsuit and presented his back to her. *Grab onto my fin.* As soon as he felt her latch on, he added, *Hold on tight, this is going to be fast.*

Swimming fast meant no longer maintaining a visual field, so Burn sent a series of continuous pulses ahead of him to navigate his way through the dark passages leading away from the tank.

The female Ylydii did her part by clinging fast to his fin and keeping her head pressed down against his hide, eliminating most of the drag her body might have caused. Burn could feel her frantic heartbeat against his spine, but he didn't dare to slow down to explain things more until he had put some distance between them and the other mercenaries on the ship.

Once they were in the hub, he slowed and rolled, swimming upside down to keep the female from being a target to any snipers possibly positioned overhead. At last Burn reached the cargo hold he had secured, and after pulsing to assure it remained empty, he secured the hatch and came to a stop. *This is safe for now.*

For a moment she clung to him, and then slowly she released her hold on his dorsal fin. *What about the others?*

He swam over to the wall panel and attached a transmitting device to it. *I'm going back to get them, as soon as I can signal for reinforcements.*

Liana watched the 'Zangian as he communicated with his patrol. Never had she seen a male so large or powerfully made. How could a female hope to control such a male? Were the other males of his kind of such size? Did they issue orders to their females as easily as he had to her? Was he never punished for such audacity?

Maybe his females do not exercise their authority over their males.

Liana had never had any personal contact with the other aquatic species, nor had she been permitted to learn a great deal about them. Her mother had once told her that the 'Zangians and their ways were very different from their own, and at the time she had not sounded as if she had approved.

Males are suitable for pleasant companionship, and breeding, Liana, but that is all. Their bodies are too weak, and they have no song, so their minds never truly develop. It would be unkind to demand more of them.

Liana caught herself staring at the 'Zangian and averted her gaze. She was glad that she had not given him her proper title, and that there was no one around to see her behaving so badly. If she had shown such attention to an Ylydii male, other females would have interpreted it as a mating claim.

He finished sending his signal and turned to inspect her. *Are you hurt? I tasted blood when I found you.*

It was not mine. Astonished that he would attend to her when he was wounded, she stretched out her petite veils. *It seems that I am only bruised.*

Let me check. He circled around her like a grandmother. *There are marks on your back and sides.*

From the bonds. They were tight. Liana turned with him, trying to keep face-to-face. His singular gray color did not repel her, but it did seem odd. *Where are your veils?* She had thought them concealed under the strange, false hide he had worn before, until he had removed it.

We don't have veiled fins like you, and I've been changed. It's a long story. The 'Zangian went to the hatch and checked the locking mechanism before returning to her. *What is your name?*

No Ylydii would ever have been so rude, and for a moment she stiffened. Then she understood: she had not given him her name, and he needed to call her something. *I am called Liana.* Although he was only a male, she made the appropriate gesture of naming oneself before a comrade.

I'm Sublieutenant Byorn mu Znora. My pod calls me Burn.

Burn. Yes, he did exactly that, with life and power and determination. She repeated it, and while she had never met anyone named for such a violent verb, she liked the sound of it. *What will we do now?*

The mercenaries will soon begin searching for us. I don't know if the patrol can get to the docking portal to send in reinforcements. Burn disconnected his transmitter. *I must fly the ship out of the battle zone. Stay here.*

If he was not with her, she might be captured again. *I can help you. I will watch your back, and show you where things are.* Thank heavens her mother had insisted she be given a thorough tour of the ship.

He regarded her for a moment before turning. *Climb onto me.*

Such intimate physical contact with an alien male was not seemly, and it was time she began behaving like an Ylydii royal should. *I can swim on my own, Burn.*

Liana, if anyone shoots at us, I can shield you better if you're holding on there. He waited, obviously certain that she would obey him.

Had her mother heard Burn issuing such orders, she would have ordered him driven from the synchrony. But what he asked of Liana made sense, and there was no one to observe her abandonment of protocol. Still, it had been much easier when she had done this in the tank, when she had been afraid for her life.

Your life is still in danger, she reminded herself.

Gingerly Liana latched onto his dorsal fin again, and aligned the lower half of her body so that it cradled the back of his. The coupling position was reversed—if they had been mating, they would have faced each other, belly to belly—but it did not make her feel any more comfortable.

Do you have a good hold on me? he asked her as he swam to the hatch. *You are so light and little I can barely feel you.*

Were we still face-to-face, you would feel a great deal more, Liana thought a little hysterically. Out loud she simply said, *Yes.*

Don't let go, Burn said, and then he opened the hatch and shot into the conduit.

Emily Kim walked out of the corridor leading to the public reading room of the Colonial Archives. She had woken up an hour earlier than necessary to prepare for her shift at Admin, and decided to visit the archive and continue learning about K-2, and possibly make some friends.

Unfortunately, she was making more headway with the planet than the people.

It wasn't the other colonists' fault. As she scanned the faces around her, she noted that her presence brought out the usual range of emotions from indifference to dislike. And as always, no one would speak to her, no matter how friendly she tried to be. It was exactly the same way her neighbors at her living quarters treated her. She tried not to take it personally—she was Terran, after all—but a week had passed and the silent hostility wasn't getting any easier to endure.

Her casual glance around the room continued, and then halted as she saw the bald, dark pink head of the one person on K-2 besides her boss who had been friendly toward her.

Don't rush over, she told herself as she walked through the aisles, making her way to him. *He's reading, so wait and don't break his concentration. Don't let on that you can't remember exactly how to pronounce his name.* She kept her pace sedate, and her expression polite, but her heart was definitely trying to hammer its way out of her rib cage.

The young male Omorr looked up before she came within five meters of his terminal. "Emily Kim of Terra."

"Hkyrim of Omorr."

He regarded her for a long moment. "Are you in need of aid?"

"I saw you and thought I'd come over to say hello."

"Hello."

"Hi." Lord, could this conversation become any more wretched? "How are you doing?"

"I do as I have always done, except now in new and different surroundings." His skin turned a darker shade of pink, and some of his gildrells straightened. "You are well?"

She nodded. "Working hard and trying to make friends."

"You must make friends easily."

"Not lately." That sounded so pathetic. Was that disgust in his eyes, or pity? It was so hard to tell, and the bottomless pit she was hoping to drop into wasn't appearing. "I didn't mean to bother you. I'll just go now."

She would have eased her way past two grape-cluster-eyed beings, but felt a delicate touch on her shoulder.

"Emily."

She had to look down to make sure, but yes, it was one of the Omorr's marvelous, spade-shaped hands on her shoulder.

He was standing right behind her.

"I was . . . bothered . . . to see you, but it is because I am not used to such attention." Hkyrim moved to face her. "I am not skilled with words, nor have I ever met a Terran before you. I worry I will say something offensive."

"I know my species is notorious for being unfriendly toward, well, basically everyone else in the universe, but I'm not like them. Actually I transferred to K-2 because it's a multispecies colony, and I thought it would be the perfect place to learn more about people from other worlds." She sighed. "The only problem is that now that I'm here, no one will give me a chance."

He glanced at the others around them. "I have not made any new friends, either. Most species have an aversion to those who handle the dead."

She felt a surge of sympathy. "That's not fair."

"I am used to it now." He looked at his wristcom. "I have not yet had my afternoon meal interval. I become very irritable when I must eat alone. Are you in need of nourishment?"

Emily grinned. "Desperately."

A short time later they were seated at a small table and being served their orders. Hkyrim had warned her ahead of time that the Omorr diet consisted mainly of insects and root vegetation, so she was not alarmed to see what appeared to be a bowl of gleaming blue crickets sprinkled over a pile of orange beet slices. She was just hoping he wouldn't ask her to taste it.

Hkyrim took interest in her selection as well. "Are those maggots?"

"No, this is a type of Terran grain." She pushed aside the mental image his question invoked. "The little round things are legumes, and these round slices are spiced synpro. It's called red beans and rice, and it's very tasty."

"Grain, legumes, and imitation flesh. That all sounds so . . . nutritious." He gave her a sudden, worried look. "Do Terrans require dining companions to share their food during a meal?"

"Generally, no. Sometimes friends offer each other a sample, but everyone generally eats their own food." She leaned forward. "Tell you what. I won't ask you to taste mine if you won't ask me to taste yours."

His eyes crinkled with relief and amusement. "Agreed."

Emily felt very self-conscious at first, and had to forcibly keep from staring at the Omorr as he used his gildrells to eat. It was somewhat bizarre—his three arms stayed at his sides while only the white tendrils covering the lower half of his face dealt with the food—but he ate with a precise sort of delicacy. She kept up a flow of what she hoped was casual conversation, but was only too aware of the attention the other diners were giving them.

Why do they have to stare at us like this? Can't they see we're just normal people having a normal meal? Emily flinched as something small and blue jumped onto the edge of her plate.

One of Hkyrim's tendrils whipped out and snatched the insect back, popping it into his mouth. "I am sorry, Emily," he said after he chewed and swallowed. "I think the cook neglected to prepare the *karaja* properly. It requires at least ten minutes of steaming to kill the oldest ones."

"Right." She gave him an uneasy smile. "Does *karaja* taste better, um, cooked?"

"No. I prefer them raw—alive—but it disconcerts others to see them hopping about the table."

"Oh."

Neither of them ate very much after that, and after the attendant came to clear, she felt miserable.

"May I ask you something, Emily?"

"Of course."

"Do Terrans eat the flesh or body of anything alive?"

"No, we eat synthetics so we don't have to slaughter our animals anymore." She rested her hand on her chin. "Does it bother you to see me using my hands or chewing my food?"

"No, but the fact that you do not have gildrells makes you seem . . ." He paused, searching for a description.

"Unattractive? Unnatural? Ugly?"

"Unusual. Emotional." He frowned. "Your features change with your feelings. I am not sure what all the changes mean as of yet, but I believe I will learn from verbal accompaniments. At present I can tell when you are happy, and when you feel concerned."

"I was pretty concerned during our meal," she admitted, taking a sip of her tea.

"Yes, you were. I wondered if that small line between your brows would ever disappear again." He ran one of his membranes over his gildrells. "When I was not afraid that I had food crawling all over my face."

A laugh bubbled up in her throat, and she choked a little. She grabbed her napkin and covered her mouth until the coughing spate was over. "I had a bad moment there when that *karaja* jumped at me." She cleared her throat and wiped her watering eyes. "I didn't know whether to swat it or ignore it."

The warm light in his eyes danced. "On Omorr you would have been expected to eat it, and then give me a portion of your meal in exchange."

"Which you would have been obliged to eat," she guessed.

He nodded. "And not regurgitate it, either."

They both laughed. The low, lovely sound Hkyrim made blended beautifully with Emily's higher-pitched laughter.

"On Terra you would have been arrested for eating that meal," Emily said when she caught her breath. "Off-world cuisine that contains alien life-forms is illegal."

"I offended a Hlagg the first day I was on-planet. Apparently they make pets of their insects, and to watch me eat made him ill."

"You didn't like the look of my food, either," she reminded him.

"Yes, well, that is because grain on my world is consumed by our milk producers," he confided. "The *temer*, or chaff, is used to stuff headrests for our sleeping platforms."

A giggle escaped her. "So to you I was eating the equivalent of cow feed and the inside of a pillow?"

"Omorr."

Emily looked over her shoulder to see an armed security officer standing directly behind her. He didn't look amused.

"Yes?" Hkyrim rose to his feet.

"Is this female harassing you?" The officer's weapon swung casually in Emily's direction.

"No. Why do you ask?"

"She's new, and the new ones are always trouble." The officer's head lowered as he said to Emily, "I saw you spitting before. You were told to keep your body fluids to yourself, weren't you?"

"She was choking, not spitting, and your interference is uncalled for." The Omorr's gildrells resembled icicles. "My friend and I were sharing a meal and not bothering anyone. You certainly had no reason, other than your own prejudice, to come over here and make your offensive inquiry."

The officer shrugged and moved on.

"You didn't have to do that," Emily said, feeling wretched and touched at the same time.

"On my world, friends defend each other. That being is fortunate I did not challenge him." Hkyrim sat back down. "I apologize for naming you as my friend before any such relationship was formally declared and established between us."

"Hkyrim," she said, very grave now, "I think you just did that."

"I am a life sculptor and barax expert," Paal told Moleon as they walked from the Hlagg embassy to the border of the forest. "How do you serve your people?"

The Skartesh hunter adjusted the straps holding his quiver to the middle of his back but said nothing. He did not even glance at Paal.

The artist did not mind being ignored; he had gone on many hunts with the Skartesh now and knew that few chose to communicate verbally. It was always good to try conversation, though; a young female he had once accompanied had shyly responded and told him much about her culture.

Paal also liked the Skartesh. There were a number of furred and lupine species on K-2, but most had shown a distinct aversion to the Hlagg's unusual bond with their insect friends, and those who did not were few in number. There were many Skartesh on colony now—some said all that were left from the military disaster that had destroyed Skart—and while they had seemed as indifferent to the Hlagg as they were to all other species, they were not afraid of insects, nor did they try to harm them.

Paal admired the stateliness of the Skartesh species, too. They were twice the size of the tallest Hlagg, and much stronger physically. The unfamiliar heat and humidity of K-2 had caused the Skartesh's fur to fall out, but one of the FreeClinic physicians had found a counteragent and had been given reluctant permission by the Elders to administer it to every member of the cult. Now their pelts were thick and healthy, just like Moleon's, and Paal thought them a very handsome species.

He had no such illusions about himself. Like all Hlagg, he was short and lean, with shiny reddish-brown fur, small paws, and a sharp-snouted face. When he was excited, he had an unfortunate tendency to forget to walk erect and instead ran around on all fours. He did not have a wide mane like Moleon's, nor would he ever be able to wear such clever braids in his fur. His small, sharp green eyes were hardly as dramatic as the hunter's large, liquid black eyes that seemed to glitter like polished volcanic rock.

The Skartesh, like most of his kind, disdained forming friendships with those outside his species. Still, Paal could make some conversation, even if it was with himself. Anything was better than this brooding silence.

"My mate is back on Sret, the Hlagg homeworld," he told Moleon. "She did not wish to leave our barax, and indeed it was very difficult for me to transfer here without them. I had hoped to establish a new colony for our smallest sculptors before returning, but if we do not soon find—"

Moleon made a gesture indicating silence and dropped down to sniff the soil. Paal watched as the hunter then stood and turned his head slowly, breathing in deeply. Finally the Skartesh nodded and pointed in the direction of a thick grove of trees.

It was not as polite as saying "That way" but Paal nodded and trotted after the bigger male. Along the way he talked, keeping his voice as low and soft as the shuffle of their footgear through the layer of fallen leaves covering the ground.

"I hear this Peace Summit being held in orbit should be something to observe. Our ambassador, Heek, offered his services, but I think he was merely being polite. I hate getting wet, and all know that we Hlagg cannot function well when immersed in water." Paal knew that the Skartesh were hydrophobic, but even the mention of the word seemed to upset the hunter, whose neck ruff bristled. He decided to change the subject. "It is so good of your people to assist us in finding our small friends. I worry that my barax are lonely for me. You can never truly tell, of course—barax are so aloof to begin with—but I have always sensed they enjoyed the sculptures we have fashioned together."

The big Skartesh hunter stopped and looked down at the small Hlagg. Had there been whites to his eyes, they would have been showing. "You have been . . . submerged?"

Paal grimaced. "I should not have mentioned it. Excuse my offense."

"I am not offended." Moleon swallowed hard. "Would you tell me how it happened to you?"

"It was during one of our monsoon seasons. The rainfall exceeded our expectations and overran our town's retention ponds during the night." What a mess that had been, too—it had taken their field burrow-worms weeks to build new irrigation gutters. "I woke up in darkness to discover my sleeping platform moving on its own around my bedchamber, and climbed off before I realized it was floating."

"You *fell* into water?" Moleon sounded utterly horrified.

Paal squelched a sharp bark of laughter. Like everyone on colony, he knew that immersion in water sent a Skartesh into shock, and could easily kill them. It must have seemed to Moleon as if he were describing a dip in a vat of acid. "Oh, yes." How could he make this gruesome tale seem slightly more amusing? "You know, I'd never cleaned my fur with anything but checrymin lice before the dunking I took that night. I found out just how water strips all the oil from your fur—when I finally dried the next day I swelled up like a ball of fluff."

Moleon didn't laugh, but regarded him through solemn eyes. "You were not afraid?"

"I was more miserable than anything." He shuddered, remembering the horrid sensations of soaked fur. "I still find it hard to believe there are land-dwellers who voluntarily submerge themselves each rotation. I wish we could have our lice here. They are so much gentler to the pelt."

"So is scrub sand." The big hunter scratched the side of his neck.

"The sonic cleansers they make us use at the compound now always leave my pelt feeling flat and too slick."

Paal tried to imagine washing in sand, and couldn't, but then imagined the use of cleaning insects might seem very outlandish to the hunter. "What else do you miss of your homeworld, if I may ask?"

"The ice hills," Moleon said, his words coming slow and hesitant.

Skart had been an ice world, Paal remembered, before the Hskt-skt's orbital bombardment had destabilized the mantle and turned it into a global volcanic inferno. "Were all your hills made of ice?"

"Most. The wind would sing to us on our hunts through the formations, and they were poetry for the eyes as well." Moleon looked up. "I miss, too, the white sky. Here it is so green I sometimes cannot tell up from ground."

"We must all make unpleasant adaptations, I suppose." Paal sighed. "I think friends best help ease the discomforts of being away from one's home place. May I call you friend, Hunter?"

The Skartesh's brief friendliness disappeared abruptly. "We do not make friends with outsiders."

"Why not?"

"Before the Knowing and Seeing, it was entirely forbidden for us to even speak to those not of the Promise," he said. "Now . . . now it is yet frowned upon by the Elders."

"But not forbidden."

"No." He met Paal's gaze. "You are very brave, and you survived water. I would know you as my friend." He slapped Paal's narrow shoulder with one paw.

Paal managed not to fall over. "Good. Now if we can find my barax, the day will be one to be remembered."

They moved deeper into the forest. Some of the trees here were not familiar to Paal, and he paused now and then to admire them. It was during one of these brief stops that Moleon went ahead, and then a crackling sound preceded his sharp outcry.

"Moleon?" The Hlagg looked ahead, but the hunter had disappeared into thin air. He hurried forward, following the same path the Skartesh had taken. "Hunter, where are you?"

"Stay there," Moleon called out. "I have fallen into a sinkhole of some kind. It is deep."

Paal saw the two-meter-wide gap in the ground and hurried to the edge. "Moleon! Are you injured?"

"No, I do not think so."

The edge of the hole was crumbling, so the Hlagg scrambled back and grabbed a vine hanging down from one of the nearby purple-leafed trees. He wrapped the vine around his wrist and tested it to see if it would hold his weight before creeping forward again. "Can you climb out?"

"It is too deep for that," the Skartesh called up. "I cannot see to find a handhold. I think this is some sort of nest; it feels as if it has been dug out. Have you a light emitter?"

Paal fumbled for the small penlight he kept in his pouch—the luminous worm inside the lens case was sealed in, so it would not escape—and held it over the edge. "I am dropping a light down to you. Be careful of your head." He released the penlight.

"I have it." There was the sound of shuffling. "Sculptor, there are your insects here, I think. I can feel them all around me."

Paal squinted, following the light's beam until he saw the familiar gleam of a small green shell. "By the Flanks of Solstra, it is a hive! You have found my barax, Hunter. Well done."

"They do not seem pleased to be found." Moleon stifled a yelping sound. "They are biting me."

"I will tell them you mean no harm." Paal released the tonal order for his barax not to attack the Skartesh.

"There. They will leave you alone now."

"They do not . . . seem to being heeding . . . your call." The hunter cried out and the light wavered wildly. "There are too many. You must help me out of here."

Paal tried the tonal order again, but heard the sound of barax swarming. Cursing, he dragged another, thicker vine to the edge of the nest and dropped it over the side. "Can you climb up?" He was not sure he could pull the hunter's heavy body to safety.

The length of the vine went taunt, and then jerked as the Skartesh hunter climbed up and emerged. Dozens of barax clung to his lower limbs, which were bleeding from as many small wounds.

Paal gave the sternest tonal order he could produce, but the barax did not respond.

"There is something terribly wrong with them." He was forced to knock them from the hunter's legs with his paw, and yelped himself as he was bitten.

"Perhaps they are hungry." Moleon shook the last of the barax from his head and backed away from the edge of the hive.

"No, they only eat roots. I don't understand why they are doing this." Paal watched the barax crawl away from him and Moleon and back into their underground hive. Seeing the wounds they had inflicted on the hunter and feeling the bites on his own pelt made him want to purge. "They have never harmed us or any other living thing. Not since the time my species emerged from their dens to build the first village."

"I might have frightened them." The hunter examined his legs. "Or they do not care for my species."

"None of our other insects have harmed your kind. Why would the barax do such a horrible thing?" Paal, who had never been bitten by an insect in his life, felt stricken to the depths of his soul. "We must not let them harm anyone else."

"I will not kill them." Moleon eyed the hive. "Whatever the reason for their change in behavior, I think they were only defending what was theirs."

"No, they cannot be killed, but others who come here may not be as understanding as you." Paal thought for a moment and removed a net from his pack. "Help me cast this over the open hole."

"Why do you wish to?"

"To keep the barax in there, and to mark this place so that no one else steps on it."

With a little difficulty, the two males spread the net over the open portion of the underground nest. Just as they had finished, the barax climbed up the sides and began using their body's secretions to seal the small holes in the netting.

"What are they doing?"

Paal watched closely. "They are sealing themselves back in."

Within thirty minutes, the net had been turned into a solid, silvery-white surface. Most of the barax had sealed themselves in, but a handful remained outside the hive. They spaced themselves around the edge of the hive at regular internals.

"These should join the others," the Hlagg said, studying them. "Why do they remain outside?"

The Skartesh hunter studied them. "They are posted. Like sentries."

Moleon used arrows from his quiver as posts and encircled the area. Following his idea, Paal brought thin vines and tied them like cord to the arrow shafts until a visible barricade had been established.

"That should keep others from stepping on it until more permanent markers can be erected, and the hive can be safely removed," Paal said. He sat down by one of the arrows and pressed his ear to the soil to listen. The sounds he heard told him that the barax were busy repairing the damage to their hive's structures.

"I saw some of their sculptures while I was down there," the hunter told him, "but they were much larger than anything I have seen at your embassy."

Paal's throat closed. "How much larger?" he asked when he could force the words out.

"It was difficult to see the exact dimensions, but what they had built was three times as tall as I, and many, many times as wide."

Such a change in barax behavior alarmed Paal even more than their attack on him and the Skartesh. "We must return to the colony at once and inform security."

"Does this indicate some danger, Sculptor?" Moleon gave the sentries positioned around the hive an uneasy look.

Paal didn't answer. He had already abandoned his dignity and was hurrying back toward the embassy, running as fast as he could on all fours.

CHAPTER 7

*T*aking Liana with him to the command center was not his wisest decision, Burn thought. She was a diplomat, not a soldier. It would have been much safer for her to stay sealed away back in the cargo bay or even on the transpod, where the mercenaries couldn't get at her again. At the same time, he felt relieved that he had chosen not to leave her behind. Keeping her close made him feel better, steadier, and she obviously did not want to be left on her own.

Now just make sure you don't get her killed.

They nearly encountered a pair of mercenaries halfway to the helm, but Burn quickly reversed in the water at the sight of them and took an alternate corridor before the two heavily armed males could see him.

Almost there. He stopped to seal a hatch behind them, then pulled some wiring out of the control panel and hooked it to the manual release latch. He felt Liana shift as she looked to see what he was doing. *If anyone touches this, they'll get a jolt.*

Tell me what to do and I will fix the hatch on the other side, Liana asked as they entered the sphere enclosing the ship's helm.

Burn quickly explained the method, then went to the pilot's console to strap in to the empty, floating harness. As he'd suspected, the mercenaries had only powered down the various functions of the ship, intending to preserve it for their own use. It was a simple matter to restore propulsion and weapons, but the communication panel had been thoroughly destroyed.

No hope of contacting Shon or the others until major repairs were made to the ship.

Burn looked at the cracks running through the ruined panel surface, and an idea popped into his head. The mercenaries had been smart enough to bring breathing rigs, but likely had done nothing to protect the equipment.

Can you fly the ship?

Burn finned an affirmative. The flight controls responded as soon as he restored power to the engines, and he checked the position of the pilots' pod before turning the huge ship and heading on a route back to K-2.

Are we not returning to Ylyd? Liana asked, swimming over to inspect the course readings.

I would, but the ship could be rigged with high-density explosives, he told her. *The mercenaries were beaming a signal to your fleet to come and rescue you. It could have been to draw them close before they blew up the ship.*

Liana looked horrified. *They would do such a thing?*

Decoys are very popular with their kind, and I can think of no other reason they would want your fleet here. He transferred weapons and flight control to one console and positioned himself behind it. *Can you monitor the outer corridors and tell me if anyone tries to get in here?*

Liana seemed startled by his request, then simply finned "yes" and took position at a terminal close to his console before strapping herself in. *Burn, how are we going to signal for help without a working transponder?*

I don't know, but I will think of something. Surely Shon would guess that it was Burn at the helm of the ship and not one of the mercenaries. On the other hand, he was flying into closely guarded space without the ability to identify himself.

Or maybe I can.

The sphere's flight controls responded instantly to his touch, although their jump into flight made both the pilots' pod and the mercenary ships break off their attacks on each other. As soon as he had every ship identified, Burn engaged the Ylydii's weapons array and charged the pulse cannons.

What are you doing? Liana asked, watching the cannon fire appear on the front viewer panel.

I'm a gunner and *a pilot,* he told her as he fired off another spread at the mercenary ships. *This is how I can say hello to the family.*

Oh. Liana returned her attention to the monitor in front of her, and when Burn glanced over a quick flash from the console illuminated her dark face. *Two males were trying to open the hatch.*

There would be more coming, and one of them might figure out how to short-circuit the panel. Burn had to stop them where they were. Looking again at the cracked companel gave him an idea. *Liana, can your people withstand sudden pressure changes?*

Rapid changes make us uncomfortable, she told him, *but they do not harm us. Only large shifts in temperature do that.*

Burn had little hope of finding any other survivors, but he still had to consider them as well. *Do you have any staff or crew members who are not Ylydii?*

No.

Burn tapped into the ship's atmospheric controls and increased the pressure to all levels and compartments except the helm. As aquatics were accustomed to shifts in pressure while diving, their bodies would automatically compensate.

Any humanoid nonaquatic on the ship would not equalize as well, and neither would their equipment. Burn turned on the ship's common area monitors and watched the mercenaries writhing.

It is hurting them, Liana said. She was also watching the effects on her panel.

It will render them unconscious.

Faint waves rippled through the water, bringing the sound of voices crying out in pain. The taste of new blood also came.

Suns. Burn immediately decreased the pressure in slow increments, knowing that to do the same rapidly would definitely kill the mercenaries. *I only wanted them unconscious.*

I think they are dead. She looked away.

He checked the monitors and saw several bodies floating motionless outside in the corridor, surrounded by a fog of blood in the water.

I killed them?

They would have killed us, Liana said.

It was not the same, but Burn had no more time to dwell on it. The sphere's auto-targeting system was too sluggish for Burn's taste, so he disengaged and put the entire array on full manual, working the weapons with one fin and the flight controls with the other. Because of the complexity of the control protocols, he couldn't give the pulse cannons his full attention. *You wouldn't happen to know how to fly this ship, would you?*

Liana slipped out of her harness and came to him. *Royals are trained to fly every vessel in our fleet.*

So she was a diplomat *and* royalty as well. That explained some things, like those distant, cold looks she had given him a few times. Ylydii royals, according to the stories Burn had heard, were very rare individuals kept segregated from the rest of their society, who only saw them from a distance or to pay homage during some cultural ritual.

At least they didn't kill a ship full of men by accident.

Liana looked at him. *What is wrong?*

Don't crash into any of those, he flicked a fin at the blips on her screen that represented the 'Zangians' strafers. *Or those.* He tapped the position of the nearest energy shunt field, left behind by the war. *You're sure that you know how to pilot?*

She gave him another of her odd, aloof looks. *Keep your harness on, 'Zangian. You're about to find out.*

"Pardon the interruption, Administrator, but we have a situation developing."

The quiet voice, along with the delicious scent of something dark and freshly brewed, dragged Ana's attention from the emergency incident report she had been reading. "Does it involve hostile barax, and, Good Lord, is that Terran coffee?"

"No barax, ma'am, but affirmative on the coffee," Emily Kim said as she carried a small server tray to Ana's desk.

It had been an interesting week since Emily had reported for her first shift. Ana had discovered that her new assistant was not only efficient and precisely punctual, but that she had taken over Carsa's duties with utter confidence and skill. To her knowledge, the younger woman had not made a single error to date.

There was an aura of mystery surrounding Emily Kim, however. Her voice and expression were perpetually serene, which gave the impression that she was wholly at ease with her surroundings. Yet Ana knew the younger woman had never left the homeworld before her transfer. Emily never spoke about her life back on Terra, or made any attempt to exchange more than greetings and simple pleasantries with Ana.

She did, however, make the best coffee Ana had ever tasted.

Ana picked up the steaming server Emily had poured for her and took a greedy sip. "This isn't my blend, is it?"

"No, ma'am. It's some Arabica I brought with me from home." She set the pot back on the tray and set it on a side table. "I'm afraid that your Colombian blend ran out a few days ago."

"Emily, you shouldn't raid your personal supplies for me."

The younger woman shrugged. "I don't drink it very often, and Carsa told me how much you enjoy a server or two in the mornings."

"Or three, or nine, depending on the current slate of crises." She frowned. "When did you speak to Carsa? I thought he was isolated with his family, awaiting a group birth on their homeworld."

"He is, as far as I know," Emily said. "Carsa kindly left a recorded message for me before he departed K-2, along with a complete procedure guide as to how to run the office."

Ana grinned. "So that's why you're doing everything so perfectly. Carsa primed you ahead of time."

The younger woman nodded. "Perfection is always easier when you have a cheat sheet."

"I'll keep that in mind." Ana indulged in another sip before she placed the server on her desk. "So what have you got developing, situation-wise?"

Emily consulted her datapad. "A Captain Noel Argate contacted Admin to file a complaint against Transport. It seems he sent in a request to have his belongings moved from temporary visitors' quarters to the URD facility out at Burantee Point. The request was denied."

"Argate." The name immediately sounded familiar, but Ana couldn't recall where or when she had heard it. "Terran?"

"Yes. A League military officer assigned out of Marine Research Division, according to his datawork."

Teresa is going to love having a complaining male Terran underfoot. Ana sighed. "Did you talk to Transport, see what they had to say about it?"

Emily nodded. "I checked with their processing drone. They claim that Captain Argate's visa has expired, and they had no choice but to deny the request."

"We should issue the captain a new visa, then."

"I was going to suggest that, but the captain only arrived here three days ago. His visa should still be valid."

"That sounds like an input error." Ana pulled up the personnel file she had on Noel Argate, the corresponding transport request, and compared the two. "I see what happened here. The captain neglected to fill in his current visa code on his request. He's still using the old one that expired three cycles ago." She pulled the new visa that had been issued and copied it onto the disk. "Send this to Captain Argate and ask him to discard the old visa chip. Copy to Transport along with the captain's request and ask them to reprocess with the newer code."

Emily accepted the disk and made a few notes. "Thank you, ma'am."

"Ana." She looked over the rim of her server. " 'Ma'am' makes me feel five decades older than you."

A dimple winked in and out of Emily's cheek. "Yes, m— Ana."

The near-smile delighted Ana. "I'm actually only three decades older, and I can get away with claiming two if no one hears it while I'm standing in the sunslight."

"I'll keep the shades drawn at all times."

An incoming signal chimed on Ana's console, and she cut short her laugh to respond. "This is Ana Hansen."

"Administrator, this is Chief Norash over at security. We have an emergency situation involving an attack on a diplomatic transport en route to K-2. The planetary patrol and Bio Rescue have responded, but your presence would be much appreciated at Flight Control."

"I'm on my way, Chief." Ana gulped down the rest of the coffee as she rose, and handed the server to Emily. "This doesn't sound good, so I'll need you to hold down the fort here. There will be a thousand signals; take messages or refer them to security if they can't wait for info. I'll take direct relays from any planetary leader, quadrant command, or patrol pilots. Norash's lines will be jammed, so forward them to my wristcom."

"Should I cancel your appointments for this afternoon?" Emily asked as she followed Ana into the outer office.

"Yes, all of them. I'll call back personally to reschedule." Ana came to an abrupt halt before she ran into William Mayer. "Liam, Norash just signaled me. Someone is attacking one of the diplomatic vessels."

"I know. I signaled him from the FreeClinic when Transport alerted Rescue Three. It's going to be a mess." He took Ana's case. "My glidecar is waiting outside."

Ana glanced back at Emily. "If you need anything—"

"I'll handle it until you return." A buzz of incoming signal alerts made her assistant hurry back to her desk.

On the brief drive to Colonial Security, Liam related the scanty details Transport had relayed about the attack. "Subcommander Onkar took Rescue Three up to provide support, and we can scramble the other two medevac teams if the casualty count is high." He glanced at her. "This might end the summit before it begins."

"One crisis at a time, please." She tried not to feel frustrated, but this rocky start wasn't promising. "Even if this kills the summit, we still have to get together with the other planetary leaders sometime and decide what is to be done about Ninra."

The Ninrana were not the only problem Ana had hoped the diplomats at the Peace Summit would address. The Skartesh, who were too sensitive to humidity to permanently adapt to life on K-2, were anxious to establish their own independent colony off-planet.

"I'm backing the proposal for the 'Zangians and Ylydii to supply water and terraforming equipment for Ninra in exchange for mineral rights," Liam warned her. "I think it's only logical."

"I feel the same way about the Skartesh's idea to colonize one of the habitable moons around Ylyd or K-2," Ana told him. "The problem is that the aquatics still don't trust either species."

"I can't say I blame them. The Skartesh came here and pretended to join the colony while planning to *invade* the entire system, while the Ninrana have been eating anyone unfortunate enough to crash-land on their planet."

"They did give them seven days to be rescued first," Ana reminded him.

"I had thought living out here would be interesting but relatively peaceful," Liam said. "Instead it's been one crisis after another, since the day I stepped foot off the transport from Terra."

She chuckled. "You know, we should be grateful for them. These are the only times that you and I see each other for longer than five minutes."

"I've got a new pathologist on board, which relieves one of the senior surgical residents who was filling in down in Forensics." He stopped in front of the security building, where an officer was waiting for them. "That should give me a few more free evenings during the week."

"You'll be home in time to say good-bye to me, then," Ana said. At his blank look, she reminded him, "I'm the colonial representative assigned to monitor the PM sessions. I'll be spending most nights up in orbit."

"I'll see if I can juggle a few shifts with mu Cheft," Liam said.

Security's command center was usually a busy hive of activity, but Ana and Liam walked into what appeared to be controlled chaos. Every terminal was being shared by two or three officers, all of whom were communicating with other entities via their headsets. Satellite vids projected on the immense wall screens showed the battle taking place far above in space, and transmissions from the patrol pilots were being loudly broadcast from an audio panel, adding to the din.

"Dr. Mayer, Administrator Hansen." One of Norash's many assistants came over and indicated a situation room off to the side. "The preliminary briefing is already in progress."

They entered the room to find a three-dim image of Norash addressing the various officials gathered there. Ana saw why the chief had chosen to send a vid as she watched him pace back and forth while speaking.

Jadaira came to join them. "Norash decided to stay in his office and hold the meeting by holoimage," she told them. "He's so agitated he was worried he might accidentally step on someone in the room without noticing."

"So we know that the Ylydii ship was boarded and hijacked," Norash said. "What we don't know is who hired them, or why. Comments, questions?"

"The Ninrana have no water on their world," someone said. "If anyone would want Ylyd, it would be them."

"That's not correct," Dair said at once. "I was there during the Skartesh occupation. The Ninrana have to drill deep, but the planet still has enough water to support life."

"Planetary engineers estimate they'll have water for another twenty more years," Liam added. "After that, the rate of desiccation will be too rapid to sustain life, and the people will have to be relocated."

"Maybe they don't want to wait until it dries up," a small, fearful-looking Tesomra engineer said. "They planned to invade us with the Skartesh, didn't they? And bring back the Hsktskt. And perhaps release the Core plague again, too."

"The Core will not attack us again," Liam told the engineer. "We have a signed a treaty with them."

"How can you make a treaty with diseased tree sap?"

"The Core inhabit the sap of gnorra trees, but they are not a disease, and we should not jump to conclusions," Ana said in her firmest tone. "It was our success with the Core that gave us the idea to hold the Peace Summit. Ambassadors from all the planets in our system will be able to meet, discuss problems, and form cooperative accords so that we can defend and help each other."

"Which is admirable, but at present someone is trying to help themselves to Ylyd," Norash said. "We need to gather as much intelligence about this raid as we can, and take steps to safeguard the other diplomats and their vessels. Doctor, there will be survivors brought in from the mercenary ships. They are to be treated and kept under guard until they are fit for questioning."

"I will need some of your officers over at the FreeClinic to set up an isolation ward," Liam told him.

"Done." Norash's image looked at Jadaira. "If the diplomats on board the Ylyd ship have not been killed or seriously injured, then we will need to arrange accommodations for them until their ship can be repaired and restored."

"I will speak to Transport and see what can be arranged," Dair promised. "If there is not a vessel suitable for them, then the coastal pod will provide private waters for them on-planet."

Norash then addressed his security supervisors. "I want to know who orchestrated this raid, and for what reason. Recover all transmissions from the mercenary ships and have them analyzed. Reports are to be encrypted and sent directly to my office. Dismissed."

"I've seen that firing pattern a thousand times," Onkar transmitted to Shon and the rest of the patrol. He had flown Rescue Three out to meet the patrol and came upon them fighting the mercenary ambush. "I know that Byorn mu Znora has control of that ship."

"The flight pattern has changed, Subcommander," Saree pointed out. "If he was at the helm, then he's no longer at the flight controls."

"But someone in league with him is." Onkar avoided a midfield collision with a mercenary ship spinning out of control. "Watch the targeting sequence. It's faster and more accurate, but it is still Byorn's pattern."

His mate's cousin was also making maximum use of the Ylydii's powerful pulse cannons. With help from the strafers, they would soon turn the mercenary ambush ships into nothing but a very large debris field.

"If he and an Ylydii pilot have taken control of the vessel, then there is a reason they are flying it away from the ambassador's fleet," Shon transmitted.

Onkar mentally raced through everything he knew about merce- nary tactics in space. Unlike military troops, they often committed un- pardonable acts to achieve their aims and collect their bounties. "The intruders may have planted explosive devices on the ship."

"Scanning." There was a long silence before Saree came back with, "No energy spikes, and the stardrive core reads normal. If you want to dust an entire fleet, you have to use the core, and you have to rig it in advance."

"Perhaps Burn doesn't know that, and has no way to tell," Shon suggested. "He may be erring on the side of caution."

Saree snorted. "That I should like to witness."

Onkar felt suddenly impatient with the wing leader's open con- tempt for his mate's cousin. "It is true that Byorn has barely grown into his skin, but he knows how to think like a soldier."

"When he's not behaving like a scar-hungry child," the wing leader said.

"Boarding an occupied vessel and finding the means to take control of it takes more than brawn," Shon broke in, his tone mild. "Shall we concentrate on how we can help him?"

Saree clikked a terse apology to the other 'Zangians. "We should flush out the remainder of the mercenaries and drive them to Byorn."

"Agreed." Onkar ended the relay and checked his fuel reserves be- fore asking for a weapons status.

Curonal, who was serving as Onkar's gunner, looked up from his console. "That last blast we took disabled the aft 'torp launcher. Dis- placer power cells at eighty percent. Primary engines, thrusters, and stardrive intact and online. Dr. Dloh reports the evac team is not happy but otherwise remains uninjured."

In the heat of battle Onkar had forgotten about the medical crew, who were harnessed back in the modified cargo hold. He switched on the ship's intercom. "I apologize for the rough ride, Doctor. We're presently engaging mercenary raiders and attempting to assist the Yly- dii ambassador's vessel."

"Underztood." There was the sound of someone regurgitating in the background. "Zome of our people are a little motion zick, but iz there anything the rezt of uz can do to help?"

Onkar admired the Aksellan physician, who had served as a medevac doctor since Bio Rescue had been initiated. Despite many rousing adventures and real brushes with death, the arachnid never seemed to lose his composure. "Please prepare to receive injured. As soon as we've neutralized the ambush, there will likely be many."

"Acknowledged, Zubcommander."

Onkar dropped into attack position behind the patrol. Unlike the strafers, Rescue Three was of Hsktskt design, a gstek-class raider built to acquire multiple targets and destroy them. It once had carried more firepower than all of the other patrol ships combined, and had easily razed more than one large colony from the surface of a planet. Now stripped down and renovated to serve as a medevac transport, the gstek still maintained enough ordnance on board to pulverize an asteroid into dust.

"Charge displacer array and ready 'torps," Onkar told Curonal. "Prepare to fire combined spread."

Like the gstek, Onkar had once been a lone, dangerous force. Living a rogue's existence in the outer currents required he attack and destroy an enemy with every ounce of cunning and strength. Joining the coastal pod and mating with Jadaira had gentled much of what the years of solitary violence had made of him, but not all.

Now he drew on that instinctive viciousness and looked ahead through the eyes of a killer at the mercenary ships, which were moving into new positions. "Belay firing order."

"Yes, sir." Curonal sequenced his panel to standby. "I don't recommend firing, not with the way they're sucking on to Burn."

Onkar studied the navigational screen, which displayed the position of all the ships within three hundred kim. A bright cluster of red around blue showed how the mercenary ships had regrouped: in very close proximity to the hull of the Ylydii ship. Burn was firing on the ships that weren't close enough to damage his own, but few strayed out far enough for him to target. Anyone firing on them also risked hitting the Ylydii ship instead.

"Parasites." Onkar engaged the secondary engines and selected his route. "Do you remember those close-impact avoidance patterns we used to practice at the academy?"

Curonal answered with a groan.

"I thought you might." The ship responded instantly to the surge of power Onkar sent through the engines, and jumped through the center of the patrol and out into the margin of space between them and the Ylydii vessel. "Wing Leader, I'm taking point."

"Acknowledged. Keep your fins down, Subcommander," Saree transmitted back.

Although Onkar was sure that there was an Ylydii pilot flying the ship, he counted on Burn recognizing his flight pattern and advising the pilot how to respond to it. All the Ylydii had to do was make no course adjustments and Onkar would take care of the rest.

"Impact in two minutes," Curonal warned him.

It took more than a little spine to fly on a head-on collision course with another, larger ship, and it was not a maneuver recommended for use by League pilots. It required complete focus from the gunner, and zero margin for error by the pilot. Eighty percent of the starjocs who had attempted it in the Academy's trainers lost their nerve in midflight, and generally ended spiraling off in a breakaway, during which they either missed their targets or were fired on and destroyed themselves.

Knowing how dangerous it was, Onkar had seldom used the maneuver, but when he had, he had never deviated from his course. If Burn could maintain control over his pilot, then it would work.

If he didn't, they were all going to die.

That ship is flying straight at us, Liana told Burn, staring at the bright green light on her panel. *It's a Hsktskt raider, why won't you shoot it?*

We reclaimed four Hsktskt raiders and turned them into medevac ships, he told her. *Maintain present course and speed.*

This is madness. She hadn't survived being boarded and captured to die from an easily avoided collision. *I can't allow your crazy medical people to destroy our ship.*

That pilot isn't medical or crazy, he assured her. *He's my cousin's mate, and one of the best starjocs in the League. Next to me, anyway. The ship will be fine. Stay on this heading.*

Liana closed her eyes for a moment. He might be large and powerful, but he wasn't female. She had never flown with a male even allowed to be present at the helm without strict supervision. And what did this 'Zangian really know of battle strategy and ship maneuvers? Were her mother here, she would be shrieking at Liana to stop pandering to the simpleminded and take over command of the situation before everyone on the ship died.

Of course, her mother wasn't here, and Burn had brought her this far. He had used their pulse cannons to destroy four of the ambush ships. Now he claimed that the pilot of the Hsktskt raider was kin and that he knew what he was doing. Were it not for him, she might still be in restraints, breathing in water tainted with Nerala's blood, or have been killed by the mercenaries.

The mercenaries Burn had tried to render unconscious and then killed.

She eased her fins back from the navigational console and left the ship at its present speed and course. *If you are wrong, 'Zangian, I will make you regret it.*

If I am wrong, Liana, he told her, *you won't have to.*

Liana had trained in Ylydii ship simulators—all royals did, in the event they had to take command of a transport—but she had never flown a real vessel. The equipment was very similar, but there was always the knowledge that a simulator could be switched off and exited.

Here there was no stopping or leaving. No dodging or evading. It was only too horribly real.

Collision impact in three minutes, she announced.

Preparing pulse cannons for stream fire, he told her. *Lock flight controls and override proximity sensors.*

Acknowledged. Liana punched in the codes that would keep the ship from automatically avoiding the collision. A polite drone voice informed her of the imminent impact, but she switched the audio off. She glanced back at Burn. *Could you eject the stardrive? Just in the event you are wrong?*

He looked up from the weapons panel. *I'm not wrong. I'm never wrong.*

I see. She wouldn't point out the deaths of the mercenaries; that would have been a petty and unnecessary swipe. The Hsktskt raider was now visible and headed straight at them. *I hope your mate appreciates what a valuable male she has.*

She will someday, when I get around to taking a mate. For now I'm content with annoying my commander and aggravating my pod.

Males cannot take mates, Liana told him, shuddering at the scandalous thought. *They are taken.*

I suppose on your world you chase down the males and force them to breed with you, Burn said, clearly enjoying the most inappropriate conversation Liana had ever held in her life.

There is no need to chase or force them, she replied. *They are eager to be bred. It is their purpose. These things are never discussed. Males do not understand the importance of such matters.*

Burn blew some air through his gillets, producing an odd sound. *Have you ever explained why it is important to them, or do you prefer keeping them agreeable and compliant through your dominance and their ignorance?*

Males do not question females on our world, nor would they comprehend an explanation for our decisions. They do not have the mentality to process such concepts. Her attention moved back to the image of the gstek raider, which was rapidly filling up the screen. *In thirty seconds it will be too late to avoid that ship. Are you sure we cannot change course?*

You'll have to rely on me and my inferior mentality, Liana. He became busy with the weapons panel, but added, *'Zangian males and females are partners. We have different responsibilities within the pod, and males are dominant to females during breeding, but the rest of the time we cooperate and help each other. I need you to be 'Zangian now, and trust me.*

That made her angry. *If I did not trust you, Sublieutenant, I would have locked out your panel controls and rendered you unconscious. What do you want me to do?*

Rescue Three will skim the starboard hull and fire on the ships it drives out of there, he said. *When they're clear, I need you to bring the engines to full stop.*

The distraction of the raider combined with such an abrupt maneuver would cause the ambush ships using the portside of the ship for cover to stray out ahead of them. *They might turn and fire on us.*

They'll never have the chance.

Something in his voice reached inside her, Liana decided. Reached like the calming hand of a parent. It was every bit as potent as luresong, and the fact that it came from a male was only slightly more surprising than the effect it had on her.

She had never been swayed by the voice of another. Not even her mother.

I am a little afraid, she told him. *If this is the end for us—*

—then we shall go from here together, he finished for her. *Into the deep and the dark, I will remain at your side.*

Liana turned to face the oncoming ship and held on to his promise. If these were her last moments, she would go with dignity, and trust that her strange new comrade would be with her.

The 'Zangian medevac ship was upon them.

At the last possible moment before impact, the gstek flipped on its side, presenting a much narrower profile as it reached the starboard hull. Liana jerked anyway, expecting the worst, but the deck around them remained intact, the ship's course steady. Bright flashes off to the right of the viewer panel indicated close fire.

Three ships in one pass, Burn muttered, as if to himself. *Duo, Onkar, you should have been a gunner.* To Liana he said, *Full stop as soon as he's clear.*

Acknowledged. Liana tracked the raider, and as soon as it was safely past the hull, she reversed the engines and brought the ship to a violent stop. Several mercenary ships shot out ahead of their position, and then began breaking up as pulse cannon fire hit them.

Beautiful, Lady, Burn said as he continued to fire the cannons. *Two more. No, one. I have you, you scum-eater.*

Liana watched the screens as the last ship was cut in half. The two sections hurtled apart before they imploded, and debris occluded the viewer. It took two sweeps before she believed what her panels were showing. *You did it.* She looked back at Burn. *You were right, you really did it.*

We did, he told her. *Anytime you want to pilot me around this system, Lady, I'm your gunner.*

Liana started to reply, but cringed as a violent impact blew in the helm door panel. Burn was out of his harness and over the console before Liana could stop him.

No, Burn, no, she said, shrugging out of her own harness and swimming forward to face the other female. *This is not one of the intruders.*

Who is this? the other female demanded, shoving Burn out of her way with some difficulty before inspecting the scene outside the ship, shown on the view screen. *What have you done? Liana, explain yourself.*

We engaged the enemy and saved the ship, she told her before turning to Burn. *This is Ambassador Carada. Ambassador, this is Sublieutenant Byorn mu Znora—*

Burn swam around Carada and pinned the small figure that had appeared behind her to the wall panel. *And who is this?*

That would be my personal assistant, Miglan, Carada told him in her iciest tone. *Remove yourself from him, if you please.*

Liana nodded at Burn. *He will not harm us.*

The 'Zangian backed away from the small, terrified Ylydii male. *My apologies. I thought you were a threat. Miglan, is it?*

The little Ylydii male squeaked and hurried back to Carada's side, where he inserted himself under the protection of her broad pectoral fin and peered out fearfully at Burn.

Carada stared out at the debris field left by the destroyed mercenary ships before whirling around and regarding Liana. *I dislike repeating myself. Tell me precisely what you have done.*

As always, what must be done to preserve life, she said, and lifted her gaze to meet the outrage in Carada's. *Just as you told me to. Mother.*

CHAPTER 8

"*I* am going to the Point this morning," Teresa told T'Kafanitana when the N-jui reported for her shift at the lab in Teresa's land dwelling. "Would you keep an eye out for that probe we launched yesterday? It should be sending in a signal any time now."

"Yes, Doctor." The chemist moved to take her place at the monitoring console, and then hesitated. "Are you meeting Captain Argate at Burantee?"

"No, I'm going to break the news about our 'shrike hunt to Dairatha." Teresa picked up the case of vids and datapads she had packed to show her mate. T'Kaf's face appeared as impassive as ever, but there were other, tiny signs that her lab chief wasn't altogether happy. "What's wrong?"

"I do not care for Captain Argate."

"Neither do I, but we can use him." She adjusted the strap of the case and slung it over her shoulder. "Think of him as a necessary evil."

"Evil is not necessary." T'Kaf made a sweeping gesture with two of her limbs. "It is deceptive, and destructive."

Teresa was surprised by the vehemence backing the chemist's statement. "You really don't like him."

"He is not what he appears to be," the chemist said, very slowly. "His interest in you and our work is not altruistic, and his motives are suspicious. He is not a male to be trusted."

"I don't trust him, but I need his resources." She patted the big female's shoulder. "Don't worry. He won't be here forever."

The N-jui gave her a long, silent look, and then nodded and turned her attention to the console.

Teresa rarely spent any time alone with Dairatha anymore. Privacy was basically impossible underwater, unless they went to the breeding caverns, and even there they could only play for a short time before she tired and had to return to the URD. She also didn't think going to the caverns was fair to her mate, who could no longer enjoy her as he would a female of his own kind. Thus, when it came time to tell Dairatha about her plan to work with Noel Argate and the military, Teresa thought it best to do so in private.

Her immersion tank was too small to accommodate him comfortably anymore, and transporting him to her land dwelling had become a major production involving evac equipment and other people, so she asked him to meet her in the study tank at the Burantee Point station. It fed directly into the ocean, so there was no need for him to leave the water, and she could stay on deck and not have to try to communicate while wearing a breathing rig.

Teresa had helped build the surface research lab at Burantee Point when she first came to K-2, but it was rarely used these days. The URD offered better equipment and an undeniably superior environment to conduct research. She wasn't at all surprised to find the lab unoccupied when she arrived and went down to tank level.

Her mate was already there, waiting for her.

"We should have the tank at your dwelling enlarged," Dairatha said as he began circling the upper level of the tank. "Then I could spend the night with you again."

"Even spending the night means I sleep on one side of the wall, and you on the other." Teresa sat down and dangled her legs into the water. The idle movement reminded her too much of Noel Argate doing the same thing, so she pulled her feet up and tucked an arm around her knees. "You know that if I could grow gills, I would, love. I hate being separated from you like this."

"You are always with me inside," he assured her, coming over to nuzzle her toes briefly before backing away. "Now, what is so important that you must bring me all the way in here to discuss it?"

Guessing he might react negatively to the idea, Teresa had rehearsed everything at least twice at home. She told him first about the increased number of 'shrike sightings, and how concerned she and the other scientists were for the safety of the 'Zangian pods. She explained how blue whales had been captured on Terra in natural inlets, and how studying giant aquatics often led to amazing breakthroughs in behavior tracking and understanding. Once she had presented him with those facts, she mentioned Noel Argate, his expertise, and how she planned to use him and his military resources to find an answer to the 'shrike problem.

"Yes, yes," Dairatha said as she paused for breath. "This is all very scientific, but what has it to do with me? Do you require assistance in the water with whatever experiment you are conducting?"

"Not this time." She couldn't keep sidestepping the issue. "Dairatha, we intend to lure a mogshrike to an inlet north of here and capture it alive so that we can study it."

He stared at her, his big form going completely still in the water, and then he released a strum of laughter. "My haffets must be clogged with chokeweed, or that was the most tasteless attempt at humor you have ever made."

This was not going the way she had hoped. "You heard me fine, and I'm not joking. We're going to catch a living 'shrike. We have to, love. It's the only way to know why their habits are changing."

He bared his teeth. "Find another way."

"A live specimen would—"

"*No.*" His hide flushed with dark color, and he rose so far out of the water that Teresa thought he might full breach. "I *forbid* it."

It was instinct. She was talking about the only thing on the planet that could kill his kind. Naturally he was upset. "I assure you, Dairatha, we will take every precaution and safeguard to insure no one is hurt. Once we have it secured—"

"*Do you know what you say?*"

Teresa clapped her hands over her ears. "Stop shouting at me." 'Zangians never used full vocal power above water, and for good reason. "We can't discuss this if you get angry; my eardrums will burst."

"There is no discussion of this."

She eased her hands down and gave him an exasperated look. "Of course we'll discuss it. We discuss everything—"

Her mate's massive head slammed into the side of the study tank, so hard that Teresa was knocked backward. Before she could right herself, a heavy fin dragged her back to the edge of the tank so that her face was an inch from her mate's furious eyes.

"No discussion."

She had never seen him like this, and it was terrifying. "Dairatha, for God's sake, please—"

"*You* will be silent now, Teresa, and *you* will be the one who listens." Blood spurted from a split along the edge of Dairatha's mouth, but he didn't seem to notice the wound he had inflicted on himself. "I have curled myself like an oversize wrill, working myself around your humanoid ways. You said it would hurt you if I mated with another, so there have been no females but you. You said you could have no pup of mine, and I accepted that. You said my only child would benefit from leaving the pod to live among the land-dwellers and protect them with their star vessels, and I let her go. Even now, when I have grown too old and large for you to be a proper mate to me, I remain exclusive to you. I have done all you have ever asked of me, whatever it cost me with my own kind." He jerked her closer. "Have I not?"

She nodded, too frightened to speak.

"This I have done out of love for you, and it is a deep and abiding love." He pulled her close, his grip not hurting her now, but pressing her to him as if she were as precious as life itself. "*Duo*, Teresa, we have let *nothing* come between us. Not the water or air we breathe. I know you have sacrificed as much to be with me. The love you feel, I know it is as strong as mine."

"It is." Her hands shook as she lifted them to his face. "I swear to you, it is."

He set her back to look into her eyes. "I hope that you mean what you say, for this time it must be my way, not yours. You will not lure a mogshrike to shore. You will not try to capture one alive, here or anywhere, at any time. You will not allow others to attempt it."

Teresa folded her arms across her waist. "You don't understand what I'm trying to do. You think I'm putting everyone in danger. It won't be like that."

"I do not care what it will be like. It will not happen. You will *not* do this thing, Teresa."

"Fine." She threw out her hands. "You're not asking much, are you? Just stand by, Teresa, and let the 'shrikes keep coming. Maybe I can record it on vid and relay it to other League worlds. Everyone can watch the 'Zangian species become extinct via live relay."

"If we are to die, then we will die defending our way of life, in our water. It is none of your business, Teresa."

"But I love you." If he had used his teeth on her, it wouldn't hurt as much as what he had just said. Anger surged inside her. "Damn it, Dairatha, this isn't just about you and me. It can't be about us. I'm trying to save all of you."

He looked ready to ram the side of the tank again, and then he swam away, circling several times so swiftly that the surface of the water turned white with froth.

"I would do anything for you," Teresa said, knowing he could still hear her. "Anything but let you die."

Slowly he approached her, and lumbered out of the pool. She tried to stop him—it was dangerous for him to do so—but he would not be moved.

"What are you doing? Get back in the water."

Dairatha picked her up with his fins and lifted her four feet off the deck so that they were at eye level. "Tell me you will not do this thing. Say it. Now."

She could have said no, she wouldn't, and that would have been the end of it. By tomorrow, Dairatha would have forgotten all about it. But his life, and the lives of the other 'Zangians, were depending on her answer. That was the only thing she considered greater than her love for him: the future of the 'Zangian species.

"I can't. I love you, but I have to do this."

His great dark eyes clouded for a moment as he stared at her. It was as if he no longer recognized her. Then, very carefully, he set her back down on her feet and pulled his fins away from her. "You are no longer my mate."

Dairatha dove from the deck into the tank and disappeared.

Teresa didn't know how long she stood there, staring into the empty tank. Of all the reactions she had expected from him—annoyance, anger, even outrage—this had not been part of it. They had pledged themselves to each other so long ago she couldn't remember what it felt like not to be mated to Dairatha.

It feels like this.

At some point a pair of gentle hands turned her around, and an insistent arm made her walk away from the tank. She moved like a drone; jerky, cold, unfeeling. Uncaring.

You are no longer my mate.

There was a change of light, and sound, and something fragrant and warm was put to her lips. She drank and swallowed tasting nothing, seeing nothing, hearing the distant murmur of a voice but not making out the words. She couldn't hear anything but his voice, and his words.

You are no longer my mate. No longer. No longer.

The clinical, scientist part of her psyche split off to one side and tried to reason it out. Had she really ever been Dairatha's mate? Everything between them had been a series of adjustments or compromises. If she set aside her emotions, it was clear that he would be better off with someone else.

Someone not like Teresa, who was no longer his mate.

A mature 'Zangian, like Kyara, Dair's biological mother, or one of the younger females, would make Dairatha much happier. He could certainly help himself to anyone he wanted now. Another 'Zangian could give him the kind of companionship Teresa never had. He didn't have to restrict himself to monogamy anymore; a pod female would never expect that of him. Dairatha might chase down more than one in the breeding caverns and, in a few seasons, give Dair five or six new siblings to love.

He didn't need a mate like Teresa, who couldn't breathe water, or make love with him, or give him a child of her own body.

"Teresa."

Teresa, who had just refused his only request in the ten years they had been together.

"Terri."

Something was brushing the hair away from her face, and something else held her close to another body. She looked up into eyes that weren't as big as her fist or the color of the sky before moonsrise. These eyes were smaller and lighter and much more familiar. Terran eyes.

Noel Argate's eyes.

"I heard what he said," Noel told her. He looked how she felt: old and tired. "Terri, I . . . I don't know what to say. I am so sorry."

She rested her cheek against his shoulder and tried to feel something, anything beyond this wrenching, tearing agony that was going to kill her, kill her slowly, so slowly, chewing her to pieces.

And I fed myself to this mogshrike. "So am I, Noel."

The battle was over, and patchy communications were established with the Ylydii diplomatic vessel. Shon volunteered to fly escort for Burn back to K-2, while Onkar and the patrol stayed behind to collect the survivors from the mercenary ships.

"I'm reading weak life signs coming from two of the derelicts," Onkar told the medical crew. "We're sending in the transpods first to check for hostiles and traps."

"Make it fazt, Zubcommander," Dr. Dloh advised him. "From the zignz, those beingz don't have long to live."

The armed gunners docked with the mercenary ships, and soon reported back that it was safe for the medical crew to board and perform triage on the wounded.

"I don't think they'll like this, Subcommander," one of the gunners transmitted. "They're all dying."

Dr. Dloh, who also monitored the incoming relays, broke in with, "We'll determine that, if you don't mind, pleaze."

Onkar sent Curonal in with the medical crew to evaluate the situation. The gunner reported back in a few minutes, but his transmission was equally dismal. "The medics are doing what they can, but the wounded are not responding. Something is wrong with them."

Onkar had encountered many ways to die. "Are they self-terminating?"

"The doctor says they might be sick with something; that they were sick when they were fighting us."

Onkar instituted contagion-control procedures. By the time the wounded were transported back onto Rescue Three, all but one had expired. Dloh did his best to keep the sole survivor alive, but the mercenary refused to cooperate. He subsequently sank into a coma and died en route to K-2.

Dloh came up to the helm to report. "I've run multiple blood zcanz on all of them. Theze men have zerious gaztric and lymphatic damage, and it could be pozzible that they're ztill carrying a contagiouz pathogen."

After landing back at K-2 Main Transport and passing through a thorough biodecon, Onkar left the helm and watched as the bodies were unloaded from Rescue Three's modified cargo bay and onto morgue transports. Engineering Chief Verrig joined him.

"If they were all sick, why would these men not seek help for their condition?" It was, according to Dair, what humanoids did when they discovered they were ill or in danger of dying.

"I can't say, but the ship is on full quarantine until we identify the source," Verrig promised. "I'll download the computer databases that are recovered from the battlefield; see what was happening on board in the days before the attack. Would they have attacked the Ylydii ship for medical stores?"

"If they did, they killed the entire crew looking for them." Burn joined them and waved a fin back toward the diplomatic vessel. "I have more bodies than you can count floating around in there."

"Where are the Ylydii survivors?"

"Over at the medical facility. They evacuated them first; took them out in emergency tanks."

Onkar noted the long gash across the younger male's face and the change in his eyes. Burn looked as if he had come back from a long swim through the outer currents. "Did you notice if the mercenaries on board the Ylydii ship were sick?"

"I don't know." Burn's gaze followed the evac unit transporting the Ylydii to the colony's FreeClinic. "I killed them all before I could check out how they were feeling."

So he had blooded himself thoroughly, Onkar thought. That explained the wound, and this new remoteness. "Was it necessary?"

"Yes, it was. And no, it wasn't." Burn hesitated, and then looked at him. "You were right, Onkar. It was not like firing on another ship. I heard them, and saw them. I could taste their blood. I felt them die."

"You will carry it with you for a time," Onkar told him quietly. "Learn from it."

"Learn what?" Burn demanded. "That I enjoy killing, but only from a distance? That one mistake costs a hundred lives?"

Jadaira hurried out from the Flight Control tower and launched herself at Onkar. He caught her and held her close for a moment before looking over her head at Burn. The subject of killing was not to be discussed in front of Jadaira. The younger male nodded in mute understanding.

"If you ever fly at another ship like that again," she began saying, and then shook her head and buried her face against the front of his flightsuit.

Onkar held her close and said nothing. She knew he would fly the maneuver again, just as she would once she was back in space, and he remained on the ground to watch and worry and fear for her.

"We knew what we were doing, Dair," Burn said. "Onkar and I both mastered that maneuver long ago."

"I should slap you both with a regs violation. I think I will, as soon as I think of one." Jadaira glanced at him and then whirled out of Onkar's arms to touch her cousin's face. "What happened—Burn, this is a *blade* wound."

He started to say something and then shrugged. "You should see the other male."

She glowered for a moment and then blew some air through her gill vents. "You'll be able to see the scar from a mile away."

Verrig tapped Burn on the shoulder. "A signal came in for you, Sublieutenant. You're wanted over at the FreeClinic. You two as well," he said to Onkar and Jadaira. "Report to the immersion tank room at the aquatic treatment center."

Onkar was tired, and hungry, and wanted nothing more than to take his mate and go home. He was also deeply concerned about Burn, who needed time to adjust to what he had done in space. "Can it not wait?"

"It's probably the Ylydii ambassador," Burn said, shuffling his flukes. "Cara-something. She said some things when she broke down the door to the helm and found me with her daughter."

"Like what?" Jadaira demanded.

"Some things about me." The younger male sounded glum. "Using another blade on me. And something about prison."

The three 'Zangians rode over to the FreeClinic with one of the evac transports. They were met outside the aquatic treatment center by the slim blond Terran administrator.

"Ana." Jadaira exchanged greeting with her stepmother's friend. "Did you summon us?"

"Yes. I thought it best, considering how upset Ambassador Carada is." She glanced at Burn. "Sublieutenant, I have to ask you not to make any remarks during this meeting. You either, Subcommander. You won't be addressed by the ambassador anyway, so please allow Jadaira and me to handle this."

"Why won't she speak to us?" Onkar asked.

"Ambassador Carada has very high rank among her species." Ana rolled her eyes. "I have been informed that Ylydii females of her position do not speak directly to males."

"Her daughter does," Burn put in helpfully.

"Yes, the daughter." Ana grimaced. "I think that Lady Liana may be at the center of this. Please, come with me."

The aquatic treatment center, designed by the best 'Zangian engineers on the planet, adjoined the FreeClinic facility but was kept separated by an air-and-water lock. Because there was only one aquatic physician on staff, the center also provided transparent viewing and treatment cubicles, built into the patient tanks to accommodate the needs of non-water-breathers.

The three 'Zangians stripped out of their uniforms and dove into the visitors' tank, while Ana entered one of the viewing cubicles. Special underwater audio allowed everyone to communicate clearly with each other.

Onkar remained at Jadaira's side as Ana introduced Miglan, the ambassador's personal assistant. The small aquatic came forward, swishing the water with mincing sweeps of his fins. He was smaller than the other Ylydii, Onkar noted, and not as brightly colored. He seemed to compensate for his diminutive size by speaking with his chest plate puffed out.

Administrator Hansen, Ambassador Carada of Ylydii was not harmed during the hostile takeover of her ship. However, my lady wishes to express her displeasure with the manner in which rescue efforts were made.

Her displeasure? Dair exchanged a look with Onkar. She did not wish to be saved?

I will speak to these persons now, Miglan.

Ambassador Carada emerged from her shrouded patient tank and entered the visitors' area, filling up half of the available space with her bulk. Liquid jewel tubes circled her head, fin bases, and waist, from which artificial veiling fluttered.

Onkar had never seen a female aquatic of Carada's dimensions. She was easily as large as he and Burn. It was not her size that bothered him as much as something else about her—something not so easily defined. Whatever it was, it had his teeth set on edge.

Her Grace Lady Carada, Ambassador of the Ylydii. Miglan quickly scooted behind the ambassador.

An aquatic nurse came out of the patient tank, but Carada turned and said, *I told you, I do not wish to be examined by any physician, and certainly not some male.* She circled around and gave Ana a baleful look. *Nor do I wish to be coddled by a lowly mouth-breather. Who is the aquatic in authority here?*

Onkar saw Ana nod to his mate.

I am. Jadaira came forward and finned gestures of respect suitable for an Elder of the pod. *Welcome to Kevarzangia Two, Ambassador. We are so pleased you were not harmed during the raid on your ship.*

Indeed. From the manner in which you carried out your rescue, I gained the impression that you wanted me and mine dead, Carada said. *Why else would you send that maniac to spread chaos and destruction as he did?*

Maniac?

She means Burn, Onkar told Dair.

Burn. I am not surprised that is his name. He all but burned up our vessel. Carada pulled her head up and her tale under, taking a vertical, commanding position in the water. Her flukes caught the hovering Miglan, who was knocked into a small spin before she plucked him out of it and tucked him under her fin like a podling. *That male savaged my daughter and nearly killed her several times. Our water is filthy with the blood of those he wantonly slaughtered.*

Onkar caught Burn by the fin, keeping him from surging forward, and then clikked a reminder for him to keep silent.

Ambassador, Sublieutenant mu Znora boarded your ship alone and at great personal risk, Jadaira said carefully. *He only acted in self-defense, and to protect you and the other survivors.*

His actions were reckless and ill-conceived. He killed these males when they might have been captured and held for interrogation. I should not have to point out that, had he failed, we all might have been murdered. Carada tightened her hold on Miglan, who squeaked. *You will imprison him and have him neutered at once.*

Jadaira was visibly fighting to control her temper. *With respect, Ambassador, we do not reprimand our officers in such a manner.*

Males should not be given rank, Carada snapped. *As for troublesome males like this one, they have to be gelded. If you do not, they will pass their violent traits on to the young.* The ambassador drew back, bumping into Miglan again. *Do not tell me you allow ones like him to freely breed among your kind.*

Onkar saw Ana shaking her head at Jadaira, who was already at a loss for words. He moved forward and addressed the ambassador's pet male. *Miglan, is it permitted that I speak to you?*

If the ambassador has no objections. The small male looked up at Carada, who was inspecting Onkar's bicolored augmentations.

He has the look of one of our males, the ambassador told her assistant, and released him from her hold. *Very well, you may speak to him. Perhaps he has some influence with these rock-headed females.*

Miglan came forward. *What is it you wish to tell me?*

Our societies are very different. 'Zangian pods are matriarchal, but our relationships are reciprocal in respect and deference. We do not elevate females above males, or males over females.

Males over females. Miglan squealed with mirth. *That is a good one, 'Zangian.*

Your people must know this is how we live from the contact they have made with us in the past. Onkar glanced at Carada, and wondered why she chose to ignore what she already knew about his kind. *I would respectfully remind the ambassador that tolerance and understanding are two of the greatest tools of peace. They are also the most welcome gifts a visiting species can bring.*

Miglan swam back to Carada's side and repeated everything Onkar had said to him. It was rather ludicrous, since the ambassador had clearly heard every word as he had spoken to Miglan, but the pretense obviously gave her some satisfaction. He waited as Carada made a show of pondering the request, and then she withdrew from the tank, leaving Miglan behind.

You will be honored and privileged to know that my lady will think on your words, 'Zangian, the little male told him. He had grown the lashes around his eyes very long, and peeked through them as he spoke. *For the interim, this male—*he gestured toward Burn—*will not trespass on the ambassador's kindness or good will again. He will not approach my lady's daughter, the lady Liana, and he will not be permitted to board our ship at any time in the future. Is this understood?*

Onkar's attention moved to a new group entering the treatment ward.

Who is that, Miglan? Carada demanded. *I did not give permission for any others to be admitted here.*

Ana Hansen glanced back and hurried to meet the two males, one Skartesh, the other cloaked but clearly Ninrana. "Ambassador Urloy-ka, Representative Bataran, welcome. If you will come with me—"

The Ninrana pulled back his hood, revealing the narrow-eyed, deeply tanned face of a desert-dweller humanoid. "Is this the male who brought the fish people back?" He gestured toward Burn with the bone staff he carried.

"Yes," Ana said. "Now if I may take you to a reception room, we can—"

Urloy-ka moved around the administrator and came to the transparent wall between him and the aquatics. "You are to be commended, 'Zangian. Never have I seen kills as clean as those you made. None of the bones or tissues were spoiled or wasted. I would know how you did it."

Burn's hide paled several shades.

"It was an unnecessary and barbaric solution," Bataran said, and glared at Burn. "For what he did, this one should be severely punished, not praised."

Onkar winced, and heard Ana smother a groan. Burn didn't respond. He was busy watching Carada.

A smaller Ylydii female appeared in the tank and pushed past the ambassador. She looked at no one but Burn. *I thank you for my life, Pilot.*

Silence, Liana. The Ylydii ambassador grabbed the small female by the dorsal fin and dragged her back. *He has earned no gratitude from us.*

He has from me. Liana struggled free and swam forward to press her snout against the divider. *I will say what needs be said. I* thank *you, Pilot.*

Onkar watched as the ambassador drove the smaller female from the tank before returning alone.

Tell all of these males to get out, Carada ordered Jadaira. *Then you will explain to me why this Bio Rescue operation is peddled as a medical treatment and evacuation effort when it is so clearly a military operation.*

* * *

"Liam."

William Mayer looked up to see Ana standing in front of the assessment desk. She looked agitated and unhappy.

"Check on him in thirty minutes, and make sure his chest tube is clear," he told his charge nurse, and handed the patient's chart to her. "Ask Dr. Tixys to cover for me." He came out from behind the desk and joined Ana. "My next surgery is scheduled in an hour. I'm yours until then."

She gave him an unconvincing smile. "I hope this doesn't take that long."

As they walked to the aquatic treatment center, Ana briefed him on the situation, and the events up to that morning.

"I asked Urloy-ka and Bataran to leave, and Jadaira is placating the ambassador until the 'Zangian Elder arrives." Ana checked her wristcom. "Which should be in ten minutes. We've got that long to figure out how to keep Carada and the Ylydii delegation from withdrawing from the Peace Summit."

Liam tugged her to a stop. "What does Carada want?"

"I don't know. She talks like a paranoid pacifist but acts like a general on amphetamines. She makes one demand and then changes it to something else. When I left, she was working up a theory on how Bio Rescue was nothing but a military operation disguised as a medical rescue effort."

"It sounds like she has a slight case of PMS."

Ana gave him an ironic look. "I don't think this is hormonal, Liam."

"Prisoner Maladjustment Syndrome. Some beings don't take too well to being captured and detained, particularly those who occupy an elevated position in their culture. We've seen it lately among the military, usually after a POW center is liberated. High-ranking officers who were steady as stone during their detainment become inordinately demanding, irrational, and sometimes violent."

"How can you tell if she's got this version of PMS?" Ana asked.

"Erratic synaptic pulses in the frontal lobe. However, my nurse over at the ATC already informed me that Carada refuses to be examined." He thought for a minute. "The patient tanks have built-in proximity scanners; I could perform a remote scan and check her brainwaves. I've treated enough aquatics with PMS that I'd recognize the pattern."

Ana gnawed at her lower lip. "If the ambassador discovers that we've scanned her without her permission, she'll be furious. It would also violate the diplomatic code, and she'd have every justification for leaving K-2 and never coming back."

"The alternative is canceling the summit until she gets over it," Liam advised her. "Untreated, the condition only gets worse. She could present a danger to herself and others."

"What is the treatment for this syndrome?"

"A low-grade stim to the nerve centers to restore synaptic balance. It sometimes causes short-term memory loss, but not among aquatics. She won't be aware of it. The sensation is like that of a mild tingle that lasts only a split second."

"Officially I'm supposed to tell you 'no way in hell' now. Unofficially . . ." It was Ana's turn to think. "Do the remote scan while I speak with Carada's daughter, Liana. As next of kin, she can give you permission to treat."

Liam took Ana's hand before she could hurry off. "Carada's behavior isn't the only problem, is it?"

"When did you become empathically gifted?" Ana tried to joke.

"I don't know. Maybe the day you seduced me." He caressed her cheek. "You taught me to pay attention to feelings as well as the physical condition."

"It's not Carada. It's her daughter." Ana lowered her voice. "I have an inkling that there's something terribly wrong with her. She has a regimented mind that's very hard to read. Beneath all that iron self-discipline, I sense that she's manipulating her own thoughts; thinking only what is acceptable or necessary and feeling nothing."

"What is the harm in that?" It described his own mental discipline perfectly.

"You can't impose that kind of restraint on yourself for very long without some psychic backlash." Ana sighed. "Her control isn't perfect, either. It's like seeing a lid clamped down over something boiling—or toxic—and knowing it could blow at any minute."

"All that from an inkling."

She frowned. "I'm serious, Liam. I've never felt a mind like hers, and I'm deeply concerned."

William rarely thought much about Ana's latent psychic talent. The scientist in him tended to doubt the reliability of her perceptions, but he'd seen her summon deadly accurate impressions too often to dismiss it. "This mental control Liana has—would it affect her ability to make an informed decision about her mother's treatment?"

"No, it shouldn't."

"Then we should address Carada's PMS first," William said. "Once we have her stabilized, we can talk to Liana about treatment for her problem. Let me clear my slate." He signaled the pre-op ward and asked Dr. Tixys to take his afternoon procedure.

As soon as he was done rearranging his shift schedule, Ana put her arms around him and hugged him tightly.

William returned the embrace before lifting her chin so he could see her face. "What's this all about?"

"I love you. I love that you're a doctor and you help so many people. I love your mind, which is beautiful and disciplined and brilliant." She grimaced. "I can't talk about your body until we have some privacy."

"Good idea." He never tired of her slim, mature figure or the exotic *togmot* covering nearly every inch of her skin under her garments. The reddish-brown markings, a legacy of Ana's first marriage, felt like silk to the touch.

She placed a hand over the left side of his lab coat. "What I really love, though, is your heart. It's always filled with compassion and generosity. You never run out of them."

"That's because you keep giving me some from yours." He kissed her the way he would if they'd been alone, and the last few, blurry emotions snapped into sharp focus. "Clear your calendar for the cycle after this Peace Summit is over."

She smiled up at him. "Are we finally taking a vacation together?"

"You'll see." William kissed her again.

CHAPTER 9

*B*urn left the aquatic treatment center with Onkar, made the uncomfortable transition from tank water to breathing air, and waited outside the FreeClinic for the females to sort things out with the Ylydii. He didn't like the big, gaudy female ambassador, but she had the right to be angry with him. Politicians seldom did or said anything that made sense in his view, but he had killed unnecessarily. It was only her suggested punishment that made him fume.

Have me neutered. "I know why the Ylydii males were so small and timid," he said out loud to Onkar. "Carada and her kind probably emasculate anyone who isn't."

Onkar didn't seem amused. "Their customs seem strange to us, but they do work. Teresa told me that the Ylydii species is as old as our own."

Burn snorted. "You don't see 'Zangian vessels being taken over by mercenaries without a fight."

"The Ylydii don't fight as we do. They sing their prey to death."

Burn folded his arms. "They sing that badly?"

"They use their voices and those flowing fins. Once they make a sort of net with their fins' membranes, the females direct a loud, tightly focused series of tonal pulses toward the center of their feeding grounds. The sound waves have no affect on the Ylydii, as their haffets evert during the song, but the prey is lured into their nets. They eat whatever they catch."

Some of the sounds Liana had made had pricked the insides of his haffets, but he had merely thought it more of her offworlder's strangeness. "Have you ever heard them?"

"My dam always told me to beware of strange females." Onkar looked up at the sky. "The Ylyd certainly qualify."

Burn eyed him. "Could you swish around a female and let her push you around the way their males do?"

"No, but I will mate with no one but Jadaira."

"I suppose she pushes you around enough."

The big male didn't take offense. "You will understand how it is when you discover a female for whom you care above all others."

That reminded him of Liana. Burn hadn't been able to speak to her, and no one would tell him where she had been taken. He had not been able to tell from her brief appearance if she had suffered any complications from the injuries she had received at the hands of the mercenaries. Carada driving her out and not knowing where Liana was now had him on edge.

We faced death together, he reasoned. *I have the right to speak with her, to know she is well.*

There had also been something strange about her deliberate defiance of her mother and the public announcement of gratitude. He couldn't quite say why, but he had the feeling she hadn't done it out of true gratitude or at all for his benefit.

But what could she accomplish by thanking me?

Onkar was a good companion. He kept Burn distracted by talking about their mission and how they might improve their response time and patrol formations during the next. He did not speak of the dead, or of the ambassador's damning remarks. By the time Jadaira rejoined them an hour later, Burn felt much more settled.

"Dr. Mayer and Elder Nathaka mu Hlana were called in to consult on the problems, and we've worked out an agreement with the Ylydii ambassador," Dair told them. "A detachment of 'Zangian SEALs will be assigned as escort and guard for her and her entourage during the Peace Summit."

"I do not think we have an adequate number of females who can serve," Onkar said.

Dair shook her head. "The SEALs will be male. They will serve as representatives both of the 'Zangian species and for Bio Rescue. Our presence will demonstrate the basic principals of the effort: to protect and preserve life, not destroy it." She faced Burn. "You have been chosen to lead the SEAL detachment assigned to the ambassador."

Burn cocked his head. "Why me? An hour ago the big glittery female proposed to part me from my penis."

"I was tempted to let her do it," Dair retorted.

"Jadaira." Onkar nudged her.

"The ambassador was very specific about having you as detachment leader," she told Burn. "I was just as surprised to witness her change of heart. But then, she's a diplomat, accustomed to dealing with hotheaded idiots and making compromises. You should be grateful she's so forgiving."

"I didn't do anything that requires forgiving, Cousin. In fact, I . . ." Burn caught the quick fin gesture Onkar made and swallowed the rest of his protest. "Very well. I'll play watchout."

"This Peace Summit is important." Dair sounded tired now. "Our people are deeply involved in what will be discussed. The settlement of the Skartesh, aquatic territorial and resource management rights, even the very survival of the Ninra species, could be decided during these talks."

Burn could just imagine the endless hours of listening to the politicians drone. What frightened him was the thought of making another mistake. This time he might kill Liana and the other Ylydii. "All that has nothing to do with me."

She scowled. "You are no longer a podling whose chattering can be indulged and overlooked. Each word you speak, each action you take could influence those making these decisions. Their decisions in turn will affect millions of lives. It is your choice, cousin, but I think it is time you began conducting yourself like a responsible adult."

Burn didn't care about his behavior. He needed to see Liana again, though, so he would take the duty assignment. He might not be allowed to speak with the ambassador's daughter, but at least he could watch out for her. And he would not make any mistakes.

"Very well. I'll escort them, guard them, and listen to that harridan purge her gullet every two seconds. I won't twitch a gillet the whole time. Whatever you say." Burn glanced back at the treatment center. "Is there anything else she wants?" He wanted to be sure there was no more talk of gelding; deserved punishment or not, he happened to be very fond of his penis.

"Besides biting the Ninrana ambassador in several vulnerable places and having her ship completely sterilized? Not at the moment, but I'm sure she's preparing a new list." Dair shook some of her gillets out of her face. "Security would like you to file a full report of what occurred on board the Ylydii ship. I'll take a copy of it." Dair's expression changed and she pressed one of her hands against her belly. "Now I'd like to get wet, before I start purging again."

"Are you feeling ill?" Onkar curled one of his arms around her narrow, sloped shoulders.

"I shouldn't have watched the two of you playing chicken," she told him as she leaned on him.

"You are short of breath." Onkar pressed his fin tips to her throat. "Your pulse is rapid."

"My heart has been fluttering all day," Dair admitted. "I had better go and see Mom. That should make her happy; she's been signaling me since sunrise."

"Chief." Shon entered the office when the head of colonial security was poring over evidence scans. "You needed to see me?"

"We picked up a tiny amount of DNA off one of the derelicts that doesn't match any member of the crew. We don't believe it belongs to a courier, either." Norash handed him a copy of the cell profile scan. "You'll recognize the profile."

The cells that had been recovered gave no indication as to the species, gender, or age of the body from which they had been shed. "This changes things."

"I thought you might be intrigued." Norash offered a disk. "Your new orders. I want you to find who this DNA belongs to, and bring them in for questioning."

Shon accepted his orders and tucked the chip in the vest pocket of his flightsuit. "How much resistance did Quadrant Intelligence give you about pulling me for this assignment?" he asked Chief Norash.

"As much as they could without making direct threats to have me assigned to waste management for the remainder of my existence." The Trytinorn came around the big console. "Let's take a walk."

Strolling with a being Norash's size required constant vigilance, so as not to stray under his massive feet, but Shon had an idea of why the security chief wanted to leave the building.

Once they were outside, Shon asked, "Find some new furnishings in your office?"

"Recording drones, yesterday. I like a clean office; Intelligence should have considered that and embedded them in the walls. Instead they attached them where they believed I do not dust." Norash paused by a communications dish, where the strong signal output would mask their conversation from any nearby or hovering surveillance devices. "Major, your orders were approved solely because quadrant wants to know what they're dealing with here. That paranoia, however, will protect you only so long. Eventually Intel will find a replacement expert or consultant to send here, and yank you back to oKia."

Shon looked out over the horizon, to where the twin suns were setting. "I will not be returning to my homeworld. Not now, not ever."

"I thought not." Approval gleamed in the Trytinorn's small eyes. "I've never had much use for intelligence operatives, but you've done some remarkable work over the short term of your career. My people believe that a life lived with honor is reborn to its reward. If that is true, Major, I envy you your next existence."

Shon left Norash and went down to Main Transport. The 'Zangian planetary patrol had landed, and the pilots who had flown their patrol shift were coming in from the docks.

One female pilot walked by herself, keeping slightly apart from the others, and bypassed the hangar where the relief shift waited to enter one of the engineering bays. Not knowing exactly why, Shon followed.

He entered the bay to see that the lone 'Zangian female was Dair's wing leader, Saree. Saree was talking to Verrig and gesturing back to her strafer, the *Sandpearl*. Verrig nodded a great deal and took notes as she spoke.

Saree was the most demanding member of the pilots' pod, Shon recalled, and always flew alone. The other pilots respected her, but her general demeanor was so aloof that few spent any time with her.

Shon personally thought she was a spectacular pilot, but didn't know a single thing about her other than her ability to handle a strafer in space. For a 'Zangian, Saree was remarkably unfriendly.

If she is a 'Zangian, the part of his brain that Shon didn't like very much tagged on.

The 'Zangian pilot looked toward him and rapidly finished her conversation with Verrig before coming over to confront Shon. "Is there something you need, Major?"

He needed more than the orders in his pocket, or the prospect of assuring that he would never return to oKia. Given the unique profile of the DNA recovered from the mercenary ship, he needed answers, and he needed them now. If he didn't obtain them, everything he had done to preserve the peace in this system would be made a total, utter waste.

"I'm going for a dive." He kept his tone casual and nonthreatening. "I thought I'd see if you were interested in coming with me."

Saree clearly hadn't been expecting such a request. "Why me?"

"You're not busy right now, are you?"

"No. Why me?"

He liked her tenacity. "I've always felt an affinity with you. You're like me; you walk alone."

"You obviously haven't been paying attention around the pilots' pod," she said, "or you'd know that my kind are never alone."

"Being alone and walking alone are two different things."

She inspected him. "This sharing a swim—it wouldn't be some sort of prelude to a mating ritual among your kind, would it?"

Shon laughed. It had been so long since he had done that; the sound came out harsh and dry. "No, Pilot. If I wanted to mate with you, I'd seize your neck in my teeth and throw you down on all fours. Or fins, to be more precise."

"How romantic." She seemed amused now. "Very well, Major. I'll swim with you."

Shon took her to the coast in his personal glidecar, which evidently pleased the 'Zangian female, from her vocal admiration of the interior.

"I thought 'Zangians weren't interested in such material things as glidecars and dwellings and so forth," he said.

"Generally we aren't, but I like these private transports." She touched the smooth upholstery with a careful fin. "They're so efficient and they can move so fast when you want them to. They make being topside almost tolerable."

"Thank you, I think."

She turned her attention to him. "If you need to confide something personal to me, it would be best to do it now. You can't do much talking with a regulator in your snout, and once we're downside, everyone will hear."

"Not a snout, a mouth. Or, at least, I *had* a mouth when I was oKiaf." He felt the elongated lower half of his face. "Now I think this classifies as a muzzle."

"Different words for the same body part." She shook her head. "You people are just strange."

"So are you. Everyone is strange to each other, even when we serve in the same military."

Saree looked perplexed. "I don't know what you mean."

"You're a fighter pilot, Lieutenant. You've been trained to operate some of the most sophisticated equipment in the League, specifically to track, disable, and destroy the enemy. Yet despite your training, you never fire your weapons to kill unless it's absolutely necessary." He glanced sideways. "I find that a little strange."

She shifted on the seat. "Wasting power and ammunition is inefficient. It can also get you killed."

"That's not the only reason you conserve fire."

"No." She stared out at the approaching cliffs. "Life is fleeting. I never wished to hasten it along to its end."

"Then why become a fighter pilot?"

"I joined the SEALs to protect my homeworld. I wasn't looking for a fight." She made a fin gesture he didn't understand. "I may not be the best-loved among my people, Major, but I love them with all that I am."

She sounded sincere enough to make him uncomfortable. Still, Shon pressed her. "If the pod asked you to do something that required you to kill—kill something innocent, for example—and you knew that if you didn't, some of them would die, what would you choose to do?"

"I would make the choice for the greater good, which would likely mean I'd kill the innocent." She moved her body in a 'Zangian version of a shrug. "War often forces us to make such unpleasant choices. You know that."

He nodded. It was the sort of answer he had expected from a member of the coastal pod. That and a DNA screen should clear Saree from his list.

"I did not agree with this war," Saree continued, startling him. "I am a territorial creature, and I understand why the Hsktskt feel the need to defend their space."

"*Their* space?"

"The League came into Hsktskt-claimed territories and established colonies without asking permission," she said. "Then came the decision to outlaw slavery, something the Hsktskt have practiced and profited from for millennia. I do not believe the Faction was consulted about that, either."

"That's called liberation, Lieutenant."

"If you're League, Major. If you're Hsktskt, you call it invasion."

He brought the glidecar to a stop and stared at her. "Are you telling me that you feel sympathetic toward the lizards?"

"I do not like the Hsktskt. I do not agree with their practices. It does not change the fact that we started this war, not them. The Hsktskt had to fight or the League would have destroyed their territories, their trade, perhaps even their civilization." She gestured toward him. "Were you in their place, what would you do?"

"I'd know what I was doing was wrong." Shon couldn't believe what he was hearing. "Just whose side are you on?"

"I side with the League, obviously. But I understand the Hsktskt better."

"Your people eventually would have been enslaved or obliterated by the Hsktskt," Shon pointed out. "Under the League, you continue to enjoy your freedom."

"Is that what you call this?" Saree seemed amused now. "The League established a colony here—without consulting us—and made great changes to our world. Teresa and others like her told us that we must learn to be more like they are. They have educated and even alterformed us to be more like them. There was nothing wrong with what we were."

"You have profited from the relationship."

"Have we? I do not see how. At this time we are told that we must provide a home for the Skartesh, and water for the Ninrana, and placate the Ylydii. All because the League thinks these things are right. There is no talk of what will be done for the 'Zangians."

"You don't need anything."

"True. Had we been left alone, we would still need nothing from you. We would not be involved in your disputes and your wars. We would have the life we once enjoyed, before humanoids came here. That is freedom, Major. What the League offers is nothing more than a benevolent and intrusive dictatorship."

Shon felt like shaking her until her teeth rattled. "With your attitude, I'm surprised anyone lets you have a ship."

"I fight for the League, and my people. I kill beings who are in my eyes innocent of any transgression, and by doing so serve the greater good. I do not have to like it, or even understand it, to do it well. Perhaps I am more suited to being League than Hsktskt." She looked out at the cliffs. "Are you certain that you still wish to dive with me?"

"Considering that I'm nothing but a puppet of a dictatorship, I could ask you the same question," Shon said.

"I've always liked you, Major. You sacrificed much to help protect the Skartesh. More than anyone knows, I suspect, and that is something that I *do* understand." She nudged him. "Come on. I want to see if you can move underwater any better than before."

*   *   *

No one at K-2's medical facility paid much attention to Liana. After her aborted attempt to speak with Burn, she was forced to remain inside another, shrouded, treatment room. As she waited for Carada's negotiations to end, she was given a quick examination by a male aquatic physician and treated for minor hide abrasions.

"If these become inflamed or painful, please report back for treatment," Dr. mu Cheft told her. "I'll start you on an antibiotic."

A medicine, she guessed. Her kind made use of some compounds to ease pain, but only after grievous injuries. Thanks to the clean, salty content of their waters, they rarely suffered infections.

A humanoid female colony administrator interrupted the examination and asked permission to speak to her about Carada. The physician left them alone, and Ana Hansen explained her concerns.

Liana wanted to shriek at the other woman; instead she gave her permission for what she wished to do. She rather doubted it would have any effect on Carada, but to refuse would seem suspicious.

"Would you like to speak to one of our therapists?" Ana asked, very tentatively.

I do not have this PMS, do I?

"No, but it might help you with . . . other problems."

I have no problems. Liana turned her back on her. *Please leave me now.*

The physician returned to complete the exam, and also insisted on scanning the contents of her stomach and blood before releasing her to rejoin Carada. By that time the ambassador had been treated, had settled matters with the organizers of the Peace Summit, and was preparing to return to their ship.

Lady Liana. Fokrej, the male valet Carada had assigned to her, led her into the ambassador's treatment tank. Slightly larger and thinner than Miglan, the valet had doubled as Liana's chaperon since they left Ylyd. His face had a distinct, sour cast to it, but he was rarely pleased with anything. *Your mother wishes you to accompany her in the transport.*

She deftly avoided the stunted veils he stretched out toward her. Fokrej liked touching her, especially when they were alone. *I thought you were killed along with the other members of the crew.* She would have prayed for it, if she had believed in a higher power.

When the intruders stormed our compartment, the ambassador risked her own life to shield me, Fokrej informed her as his gaze moved with an oily slyness over her body. *If not for her gracious protection, I would almost certainly be dead.*

Oh, well. There's always the next time we're attacked. She swam past him.

Carada was being adorned by Miglan with a new collection of ornaments, and barely glanced up as Liana presented herself. *You took too long. Did they find something wrong with you?*

Liana could tell no difference in Carada, and assumed the furtive treatment had, as she had guessed, no effect on the big female. *Not really. The doctor was concerned that the cuts from my bonds may become infected. He wishes me to return for treatment if they do so.*

They will not, the ambassador said. *These 'Zangians have replaced the ship's atmosphere. It is only a synthetic seawater, but it is clean and free of contaminants, and will serve until fresh replacement can be brought to us from Ylyd.*

We will not be able to wait long for the water, Liana said, and flinched as Fokrej came and draped one of his veils across her back in a familiar, friendly manner. Small barbs hidden within his veils bit deep into her hide.

I know this, Carada said as she shrugged into a bifold cape that dangled polished shells across her wide upper torso. *The fleet is en route here, and then we may proceed with the summit.*

Liana waited for her to explain herself. Fokrej was doing his best to provoke a response, as always, but she had learned that reacting to the tiny, furtive injuries he inflicted on her was exactly what he wanted. Pretending she felt nothing infuriated him, and he drove his barbs in deeper.

Liana would have done anything to escape him—and would have bitten off one of her own veils to retaliate—but Carada was watching.

Carada knew the valet enjoyed tormenting her. She also knew what Liana was willing to tolerate to accomplish their goals.

You defied me in front of everyone today. Carada came forward, knocking Fokrej away and crowding Liana into a smaller adjoining space. It turned out to be the transport tank to the Ylydii ship. *You will be punished for it.*

Liana stared back at her. *Have you not punished me enough?*

I do not know. Carada frowned. *I cannot remember.*

Terror spiked through Liana. *What else do you not remember?*

The big female met her gaze. *I remember why I am here, and what you will do for me. Never fear that.*

Fokrej swam in behind them, and a hatch closed. *May I be of service, my lady?*

The marks on my body have been examined. Liana bared her teeth. *They have been scanned. New marks will be questioned.*

Carada said nothing. Neither did Fokrej, who sidled against the big female while smirking at Liana.

It did not take long for the transport to cross the land between the medical facility and the docking pads at Main Transport. Along the way Liana had the chance to look out and see the land-dwellers going about the business of their daily lives.

How bizarre it was, to see soil not covered by water, and the erratic, sometimes jarring motions the land-dwellers had to make to cross it. They seemed almost like two-dimensional bottom-feeders, for they could only go back and forth in linear directions, their lower limbs barely clearing the ground before returning to touch it again. It must be like living forever bound and tethered.

Burn can do that. She knew 'Zangians could live above or below, although they preferred the water. His people were also making an evolutionary shift that would drive them out of the sea, and in ten or twenty centuries they would be forced to live on the surface permanently.

Liana.

She tore her gaze away from the viewer to see the valet hovering, and Carada gone. *What?*

He gestured toward a docking ramp that led from the transport to the waiting ship. *The ambassador is waiting.*

The ship had been attended to by the Transport workers and was restored close to its original condition; the bodies cleared out and the liquid atmosphere drained and replaced. The new liquid felt cooler and tasted less salty than Liana was accustomed to, but it was acceptable.

I will go and see to my quarters, she said, moving past Fokrej.

He allowed her to make it all the way to the corridor before he caught up with her. *The ambassador's orders were very specific, my lady.* His barbs latched into the soft surface of her hide again, but there was nothing secretive about the way he touched her now. *You are to come with me.*

Liana showed no emotion as the valet guided her through the corridors to an isolation tank. She had been brought here three times since they left Ylyd, and she had learned that resisting only made it worse, and the punishment harsher and longer.

Fokrej left her to seal the access hatches. Once they were locked in and alone, he dropped his pose of the obsequious servant and darted at her, his veils spread wide. A fine, netlike, iridescent material now covered his barbs completely.

Put on your correction tether, he ordered her.

Liana slipped her flukes into the floating straps anchored to an alloy anchor at the bottom of the tank.

Fokrej came over and secured the straps. *It has been too long, hasn't it? But you have been so good before today.*

Before he had joined Carada's staff, Fokrej had been one of the few males to serve in Ylyd's security forces. Too physically weak to serve as a soldier, he had concentrated his efforts in their intelligence division, where he had been taught his specialty: the effective and relentless interrogation of prisoners.

You humiliated the ambassador. You openly defied her and spoke when you were told to be silent. Part of Fokrej's routine was to list Liana's imagined crimes, and give her the opportunity to argue or plead. He seemed to think any protest she made was a form of groveling. *Do you wish to deny this?*

Liana merely stared at him and waited.

Nothing to say? A shame. You were so verbal earlier. He darted around her, drawing it out, waiting for her to make the slightest movement. *Thanking that butcher for your life the way you did; that showed an enormous lack of taste, dignity, and self-control.*

Liana felt him slow as he came around behind her, and then the first slap landed. A sensation like a hundred thousand barbs stung her hide before pain radiated down into her flesh. Water rushed into her gillets and out through her gill vents as she tried not to fight the pain.

The ambassador gave you specific instructions, and you ignored them. Fokrej struck her a second time, this one landing across the base of her back veil. *You have been told repeatedly that such public disobedience will not be tolerated.*

Liana panted. The neural web Fokrej used to lash her hide was a clever device. It sent bioelectrical charges through her nerve endings and into her brain, where it stimulated her pain receptors. The intensity of the charges could be adjusted to inflict anything from mild discomfort to mind-rending agony. The effects lasted several minutes, but never left any permanent physical wounds or damage, and could be administered as often as desired without fear of killing the recipient.

That was the beauty of the device, and why Fokrej enjoyed using it so much. With the web he could torture someone as much as he wished.

Liana understood the power of pain. In the right hands, it became a tool to shape and bend a mind to another's will. Because of her unique affliction, she was also able to think through pain, and isolate it, and in many ways disconnect it. She had used that enormous self-discipline before, to great effect. The last time Fokrej had beaten her, she had endured in silent indifference until she had lost consciousness.

It was different now. The male who had helped her—who had saved her life—was probably only a short distance away. Knowing Burn was so close and yet had no idea of what was happening to her made it impossible to disconnect. Liana found herself fighting the need to cry out and call to him. She didn't want to leave his world. She wanted to latch onto his back and have him sweep her away from this hideous trap that her life had become.

Remember the one. Endure for the one. Fight for the one.

Fokrej had once told her that his favorite fantasy was wrapping someone in the web and leaving them in it, so that he could see how long it would take for insanity and death to set in. He thought, if the victim were regularly fed, it might take years.

Liana lasted an hour. *Stop it, stop it. I am sorry. I will never do it again.*

You are begging? Already? Fokrej glided against her, rubbing himself against her oversensitized hide. *But you have taken twice as much punishment before and not capitulated, Lady Liana.* He lashed her again. *I do not think you are ready to surrender yet.*

Liana didn't know what to do; before this he had always stopped. Being tethered as she was prevented her from fleeing. Fokrej was aroused—obscenely so—and it made her sick to realize that perhaps he couldn't stop himself now. *I am. I will obey her.*

You will obey me, Fokrej corrected. When she repeated it, he shook his head. *I still do not hear sincerity in your voice. You must do a better job of convincing me that you mean what you say.* He came around to face her and raised one webbed fin, intending to slash her across the face with it.

Enough, Fokrej.

Carada entered the tank and moved between the valet and Liana. When Fokrej began to whine, she used a fin to sweep him aside.

Liana concentrated on her breathing, but never took her eyes from Carada.

I had hoped this would not be necessary again, the ambassador said. *It is not what I desire for you.*

Liana knew what she desired, and knew she was powerless to deny her. *The dead cannot be bled.*

Fokrej made a sulky exit from the tank. Neither Liana nor Carada acknowledged his departure.

I have promised to obey, Liana said. *What more do you want from me?*

Only this. The ambassador swam closer, so they were eye to eye. *One more rebellion will result in immediate and dire consequences for*

Ylyd. Life or death, Liana. If you wish the consequences to be life, you will do exactly as you are told, and nothing more, from this point forth.

Yes. That single word hurt more than Fokrej's beatings. Liana closed her eyes. *I will do whatever you want.*

"If I don't speak to Administrator Hansen today, I will petition the council to have her removed from her position," the Transport supervisor warned, the hundreds of thousands of spines covering his body bristling.

"I will make note of that, sir." Emily added the threat to the lengthy message she had already recorded. "Is there anything else I can help you with today?"

"Unless you can pilot a transport, no." The relay terminated.

Emily closed the channel and added the message to the pending queue. When possible she had done what she could, but most of Ana's callers wanted more specific information or actions than she could give them. As a result, there were almost three hundred requests, messages, and threats piled up and waiting for a response.

"If I ever think about applying for administrator training," she said to the potted Jorenian windfern next to her console, "I'm depending on you to talk me out of it."

Her console had been so busy that she hadn't been able to accomplish much of her own work, and a stack of transfer datawork still waited to be input. As she closed down the office channels for the day and forwarded all calls to the emergency contact center, she resigned herself to eating yet another solitary meal at her desk. She was tired of prep-unit food, so she called a café at the Trading Center and placed an order to be delivered.

The door panel chime sounded. She released the lock and smiled as her new Omorr friend bounced in. "Hello, Hkyrim. What brings you to my side of the colony?"

"I have not seen you for six days, so I made some inquiries. I also intercepted your meal order downstairs." He placed two food containers on her desk.

After Hkyrim had learned what Terrans ate, she'd never expected him to agree to dine with her again. "This is so nice of you."

"I truly do hate eating by myself. This"—he checked the label—"chef's salad sounds . . . interesting." He gave her an uncertain look. "Is it made from real chefs?"

She grinned. "Afraid not. It's synpro cut into matchstick shapes—none of which are or remotely resemble a chef—and sprinkled over chopped up botanicals. With the dirt washed off," she tagged on quickly.

"I will admit a heartfelt sense of relief to hear that." He tapped the second container. "I was rude enough to assume you wished some company and brought my meal as well. It is all dead this time."

"Hallelujah." Emily pushed aside the backlogged datawork. "Let's eat."

Sharing the meal was much easier this time. They didn't concentrate on their different cuisines, but rather each other, and chatted about work and the new acquaintances they had made. Hkyrim spoke of finding friends among the hospital staff who did not mind his occupation, but still found little time to socialize. Emily confessed that she had been too busy working to put much time into friendship starting.

"I am hopeful that our chief pathologist will request more forensic technicians to supplement the staff," the Omorr said. "We have had so many procedures to perform that he canceled all of our off-duty days until after the Peace Summit."

"I heard about all those mercenaries who were killed," Emily said. "Are you working on them?"

Hkyrim nodded. "I had a protracted disagreement with the chief pathologist regarding the cause of death. Most were exposed to a rapid and extreme increase of atmospheric pressure, which was thought to have killed them. It is true that exposure to suddenly increased pressure can create equalization problems, but it is usually a sudden decrease of pressure that is fatal."

"I know divers on my homeworld used to suffer from something called 'the bends' before rebreathers were invented," Emily said. "But how does pressure change hurt someone on a ship? I thought the atmospheric equalizers would compensate."

The Omorr briefly explained how tissues and blood cells respond to pressure, and the problems air cavities such as the lungs and ear canals present in equalizing. "Even with compensators, people sometimes black out at extreme pressure shifts. The higher the pressure, the more air becomes compressed and harder to breathe. Carbon dioxide levels in the blood rise as well, because exhalation becomes inefficient. But it is too-rapid decompression that causes undissolved blood gases to bubble and block blood vessels."

"You don't think that's what happened."

"No. From the tissue biopsies I've performed, I would theorize instead that these males experienced exposure to a toxic substance. I found evidence of well-established gastric and glandular distress, and progressive systemic failure—all of which apparently occurred over a period of several days, not hours." His gildrells bunched and released in what Emily had learned was an annoyed gesture. "My supervisor dismissed my findings and certified the deaths due to nonequalization of pressure."

Absently she caught a round, gleaming cephalopod that his gesture had sent flying and politely returned it to the rim of his container. "What else could have killed them, Hkyrim?"

He glanced down at the remaining food and then pushed it away. "Emily, I think these men were poisoned."

"Poisoned? In the middle of a battle in space?"

"It would have happened several days before they engaged the planetary patrol. There are several slow-acting substances that can be administered discreetly through air, food, or water sources. The symptoms come on gradually and resemble those of influenza or a bacterial infection: fainting spells, weakness, nausea, and anxiety. Lymph nodes swell and the gastric system responds with vomiting, cramps, and diarrhea."

She shuddered. "But if they were all sick, wouldn't they have noticed? Wouldn't they have tried to signal for help?"

"Perhaps; perhaps not. These men are not welcomed on most civilized worlds. Also, the changes in the nervous system that poison causes sometimes induce paranoia and irrational thinking. Adrenaline may have accelerated or masked symptoms, depending on the individual's level of stress." He made a frustrated gesture. "I could prove this if the toxicology scans I've performed showed a noxious substance or compound, but each test result reads normal. Whatever was used to kill them left no trace behind."

"That's not true," Emily said, surprising him. "You said there was evidence of problems with their gastric and . . . and some other system—"

"Lymphatic."

"Exactly. If pressure can't cause that kind of damage, then there's half of your proof. The other thing would be the poison. You have to find it."

"The most coveted poisons break down into ordinary components after the death of the victim. What killed these men appears to be in that category, as I can find no trace of toxins."

"You said it was given to them in their air, water, or food, right?" He nodded. "Then you just have to check their ships for trace amounts in the air, water, and food systems, because those things don't die." Emily smiled at his wide-eyed look. "We've impounded the derelicts from the battle. I just sent the approved datawork over to Transport."

Excitement gleamed in his dark eyes. "Would they allow me to board those vessels?"

"The ships are under quarantine, but medical people happen to be the only ones besides security who are permitted access. You'll need authorization, though." She turned to her terminal and punched a few keys before extracting a chip and handing it to him. "There you are. Administrative approval for one Omorr Hkyrim to perform a detailed inspection of the mercenary derelict spacecraft—and pieces thereof—for possible contaminants and pathogens."

He examined the chip with wonder. "You can personally approve such things? Just like that?"

She nodded. "I can also transfer your living quarters, send your annual compensation to your mother, and give you permission to walk without wearing garments through common areas of the colony. You may need some suns screen for that last part. The UV index is pretty high during this part of the revolution to be going around naked."

His eyes crinkled in an Omorr's smile. "I had no idea you held a position of such power."

"Administrative assistants, Hkyrim, rule the worlds. We just don't tell anyone that we do to preserve the illusion of order by elected government." Emily tidied up their containers. "Now I must get some of this work finished. You'll let me know what you find on those ships?"

"Absolutely. Tomorrow night, after my shift ends?"

Emily gave the stack of waiting datawork a rueful pat. "Oh, I'll be here."

CHAPTER 10

*C*arada had watched Liana's punishment from the beginning. She didn't take pleasure from it, or playing spectator, but her presence seemed necessary to assure the correction did not violate the acceptable limits.

Liana had nearly reached the final threshold.

Fokrej, on the other hand, was having more trouble than usual with keeping his twisted libido in check. The little sadist's perversions made him an effective, if somewhat flawed, tool, but he might soon become a liability. Carada appreciated his talent, which had proved extremely useful in compelling others to do as she wished. She also knew that the puny coward would soon become so depraved that nothing would satisfy him, not even covering himself from snout to flukes with the gore of his victims.

Carada was still puzzled over some odd, unexpected gaps in her memory. Since coming to K-2, several things had slipped her mind. She felt sure that they were largely unimportant, or she would have remembered them.

Carada sent Liana to the tank reserved for her personal use, and returned to her own with Fokrej. When they were alone, she isolated the tank from the ship's communication systems, so that signals could be sent but no one could use the audio to listen in on their conversation.

At once the interrogator began to whine. *Why did you stop me? I had her.* He was still tumescent—using the web was love play for him—and extremely agitated. *A few more lashes and she would have done anything for me.*

There is only so much abuse Liana can take, Carada said. *You were *told to correct her, not brutalize her.* At least, she hoped he had been. It was one of the things she couldn't recall.

She can take more than that.

No, Fokrej. You go too far.

He tore the neural web from his fins. *If you are worried about the physician's examination, it leaves no trace, I promise you.*

Carada wasn't worried. She knew the device and, physically, the web did no harm. Mentally it turned even the most ruthless and disciplined mind into a quivering, acquiescent mass. *She had enough.*

But you promised. Fokrej sidled up against her, pricking her thick hide with his little, ineffectual barbs. *I don't want to wait anymore. I want her now.*

She couldn't remember the promise, but she understood his impatience. For some reason she felt as if she suffered from the same, as if long years of deprivation weighed on her. Yet she was so close to her objective, she could almost see the end as it might happen.

As it must happen.

Liana knew that she could destroy everything with a few words. Until it was done, Carada was taking no chances.

She rolled over onto her back, cradling the smaller male on the wide plain of her belly. *I still have need of her. When I am through with her, you may do as you wish. Until then, I expect you to control yourself.*

I want to hurt her again. Soon. Fokrej rubbed himself against her, trying to penetrate her. Unfortunately his erection had wilted, and his penis had retreated back into his genital sheath. *I want you to watch me do it. I want you to smell her pain on my hide.*

Carada recalled that she had allowed—even encouraged—Fokrej to think that observing his pathetic torture sessions also provided some sexual stimulation for her. She felt no desire for him, and suspected that it had been years since she had toward any member of the opposite gender. The physical release sex provided didn't seem important anymore. The need to continually coddle her small sadist, however, was beginning to wear thin. The thought of teaching him what real pain was tempted her for a moment.

A chime from the panel dragged her from her own dark thoughts. *What is it?*

Ambassador Carada, the ship's captain signaled. *We have established orbit above the planet. There is a passenger shuttle requesting permission to dock, and they are using your private approval code.*

Finally.

She pushed Fokrej off and flipped over to answer. *Give them permission to dock, and have the pilot brought to my quarters at once.*

"Mom?"

Dair walked through Teresa's dwelling, turning on lights as she went. Onkar and Burn followed. All of the outer access panels had been secured and locked down, indicating her stepmother was in residence. Yet Teresa didn't respond to the chime or their request to enter.

"This is a violation of privacy," Burn said as he looked into one of the lavatories.

"I know." Dair didn't like using her override code, but her stepmother wouldn't answer the door panel. "Mom?"

"Someone is in there." Onkar pointed to the sitting room.

Dair heard a muffled, crackling sound coming from the room as they approached the open door panel. None of the lights in the room were on, either, but someone inside was standing on a lift platform and removing something from the wall panel. "That you, Mom?"

"Go away." More crackling sounds, and some light, rattling thuds.

It was Teresa's voice, but she sounded strange, and she had never sent Dair away from her in Dair's entire life.

"I'll go if you let me turn the lights on," Dair said, peering in, "and you tell me you're okay."

"Lights."

The emitters flared on, revealing Teresa at the wall. She had been ripping off the photoscans she had pinned there, balling them up and tossing them on the floor. The light traced wet tracks from her cheeks up to her eyelids, which were so swollen and red they had become thin slits.

"I'm okay," Teresa said. "Now get out."

Dair looked at Onkar and Burn, who looked as shocked and puzzled as she was. "Go on ahead without me. I need a few minutes alone with her."

The two males left, and Dair closed the door panel before adjusting the lights to a softer, dimmer level. She bent to pick up one of the crumpled scans on the floor. It was an image of Teresa with her father; one of Teresa's favorites. "Mom, what are you doing? Are you ill?"

"I'm terrific." Teresa tore a large portrait of herself with members of the coastal pod in half and let the pieces flutter away. "I'm not your mother, though."

"What are you talking about?" Dair moved forward, and then went still as Teresa flung out a hand and made the fin gesture for stay-away. "Of course you're still my mother."

"Sorry, but not anymore." She climbed down from the lift and moved it over to another section of the wall panel. "Your father in his infinite wisdom and affection has terminated our relationship."

"What? *Why?*"

"I decided to do something about the mogshrikes attacking the pods," Teresa told her in a blithe, conversational way. "Your father objected. We argued. He gave me an ultimatum, and I made the only logical choice." She bunched the ends of her fingers together and then thrust them apart and out. "Poof! End of relationship."

"You argued over mogshrikes?" Dair couldn't follow what she was trying to tell her.

"Try to keep up here, honey." Her stepmother tore another photoscan down. "Your father and I argued over my plan to catch a mogshrike alive so that we can discover why it's coming inland and attacking in warm waters."

Dair felt a deep, wrenching sense of revulsion. "You can't catch a live mogshrike."

"I can now." Teresa gave her a bright smile. "See, your father and I are no longer a couple. That means I'm no longer subject to follow 'Zangian customs. Not that I ever was before, you understand, but I tried to toe the line for his sake. Legally I'm not even obligated to ask the Elders for permission to catch a 'shrike. So in actuality, your father did me a big favor, tossing me out of his life. I can do whatever I want now."

And it had made Teresa cry so much that now her eyes could barely stay open.

"You can't catch a mogshrike in the outer currents. They're too strong and fast out there." Dair suddenly understood. "Mom, no. Not here. You can't bring one here. We have twenty-nine pups in the pod this season. It would go after them first."

"Just like your father." Teresa shook her head. "For your information, I wouldn't ever put the little ones, or the pod, in any danger. We're going to lure it in north of your waters, in an uninhabited area."

"Every coastal area is inhabited. Perhaps not every hour of every day, but we all make use of the waters along the entire coast." Dair felt exasperated. "It doesn't matter where you bring it in. 'Shrikes are too large and too dangerous to capture. Don't be an idiot, Mom."

"Thank you so much." Teresa gave her an ugly look. "Would you like to bite me now? Your father almost did."

Dair smothered a groan. "I'm sure my father was only angry over your plans, Teresa. He loves you very much. He doesn't want the pod or you to get hurt."

"I don't know about that, Jadaira. When you love someone, you generally don't break off a ten-year relationship and swim away without looking back." Teresa looked blindly at the photoscan in her hands. "This is a nice one of him when we were out charting the currents around the southern bend. You weren't even born yet, so you don't remember." Slowly she twisted it into a ball and stared down at it. "You know, I fell in love with your father on that trip." With a sudden, violent motion she threw the crumpled scan across the room.

"That's enough." Dair went over and lifted Teresa from the platform, setting her down and resting her modified fins on her shoulders. "You can't destroy ten years of happiness by tearing up a bunch of pictures."

"No, but it makes me feel a hell of a lot better." She looked around them as if seeing the mess she had made of her mementos for the first time, and then it was her face that crumpled. "I'm getting hysterical again, I guess. Only your father could reduce me to this." She pressed her fists to her eyes. "*Damn* him."

The fluttering sensation in Dair's chest increased, and her grip changed as she held on to Teresa. "You'll have to curse him later. Something is wrong with me."

The last thing she heard was Teresa crying out as she fell forward and collapsed in her arms.

New attendants and guards had been summoned from Ylyd to replace those killed by the mercenaries, and Liana was allocated a middle-aged female named Graleba. The older Ylydii, a low-ranked but cheerful sort, had served as a companion to a grand matriarch and knew proper protocol. She also liked to gossip a great deal, which Liana encouraged whenever they were alone.

I have some trebelet *today, my lady,* Graleba said as she released Liana's meal into the tank. *Very lively and sweet, fresh from the homeworld.*

Liana had little interest in eating, but fresh food meant that a supply ship had docked with them. *Did anything else arrive?*

Only a delegate's aide from another ship, and those mono-colored brutes. Graleba snapped the edges of her veils at the trebelet, inciting them to dart over to Liana. *You really should catch something, my lady. You look thin and sickly.*

Liana caught one of the smaller iridescent teleosts in her petite veils and made a show of killing and eating it. If she displayed too much curiosity, Graleba might mention it to Fokrej, who was attending Carada but would use any excuse to serve as Liana's valet again. Misdirection, that would serve. *What manner of brutes?*

Males, if you can believe it. So scarred up they were that you'd think they were clever food. They came on a separate transport from the planet. Graleba gestured toward K-2.

Did they bring the delegate's aide with them?

No, he came on his own shuttle. Do you know their females allow them to carry weapons? She rolled her eyes. *As if they'd know which end to point at an enemy.*

They know. Liana wished she could use the ship's database to learn exactly who had boarded, and why, but Carada had changed all the codes. *One of the 'Zangian males saved us when the ship was captured.*

That one was the leader of the group, Graleba told her. *He had a funny name. Now, what was it? Born. Borg.*

Byorn.

That's it. Graleba finned gratitude. *Miglan pointed him out to me and told me who he was. He also said the brute was not to be permitted to speak to you.*

Naturally. Carada would not let her speak to any offworlder, especially not a League pilot and gunner who might tempt her to do something reckless.

Where are these males now?

They've stationed them all over the ship. They're guarding all the members of the delegation. The older female nudged her with a gentle fin. *Come now, my lady, you must feed or your mother will have me beaten.*

Liana thought of the web and seized her. *Did she say that to you? Fokrej, has he touched you? Threatened to hurt you?*

He—oh, no, my lady. Graleba looked horrified. *Forgive my ridiculous tongue—it was only an expression. Your lady mother would never do such a thing, much as I deserve it for upsetting you.* Her eyes went soft and sad. *You poor thing, you've likely been on spines and barbs since those criminals took the ship, and here I am making you more nervous. I'll ask to have someone else assigned to look after you.*

Someone else who wouldn't gossip like Graleba.

Liana forced herself to relax and resume her authoritative role. *You will do no such thing. I am very pleased with your service and attention to detail. I am only weary of being cooped up in here.*

Your lady mother said it was safer for you and her to remain in seclusion until the summit begins, Graleba said. Her gaze went to the access hatch and then back to Liana's drawn face. *Of course, when I want to take a little swim, I don't bother with the main corridors.*

You don't.

Not when I can swim in complete privacy and seclusion through the recycling conduits. Graleba pointed to the small hatch overhead that was the source of the tank's water. *Now that the ship's atmosphere has been replaced twice, they're very clean. No one uses them or monitors them. If I wanted to, I think I could swim through them around both wheels of the ship.*

How common and revolting. Liana tried to look and sound bored, but she gave the attendant a furtive wink.

Graleba hummed a laugh. *Yes, well, you royals are used to your space and your luxuries. And why shouldn't you be? Now come, my lady, and eat something. In a few days these trebelet will be too old and stringy to eat without giving you indigestion.*

Liana shut down her lighting after the attendant left her and waited in silence for a long time. She was depending on anyone monitoring her tank to assume from the silence that she was asleep and would not wake for several hours.

It was harder than she expected to move very slowly toward the access hatch and open it without making any noise. Her entire body wanted to shake. *If I'm discovered, she will give me to Fokrej—or worse.*

She also knew that the delegate's aide who had arrived was likely not Skartesh, the people with whom Carada most wanted to form an alliance, because he came on a separate ship. The Skartesh had no ships, and were constrained to use 'Zangian transports. If Liana didn't discover what of the plan had been altered, she might as well give herself to Fokrej for his sickening pleasures, for she would be unable to change or stop anything.

The recycling conduits were round pipes three times as wide as Liana's body. Their mechanism removed solid waste and debris, and replenished fresh liquid atmosphere to all the Ylydii-occupied tanks within the vessel. Usually the sides of the conduits were perpetually scaled with sediment contaminants from the waste materials they channeled to the ship's incinerators, but Liana saw Graleba's claim was correct—the pipes were now very clean.

She slid through the narrow hatch, dropped into the rushing current within the conduit, and let it carry her away from the tank. It was strong, but not enough to sweep her into the fiery disposal equipment in the center of the ship.

Each tank had its own supply and return to the conduit, and it was a simple matter to stop and look through each hatch until she found Carada's private tank. Staying there with the current rushing around her would be difficult, and Liana decided to wedge herself in the short space between the hatch and the conduit pipe, where the rush of the water was not as loud.

Almost immediately she could hear Carada speaking to someone. "—paying a personal visit."

"Ambassador Urloy-ka was not amused," a harsher, humanoid voice replied. "Considering what was said to him, he did not wish to send me as his representative."

Liana shifted so she could see through the grid of the hatch. The ambassador was hovering in her water and speaking through an audio panel to a humanoid male standing in one of the air locks. He was dressed in Ninrana robes and had two heavily armed guards standing on either side of him.

Liana had never seen him before. *Why did she summon him?* There was no advantage to an alliance with the Ninrana. Her mother had told her a hundred times that their world had nothing to offer but some metals that, given the degraded environment, would be too much trouble for the Ylydii to mine.

"Urloy-ka is too sensitive," Carada said. "Nevertheless, I will make do with you. I have a proposition for you that may benefit both our peoples."

"Such matters are to be discussed at the Peace Summit, with Ambassador Urloy-ka," the aide reminded her. "Only he can negotiate with you."

"You have auditory canals. You may listen and relate what I offer to him." The ambassador bared her teeth. "I would transmit this proposal, but it is a private one and not to be openly discussed with the other members of the summit. You will tell Urloy-ka this. And send your escort out, too."

The Ninrana looked impatiently at his guards, and then nodded once. The two other males left the air lock.

"What do you propose?" Urloy-ka's aide demanded.

Carada moved to hover vertically in the water, casting her wide, long shadow over the Ninrana. "Ylyd will provide all the water and terraforming equipment Ninra needs. In return, you will disband your armies and your government, and henceforth live under Ylydii rule."

The Ninrana made a strangled sound.

"For our investment, it is a fair return," Carada added.

"Yes, you are only asking us to surrender our world, our leadership, and probably our freedom. I will relate this to Urloy-ka. I advise you pray he does not attack your vessel." The aide turned to leave.

"So you think you are outraged, little male?" Carada's hum of mirth rang out. "Tell me, do you Ninrana have something else to offer the Ylydii in return? Lifeless sand and endless heat have no value. Nor do the bones of all the poor people you have eaten."

"They were sacrifices, delivered into our hands by the gods." The aide gave her an angry look. "We offer minerals that can be mined. The Ninrana are willing to consider temporary mining operations to be carried out while we are rejuvenating our planet."

"It will only take ten years to terraform Ninra, brainless one. Ten years of mining is not enough to repay the cost to do so." Carada swam closer. "You would do well to remind your ambassador that in twenty revolutions your world will be a cold, dead, red rock. We are your only hope to keep it alive."

"I will relay your offer." The angry aide left.

"I can't find anything wrong with her or the pup," William told Teresa. "Both of them show steady vitals and their organs and blood scan clean."

It had been a week since Dair had fainted in Teresa's arms. She had rushed her stepdaughter to the FreeClinic, but by the time they had arrived in Trauma, Dair had regained consciousness and seemed perfectly normal. The pup developing in her womb also showed no signs of trouble. As they had every day since.

Teresa looked at Dair, who was swimming idly around the immersion tank. "You ran the cardiac scans again?"

"Five times. Teresa, her heart is strong and more than meets the demands the baby places on it. She's not sick, or diseased, or injured." William handed her Dair's chart. "Unless you can think up a test I haven't performed, or a valid reason to keep her under observation, I have to discharge her."

"If she dies, I'll have nothing," Teresa muttered.

"If she were going to die, she'd have done it when she fried herself saving the Skartesh." He patted her shoulder. "I've got to make rounds in post-op. Have the nurse signal me if you need me."

Teresa went to the tank and told Dair the good news. "I don't want you discharged if you're still not feeling right."

"I feel good." Dair climbed out of the tank and cleared the water from her gills. "I'm getting fat, though." She spread her hands on the growing bulge of her abdomen, and then glanced over Teresa's shoulder and grinned. "Onkar."

Dair's mate came to embrace her in his arms. They began speaking in clik so rapid that Teresa couldn't follow the conversation.

Why should I? She doesn't need me any more than Dairatha does. Like he said, it's none of my business.

Teresa withdrew and left the aquatic treatment center alone. Work had been piling up for the past seven days at the URD as well as her home lab; T'Kaf had sent her several signals. She'd sent regular reports on Dair to the pod via Burn or Onkar, but she couldn't bring herself to go back underwater.

"I know you're in there somewhere, Dr. Selmar."

Teresa dragged herself out of her thoughts to see Noel Argate standing in front of her and waving a hand in front of her nose. "Noel. What a surprise."

"Everything all right with Jadaira?"

She nodded. "She's with her mate. Mayer is going to spring her; he can't find anything wrong."

"Good, then you'll be free to help me with the last of the prep work at the inlet." Noel indicated a military glidecar waiting at the curb. "I'll drop you over at your place so you can pack a few things."

Teresa frowned. "What prep work at what inlet?"

"I'm sorry. I thought your lab chief would pass along what we were doing. We're almost ready to go after a 'shrike."

She stared at him. "Almost ready. Noel, we only discussed a few possible methods of capturing a mogshrike. That was where we were last week, when Dair fell ill."

"I consulted with your people during your absence, and we agreed on what would be the best method." He made a face. "I'm sorry, Terri, but I'm not going to be here much longer, and I couldn't see waiting."

"No, of course not."

"I'm not here on vacation. My superiors want regular progress reports. There have also been a bunch of new 'shrike sightings." Noel gave her a searching look. "Listen, once the military gears start turning it's not easy to go back to a standstill. It doesn't matter. If you want me to call a halt to it, I will. This is still your turf, Terri. You have the last word."

She rubbed her eyelids with her fingertips. "How many new sightings?"

"About fifty. Twenty or so rogues, the rest were multiples of twos and threes. Mostly young 'shrikes." His mouth flattened. "They come to scout first, don't they?"

She nodded. "If there's a reliable food source, then they come back to hunt."

Jadaira was going back into the water today, and nothing would keep her out of it. Teresa couldn't stand the thought of her child and her grandchild dying in the teeth of one of those monsters.

"What do you want me to do, Terri? I can signal my people and call them off the site now, if you like."

"No. Let's go to my place and you can bring me up to speed."

Noel had accomplished an amazing amount of work over the last week. Using one of her station monitors, he pulled up a satellite shot of the inlet and the work going on there.

"The reef extension walls are in place under the surface; they'll lie flat under a layer of silt until the 'shrike is well inside our surround. Reinforced observation posts have been staggered around the perimeter every hundred yards, and those will be manned by my troops. I have a hover pod for your scientists so they can observe without any risk to themselves."

"Very efficient." And much better than she could have done with her people and limited resources. "Once we have it inside, the extensions are raised and charged?"

"With contact charges only," Noel said. "The trapped 'shrike will have to swim right into the extensions to trigger a feed burst from our onshore power plant. I didn't want to take the chance of running that much current continuously; it would kill everything in the vicinity."

Teresa had to admit he was doing everything as she had asked—with respect for safety and life—but she still wasn't convinced his idea would work.

"Right. So we get the 'shrike in, and trap it, and keep it in." She gestured toward the inlet image. "How do we get it out of the water and transport it seventy kim over land and dump it in the study tank at Burantee?"

"That's the beauty of being a part of the Allied League of Worlds," Noel said, and put a new image up on the screen. "We have a lot of worlds to contact and consult with on our problems."

The image at first didn't make sense. It hovered over remote mountainous terrain the way a transport would, but the design was unlike anything Teresa had ever seen.

"We turned our transport problem over to our intersystem jaunt experts, and they suggested we use this baby."

"It looks like a big, floating dandelion."

"That's not too far off the mark, actually. It's a P'Kotman life flyer, constructed from one of their giant wind plants. The League tells me the natives use it to retrieve and transport the injured from remote areas of P'Kotma."

Teresa studied the dimensions. "You're telling me that that thing is made out of organic botanical materials?"

Noel nodded. "Part of it is fossilized, but the lower half is living tissue. It actually envelops the passenger and can carry up to forty metric tons of weight."

"A ship that eats people."

"It would if you left the people in it long enough, but the short flight time doesn't give it the opportunity to start the digestive process. Instead, it holds the enveloped victim suspended inside a harmless gel, along with a small bubble of oxygen so it won't smother. The P'Kotmans are delivering one that has been trained to hold liquid atmosphere so our 'shrike can keep breathing."

"How do you get the victim back out of it?"

"An even exchange." Noel put up another image of the bizarre vessel hovering over a pen of benign-looking herd animals. "The ship will release the victim for something fatter and weaker and stupider, like these *casein-orwfs*."

The alien ship was starting to make her sick. "I don't want to see a vid of it, okay?"

"Sure. I have a couple of computer models of how we're going to bait the 'shrike. If you'd like, we can run them on the tri-dim down at the URD this afternoon—"

"*No.*" She knew if she saw Dairatha that she would call the entire operation to a halt and plead for him to take her back. The work was more important, and she wouldn't give her ex-mate the satisfaction of seeing the wreck he had made of her.

"Terri?"

"Not at the URD," she said in a more normal tone. "We'll work out of Burantee Point until we have your onshore installation up and running."

"I should also tell you that as soon as we began work at the inlet, the 'Zangian Elders filed a protest with the Colonial Council," Noel admitted. "They're fighting to block the capture."

Dairatha had been busy. "The Elders can do whatever they like. I have it on good authority that the council is tied up with the Peace

Summit and they won't get back to regular business for several days."
She turned to him. "I want a 'shrike in captivity before their grievance
goes before the council, and I want to keep them from killing it if they
are granted the block. How do we swing that?"

"Good question." Noel considered it for a few moments. "We can
start hunting in two days. If the Elders sway the council, my people
will transport the 'shrike we catch off-planet."

"That violates most of the stuff written in the colony charter."

He shrugged. "This region is still under full military jurisdiction.
Your council can file a grievance with quadrant. I've heard that, with
the war demanding so much time and attention, civilian grievances are
pretty backlogged. Should only take, oh, two or three years for theirs
to be reviewed."

Teresa sat back in her chair. "We're really going to do it, then.
We're going to catch this nightmare."

"No, Terri." Noel took her hands in his. "We're going to put an
end to it." He leaned forward and brushed his mouth over hers.

She hadn't been touched by a Terran male since she had left the
homeworld, Teresa thought. She hadn't been kissed at all since Noel
had left her. 'Zangian males used their mouths for feeding or biting.
Dairatha had marked her more than once in passion, but he couldn't do
this.

She had missed this. Missed Noel.

That foreign thought made her jerk back. What was she doing?
This man was the biggest reason she had left Terra. Him and his lies.
"Don't ever do that again."

"I'm sorry. I can't agree to that. But I'll wait for an invitation next
time." He tucked a piece of her hair behind her ear. "You can't stop me
from thinking about you. We had some wonderful times together,
Ter."

"You think you can jump back into my bed now that it's empty?"

"It's always been empty, hasn't it?" His expression turned quizzical.
"Your 'Zangian lover could never sleep with you."

"He was my mate, and you'd better just shut up right now." She got to her feet. "I have some signals to send. I'll meet you up at the point in a few hours."

Noel left without making a fuss, and Teresa studied the images of the inlet surround and the P'Kotman carrier vessel for a long time. She could see a thousand ways in which things could go wrong. The 'shrikes were excellent breachers; something would have to be done to keep them from jumping over the tops of the reef extensions. Then there was subduing the monster—they still didn't know if a standard neuroparalyzer would have any effect on it—and assuring the study tank was durable enough to contain it.

She lifted a hand and touched her mouth, which still tingled from Noel's kiss, and then glanced at one of the few photoscans she hadn't torn off the wall. It was of Kyara, Dair's biological mother, who had died giving birth to her. Kyara had been her best friend.

So had Dairatha, even if he never had slept in a bed with her.

Teresa tapped her console and signaled the FreeClinic. "Put me through to Dr. Mayer, please."

Burn terminated the relay from the surface and swam out of the communications room to meet with three members of the 'Zangian detachment preparing to go on duty. "Dair is out of the hospital. They say she and the pup are fine."

"Of course they are." Loknoth tugged at the collar fastened under his gillets. "Dair doesn't have to swim in a full dress uniform through ship corridors all day and night."

Burn understood their discomfort, but the delegates all wore clothes, and the colonial administrator wanted the 'Zangians to blend in. "You can strip as soon as you're off duty."

"How much longer will we have to be here, Sublieutenant?" Gharain, one of the youngest males, asked. "I think I'm starting to chafe in unmentionable regions."

"Until they make peace or kill each other," Curonal guessed. "I'd wager that big female could easily dust both of those mouth-breathers."

"I don't know," Loknoth said. "They move fast when they want to, I know they haven't surrendered all their weapons, and she can't breathe in their air locks."

"They'll make peace and then we'll go home." Burn felt like knocking his detachment's heads together. No wonder being in command made one surly—everyone did nothing but complain—and he intended to apologize to Dair in person the minute he saw her. He turned to Loknoth. "What do you mean, they haven't surrendered all their weapons? I personally disarmed every Ninrana before they boarded." What a happy task that had been, too—Burn had thought at one point the fierce desert-dwellers might attack him en masse.

"Did you search that sea of fabric they wear?" the other male asked, referring to the Ninrana's voluminous robes.

"You know I didn't." Burn would have, but the 'Zangians weren't permitted to touch any of the delegates. "But I scanned them thoroughly."

"They're carrying them," Loknoth insisted. "I've seen them tuck their hands under the fabric a number of times when they're angry or startled. Not to take whatever they have under there out, but to be ready to. You know, the same way we'd bare teeth at big shadows in the current."

"The only things that don't show up on scanners are organics or body parts," Curonal put in. "I doubt they're going to beat someone to death with a spare arm or a weed."

Burn remembered the platform upon which the Ninrana had sacrificed the ship crash survivors they found on their world. It had been made of bone. So had parts of their dwellings.

Bone was one of the oldest tool-making materials among landdwellers, Burn recalled from his Academy training. Among primitive species it was still used to make darts, clubs, even blades.

"Lok, signal the council and see if you can have the no-search order reversed." To Curonal and Gharain he said, "You two patrol the stern corridors. Keep alert and signal me at the first sign of trouble."

Burn went directly to the conference area being used by the summit delegates. The main entrance was guarded by two 'Zangians, whom he stopped and briefed before moving on to the adjoining observation chamber, where the delegates' aides and members of their entourages waited during the talks.

Everything that was being discussed could be heard over audio panels, and several monitors had been posted that showed the delegates in the summit room. The room had been divided in half, with an air lock for the land-dwelling Skartesh and Ninrana, and a water tank for the 'Zangians and Ylydii.

Burn listened to the voice of the intermediary drone, which was still reading off the various clauses and demands filed by each of the delegates. He couldn't understand why they had to use such frilly speech when the issues were so simple to understand. The Ninrana wanted water, because their planet was dying. The Ylydii wanted order and some control over what happened within their system. The Skartesh wanted their own colony away from K-2 because they couldn't adapt to the climate. The 'Zangians simply wanted the fighting to stop and everyone to live together in peace. In his mind, these were all reasonable requests.

It was what they wanted for each other that created the conflicts. The Ylydii wanted harsh trade restrictions placed on the Ninrana, who weren't too particular about how or from whom they got the water they so desperately needed. The Ninrana in turn thought that one of the aquatic species should provide them with water without any conditions attached. The Skartesh thought the 'Zangians should be happy to deed one of K-2's moons over to them, since the aquatics could never live on them. The 'Zangians thought the Skartesh's cult should be outlawed and the species strictly supervised until it was fully deprogrammed.

Ana Hansen spotted him and left a group of Skartesh to come over to the panel used to communicate between the air and water locks. "Sublieutenant, is something wrong?"

Administrator, some of the Ninrana delegates may be armed, he typed on the panel pad so that she saw the words appear on the vid screen only. Out loud he said, *How are the talks progressing?*

Ana's mouth tightened before she played along with his ruse. "As well as can be expected, considering the trouble we've had with the translation equipment." She used the pad to type, *Smuggled weapons past the scanners?*

Weapons made of bone wouldn't register, he typed back. Some of the delegates were looking at them, so he discontinued using the keypad and wiped the screen. *Shall I advise security on-planet about the problem?*

"I don't think that will be necessary, Sublieutenant." As Ana said that, she moved her head in a barely perceptible nod. "Chief Norash should only be consulted when there is something that might compromise safety for the delegates and their parties."

Understood, Administrator.

"How much longer must we listen to this machine?" Ambassador Urloy-ka demanded from the air lock side of the summit room. "Every day we spend talking, my people and planet die a little more."

"They will survive the week, Ninrana," Bataran said. "My people had suffered for months, and will keep suffering every minute we stay on the surface of K-2."

The Ninrana made a strange, hissing sound. "You would compare your pelts shedding to my species' coming extinction? We need water or we will die. Do not think that because we agreed to these talks that we will be denied. We will have water, or we will use whatever means are necessary to take it." He plunged his hand into his robe.

Burn exchanged a quick look with Ana and went to one of the door panels leading directly into the chamber.

It is vital that we each detail our concerns, so there can be no misunderstanding between our species, Nathaka mu Hlana said. *There is a priority of need to be established, but no planet or people can be regarded as more important than another. We are all equals here.*

Carada gave the other aquatic a pitying look. *You three are males. Here or on Ylyd, you can never be equal to me.*

Ana Hansen slipped into the room and took position in the center of the air lock. "Delegates, forgive my intrusion, but I would remind you of your agreement to set aside personal animosity as well as status for the duration of this summit. What you decide here will determine the future of this system, and the millions of beings who inhabit it.

Antagonism and threats will never serve them the way tolerance and cooperation can."

The Terran woman seemed to have a calming effect on the Ninrana, who fixed his gaze on her lovely face and golden hair. "You are good to remind us of this, *yahleha.*"

Burn kept close watch on the monitor, and input the code that would allow him immediate access to the summit chamber. On screen the administrator looked very pale and was staring back at Urloy-ka as if he'd just threatened her life. Only when the Ninrana delegate removed his empty hand from his robe did Burn disengage the emergency override.

"Again, forgive the intrusion." Ana inclined her head toward Urloy-ka and then to each of the delegates before silently moving back out to the observation chamber.

Burn moved to Ana's side. "You look ill."

"I'm a little nauseated. Too much coffee, not enough sleep." She gave him a wan smile. "Sublieutenant, please ask your people to keep the Ninrana delegation under close watch until I can sort out what to do about the weapons they've smuggled on board."

"You think they are carrying them, then?"

"No." She glanced at Urloy-ka. "I know they are."

CHAPTER 11

"*L*et me talk to my hardware experts," Norash told Ana Hansen. "If there's a security scanner that can pick up bone shapes, we'll deliver one to you in orbit."

"Bone shapes . . . of course." Ana felt like slapping herself in the head. "I'll ask Dr. Mayer to lend us a handheld medical bone scanner. We can use that to detect the weapons the Ninrana are carrying."

"Don't approach them about this until I can send up more security teams to assist with the searches," Norash warned. "I don't want you trying to disarm these people by yourself."

"Acknowledged. I'll send update reports as things progress. Hansen out." Ana ended the relay and sent a new signal to the colony FreeClinic.

Luckily the chief of medical services was in his office for once. "William Mayer."

She took a moment to enjoy his image. "Can I borrow a bone scanner, and a very large vial of painkillers?"

He peered at the screen. "Do you have a broken arm, or a headache?"

"No broken bones. I *had* a headache. Now I believe it's blossoming into the dimensions of a supermigraine." Ana explained the need for the bone scanner, adding, "I'd like to keep one up here on the ship if you can spare it for a week. I may be able to disarm them during a search, but they may have hidden other weapons around the ship."

"We had some extra units come in for the Bio Rescue ships," he said. "You can use one of those for as long as you like. Now, what about this migraine?"

"Not as easily curable, but it's my own fault." She slid a hand under her hair and rubbed the back of her neck. "I know better than to stand in a room filled with angry and imaginative beings."

"Imaginative?"

"Empaths sometimes pick up more than impressions, particularly when emotions are running high. Take the Ylydii ambassador, for example—when Carada *wasn't* thinking about releasing the air lock into space, she was wondering how much effort it would take to force Nathaka to have sex with her."

"A lot," Liam said. " 'Zangian males are very strong, and have more teeth than the Ylydii."

"I know. While Carada was thinking all that, Nathaka was fantasizing on where he could bite Carada to keep her away from him. Evidently he picked up on her attraction."

His lips quirked. "So much for it being mutual."

"I prefer all that to what I picked up from the other two. Bataran was muttering passages from the Scroll of the Promise, so I tapped his mind and found out why he was doing it. To keep himself from ripping out Urloy-ka's throat."

"No love lost there."

"No love, period. Meanwhile, Urloy-ka was . . ." She trailed off as she remembered how dark and disturbing the Ninrana's thoughts had been, particularly when he had focused on her. Sex and death excited him equally, and both featured prominently in his private fantasies.

When he had thanked Ana, he hadn't been thinking of gratitude. He had been studying her hair—there were no blondes on Ninra—and wondering how it would feel in his hands. He also imagined it stained with her blood. His fantasy had been so lucid that Ana had nearly thrown up on him.

"Counting the ways in which he could gut Bataran?" Liam guessed.

"Yes," she lied. "The delegates were all tired and hungry, too, which didn't help." She propped her throbbing forehead against her hand.

"You need some physiotherapy." He looked away from the screen and nodded to someone who handed him a chart. "Excuse me for a moment."

Ana watched his frown form as he skimmed the data. "I'd better let you get back to work. If you could send up the bone scanner today—"

"I will, but don't close the channel yet." Liam copied the chart's data chip. "I'm sending this to you for your review. The short version is, one of the newly transferred forensic technicians down in Pathology—I can't think of his name, but he's Omorr—performed an inspection of the quarantined mercenary ships. He found traces of a slow-acting neurotoxin in samples taken from the water and food stores." He looked up at her. "You did right sending him in, but what made you suspicious? Was it something with the original autopsy findings?"

"Liam, I didn't send anyone to inspect those ships." Ana thought of her new assistant, who according to rumor had been seeing an Omorr during her off-duty hours. *Emily, what are you up to now?* "I think I know who did. In any case, what does this boil down to? Are you saying that the mercenaries didn't die from pressure sickness during the battle?"

"No. They were poisoned. Long before they attacked the Ylydii." He pulled up a file on his data terminal. "The only recorded cases involving poisoning by this particular neurotoxin involve detained drug couriers. Their suppliers often poison them before they transport shipments. If they deliver, the counteragent is given to them and they live. If they're arrested and detained, they die before they can give any information to the authorities."

She tried to fit what he was telling her into the scenario with the mercenaries. "We know someone hired these men to attack the Ylydii. Maybe the poison was administered for the same reasons: to control them, or kill them if they were captured."

"There aren't too many sources for this particular neurotoxin, and what's available is extremely expensive. Norash may be able to track down who used it by following the credit trail." Liam copied the chart. "I'm sending you a file copy of the report. I'd distribute it among the delegates and see if they have any enemies who might resort to such tactics."

"I don't know if that's such a wise idea. All four of the delegates are extremely agitated and unhappy; what little progress we're making here doesn't suit any of them. They might use this as an excuse to begin hurling blame or suspicions at each other."

"That will have to be your call. I'm going to have Burn and his men discreetly check your prep units and ship's stores, and assure that no one has tampered with those." Liam reached out and touched his screen. "I miss you, Ana."

She reached out and matched his fingertips with her own. "I'm sorry this is taking so long. When it's over we'll go somewhere quiet and beautiful and not inhabited by anything with a brain stem."

His expression became stern. "Rushing off to snatch a couple of days by ourselves, knowing the entire time we're gone our respective workplaces will descend into utter chaos? Then to return and field hundreds of complaints while we kill ourselves putting it all back in order? A vacation's just not worth it, Ana."

Disappointment made her lift her hands. "Well, then, I'm open for suggestions. You name it, I'll try it."

"We'll have to have the ceremony first, so we can make it public and official. That way there is a slim chance—very slim—that everyone will be on their best behavior. If not, when we return from the honeymoon, we'll remind them that we're newlyweds and they'll feel too sentimental to complain much."

"Honeymoon . . . newlyweds . . ." She was on the verge of stuttering. "Liam, are you asking me to—"

"Marry me. Say yes, Ana."

Her Grace, Lady Carada, the ambassador of Ylyd will see you now, Miglan said to Burn. Although he was smaller than most of the youngest pups in Burn's pod, the diminutive Ylydii male managed to look down his snout at him.

Do your kind bite each other when you fight over a female? Burn asked him idly.

Males do not have to fight over females on Ylyd, Miglan informed him smugly. They *fight over us.*

Burn inspected him from gillets to flukes. *Oh, I get it. They fight, and the loser has to breed with you.* While Miglan sputtered, he swam past and entered the ambassador's private chamber.

Carada was in the process of being groomed by another little male, a process which required him to delicately pick off dirt and pieces of loose hide with his teeth. Seeing another male reduced to the level of a cleaner fish had shocked Burn at first, but he had been called to the ambassador's chamber several times now, and she liked being groomed. Now he turned his gaze to a spot on the tank wall and waited in silence.

So, the psychopath can behave like a well-mannered being on occasion. I am astonished and pleased. Carada dismissed her hide-cleaner and swam a circle around Burn. *You are learning, 'Zangian. Perhaps someday soon I will allow you to groom me.*

Not as long as I breathe, Burn muttered.

What did you say? The ambassador came around and assumed her favorite position when he reported, which was hovering an inch from his face.

He schooled his expression to blankness. *I said, I am glad you are pleased, Lady Ambassador.*

Are you? She treated him to a long, skeptical look before continuing. *There were problems reported to me today by various members of my staff. You will attend to these immediately and assure that they do not happen again.*

Carada began to recite a list of complaints ranging from 'Zangian guards who had interrupted an Ylydii female while she was speaking to a demand by the male members of her entourage that the aquatic soldiers not feed in the same area with them.

Burn made one half-hearted attempt to reason with her. *We do have to feed, Lady Ambassador.*

Our males are quite intimidated by your men, Carada said. *They cannot compete with them for the food released. You will refrain from feeding until they are through.*

In other words, starve. The little Ylydii males were greedy, and could clear out a feeding area within a few minutes. He'd have to talk to Ana about getting more supplies from the surface, and maybe having a separate tank designated for their meals.

Burn pretended to listen to the rest of Carada's demands and complaints as his gaze drifted around the tank. He thought he could taste Liana on the water, but she wasn't here.

He had caught several glimpses of Liana since coming on board, but had not yet found an opportunity to speak with her or be alone with her. It didn't help that she was always escorted, either by her female attendant or by a skinny, wall-eyed male who liked putting his fins on her whenever he thought no one was looking.

Whenever he did see Liana, she didn't act as she had when he'd taken the ship back from the mercenaries. In fact, if he didn't know her taste and her colors, he'd swear she was another female altogether. This Liana was silent and thinner, her eyes dull and her manner completely cowed, as if she feared everything around her.

Liana had been afraid during the battle, but not like this. What was wrong with her?

Well, 'Zangian? Carada was asking him. *Will you give me your assurance that these matters will be dealt with swiftly?*

Of course, Lady Ambassador. He had no idea what they were, but he'd get the complaint list from Ana Hansen later. Carada always sent the administrator a copy. *I'll see to it personally.*

Excellent. You may go.

Burn left Carada's chamber so fast he left Miglan tumbling in his wake. He ignored the Ylydii's indignant yelp and moved out to the corridor, where he stopped to taste the current. Liana left a very faint but distinct signature in the current, and he had tracked her before by following it when it was strong enough.

There it is.

Burn rolled the essence of her over his tongue. This time it was much stronger—that or he was becoming sensitive to it—and more than enough for him to track. He shot off down the corridor.

Burn knew he couldn't have tracked Carada like this, and he had spent much more time in her vicinity than Liana's. It might be because

Carada was older, or Liana was preparing to go into season. The thought of her wandering the ship while in estrus made his hide prickle all over. There were fifty young, very fit 'Zangian males on board guarding the delegates and their people. If they picked up the taste of her and decided she was ready to mate . . . he really didn't want to think about the consequences.

Liana's track led Burn to an unoccupied chamber that he swam around twice before stopping and drawing the water there through his gillets. She had either just been in this area, or spent a great deal of time here; the taste of her was all around him.

Where are you? Since he was alone, he said it out loud.

A bumping sound made him look down to the makeup hatch for the tank's liquid atmosphere. There, just beneath the grid, a pair of very black eyes stared up at him before moving past him and narrowing.

Behind him came the sound of the tank hatch opening.

Pretend I'm not here, Liana said before she disappeared.

Lady Liana?

The skinny male with the bulging eyes who had been skulking around Liana entered the chamber. He regarded Burn with his thin lips pulled back in a snarl of dislike. *What are you doing here? This is not an approved area for guards. I will report you to the ambassador at once.*

Burn turned away from the hatch and blocked the sight of it with his body. *You'll do what now?*

You're not supposed to be here, and I have to report you. When Burn edged closer, the small Ylydii flared out his fins. Abbreviated veils with muddy coloration flared like stumpy flags. *Get away from me, you brute.*

Burn caught the glitter of tiny barbs among the veils and showed his amusement. *Or you'll what? Scratch me to death? What is your name?*

I am Fokrej, valet to the Lady Liana. Not that you may address me, 'Zangian. I am—

Boring me into a coma.

The little male drew back in the exact same way Burn's mother did when she was highly offended. Which was pretty much every other hour of the day. *You will be punished for this,* Fokrej promised. *I will see to it.*

I am using this space, and Liana is not in this tank. Burn surged forward, crowding the other male toward the hatch. *Go flash your infant spines somewhere else.*

Fokrej's flukes hit the hatch and he scrambled to open it. *Ambassador Carada will hear about your insults to me. She will have you severely punished.*

I'm terrified, Burn assured him as he covered the male's face with his fin and shoved him out into the corridor.

Once the hatch was secured, Burn swam back to the grid. He wrenched off the alloy lattice and reached in until he felt warm, smooth hide.

Liana gripped his arm tightly. *Pull me through.*

He eased her out of the conduit, through the hatch and into the tank. She was covered with bits of food and dirt. *What were you doing down in there?*

Hiding. She leaned against him, her body trembling. *The current is much stronger than it was before.*

He brushed some scales from her face. *You make a habit of hiding in waste pipes?*

Her black eyes sparkled with amusement. *Lately it seems that is all I do.*

He held her, sensing she was regaining her balance, and looked down into the conduit. The current was rushing as fast as any major sea stream. *How long were you in there?*

I do not know. Perhaps an hour. She shook off a bit of vegetable matter clinging to one edge of her fins. *Fokrej still thinks himself my . . . valet.*

Fokrej could be eaten in two bites. He didn't comment on her hesitation but instead surveyed her hide. *You're in need of a good cleaning. Do you have any* mvrey *on board?*

She swiped at the grime on her face. *My attendant will scrub me off later when I return to my chamber. She knows I use the conduits.*

Not after this time. Burn lifted her face so that her gaze met his. *Lady, I would rather not pull your bones out of the incinerator strainers. Stay out of those pipes.*

She stiffened. *Males do not tell females what to do on my world.*

Remind me of this when we are on your world. While you are on this ship, you will stay out of the pipes.

I suppose it is too dangerous to keep using them. She pulled away from him and glanced at the secured hatch. *He'll be back soon; I must go.*

Where else can you go that he will not find you? Burn was struck with an idea. *I know.* He tugged her toward the other exit. *Come with me.*

She tugged back. *The last time I went somewhere with you, 'Zangian, I had to fly a ship.*

You won't have to fly this one.

Burn was glad he had insisted on keeping the detachment's strafers docked with the Ylydii ship and held ready for launch. He led Liana through the next tank and into the corridor that led to the launch bay, where the carousel dock provided access to the *IceBlade.*

Is this your vessel? she asked as he opened the water lock to pass through the docking portal.

The ship was assigned to Shon Valtas, but the major had been re-called to K-2. In the absence of his pilot, Burn technically had command of the ship. He began to tell her that, but it was too close to a lie. He valued the truth, however unpleasant it was, and he would start off with her as he meant to go on.

Not yet. I am still in pilot training. He opened the canopy and disabled the weapons panels before moving back. *Hop in.*

Hop? She gave him a puzzled look before gliding into the strafer's cockpit.

He made a face. *It's one of my cousin's expressions. She's part Terran.*

The gunner's section had been specially retrofitted to accommodate his bulk, so Liana had no trouble slipping into his harness. *Now what?*

He adjusted her harness securely before moving into the pilot's position at the helm and strapping into his own. *Now we go for a ride, Lady.*

Burn sent a quick signal to the Ylydii ship's captain and the second-in-command of his detachment, informing them that he was taking the *IceBlade* out for a practice run. The thrusters engaged smoothly and the docking portal retracted, allowing the strafer to drop down into flight position.

I did not give you permission to launch this ship, Liana said, her tone severe.

I didn't ask for it, Burn told her as he spun away from the big Ylydii vessel and engaged the stardrive. He didn't laugh when he heard the startled sound she made, but he took pleasure in the lengthy and imaginative way she cursed him after.

Are you giving me a ride, 'Zangian, she demanded when she ran out of vile words, *or trying to frighten the wits out of me?*

It would take more than a little razzle-dazzle drivejump to steal your wit, Lady. He altered their speed and course and entered a safe region of the system where the views of the stars were spectacular. *Do you ever look up and see them reflecting on the surface at night?*

Yes. Sometimes, when I was little, I would swim up and try to eat them. One of my grandmothers tried to tell me that they were the eyes of the goddess looking down upon me, but I didn't believe her. I already knew that there was no goddess, and nothing could have so many beautiful eyes.

You do not believe in a higher power?

No.

Burn found that a little alarming. His people had worshipped *Duo,* the nameless twins represented by the two suns that warmed his homeworld, since anyone could remember. *Why not?*

I watched my father die. He was kind and gentle and made me laugh. He wasn't afraid of my mother, and he didn't suck onto her hide like other males did. He only wanted to play, all day long. Her tone changed to one of bleak bitterness. *My father died slowly and in great pain, and if there is a higher power that might have answered my prayers and saved him, then she or he or it ignored me.*

Burn had never known his father, who had been killed by a 'shrike attack when he was a newborn. It was not the same as watching a parent die before your eyes. *There are no words to ease your pain, but I am sorry, Lady.*

Burn, will you take me away from here? she asked suddenly. *Just keep flying until we reach a world where they can't find us. No one will ever know I went willingly.*

I would take you wherever you wished to go, he said, *but then you would have to watch me die. 'Zangians cannot be parted from our home-world waters for more than two rotations of our planet. Being away from it kills us.*

How can this be? Liana asked. *You are not like the Ylydii. You can breathe air, like the land-dwellers.*

Not indefinitely. SEALs like me can stay away longer, but eventually we have to go home. He turned the strafer back toward the diplomatic vessel. *As you must, Lady.*

Yes. Now she sounded dull and defeated. *As I must.*

Going with Burn in the strafer had been a wanton taste of freedom for Liana, until he had spoken of obligation, and home. She had never felt more ashamed of herself than in that moment.

With the work she had to do now, however, she might surpass it.

The two delegates are alone, my lady, Graleba told Liana. *They appear to be finished their feeding, although it is hard to tell.* She made a face. *Did you know that everything they eat is already dead?*

Yes, I did. Thank you, Graleba. Liana finished sluicing off her hide un-der the sonic port and moved out of its tight, soothing waves. *How do I look?*

Beautifully clean. The attendant's eyes widened as she watch Liana extend all but one of her veils, revealing most of the intricate, blazing pattern the green stripes among the individually colored segments formed. *My lady, I had no idea you were . . .*

Liana furled her veils. *Afflicted? Does no one gossip about me anymore?*

Graleba looked uncomfortable. *Some of the other attendants who have served you before . . . but my lady, you are under tremendous strain. It is no wonder you have not been like yourself since leaving the homeworld.*

Liana did not want the older female to fear her. *I have never used my affliction purposely against another,* she told her. She could not promise Graleba that she never would.

The attendant finned acceptance, and then gave her a curiously sympathetic look. *Is it as terrible as they say?*

No. I hardly notice it anymore. That was how well Carada had neutered her. *I will go and speak to the delegates. If the ambassador summons me, you will tell her that I am with Fokrej.*

Yes, my lady.

The land-dwelling delegates were quartered in the hub of the ship, where there were compartments kept permanently dry for their use. Running through the hub was a water-filled transparent passage so that the aquatics on board could visit their passengers and friends easily. It was through this passage that Liana made her way to the galley, where the Skarresh and Ninrana delegates were having a meal together.

The two had become allies over the last week, and Liana had observed them going off to talk privately together several times. It was clear that they had settled the differences between them and were working cooperatively toward peace.

Which was the last thing she would allow them to do.

Gentlemen. Liana was pleased to find them alone. Witnesses to what she had planned would only interfere, and if Carada discovered what she was doing . . . no, she couldn't think about that. She had to do this, and quickly, before she was detected. *I was hoping to speak with you.*

"Indeed." Bataran rose politely and bowed. "Has your mother sent a message for us to reconvene? The 'Zangian ambassador has returned to the surface to replenish himself."

No, I came of my own accord. Liana watched Urloy-ka, who had not risen or shown her any deference. That she could use. *Bataran, I have done as was requested and found a suitable moon of Ylyd for your new colony, but it is rather small and airless, of course. I wish you would reconsider taking over the governorship of Ninra instead.*

Urloy-ka jumped to his feet. "What is this? The Skartesh will never govern Ninra. My people will never accept them."

"There must be some mistake, Lady Liana," the Skartesh said carefully. "I have not requested such, nor agreed to such."

Oh. Liana pretended confusion. *I thought you were the one to meet privately with my mother. It must have been one of your aides.*

"So this is how you conduct a friendship, Skartesh," the Ninrana said, his dark face scowling. "All for show in the front, and with a knife poised at the back."

Bataran turned on him. "I never agreed to a governorship, nor would any of my people. It would be good to have someone in authority over your people, however. Your religion was barbaric, and your tempers are far too volatile. As you demonstrate now by leaping to a false conclusion."

Liana backed away. *I should not have spoken about it here. I apologize, I am only the messenger*—She halted as she bumped into a much larger form. A glance over her shoulder revealed an unhappy-looking Burn hovering just behind her.

Aquatics were told to stay in their areas when the talks were not being conducted, he reminded her, *and you are not authorized to conduct any negotiations here.* He looked past her to where the two delegates were shouting at each other. *Or did you provoke this for your own personal amusement?*

I am not amused, she flared. She would have said more, but Urloyka's aide appeared and pulled a white, dagger-shaped object from his robe. He used it to stab Bataran in the shoulder.

Neither am I. Burn shot into a transition lock and sealed it, draining it of water.

Liana had never seen him leave the water before, and it terrified her until she saw him stand erect and take a breath before lunging at the Ninrana delegate's aide and disarming him.

Enough. Burn caught the crazed aide under one arm and held him. To Urloy-ka, he said, *Summon the medics.*

Frustration filled her as she watched Burn restrain the aide and help the medics treat Bataran for his shoulder wound. The 'Zangian also pulled Urloy-ka to one side and spoke with him at length. She couldn't hear what the two males discussed, but the Ninrana soon lost his ferocious expression and left the deck. Bataran was carried off by the medics, and the aide was taken by two security officers. That left her alone with Burn, who had ruined everything.

The 'Zangian reentered the transition lock and came back into the water with her. *Tell me why you did this, Lady.*

You should not have interfered in this, 'Zangian, Liana told him. *It was none of your concern.*

Burn wouldn't let her swim off. He blocked her against one of the retaining walls and held her there. *You know the Ninrana are desperate, and yet you tell lies to provoke a fight? Why? Bataran could have been killed.*

She finned indifference. *I was bored.*

If you try a stunt like this again, I don't care who your mother is. I'll throw you in a detainment tank and keep you locked up until the summit is over.

You will do nothing to my lady.

Liana smothered a groan as Fokrej swam in behind her.

Lady Liana is the future ruler of Ylyd, and you are not fit to eat her waste, the outraged valet told Burn.

If I kill him, will he be missed? Burn asked Liana.

Fokrej bared his tiny barbs. *You were told to keep your distance, 'Zangian. This, and your death threat against me, will be reported. Just what do you think you were doing, handling my lady so?*

Liana closed her eyes. Burn was going to tell Fokrej what she had been doing, and that would be the end of everything.

I can't help myself, Burn said, staring hard at Liana. *Whenever I see her, her beauty pulls at me like a hook.*

Liana's relief was so great that she nearly wept. Instead, she went along with the ruse. *Do not let it happen again, Sublieutenant.* She turned to Fokrej. *Would you escort me back to my chamber?*

With pleasure, my lady, the valet said, and slapped one of his barbed fins across her back.

Burn watched them go, and the last sight Liana had of his face was to see it darken to a furious shade of black.

CHAPTER 12

"What have you found out?" Norash asked when Shon entered his office.

"I know it's not a 'Zangian." Shon handed over copies of the scans he had performed. "DNA samples on every SEAL in the pilots' pod, except one."

"How did you obtain them so quickly?"

"I've been swimming with them every day for the last week." Shon showed him one of the palm slides he had used. "It's easy enough to make casual contact underwater and scrape off a few cells without making anyone suspicious."

"Who's left?"

"The wing leader, Saree."

Shon had done his best, but somehow Saree had evaded every attempt he'd made at physical contact. It bothered him that she had treated him underwater as she might a floating corpse, until he saw it was how she treated everyone. He had obtained a sample of her DNA from a few tissue cells she had left on the flight-control console of the *Sandpearl*, but that was not enough to clear her. Cells could be planted; DNA had to be taken directly from the body.

"You'll have to clear her another time." Norash copied the scans and handed Shon a new set of orders. "Quadrant wants you to replace Bataran as the Skartesh delegate at the summit."

"The other delegates won't accept me speaking on behalf of the Skartesh," Shon warned him. "They'll know I'm a plant."

"Not when you have the blessing of the Skartesh people. They have always wanted you as their chosen leader, and they've been very vocal about having you replace Bataran."

"Intel wouldn't put me in merely to have eyes and ears at the negotiation table," Shon guessed. "Am I going in to scrape cells?"

"This information is not to be repeated and released to anyone," Norash warned him as he switched on a wall screen. The image of a humanoid in a critical-care medical berth came into view. "This is Lep Falsma, one of the mercenaries who attacked the Ylydii ship. He was found hiding in one of the derelicts."

Shon frowned. "I thought they were all dead of poison."

"They were. Lep, it seems, didn't like shipboard fare and brought his own food and water stores with him when he signed on. He's the only one who didn't get poisoned, although he was badly injured in the battle." Norash enabled the vid to play.

"We were hired to attack the delegate's ship, and two others," Lep told the security officer standing by his berth. "We don't take many jobs like this—too much exposure—but someone musta waved a lot of credits under the captain's nose. He ferried out five other jobs to do this one."

"Who paid you to carry out the attack?" the security officer asked.

"Unknown. He used Bartermen intermediates to buy us, but word went around. Captain wouldn't say which delegate ship we weren't supposed to touch, but everybody said that was the backer, 'cause he'd be the only one left alive after we were through."

Norash paused the playback. "Bataran and the Skartesh have been cleared, as the cult's assets were seized after the invasion of Ninra. That leaves you three suspects."

"You mean two."

"Carada survived the attack when she should have been the first person killed on that vessel. Until you can clear her, I'm going to consider her a suspect."

"What about the daughter? She's known to be in opposition to her mother, and she's going to be the ruler of that world once the present Matriarch dies. Maybe killing Carada would remove one more obstacle to the throne."

"Check out the particulars and, if she has a motive, add her to the list." Norash thought for a moment. "You'll need someone to carry secured messages back and forth to the planet; I'm not trusting any space-to-ground communications until this is over. Draft one of the pilots to work with you."

"Saree," Shon suggested. "She flies alone, so no one will question her going off by herself."

"You don't have clean DNA on her. She can't be trusted."

Shon thought of what the 'Zangian had said to him about serving the greater good. "I'll get the DNA sample."

Dair left the FreeClinic and went immediately to the coast with Onkar. A week in the immersion tank was enough to drive anyone sand-belly, but she was more concerned about the breakup of her father's relationship with Teresa.

Nearly every member of the coastal pod was waiting for them at the seamount ridge. Dair's first hour underwater was spent exchanging greetings and assuring the pod that she was well, until she came face-to-face with Burn's dam.

Znora looked her over. *So you've cheated death again, Jadaira. I begin to think nothing can kill you.*

The older female had never in Dair's memory addressed her by name. Onkar made an aggressive move forward, but Dair caught his fin.

Has Burn returned from the summit ship? she asked Znora.

Only long enough to rejuvenate himself, and then he goes right back. Znora swam a little closer. *He listens to you. Tell him to come home before one of those mouth-breathers harms him.*

So that was why Znora was being polite. *Burn is a grown male now, Znora. He has to make his own choices.*

I have watched a sister and a mate die, Znora told her. *I will not lose my only child.*

Dair understood how Znora felt. She had spent the last week in silent terror, waiting to feel any sign of cramping or pain that Teresa had warned her would herald the loss of her own child. *Burn is smart and strong. Whatever happens up there, he will come out of it alive.*

He is not like you, Znora said bitterly. *You are not there to protect him. He will do something foolish, and die, and it will be your fault.* She suddenly turned and swam away as if she couldn't bear looking at Dair another second.

Dair watched her go. *Onkar, I need to find my father.* Dairatha had not been present to greet them, and that was also something that had never happened in Dair's memory.

I think I know where he is, Onkar said, and led her away from the reef.

The coastal pod's feeding grounds were extensive, stretching along a twenty-kim region of the reef, and were rich with all manner of life. Onkar led Dair into the strong boundary current that took them past the grounds and into one of the older areas, where ancient volcanoes had formed a lattice of rock and sunken caves.

No one comes out here, Dair said as they swam over the dark rock formations.

Your father does, her mate assured her, and cruised to a stop to taste the water before pointing to a run through the rock. *He's down there.*

Dair peered and saw the faint outline of a large 'Zangian male resting under a natural arc in the stone. Or was he hiding? Surely Dairatha had heard her pulse when she'd returned to the water. *You'd better let me talk to him by myself.*

Onkar finned his agreement. *I'll wait here. Jadaira, if he does not wish to speak with you, leave him be.*

He will speak to me.

Dair approached her father slowly, and released a pulse of greeting so that he would know it was her. His eyes moved up as he caught the sound, but he didn't look very welcoming.

She stopped beyond the arc and looked in at her father. *Have you decided that I am no longer your daughter, too?*

Dairatha slowly emerged from the rock niche. *I am glad to see you are well, Jadaira. Now go back to the home waters and leave me alone.*

I spent a week in the hospital, and all you have to say is that? Dair finned her disgust. *Some father you are.*

I am upset and angry. It is best no one is around me now. Dairatha eyed her belly. *You still have my grandchild in there?*

The pup kicks often. Like now. Dair rolled to show him her undulating belly.

He came over and rested a fin against the moving bulge. *It will be a male. Or did that Terran idiot female confirm the gender?*

My stepmother, Teresa, who saved my life in the event that you've forgotten, wanted to tell me. I wouldn't let her. Dair flipped so she could be on eye level with her father. *Why are you doing this to each other? You love Teresa. She adores you. If you went at each other with your teeth until the water turned scarlet, it would not hurt this much.*

She is going to catch a mogshrike and study it, Dairatha said. *That is what will hurt, daughter.*

I hope not. Onkar and I are going to help her. Dair cringed a little as she saw his hide blacken. *Father, someone must, and we have dealt with the 'shrikes before. We could use your help, though. No one has seen more 'shrikes than you.*

Don't you try to flatter me. You are not content to involve yourself in this madness, no, you must drag me into it? Never, Jadaira. I will never help her bring one of those monsters into our water.

If Teresa can discover why the mogshrikes have changed their habits, she can—

No. She cannot. Dairatha surged forward. *She has no inkling of what she faces, and neither do you. Have you ever seen a 'shrike kill a 'Zangian, Jadaira?*

You know I have not.

Then you don't know what horror is. I will not be a party to bringing that horror into our waters, and I will never acknowledge you as my child again if you do. Her father looked up and released a warning pulse as Onkar came hurtling down toward them. *Don't interfere in this, rogue. You may be my daughter's mate, but she is still child of my body.* He turned his eyes back to Dair. *You will not assist Teresa in this capture. Do you hear me? If you do, you are no child of mine.*

You want me to choose, is that it? Choose between you and the only mother I have ever known? Dair was outraged. *I'll tell you who I choose, Father. I choose the life of my child. I want this pup to live in waters that are safe. I never want to see the rest of the pod fighting to protect it from something that could gulp it down in one swallow. That is my choice.*

Dairatha seemed to wilt. *You must do what you think is best, child. I can only do the same. Good-bye, Jadaira.*

Onkar came to her side and watched the big male swim off into the rock run. *He will not be swayed.*

Neither will Teresa. Dair's heart constricted as her father's flukes gave a final lash before he disappeared from sight. *How can this be the thing that divides them? They stayed together after my birth, after the pod rejected me, even after my father could no longer leave the water. Why aren't their feelings for each other strong enough to overcome this?*

Give them time, he advised her. *Perhaps they will.*

Although her nest-mother was a prodigious breeder, T'Kafanitana had never personally considered consuming a male. First, it was not T'Kaf's place to eat males of her species, or any other, for she was sterile. Only a fertile female like her nest-mother had the right to devour a male's body and use its nutrients to manufacture shells for the unborn hatchlings with which he impregnated her.

Devouring another being seemed so uncivilized, too. Granted, it was classified as a criminal act almost everywhere outside the N-jui homeworld, and that attached quite a stigma to offworld male-consumption. And while T'Kaf didn't care very much for the gender as a whole, she had been persuaded to view some males as a viable part of a multispecies community. Certainly some could be trained to function as usefully and normally as females, and males of other species— with the exception of Rilkens—did not scurry about trying to hump the nearest erect-standing being.

Besides, if males were, as her mother claimed, very good eating, surely other species would have adopted the practice by now.

Those were not T'Kaf's thoughts as she watched Captain Noel Argate using his persuasive charm on Dr. Selmar. No, thanks to the Terran male, T'Kaf was debating the matter all over again.

"The expedition vessels will be delivered within the week," Argate was telling Teresa. He had a hand on her shoulder and was pressing his fingers to that portion of the Terran female's body with rhythmic intent. "There is no reason to wait any longer."

His neck is not so wide, T'Kaf thought, a little saliva pooling in her inner mouth. *One snip of my mandibles would take his head off easily. I could probably swallow it whole.*

More would be lost than the Terran male's head if T'Kaf did that, however, and that was all that restrained her. Had there been no other consideration, nothing would have kept her from snatching him up in her strong arms and cracking his skull open to suck out his brains.

The brains and the tongue, her mother had told her. *Raw, with just a tiny bit of* rey-was *spice sprinkled on top. Absolutely delicious.*

Teresa chose that moment to glance at the N-jui chemist. "T'Kaf, I'm sorry, what were you saying?"

She had been detailing the condition of the latest wrill samples harvested from their deep-sea probes, not that the doctor had been paying attention. No, from the moment Noel Argate opened his ridiculously bare slit of a mouth, Teresa seemed to hear only his voice.

"I will speak to you later, Doctor." She took a final look at Argate's neck before she left the Terrans and returned to the lab.

The wrill samples used to be important to Teresa, before she had joined Argate in his quest to capture a live mogshrike. Now, like T'Kaf, the tiny crustaceans sat waiting, unwanted and ignored. The fact that the probes that had captured the wrill might not do so again for another decade didn't seem to trouble Teresa.

"The wrill population is fine," she had assured T'Kaf during one of their recent debates on the value of continuing the experiment. "Set the probes to monitor and transmit bloom densities and randomly collect samples, and leave it at that."

T'Kaf could not leave it at that. She still kept records, careful records, for the future. For the not-very-distant future.

An alarm went off, and the N-jui went to one of the tanks containing specimens from the farthest reaches of the monitored currents. Among the tiny wrill was a single, much larger, specimen floating upside down. Its death had triggered the alarm, but she scanned it a second time to assure that it was dead before she removed it from the sample and placed it under a scope.

The dead wrill was one of the millions Teresa had augmented and released during the opening of the URD. Bioengineered to be three times larger than natural wrill, the dead crustacean had been created to live much longer and breed five times more often, to provide more food for the aquatic species who made it their main food.

T'Kaf began a series of standard dissection scans. The wrill, a male, was in the mid-adult stage of its life cycle, well fed on algae-plankton and quite healthy. The specimen's pin-sized brain, on the other hand, appeared under the scope to be both enlarged and internally damaged. The wrill's condition was consistent with a compression injury, obviously acquired during the collection process.

The scan readings told a far different story.

T'Kaf moved back from the scope and looked around for a specimen dish in which she could destroy the specimen. Only then did she see the scan flags scrolling up the screen of the analysis console, which she had left running on auto while she went to make her status report to Teresa.

The readings were already being stored in the analysis console's database, and the only way to remove all traces of them required a reinitialization of the entire system. Teresa had redundant storage systems feeding off the analyzer as well, and while T'Kaf could wipe out the lab console's memory, she could not get to all the other systems and do the same before someone would raise an alarm.

She had not asked to be placed in this predicament, and she bitterly resented the fact that the twin burdens of knowledge and deception had fallen on her. Until she did secure a release from this unwanted obligation, she had no alternative but to continue on.

It is my misfortune that no one snapped your head off, little male.

There was a possibility of concealing the truth in another manner. The N-jui stared at the display of her scanner before moving to the console. She could not erase the scan flags, but she could refine some of their parameters.

It took less than an hour to make the necessary adjustments, and then it was time to stage the accident that would destroy the evidence. A small measure of acid in a cracked beaker did the latter quite sufficiently.

Teresa answered her signal a few moments later. "What is it, T'Kaf?"

"I'm sorry, Doctor, but there's been a slight accident in the lab." T'Kaf stepped aside so that her supervisor could see the smoking ruins left by the beaker. "One of the outer current specimens was destroyed."

The Terran woman sighed. "Par for the course today, my friend. Don't try to deal with that yourself; have one of the housekeeping drones come in and clean it up."

"I will, of course," T'Kaf said, and looked past Teresa into Noel Argate's interested gaze. "Before I do, would you mind coming over here? There's something that I believe you should see."

"Could you be a little more specific?" Teresa gestured at the worktable she was sharing with Argate, which was covered with datapads and sea stream map scans. "We're rather busy right now."

"The specimen that was destroyed was one of the bioengineered wrill you released. It was recaptured by our probe, but it died in the tank." T'Kaf looked into Noel Argate's interested gaze. "It was also apparently contaminated with a new strain of microparasites."

"Sublieutenant, I think that we have a problem."

Burn had nothing but problems. From the day he had prevented Liana from causing an interspecies incident, everything had gone sandbelly in a hurry. First the summit talks were suspended until the injured Skartesh delegate could be replaced, which was taking forever. Then Security had sent a request for voluntary DNA testing of everyone on the vessel, which had created a complete uproar among the remaining delegates and their entourages.

"No one is taking pieces of my body," Urloy-ka told Burn after he threw the medical team out of his quarters. Even when it was explained that only a few cells were required, the desert-dweller had flatly refused to cooperate. "If you doubt who I am, contact my planet."

Because the Ninrana delegate refused DNA testing, the rest of the delegates followed suit. The medical team was sent back to K-2 empty-handed.

That had only been the beginning of the trouble. Since then, Burn and his detachment hadn't enjoyed a single rotation without some sort of problem on board the Ylydii vessel.

Three days before, the liquid atmosphere temperature regulators failed, and ice crystals had begun forming inside the tanks. A blue-lipped Miglan had come to inform Burn that the Ylydii were in danger of freezing, and then it had taken another hour to find the envirocontrol component that had failed. On the heels of that incident, the 'Zangian delegate had nearly been electrocuted by a dangerous short in the communication console in his quarters. Nathaka had returned to the surface, ostensibly to rejuvenate, but Burn had the feeling they'd be lucky if he returned at all.

Now the ship's captain, a sensible and hard-to-excite Gondian, looked ready to abandon ship. "Is it a matter of life and death, Captain?"

"I don't know. We were contracted to crew this ship, Sublieutenant, and while I understand the design and how to operate it, this . . . this is something outside my experience."

Burn rolled his fin.

"My propulsion crew performed a routine inspection on the propulsion deck a few hours ago, and reported finding an unauthorized device attached to the cell feed lines. It wasn't there during the last inspection, so I went to have a look." The captain handed him a photoscan of the cell feed panel. "I thought it was some sort of regulator, until I checked the ship's schematic, and it's not listed anywhere."

Burn glanced at the photoscan and then went still as he recognized the device. "What did you do to it? Did you touch it?" No, of course he hadn't; the ship would be a pile of rubble if he had.

"Nothing. I've asked the crew to leave it alone." The Gondian frowned. "It's not a regulator?"

"No." Burn used his console to issue rapid orders to the detachment. "Evacuate the propulsion deck and seal all the access hatches. I want everyone on board moved to the starboard wheel. Now, Ensign." He terminated the signal and looked at the captain. "Have you ever separated an Ylydii vessel?"

"Simulated, yes." His eyes went to the photoscan. "Is it a bomb?"

"No. It's a detonator. It turns the ship into a bomb." Burn came from around the console and picked up his weapon harness. "Take me to it."

Burn stopped long enough to brief the guards evacuating the portside wheel. "Be alert and keep your weapons ready. Two men on every delegate until we're clear. This could be some kind of diversion tactic to draw our attention away from them."

"Do you think all the accidents we've been having were veiled attempts to harm the delegates, Sublieutenant?" the captain asked as they continued on to the propulsion deck.

"Probably."

"That means the saboteur is on board with us, and he, she, or it will die with us." The Gondian shook his shaggy head.

Burn thought of Nathaka and Bataran. "Whoever planted it may have already left."

As soon as Burn saw the device, his blood ran cold. Displacer detonators weren't unknown to League militia, as the Hsktskt had used them extensively throughout the war, but whoever planted it had hooked it into the coolant and power cell feed lines. The small charge would mix the two chemicals and destroy the entire deck before the ruptured coolant lines allowed the stardrive to go critical.

"All right, I'll take it from here," Burn told the captain before he yanked open a tool storage unit and started pulling what he needed from the shelves. "Get over to command and prepare to separate the ship."

"Shouldn't I wait for you?"

Burn checked the display on the front of the detonator. "Not enough time. You'll want to engage the emergency buffers and take cover behind one of the moons. I need a headset that will give me a channel to the surface."

The captain found and brought him a hands-free transponder. "Stay in communication with the helm if you can, Sublieutenant. Good luck." He left the deck at a fast trot.

Burn slipped on the headset and signaled Norash on the surface. "Chief, I have a displacer detonator hooked into the stardrive coolant and fuel power feed. It's active, counting down, and set to fire in three minutes."

"You had demolition training at the Academy?" Norash asked, his tone brisk.

"Expert course, which means I have one chance in three of defusing this bitch without killing everyone within a hundred kim."

"One in two," the chief said. "I worked armament division retrieval when I was in uniform, and displacer tech was my specialty."

Burn chuffed out some air. "All right, here's what I'm looking at." He described the detonator, peering around all sides of it without touching the casing. "I see thermal and motion sensors, so I can't detach. The hookups are alloy-cased and multiheaded; pulling the lines is out. I'm not seeing a power core."

"You won't," Norash told him. "That type feeds on the accelerant."

Both the coolant and the fuel feed were excellent power sources. "Which one?"

"If I were rigging it, I'd leech coolant—no flow fluctuation in the line."

Burn placed the edge of one fin just above the third line siphoning into the center of the detonator. "It has to be coolant. The line is frigid."

"How many heads on the leech?"

"Two, and a reg valve set to full flow. Sensors on the valve, so that's out." Burn peered under the detonator and saw an isolated feed head. "I think I've got a back door."

"What?"

"An accessible tap into the works." Which would allow him to get at the internal workings of the detonator. "Or maybe I'm hallucinating."

"It has to be a decoy. If it isn't, you'll still need something to keep the conductors from firing. Stand by." The sound of Norash arguing with someone else came over the headset. "Scan to verify the tap isn't rigged."

"Scanned and verified. It's completely open." Which certified the bomb planter as an idiot or an incompetent. "What would keep the conductors iced? Ice." Burn backed away from the device and looked around the deck. "I've got three possibilities. Liquid oxygen, liquid methane, and liquid nitro."

"Use the nitro; it's the closest in temp to the coolant."

Burn lugged the barrel over to the power array. "How long will the ice hold it after I flood the works?"

"Two, maybe three seconds before the thermal kicks in and completes the backup circuit."

"Make my farewells for me, Chief."

Norash grunted something wholly Trytinorn and untranslatable.

"Establishing connection to open port." Burn carefully ran a supply line from the barrel of liquid nitrogen to the center, unused port of the detonator. Because touching the device would have triggered it, he used the detonator's weak magnetic field and a buffer connection to secure the end of the line. Before he initiated the flow, he tapped into the ship's com. "Captain, I'm preparing to disarm the device. Tell me you're on the other side of the moon."

"Separation successful and we're presently in position."

"Acknowledged." Burn picked up one of the flow regulators— which also did not need to touch the device—and opened the supply line on the barrel. The display fluttered as the liquid nitrogen entered the detonator casing. "It doesn't like the taste."

"Get out of there," Norash bellowed.

Burn saw the sequence indicator lights flash and stopped thinking. He yanked the liquid nitro line without a shutoff, spraying the entire device with the subzero liquid. The layer of ice that encased it was instantaneous, and scalded Burn's fin as he tore the detonator off the lines and threw it across the level at some storage bins. By the time he hit the deck the detonator had exploded, showering him with icy shrapnel.

Moments passed by as the dust and debris cloud settled. The atmosphere remained intact, and nothing sucked Burn out into space.

Cautiously he lifted his head and looked over at the blast site, which had vaporized three bins and melted a dozen others. His frost-covered fin shook as he reached up and enabled both channels on his headset.

"Device disabled." He saw frozen blood on the floor, and darkness crowded in on his vision field. "I'm going to need a medic down here."

"That's a nice addition to your scar collection," Shon said as he inspected the wide gash being sutured shut on the side of Burn's neck.

"I offered the sublieutenant a follow-up appointment for next week so that we could remove the scar tissue," the nurse working on the 'Zangian told Shon, "but he refused."

"I told you, scars are attractive." Burn lifted one of his fins, the ends of which were smeared with a colorless dermal gel. "Frostbite, in contrast, just hurts."

"You wouldn't accept any painkillers, either," the nurse reminded him. It took another minute for her to finish the suture and apply a light dressing. "Stay out of the water for twelve hours, please, and come back if there is any significant bleeding or further loss of consciousness."

"I won't be going anywhere if I pass out," Burn said.

"That's why you shouldn't be alone for the next twelve hours." The nurse smiled at Shon before leaving the treatment room.

"I knew I should have taped it up myself," Burn grumbled as he gingerly touched the bandage.

"Let them fuss." Shon secured the door panel and leaned back against it. "You're a hero to every person on this ship."

The console beside the berth flickered on, and black eyes in a black-and-green-striped aquatic face looked out. *Burn? What happened? They made us go over to the other side of the ship. They won't tell me anything.*

Burn exchanged a look with Shon before enabling the com panel. "I'm fine, Lady Liana. There was a problem in engineering. It's fixed now."

You're bandaged. What is wrong with your fin? The Ylydii female swam closer to the screen, and the fins on the sides of her body unfurled. *Who did this to you?*

"Liana, it's nothing. I'm fine. You'll be briefed later." Burn reached over and shut off the console before he rubbed his brow. "Females."

Shon didn't see any annoyance on the 'Zangian's face. "She's beautiful."

"She should be. She's royalty."

"So she's the one." Shon recalled the panic in the Ylydii's eyes. "She cares about you."

"It doesn't matter. The Ylydii don't crossbreed, and, even if they did, Liana will be returning to her homeworld in a few weeks. She'll rule it someday, and have plenty of meek little males eager to suck on her flukes." Burn used his uninjured fin to scratch around the base of his gillets. "Twelve hours until I can get wet."

Shon chuckled. "You could be dead, Burn. Count your blessings."

"One being an incompetent bomb maker." Burn swung awkwardly off the berth and tested his legs. "If he really was so stupid."

Shon tensed. "What makes you say that?"

"If you wanted to blow up a ship, would you build a device that could be disarmed by a pup?" Burn shook his head. "The tech is all wrong, too."

"He got the detonator components from the Hsktskt," Shon said. "Displacer tech is all they use."

"Which is why every League soldier is extensively trained on how to handle it." Burn wobbled on his flukes and clutched the berth rail. "You'd also plant the detonator in an area that isn't inspected daily by the crew, right? Not slap it on out in the open." Burn decided he could stand and released the berth rail.

"This bomb was never meant to explode," Shon said, lending an arm to help steady him.

"I'm okay, Shon, thanks. No, this was done for another reason."

"A dry run to test response times and reactions?" Shon guessed.

"That, or he's telling us that he can destroy the ship whenever he wants." Burn began fastening up the front of his flightsuit. "I wish I knew what was really going on here. I can't guard against a theoretical motive."

"We'll find out. In the meantime, I'm the new Skartesh delegate to the summit."

Burn gave him a sideways glance. "You're pulling my tail."

"I wish I was." Shon looked out through the viewport at the stars. "The other delegates are refusing to continue the talks until we've changed locations. Representative Nathaka has suggested we move the summit on-planet and hold it in the coastal waters."

"Great idea. Nathaka and Carada can chat while you and the Ninrana drown."

"A surface meeting place would be harder to arrange, as the Ylydii have to remain submerged. Urloy-ka and I can stay at the URD for the duration."

Burn regarded him. "I don't like this, Shon. All that open water provides a lot more exposure than this ship. This smells like rotflesh."

"I agree," Shon told him. "But what smells can be tracked."

CHAPTER 13

I am not pleased about any of this, Sublieutenant, Carada said to Burn as she moved into the submersion transport. *Two of the delegates will be physically separated from us. We Ylydii will have nothing between us and whatever is trying to kill us.*

The Skartesh and Ninrana parties will have open access to communications with the aquatic delegates at all times, Lady Ambassador. Burn didn't twitch from his guard post at the docking portal. Nor would he look at Liana. *Everyone will be made as safe as is possible.*

We weren't even safe on our own vessel. Carada swept past him. *Come, Liana.*

Liana wasn't sure why Carada had agreed to accept the 'Zangian delegate's invitation to relocate the summit to the coastal sea waters on K-2. The few times in the past that Ylydii had made contact with the 'Zangians, they had brought the aquatics up to their ships. This would be the first time any Ylydii had ever entered water populated by another aquatic civilization.

The submersion transport shuttle was a recent triumphant melding of aquatic ingenuity and land-dweller engineering. Designed to ferry large numbers of aquatics from the surface into orbit, where they could be transferred to larger passenger transports, it provided most of the comforts of the sea within its liquid-atmosphere-filled decks. Small compartments designed to mimic different regions of the 'Zangian oceans were made available for passengers who wished to rest or have privacy during the flight.

It was into one of these compartments that Liana was sent. *Take this opportunity to rest,* Carada told her before swimming off to consult with her advisors. *You look tired.*

Liana wasn't fooled by the show of concern. Someone—probably Miglan—had reported the transmission she had made to medical to check on Burn after he had been wounded. Since then she had been treated like a wounded invalid herself, and hadn't been left alone for a moment.

Like time, the opportunities to take action were quickly running out.

The compartment was only a third of the size of the tank she had occupied on the ship, but the feed was plentiful and the décor as natural as any real underwater reef. Liana watched the flat-headed, wide-tailed *orasa*, specially imported from her homeworld, dart in an orchestrated mass of flowery color through the dazzling red branches of synthetic flame rock. Beyond them, a wide, transparent panel provided a view of the planet, which seemed to swell larger as they descended.

The entry portal flowered open and closed behind her. *Aren't you hungry, my lady? Or are you eager to get to the surface?*

Liana turned to stare out the viewport. *This is my space, Fokrej. Leave it.*

The valet ignored her order and swam to her side. He looked down at K-2. *There are monsters down there. Did Her Grace tell you about them?*

I know about the 'Zangians. They're not monsters. She held her fins furled so tightly that they ached. *Get out.*

Such deliberate discourtesy. You must have missed my special attentions. Fokrej slapped her across the face, his barbs creating a dozen shallow scratches.

If she killed him, Carada would punish her unmercifully. Liana knew this, knew she had to endure whatever he did to her as a result, and still her veils ached.

The valet drew in the water stained with thin ribbons of her blood, savoring the taste of it. *The monsters I refer to are those that prey on the 'Zangians. They're called mogshrike.*

Naturally he would know about them. *Everyone knows of them. They're as large and mindless as the* zodsio *who lumber through our seas.*

Large, yes, but not mindless. The land-dwellers call them killing machines. They live to hunt, and they hunt everything. Imagine mouths as wide as caves, lined with very keen-edged teeth. Fokrej darted forward, as if to snap at her face, making her flinch. *They move much faster than that, my lady. You'd never get away.*

I will never be around them.

Didn't you hear? They're not staying in the cold waters anymore. They're coming into the shallows to hunt the 'Zangians. They hunt by scent. Blood scent, rot scent . . . change scent.

Sickened, Liana closed her eyes. Somehow Fokrej had guessed her deepest fear. Nothing revolted her more than the thought of being made prey, of being devoured alive. *I am not afraid.*

I think one of these mogshrike will recognize you. You're so close to it now that I can smell it. Instead of hurting her again, he stroked one of his blunt fins down her side. *It excites me to think I will be here to see it as well as taste it.*

Why was he trying to make her angry? Didn't he understand how close she was? *It will never happen.*

You've waited too long, my lady. Fokrej was already so aroused that he was shaking. *Nothing can stop it but your death.*

Liana could no more hold back her anger than she could a tide. *Is that what you want? To see me dead, or to watch me kill? Why are you like this? What is the matter with you?*

I am the normal one here, my lady. Fokrej glided against her. *But you need not be afraid. There is always the third alternative.*

Liana's vision sharpened, and her own body trembled. The forces at war inside her were so strong that resisting them took all her concentration. *Leave me now.*

I haven't properly attended to you, my lady. You know how much you need me. We were born soul mates; now we have only to consummate our love. He latched onto her and tried to roll her. *Take me inside you.*

For a moment she nearly gave in. Although the thought of the child that she and Fokrej might produce made her belly surge, it would be the simplest solution. This way she would have the pleasure as well as the pain. It would take several attempts for him to impregnate her, but if she allowed her body to dictate matters, he would. Her body didn't care who or what the valet was; he was a male, and ready to mate. It was enough.

It wasn't enough. She had never wanted Fokrej, or any other male. She had mated out of duty, but the act repelled her. She had never desired another male except the big 'Zangian.

Take me, Fokrej crooned. *You know it is what you want. Take me. Hurt me.*

Burn would never say that. He would never want to be hurt, and he would do the taking. He had even said so.

I would take you wherever you wished to go.

The memory of the 'Zangian's voice made the bile rush up Liana's throat, and she opened her eyes to see Fokrej positioning himself against her, upside down. It made him the perfect target, so she released the contents of her stomach into his face.

Fokrej was still choking on her vomitus as she swam out to find a steward and request another, cleaner compartment with a door panel that could be secured from inside.

"I was hoping to contact Dr. Selmar," Ana Hansen told T'Kafanitana. "This underground barax hive on the perimeter of the colony might constitute a hazard to some of the agricultural projects, according to the dozen botanists who have been signaling me about it since it was discovered. The Hlagg are also quite upset, as it could represent a cultural disaster for them."

"I will relay the message, Administrator," T'Kaf told her, "but I fear that Dr. Selmar will be occupied for some time with the 'shrike capture project. Perhaps I can be of assistance?"

Ana looked puzzled. "Do you have some background in xenoentomology?"

T'Kaf discreetly masked her amusement. "No, but I am an exo."

"An exo?"

She found it hard to believe Ana had never heard the slang term for her kind before this. "Exoskeletal or insectile life-form. As such, I may be able to contribute some insight as to the reason the barax have built and are actively defending their hive."

"I see." The Terran female frowned. "Just out of curiosity, do you call us—life-forms with internal skeletons, I mean—endos?"

"That, or bonies."

"I see." Ana chuckled. "Forgive my nearsightedness, T'Kaf. I tend to think of you as a person, not a type of life-form."

"That is why you are so suited to your position here. You see every colonist the same." The N-jui checked her schedule. "I have a few hours of personal time this afternoon. Would the two hunters who found the hive be available to meet me and take me to the site?"

Ana confirmed that they were, and the N-jui made arrangements to meet the two at the Hlagg embassy before ending the relay.

T'Kaf left her console and scanned the last of the specimen batches brought in by the deep-sea probe collectors. Another bioengineered wrill had been caught in the bloom sample, but this one was still alive.

Her four eyes glittered as she carefully separated it from the other, normal specimens and placed it under the scope in a dry dish. Deprived of water, the wrill tried to curl, but its body could not control the weight of its enlarged head, and its spine snapped soundlessly.

As soon as its life functions stopped, the wrill's transparent skull split open, spilling its swollen brains out into the dish.

T'Kaf returned to her console and prepared a standard specimen container, labeling it to the attention of Dr. William Mayer before taking it to one of the housekeeping drones. "Send this over by courier to the FreeClinic. Have it delivered today."

"Acknowledged."

T'Kaf had ample time to finish her work in the lab before leaving to meet the two insect hunters at the prearranged place. She took a field collection kit and, almost as an afterthought, a stunner.

The Hlagg named Paal greeted her with the open-mouthed admiration of a true insect-lover. "Chemist T'Kafanitana, a pleasure to make your acquaintance. This is my companion, Moleon."

The Skartesh looked up at her and gave a single nod of acknowledgment before silently walking off into the forest.

"Administrator Hansen told me few details about the underground barax hive you found," T'Kaf told Paal as they followed the Skartesh. "Have there been any incidents similar to this one on your home-world?"

"No, and I do not understand what has changed them." Paal's eyes shimmered. "The barax have never been specifically interactive with my kind, but they have never displayed such overt hostility, either. We thought we had a relationship of mutual respect and admiration."

T'Kaf knew endos regularly projected their emotions onto other, different species. Despite the appalling amount of ignorance that indicated, she always tried to consider it part of their charm. "Have you ever attempted to ask them how they felt about this relationship?"

Paal shook his head. "We cannot communicate with them, I fear." He gave her a hopeful look. "Would you be able to?"

"I don't know. Can you hold a conversation with a paramecium?"

"Ah. I see your point."

"I am sensitive to chemical messages and exo behaviors, so perhaps I can interpret something." T'Kaf felt sorry for the downcast Hlagg. "How long have the barax been building this hive?"

"Almost a cycle, we believe." Paal sighed. "They tend to build quickly, and they're not that far from the embassy."

"Long enough to start a second generation?"

"And a third, and eggs to start a fourth. Barax breed faster than they build." He peered up at her. "Does that present a problem?"

"Exos usually are not sentimental, and primitives like these do not store memories as your kind do. The longer the barax are separated from you, the stranger your chemical scent becomes to them." T'Kaf looked ahead and saw that the Skartesh had stopped walking and was sniffing the air. "Subsequent, new generations may have been the ones that attacked you when you found the hive. What is wrong with that one?" She indicated Moleon.

"Moleon?"

The Skartesh made a quick hand gesture demanding silence, and drew in a deep, slow breath.

"He will do this several times," Paal whispered to the N-jui. "It is how he scouts the area."

T'Kaf breathed in and picked up some scent, but the chemicals were too sophisticated and evolved to belong to the barax. "Someone has been out here before me to visit this site."

Paal looked confused. "I do not think so. The area has been declared off-limits to the colonists."

"Likely some curious children." The scent trace was rather strong. She saw Moleon swiping the air with his hairy arm. "I think that male wishes us to join him."

They moved quietly toward the Skartesh hunter, who was staring across a cleared area at a group of purple-leafed trees.

"This is not where we found the hive, Moleon," Paal said to him.

"It is bigger now." The Skartesh pointed to the middle of the clearing. "Look there."

"It cannot be here," Paal protested. "There is another quarter kim for us to walk before we reach the place."

T'Kaf stretched her head to study what appeared to be a roughly oval area of ground covered by short, thick, brown and green plant life. Small, sculpted mounds of dark soil appeared at regularly spaced intervals. "Entries."

"I beg your pardon?" Paal asked.

"The mounds of dirt. They are entryways into the hive." T'Kaf caught a tiny amount of movement under the cover of the plant life. "Please, stay here."

Using her wings was rude—one should never fly when others could not—but they allowed her to move over the clearing without disturbing the soil or what lay beneath it. Vibrations from the subterranean excavation and construction washed over her, and carried the same strong scent she had picked up before. She studied the few insects on the surface, mostly sentries posted at the mounds to protect against invaders, and spotted a quartet dragging a large chunk of dead wood out from where it was buried under fallen leaves. Two others emerged from the hive and trundled over to meet them.

Workers.

T'Kaf moved to hover as quietly as she could over the barax, and lowered a nictitating membrane over her fourth eye to pick up the colors of the conversation being transmitted between the workers. The chemicals that had filled her nostrils since entering the area *were* coming from them.

She had once tried to explain a chemical conversation to Teresa Selmar, who, like other endos, depended almost exclusively on sound to transmit information. "You already know nonverbal species that use body language or specific behavior to communicate. Chemical conversations are conducted in much the same way, although specific shared concepts are expressed through taste or odor, often in combination with some body movement."

"But what is the language of a chemical conversation?" Teresa asked.

"Not words as you understand them; exo brains don't function in that manner. It is more like a shared series of images. Let me demonstrate." T'Kaf released a bit of plant sap she had gathered and stored in one of her leg parts. "Breathe in and tell me the first thing that comes into your mind."

Teresa closed her eyes and tested the air. Her lips curved. "Mmmmm. Pancakes with maple syrup."

"*Rellim* tree sap does strongly resemble that of Terran maple, although I would not recommend pouring it on your cakes from the pan. It is highly toxic to your kind. This is how I say where I found it." T'Kaf made the appropriate accompanying motions with her arms, legs, and head.

Teresa admired her body-speech. "It's as if you're dancing."

T'Kaf was not dancing now. From the conversation she was tasting, the barax were feeling particularly irate about the two males at the edge of the clearing. They had noticed her as well, but dismissed her as a nonthreat because she was on wing. She listened for another few exchanges before flying back to where Paal and Moleon waited for her.

"You cannot move into the clearing," she told the males. "These creatures know you are here, and they have memories of the last time they encountered you. They will not permit you to damage the hive again."

"That was an accident," Paal said at once, "and barax do not attack people."

She looked back at the workers, who had abandoned the wood chunk and were hurrying toward a mound entry. "They do now."

"How will they defend the hive?" the Skartesh asked.

"With their numbers." She made a sweeping gesture toward the center of the clearing. "There are millions of drones under the surface, and the sentries are prepared to signal them if you walk out over the hive. They will not spare your lives this time."

Paal became agitated. "How do you know how many there are? And their intentions?"

"They have a very sophisticated vocabulary, almost as complex as the one my species uses." T'Kaf took out a live specimen container from her pack. "I will capture one of the barax for further study, but you must leave the area first."

"Why?" Paal demanded.

"The barax cannot attack me while I am in the air. They now see the three of us together, so they will come for you."

"If we leave, will they attack the colony instead?" Moleon asked.

She shook her head. "It is too far from the hive for now. People will not be in danger for several weeks."

"What are you talking about?" Paal demanded. "The barax do not pose a threat to us."

"They will when they finish building their hive," T'Kaf told him. "Their excavators are continuing to dig east, and will not stop."

Paal looked back toward the embassy and, beyond it, the structures built on the outskirts of the settlement. Comprehension rendered him speechless.

Moleon looked into the forest, then at the clearing, and back at the way they had come. "They are tunneling directly toward the colony."

Emily could barely contain her excitement as she rushed from work to meet Hkyrim at the Trading Center. Ana Hansen hadn't been angry about the official approval Emily had given Hkyrim to search the mercenary ships for poison; rather she had commended her on her quick thinking.

"Now that we're moving the summit down to the surface, I should be able to make it into the office more often," the administrator told her. "But in case I don't, keep doing what you're doing."

Earning her supervisor's trust made Emily feel like singing. Ana had always been kind and considerate, of course, but a wall of reserve had been kept firmly in place. Emily felt as if she had knocked down the wall for good.

She couldn't wait to tell Hkyrim about how his investigation had helped Ana and the other people running the summit better safeguard the delegates, as well as leading to the discovery of a survivor in one of the derelicts. He needed to know how valuable his work was.

What slowed Emily to a full stop was the sight of Hkyrim sitting and talking with a group of other Omorr.

So he's made some new friends.

The fact that Emily hadn't done the same didn't bother her so much—she had been insanely busy at the office—and she knew he missed being around his own kind. With the exception of Ana, she wouldn't care if she ever saw another Terran again for as long as she lived.

Oh, no, you're not jealous.

Emily turned to move in a different direction and promptly bumped into a very solid chest covered by greenish-gray scales and an intricately scrolled white tattoo. She looked up and saw fangs the size of daggers flash.

"Watch where you walk, Terran," the snake-headed being said.

"Sorry. I mean, I will, and I'm sorry." She went around it and walked blindly until she saw a sign posted in stanTerran. She went to the serving counter of the outdoor café, behind which stood a statuesque Terran female with long, curly golden hair and lovely, dramatic features.

Emily wondered if every other Terran woman on colony was beautiful and blond. If they were, she was going to get a complex.

"Well?" The proprietress had a gorgeous French accent to go with her commanding presence. Naturally. "Do you wish to order, block my counter, or ask for a job?"

Emily wasn't sure what she wanted, but she was going to need a tissue in a minute.

"I usually don't hire other Terrans," the Frenchwoman said. "Too much trouble with the customers; they think they will spit in their food."

Was she being funny, or serious? "I have a job already."

"No crying, then." The tall woman pointed to a nearby empty table. "Go and sit down."

Emily went and sat down. A moment later the café owner brought two long-stemmed servers of wine and a plate of bread and cheese to the table. "I'm sorry, but I don't drink."

"You do not drink this. You bask in it." She handed Emily one of the servers. "I am Lisette Dubois. You are Ana Hansen's new assistant, *oui*?"

Emily nodded. "I'm Emily Kim." She gingerly sampled the wine. It was cold and soft and tasted like flowers smelled. "This is wonderful."

"*Naturalement.* It is from my cousin's vineyard. He cannot keep his wife happy, but he is the genius with grapes." Lisette studied her. "What are you doing here?"

Emily told her about her safe, quiet life back on Terra, and how much she had hated it, and her decision to strike out and find a new place in the universe for herself.

Lisette listened and when Emily was finished, asked, "Good. Now why are you wandering the Trading Center and walking into Tingaleans?"

It took a moment for Emily to connect Tingalean with the snake-headed being she had bumped into. "I was going to meet a friend, but he was busy, and I guess I got distracted."

"He is the Omorr I see you with sometimes?" Lisette smiled at Emily's wide-eyed reaction. "You are Terran. He is not. You stand out like the banged thumbs. I am surprised no one has started a petition against it."

Emily took another sip of the wine, but she couldn't taste it anymore. "I thought I left all the prejudice back on Terra."

"*Non*, it follows you, like the *le petite* yapping dog." The French-woman made a dismissive gesture. "You have two choices."

"I do?"

Lisette nodded. "You can run away and cry and mope over him alone in your room. You will write much bad poetry, get the hiccups, and sleep on damp pillows."

Emily could see herself doing that. "What's the other choice?"

"Go to him, as you planned. Meet his friends. If they are rude to you, say nothing, but smile as if you know a secret." Lisette leaned over. "Omorr have to know everything, so this makes them crazy."

She toyed with the thin stem of her server. "Pretend it doesn't matter, in other words."

"Oh, it matters." Lisette waggled a finger at her. "You do not show them this matters. You show him, later."

Emily drained her wineglass and stood up. "I'm going to him." She paused and reached for her credit holder.

"*Non, non.*" Lisette waved her off. "You only pay if you are running home to weep."

Emily grinned. "Then next time, I buy the wine and you tell me how you ended up here."

"Of course. Only there is much crying and damp pillows in my tale, I will warn you now." The Frenchwoman lifted her glass in a toast. "*Salut.*"

It was easier to say she was going to walk over and see Hkyrim than to actually do it, Emily decided as she drew near the group of Omorr. In fact, leaving the homeworld hadn't been quite this hard. "Hello, Hkyrim."

"Emily." Hkyrim seemed surprised to see her. "Come, join us."

The other Omorr didn't look as happy to see her, but two of them moved over as Hkyrim found an empty chair and pulled it up to the table.

"I did not know you were contracted, Hkyr," the thinnest of the Omorr said, rather snidely.

"Her name is *Emily*," Hkyrim told him.

The thin one waved some gildrells in a negligent fashion. "Pardon my error, if that is what it was."

Some of the other Omorr made a snickering sound.

Emily tried not to notice that, along with all the things that were hopping, crawling, and chirping in the bowls on the table, and instead focused on Hkyrim. "I spoke with Administrator Hansen today, and she was very pleased with the results of your investigation. I'm pretty sure she's going to speak with Dr. Mayer about it."

"It doesn't matter if she does." Hkyrim looked pleased, though. "I was glad to be of assistance."

"I know you were a big help." Emily smiled at him.

"Hkyr lives to be of assistance," an older-looking Omorr said. "You should consider that in any future negotiations."

The other Omorr seemed to find that very funny, too. Emily was starting to feel like the only one not in on the joke.

"Let me introduce my friends." With icy politeness, Hkyrim identified the others sitting around the table, all of whom worked either at the FreeClinic or in Environmental Services.

The names were confusing, so Emily didn't try to remember them all, but nodded to each one in turn. "I'm pleased to meet you."

"Would you care to share my meal?" one of the Omorr sitting beside her asked, and offered a bowl filled with something green and long and slithering.

"Careful, Tpyg," another said. "You don't know where her mouth has been." He gave Hkyrim a direct look. "Do you, Hkyr?"

More snickers, quickly smothered.

Emily had eaten with Hkyrim often enough not to show any repugnance over the food, but she was having a hard time doing the same for his friends. They didn't like her, she got that much. If she fell into a ten-thousand-foot hole, they'd probably stand around the edge, criticizing the way she fell and waiting to hear the thump when she hit bottom.

You do not show them this matters, Lisette had said.

"Thank you for offering," she told the one with the bowl, "but Omorr food doesn't appeal to me."

The one named Tpyg nudged Hkyrim with one arm. "Good thing she doesn't feel that way toward all things Omorr, eh?"

Hkyrim nudged back, and not very gently. "Quiet, Tpygon."

"Terrans do not eat their food alive, I understand," another Omorr, the only one who had not been laughing at her, said. "How do you absorb the nutrients properly if you process and burn everything?"

"I can't really say," Emily admitted. "Nutrition isn't my field. I'm an administrative assistant."

"Not much value there," a third mentioned, as if she were some sort of commodity.

"Emily and I are friends," Hkyrim said, his voice taking on a hard edge. His gildrells were so stiff they barely moved. "If you'll excuse us, there are matters we must discuss privately now."

The other Omorr exchanged some knowing glances before they all rose and collectively bid Hkyrim farewell. No one said anything to Emily, who sat with what she hoped was a mysterious smile pasted on her face.

"I apologize," Hkyrim said as soon as they were alone. "I never realized how rude my kind can be until now."

"It's my fault." She felt miserable again. "I shouldn't have interrupted you."

"If they cannot accept our friendship, then I do not require theirs."

Emily could tell that he meant it, and knowing that made all the difference. "What was all the business about contracts and negotiations?"

Hkyrim sighed. "It is your name. At first they thought I called you 'Adorelee.'"

"That's pretty."

"It is the word for a female to whom one wishes to contract marriage. The male word is 'Adoren.'"

"Oh." Could that ten-thousand-foot hole appear under her chair? Sometime within the next three seconds?

"Your name, Emily, is not so similar in sound, but I think they were making assumptions out of turn. Our friendship . . . disconcerts them."

Right. They hate me. "If you remove the first vowel sound of your name, Hkyrim, it would be identical to my surname." She tried to sound droll and witty, so that when he told her he didn't want to see her anymore he wouldn't think she was crushed. "That doesn't require you to marry me, by the way, and no one would mistake us for relatives."

"No, I suppose they would not." His gildrells relaxed a little more. "Names are overly important to my species. They are used to convey more than the individual's identity. They reflect status, social place, and importance. One could say they sometimes reflect the hope of another, as Adoren and Adorelee do."

"You could call me Terran when we're around your Omorr friends, if that would make things simpler." She liked the unique intonations that he gave her name whenever he said it, though, and it was something of a wrench to make the offer.

"I do not wish to call you what you are not, Emily Kim."

"I don't understand." She looked down at herself. "You don't get more Terran than this."

"You may be biologically Terran, but there is more to you than your species. You may lead an evolution."

He seemed serious. "We Terrans aren't evolving very much these days," she said sadly. "The war has made things so much worse on my planet. Everyone is fighting about whether we should stay in the League or break away from them. If anything, my people are becoming more bigoted than they ever were."

"You must stand and challenge that which your people—and mine—accept as standard view. Claim more for yourself than the strangled, frightened existence of those narrow minds. I wish you had been born Omorr." He looked in the direction his friends had walked. "Or more Omorr were like you."

"If I had been born to your species, we might never have met," she told him. "I don't think I would have wanted to leave your homeworld." Or you, she added mentally.

"If I had met you on Omorr, I doubt I would ever have left." He stood and offered her one of his spade-shaped hands. "Would you care to walk with me before I report back to the hospital for my shift?"

Their friendship was odd, and they did stand out, as Lisette said, like banged thumbs. Suddenly Emily didn't care what anyone thought of them.

What we think is important. "I'd be delighted."

The membranes that functioned as his fingers were soft and sensitive, and wrapped with gentle strength around her hand as soon as she touched his.

"Just one more question," she said as they left the Trading Center. "Were those green things worms?"

This is a beautiful world, Graleba said as she swam with Liana over the elongated, colorful reefs bordering the 'Zangian coastal pod's territory. *Although I must say it takes some getting used to the water. Even after three days I find it tastes strange. What do you think, my lady?*

Liana thought she might bite her attendant if she didn't get away from her soon. *It is time for you to feed. I will go and find my night guard.*

I am not supposed to leave you alone, my lady, Graleba said.

Liana faced the older female. *It is not as if I will cast myself into the depths and sacrifice myself to one of their monsters.*

As you say. Graleba suddenly came forward and glided her cheek against Liana's. *Do not be so sad, child. We will return home soon.*

Liana returned the maternal caress. *Thank you, Attendant.*

She watched Graleba wander cautiously into the 'Zangian feeding grounds, and then shot into a nearby powerful current that helped speed her away from the summit and the ever-inquisitive members of the 'Zangian coastal pod.

They had all been briefed about where to go, and what to avoid. The dark column of water at the very fringe of the pod's territory was too cold to be mistaken for anything but what it was: the outer currents, where civilization ended and the monsters roamed freely.

Liana headed for dark water.

Fokrej's story about the mogshrike had terrified her, as he meant it to, but for another reason than he intended. It offered balance, a life for a life. Her death so that the one could live.

Here she could think of the one, and no one would know. She could offer an exchange to the bitch goddess of her people, and it would be accepted.

The water began to turn cool, and then cold. Liana did not have her winter layer of fat to insulate her body, so she had to swim faster to keep her blood circulating and her limbs warm. She was glad of the cold, however. It would numb her, and she was childish enough to wish there would be little pain involved. The manner in which she died counted, but surely there didn't have to be horrendous pain. She only wanted it to be done, finished.

The mogshrike would be fast. They were hunting in packs now, it was said, so there would be more than one. They would tear her apart, fighting over her body. They would rip into her and gulp her down, and that would be that.

A life for a life.

She had thought she had lost her faith long ago, but that faith still existed somewhere inside her. She knew the legends. Self-sacrifice, to die by the worst means possible, would appease the higher power. It was the only way salvation could be earned; the grandmothers had taught her. And it made sense, too. Nothing came for free.

The outer currents of the 'Zangian sea were beyond frigid. Liana could see the glitter of ice crystals in the current. She could no longer feel her fins beyond the base of each one, and her flukes had gone so stiff that she could barely make a proper downstroke with them. There was little light in the water, and none at all below, where the soundless, blind depths opened up, an endless nightmare of black. That was where she would go, where she belonged—

Liana.

She closed her eyes. She had never heard her name pulsed with such urgency, not even when she had lost control as a child. Now she felt impatience. Could she not even kill herself without some annoying distraction?

Liana.

It was not Fokrej; he would hover in the safe warmth behind her so he could watch and stimulate himself, or whatever grubby act he performed when there was no female to take him. Carada was wholly occupied with the summit; she would never leave it to look for Liana. Graleba would never venture this far from the others. . . .

Stop, Liana.

She felt the body come up from beneath her, displacing the water and fighting the current to reach her. It was strong and determined, but it didn't savage her or even bite her. The body curled around hers, wrapping strange appendages around her. Perhaps it was some sort of tentacled thing that meant to drag her into the black. She hoped it had a good hold on her, for she would blend into the darkness, and if it dropped her it might not find her again.

Something was vibrating in her ears. Something soft and tender. Strength and power cradled her limp form as gently as a grandmother. The body warmed her and tugged her out of the strong, glacial current. The cold seeped away, replaced by a stream of soothing sounds and gentle strokes.

Had it happened already? Was this the afterlife that she had been promised? She was glad if it was. It hadn't hurt very much at all.

Liana.

It was the 'Zangian. She frowned but kept her eyes closed. *What are you doing in the afterlife, Burn? Did they kill you, too?*

We're not dead.

CHAPTER 14

*P*atrolling the coastal waters was much more fun than being locked up in space on the Ylydii ship, Burn had decided. He was home, the water tasted right, and every pulse he sent out bounced back with the comforting, familiar shape of his native landscape.

Everything had been fine, until that one pulse bounced back to him with an unmistakable shape in it.

Female, Curonal, who was on patrol with Burn, said as he caught the return wave. *Not one of ours.*

It's Liana. Burn released another, more focused pulse, and went still as it returned with her location. She was far from the breeding caverns and swimming very fast in the wrong direction.

Loknoth turned into the wave. *She's nearly reached dark water.*

Burn had then broken away from the patrol and shot into the nearest, fastest current he could find. By the time he reached her, Liana had already crossed the thermal border of 'Zangian territory and was freezing herself in the outer currents.

Once Burn had found her and wrenched her out of the icy darkness, he kept her close. The outer currents' frigid temperatures seemed to have sent her into a state of thermic shock, and she wouldn't answer him when he called her name. Holding her against him seemed the only sensible way to bring her out of the icy stupor. It wasn't what he wanted to do to her for being so brainless—hadn't she been briefed about the dangers of dark water?—but for now he'd concentrate on keeping her alive.

Later, when she was herself again, he'd shake her until her fins snarled. Until then, he kept murmuring her name and swimming as fast as he dared.

Slowly the warmer waters and heat of his body roused her. *What are you doing in the afterlife, Burn? Did they kill you, too?*

They? Who were they? She must be having hallucinations. Out loud to her, he said, *We're not dead.*

That made her dark eyes pop open. *What are you doing?* She struggled against him. *Impudent 'Zangian. Release me at once.*

The impudent 'Zangian just saved your tail, you twit. He was so relieved and angry that he almost nipped her hide. *Didn't you know where you were?*

Something flashed in her eyes. *You have no right to question me.*

Back to the royalty routine. *Maybe not, but I know someone who does. Now be still or I'll call for your mother and tell her what a thoughtless, reckless, silt-brain she has for a daughter.*

Liana stiffened but stopped trying to wriggle away. *There is no need for you to threaten me. I went for a swim. I must have gotten lost.*

Right. And I was whelped yesterday. He brought her around from the far side of the breeding caverns and guided her through a seldom-used entrance. *Go back to your chamber and stay there. If I so much as smell you looking out in open water, I'm going to have you locked up in a tank on the surface.*

She drew herself up as Carada often did in the vertical, commanding position. *You would not dare.*

Burn moved in until she was trapped between him and a corridor wall. *Try me.*

An older Ylydii female swam up beside him. *Forgive me for intruding, but you are threatening my lady. Please desist or I shall have to poke you with this.* The female displayed a diver's prod.

He backed away and turned to the older female. *She nearly froze to death in the outer currents. Summon one of the medics to have a look at her, but don't let her out of your sight.*

No, the Ylydii said, visibly shocked. *I will not.*

Burn gave Liana one last, frustrated look before swimming out and rejoining the patrol. Curonal and Loknoth said nothing to him, for which he was grateful. He needed time to cool his own blood and set his thoughts in order.

Nathaka has assigned some of us to guard the breeding caverns at night, Loknoth mentioned. *There will be no opportunity for anyone to . . . become lost with us there.*

She wants to kill herself, Burn muttered. *Or she thinks someone is trying to kill her. I don't know. She talks the way the* enilcalliw *do when they're sick and try to beach themselves.*

She could be sick, Curonal suggested. *Why else would the future ruler of Ylyd seek death?*

Burn glanced at Loknoth. *Who has the duty to guard Liana tonight?*

Kirrgel mu Chetori. He was complaining about having to feed early so he could report on time.

I will speak to Kirrgel, then.

Loknoth finned caution. *Her dam does not like you, Burn. She has repeatedly asked that you be kept away from her and her daughter.*

The reason Liana had escaped the breeding caverns was because no one had been guarding her. *I'm not letting her harm herself. If Carada doesn't like it, she can bite my flukes.*

As you say, Curonal put in. *Just be careful she doesn't decide to bite the other end of you.*

One of the older 'Zangian males swam up to meet them. *We need you over at the caverns at once.*

Did that blasted female escape again? Burn demanded. *She's going into a tank, just as soon as I put fins on her.*

No one escaped, the older male told him. *We think someone was killed.*

Shon changed out of his uniform and wore civilian garments for the first summit meeting on K-2. Bataran had worn a prayer chain around his neck, but he saw no need to do the same. No matter what anyone thought, he was not Skartesh, and he did not practice their religion. He also made sure all the other delegates knew that he was an intelligence officer and an oKiaf as well as the chosen representative of the former cult.

Shon expected objections, particularly from Urloy-ka, who had good reason to suspect him of duplicity.

Because Nathaka and Carada could not leave the water—it would kill the Ylydii, and the 'Zangian was too large and old to stay topside for very long—Ana Hansen had suggested they convert one of the large collection tank rooms into a meeting place for the delegates. The tank, which could be left open-ended on the sea side, acted like a view panel, and its audio monitors were converted to provide voice-activated, two-way communication.

All we need, Shon thought as he took his place at the table provided for him and Urloy-ka, *is some food, hot beverages, and whatever analgesics are applicable.*

Ana Hansen opened the meeting as she had all the previous gatherings, with greetings to all four delegates. "We appreciate your commitment to this endeavor, and will be on hand to provide whatever you need during your discussions." She gestured toward another pair of transparent panels. "Aquatic delegates, please notify the guard posted outside the URD with any requests. Nonaquatic delegates, please signal one of our attendants from the observation room."

"I have filed a grievance with colonial security about you, Major Valtas," Carada said. "It is outrageous that a League military officer should be drafted to serve as a replacement for our Skartesh delegate, Bataran. You do realize that your appointment may place the entire peace process in jeopardy."

Unless she did it first, Shon thought. "Lady Ambassador, I would not be here if not for the will of the Skartesh people. I do not come here representing the interests of anyone but them." He saw Urloy-ka shift in his seat. "I have done what I could to protect this species in the past. My record speaks for itself."

"That would be the record that details how you underwent physical alteration in order to impersonate one of the Skartesh's most sacred leaders in order to infiltrate the cult?" the Ylydii asked, her tone sugary.

"What Major Valtas did saved many lives among my people," the Ninrana delegate said unexpectedly. "I will not have him disparaged for the role he played in the defeat of the cult takeover on my homeworld."

"We can debate suitability for the remainder of this session,"

Nathaka said, "or we can discuss the issues that need resolution among the species we represent."

Carada wasn't finished. "I want it on record for this, and every other session, that I object to the selection and presence of this intelligence officer."

"That has been done, Lady Ambassador," Ana Hansen said over the audio panel from the observation room.

There was a long, awkward silence as everyone inspected each other.

"When we last met," Nathaka said to Shon, "we were discussing a number of possible sites for establishment of an independent Skartesh colony, as well as to conduct research with replenishment technology to restore and maintain a viable water source on Ninra."

"The Ylydii are still pleased to extend the use of one of our moons to the Skartesh, and the financial and technological means to bring water back to the Ninrana," Carada said. "I have stated this before: We are a generous people, and we wish to help."

"As long as both species accept Ylydii law, and aquatic governments to rule over them," Urloy-ka tagged on. "As I said before, Lady Ambassador, that is unacceptable to my people."

"I must refuse on behalf of the Skartesh as well," Shon said. "They wish to be isolated from constant contact with other species, and will only accept a colony where they may be self-governing."

"You see?" Carada said to Nathaka. "I offer them what they wish, and they refuse."

"We do not wish to be ruled by aquatics, or anyone else," Urloy-ka snarled. "We can do that ourselves."

"Have you forgotten about the civil war presently raging on your planet?" Carada asked him. "If someone does not step in and take charge, you will *kill* yourselves long before the water dries up."

"Nearly every species experiences civic turmoil when great change comes upon them," Shon said. "War cannot always be avoided, but fighting one does not indicate the lack of quality leadership. In fact, wars often result in a long period of peace, as leaders and their people learn from their mistakes."

"I have provided a viable solution to all the issues at this table, Delegate Valtas. What do you propose as an alternative?" Carada demanded.

"Help each other through exchanges rather than concessions," Shon said. "Ninra is rich in mineral ores, many of which the Skartesh will need to build their colony. The Skartesh may teach their methods of agriculture, which will give the Ninrana the ability to raise crops with minimal irrigation and reduce some of their dependency on water."

Urloy-ka nodded. "We would be willing to participate in such an exchange. But that does not solve our need for water, or the Skartesh's need for their own settlement."

Shon turned to Nathaka. "There are a number of moons around Kevarzangia Two that could provide a colony for the Skartesh, and a testing site for the technology to replenish Ninra's water supply. Since your species cannot live off-planet, you will never be able to use them. However, the war is not over, and K-2 needs strong allies. Skartesh warriors would defend their settlement and your world."

"So would the Ninrana," Urloy-ka said.

Nathaka appeared taken aback. "We came to these negotiations seeking peace among our species."

"The best peace," Shon told him, "is one that is well protected."

The 'Zangian delegate nodded slowly. "I would have to speak to our Elders, but if there are no objections—"

"I object," Carada said. "You are forming a triad alliance which completely cuts out Ylydii involvement, and I will not have it."

Shon had been expecting this. "You are not being deliberately excluded, Lady Ambassador," he lied. "But what can you offer to help enhance his plan?"

"You would allow the Skartesh and Ninrana to operate without any management, when I feel sure that both species have every intention of taking over this system. All they need are the means to do so. They must be closely monitored by species who do *not* wish to invade planets that do not belong to them."

"Such supervision *is* a type of invasion, Lady Ambassador," Shon told her. "Given the history of the Ninrana and Skartesh, extending such trust may seem perilous. Yet if we do not take risks, we cannot change, and we cannot grow."

"You are a male, Major Valtas. A violent, deceitful male who has participated in selfish and meaningless acts of aggression. It is our view that enough destruction, death, and chaos have been wrought by the male-dominated species in this system."

"I object to bringing gender into this," Nathaka said. "Cultural differences have no place here."

"It is time someone placed the blame where the blame belongs." Carada moved into a vertical position in the water. "The Ylydii are willing to teach you how to live in peace, as we do, but you cannot be allowed to run free. As younglings obey their mothers and grandmothers, so you, too, must be brought into the center of the circle. It is the only sure method to keep you from harming yourselves until you gain the maturity and experience to curb your hormonal tendencies."

Urloy-ka rose. "Several centuries ago, females on my world were not allowed to assume positions of authority. We considered them too simpleminded and emotional to make sound judgments. We have since learned that both males and females are necessary to a healthy and balanced society. Gender bias no longer exists on Ninra."

Carada's mouth peeled back into a sneer. "A healthy and balanced society of cannibals."

"Excuse me, Lady Ambassador, but did your last meal die of natural causes?" Shon asked.

The big Ylydii female gave him a nasty look. "It did not beg me to spare it."

The door panel opened to admit Burn and several of the 'Zangian guards in uniform. "Excuse the interruption, Major, but we need you out at the breeding caverns."

"What's happened?"

"Two guards are missing from their posts, and there are signs of violence." Burn looked grim. "We don't know what attacked them, but from the blood in the water, it probably killed them."

*   *   *

"Dr. Selmar, what you're proposing to do is dangerous. Once accomplished, the results would be irreparable." The image of the League xenobiologist wavered as the signal scattered for a moment, and then resharpened. "Have you considered other options?"

The idea had come to Teresa in the middle of the night, when she had woken from a nightmare in which Dair had given birth to a mogshrike. Feeling more useless than she ever had, she had wept and paced the floor and cursed the universe for making her who she was and Dairatha a stubborn, blind fool. She had felt wretched beyond belief, until a thought popped into her head that was so outrageous it nearly made her question her sanity.

It was having the same effect on the League's SEAL project manager.

"I know what I'm asking you to do, Dr. Wupga," she told the screen. "I also invented alterforming, so I know better than anyone precisely what's involved here."

"It would have to be done off-planet," Wupga warned. "The procedure violates the current colonial ban on alterforming, and I will not put myself or my staff at risk of detainment."

Of course he wouldn't. Never mind what she was going to have to sacrifice. "I understand. There is an aquatic medical facility on Qi-iq, about half a light-year from K-2. All you need do is bring the surgical team; I'll provide the necessary tissue and organs and so forth."

Wupga wasn't convinced. "Forgive me, but I believe such harvesting is also illegal on your world now."

"Presently, yes. However, before the ban was made into law, I was able to salvage and cryonically preserve enough tissue, organs, and bones to do a hundred such procedures." She had never considered using them for this purpose, but the only way to advance science was to keep an open, fluid attitude. An attitude that had to go both ways, even if this procedure could not.

"You do not feel a conflict of interest here?" Wupga asked. "Do you know how people will regard you after this is done?"

She would be despised and reviled, but not by anyone she cared about. The people she loved would understand her motives. If they didn't . . . "It doesn't matter."

"Very well. Please notify me when you have a target date and transport arranged, and I will assemble my team and meet your party on Qi-iq."

"Thank you, Doctor." Teresa grabbed the edge of the console as the ship lurched, and the sound of the shore lines being retracted buzzed outside the cabin.

"We're ready to launch, Terri," Noel called from the helm. "Would you like to take her out?"

Teresa terminated the relay, encrypted her notes, and saved everything to her personal database before walking out of the cabin. "I think you should do the honors, Captain Argate."

Noel grinned at her. "Take a seat, then, and fasten your harness."

The *Briggs* was the sleekest long-range expedition vessel Teresa had ever boarded. Designed to function under any sailing conditions, the ship's gleaming arutanium deck stretched ten meters wide and twenty meters in length, with a Haazen free-form hull that could be altered to cruise, break through ice floes, or ride the wildest of waves. Outfitted with the newest League tech, the ship also carried four roomy surface inflatables and a sea-to-air shuttle, which could be used to evacuate the entire ship's complement and an additional twenty under rescue conditions.

Teresa didn't know any of the crew, made up of MRD veterans who had served with Noel, but found them to be like most crews, a fairly taciturn bunch. On the other hand, the staff members she had selected to come on the 'shrike hunt were brimming with enthusiasm.

"Have you been to the observation deck?" one of her researchers asked earlier. "The hull walls are completely transparent from stem to stern. It's as if they put engines on the URD and launched it."

Noel took position in the command tower and slipped his hands into the master control grips as he powered up the ship's engines. "Here we go."

They were launching out of the same inlet where they hoped to lure a 'shrike, so the hull was currently retracted to its flat, reef-skimmer form. As soon as they cleared the delicate formations and were in the open sea, Noel changed the hull to a pointed, wave-breaking plow.

Teresa checked the console in front of her seat, which displayed the keel's depth scanners. They had clear water ahead of them, and the twin pulse-screw engines were bringing the ship up to optimum speed. The wind whipped her hair back, salting it with spray from the bow plumes, and she felt a laugh bubble up in her throat. She had stayed too long on land; out here was the wonderful sense of true freedom that she hadn't even realized she missed so much.

Two streamlined forms, one dark, one light, breached through the starboard wake and dove back into the depths. Both were wearing special thermal wraps to boost their protection against the colder water of the open sea.

"There are Jadaira and Onkar," Noel called back to her. "I was wondering if they'd show up."

Teresa had, too. She knew that Dair had gone to confront her father, and she hadn't been all that sure that her stepdaughter would keep her promise to help with the hunt afterward. The 'Zangians were as fiercely loyal to their parents as they were to their natal pods.

I'm the only mother Dair has ever known, she told herself, fighting a new wave of guilt. *She knows I'm right, and that's why she chose to be loyal to me.*

As soon as Noel eased back the engines to cruising speed, Teresa unfastened her harness and joined him in the command tower. "I'll go below and monitor the mass tracker," she told him. "Once I lock on to a 'shrike, I'll signal Dair and Onkar. I want them out of the water before we release the bait. They are strictly for backup at the extension wall when we return to the inlet."

"Ten minutes into the expedition, and you're already worrying something will go wrong," Noel teased.

"Habit. I've been doing it since the day my kid was born," she told him. On impulse she leaned over and kissed his cheek.

He touched the spot with one hand. "What was that for?"

"For saving the people I love, and for not being such a selfish dolt anymore." She looked back, but she could no longer see the coast. "We're really going to do this. Catch one of these things." She shook her head.

Noel's smile faded. "Don't tell me you're having doubts at this stage of the game."

"That's just it. It's not a game." She dragged a hand through her hair. "This is as real as it gets, Noel. People's lives are on the line. So is the future of an entire species."

He nodded. "Then let's get to work."

Graleba kept her word to Burn and hovered and questioned Liana until she thought she might utter a continuous pulse of shrieking frustration.

Are you hungry? Shall I clean you? The older Ylydii made as if to touch her fins. *If you are still cold—*

I am not hungry, or dirty, or cold, she told her attendant. *I do not need a grandmother.*

I know you do not, my lady. Graleba gave her a hurt look. *I was so worried when that 'Zangian brought you back. Your fins were covered with ice. Do you know that you might have died out there?*

Yes, she might have, no thanks to the 'Zangian.

If only a 'shrike had found her before Burn had. All she had wanted was a fair exchange, and a swift end to her misery. Was it so much to ask? Now she would be watched and followed and controlled every moment she spent on this world.

Everything Liana had done had been for nothing.

Graleba stayed with her until the night guard came, and only then did she reluctantly agree to go to feed and rest. *I will return in the morning, my lady. Sleep well.*

Liana, who had been restlessly circling the chamber, said nothing. There was nothing to say, but at least now she could be alone with her thoughts. Thoughts of the one, of what could not be said, of the utterly useless thing she had been reduced to.

No, not yet.

If she was lucky, the guard might not be as vigilant as Burn. Liana edged toward the opening of the chamber, trying not to disturb the water. She could see the outline of him—another huge male—and stopped breathing in as she eased around the corner behind him. He was paying no attention, and if she allowed herself to drift all the way to the bottom, surely her coloring would blend—

Without turning around, the guard said, *Going somewhere?*

Liana froze, and then darted back into the chamber. And then darted back out again to face him. *What are you doing here?*

Preventing yet another act of idiocy, Burn said. He inspected her. *Recovered from the last one, have you? Well, my lady, you can haul your little tail back in there, because you're not getting past me.*

Her gillets bristled. *You are offensive.*

Offensive is better than stupid. He cocked his head. *Maybe I should petition the summit and see if they'll make me the next leader of Ylyd.*

Liana started back into the chamber before circling back to him. *I do not require a night guard who disparages my government and my person. You are dismissed.*

I don't take orders from you.

In that moment, she wanted to kill him. *I am your superior.*

You probably are, but that doesn't matter. It's me, he said, and pointed toward the surface, *or a week in a tank. You choose.*

Liana surged forward and hit him as hard as she could. Burn didn't flinch, didn't grunt, and to add insult to injury, didn't even move. *I don't need you,* she told him in her coldest voice, *and I'm not afraid of you. Go away.*

Burn lifted one of his fins and Liana closed her eyes, waiting for the blow. It never came.

The ends of his fins had been altered to function more like humanoid hands, with articulated digits that mimicked fingers. These he threaded through the gillets on one side of her face, very gently, and lifted until she opened her eyes and looked directly into his.

You can beat me bloody if you like, but I will never hurt you. I will never let you hurt yourself.

Everything hot and tight and outraged inside her collapsed into a muddle. She wanted to nuzzle him, and take refuge against his warmth again, and stay there until all the storms in her life had passed. And she couldn't.

Please, Burn. If orders wouldn't work, perhaps demeaning herself and begging might. *Please go away. Please leave me alone.*

No, Liana. He put one of his fins across her back and led her into the chamber. *If you want anything, I'll be right outside. Rest now.*

"Honey." Ana closed the door panel. "I'm home."

Liam looked up from the medical chart he was reading and frowned. "Is the summit over? I thought you had another week."

"It isn't. Norash decided that the most overworked and underappreciated official presiding over the summit should take the night off." She set down her case and held out her hands. "Come and appreciate me before I fall unconscious."

"I don't know whether to kiss you, or admit you for exhaustion." He came over and, after making a show of checking her pulse, brushed her mouth with his. "Dare I ask how things are progressing?"

"We're making a little headway, despite Ambassador Carada's best efforts to derail every discussion. She's been in high dudgeon since her daughter blundered into the outer currents. Two 'Zangian sentries disappeared three days ago while they were guarding the Ylydii; Major Valtas thinks they may have been attacked and killed." She sighed. "Did you do the smart thing and not check messages?"

"No, I was stupid. Three hundred or so signals came in just today. Two hundred and ninety-nine are mostly bureaucratic nonsense, but there is one I think you should hear."

Ana sighed and went to the companel, where Liam had queued a signal.

"What's wrong with Teresa's lab chief?" she asked, and then answered herself. "Oh, right, T'Kaf went to have a look at that barax colony." She enabled the recorded message and listened as the N-jui chemist described the disturbing changes with the barax and the direction their new hive was taking.

"Send a copy of message T9843 to Security Chief Norash," she told the companel. "Mark urgent, highest priority, and encrypt for his pass code only." She glanced at Liam. "Does spicewine induce insomnia?"

"Not unless they've changed the ingredients."

"Good." She went to the prep unit and prepared a server for each of them, and then went to sit with Liam on the sinfully comfortable couch. "To invading insects," she said, lifting her spicewine in a toast.

"To the availability of competent exterminators." He clinked the edge of his server against hers. "T'Kaf sent a wrill specimen over to me and asked me to look at it. It was riddled with some sort of parasites that aren't Hlagg and can't be identified by our species database. I sent it down to Pathology for our bright new resident Omorr to have a look. We'll have to isolate them and find out what they are before they attack the aquatic population."

"One by land, one by sea." Ana took a large swallow of wine and slipped off her footgear. "Do you ever think about transferring to someplace a little safer to live? Say, the Hsktskt homeworld?"

"Before we start packing, we'd better find out why the barax intend to undermine and attack the colony." He saw her expression change and put his arm around her shoulders. "Ana, what is it?"

"I had a funny feeling when I read the initial report, but now I think I know." Ana felt chilled. "The barax began building their hive in a gnorra grove."

It didn't take him long to make the connection. "The Core."

"Since barax bore into root systems, there's little doubt they came in contact with the Core." She stared down into her wine as memories of thousands dying crowded into her mind. "Well, that's it, then. Another plague."

"Not necessarily." His hand stroked her upper arm with a soothing motion. "We negotiated directly with the Core. They understood that our removing them from the trees was accidental. They promised to let us live here in peace."

"The barax didn't. If they're under Core control now . . ." She didn't want to complete that thought. "I wish Duncan Reever were still here. He was the only one who could communicate with the Core directly. I'll have to send in orders to have the entire area quarantined until we figure out what to do."

"We can't make it public knowledge," Liam said, his expression grim. "The last time the Core were removed from their environment, they killed thousands of colonists."

"Trying to escape the bodies in which they were trapped," Ana pointed out.

"I don't think anyone will remember that part of it." Liam picked up his planner and made a note on it, then looked down at her. "You need to go to bed."

Ana could barely keep her eyes open, but she had wanted to spend at least a few minutes with him.

"Do you know why our relationship is so perfect? We're both sleeping through it. Hey." She clutched at his shoulders as he swung her up into his arms. "Keep this up and I may just marry you."

"Oh, you'll marry me," he assured her. "You like sleeping with me too much."

Ana didn't think anything could have woken her up that night, until she heard Liam's voice as she had never heard it, hoarse and desperate, calling out in the darkness.

"I won't let her die. She can't die," he was saying, over and over.

Ana sat up and saw that Liam was rigid, his hands fisted in the bed linens, but he was obviously still asleep. The emotions radiating from him were so strong they made her gasp. He was in agony, trapped in a nightmare with a dying woman he couldn't save.

He's dreaming about Rosalind. Very gently she shook him. "Liam, wake up. It's only a dream. Wake up, darling."

Liam came out of the nightmare with a terrible cry, and for a moment looked at her blankly. "Oh, dear God." He jerked her into his arms and held her tightly. "It was so real. I couldn't do anything. I tried, but nothing worked."

Ana knew her lover had lost his first wife to a brain tumor for which she had refused to seek treatment, and had blamed himself for her death ever since. Her heart wrenched as she stroked his back with her hands and tried not to feel jealous. Rosalind was only a memory; she couldn't fight that.

"Forgive me for disturbing you," he said after a long time. "I don't know what brought that on. I haven't had nightmares in years." He looked down at her. "Thanks for waking me up."

"You know, if you ever want to talk about her, I'm always here and ready to listen."

"Her?"

She moved her shoulders. "Rosalind. It might help to resolve things if you talk about it."

"Sweet Ana, I didn't have a nightmare about losing Rosalind." He wrapped his arms around her and shuddered. "It was you. I dreamt that the Core plague returned, and I was standing in the hospital, watching you slip away. Some fool had sealed you in an isolation room and I didn't know the codes. I couldn't get to you."

They had both been among the last colonists infected with the Core, and Ana remembered only too well how many friends she had watched die before her own lungs began to fail. "I want to get married," she said suddenly.

"We will."

"No. I want to get married today. Tomorrow. As soon as we can." She pulled back so she could meet his startled gaze. "I don't care if we have thirty years or three months or seventy-two hours left to live, but I'm going to live them as your wife."

For three nights Liana tried to escape her chamber, but each time she tried Burn was outside, waiting for her. He wouldn't obey her orders, and he only laughed at her threats. She hadn't tried physical violence after her first, pitiful attempt—he was too strong—and so was trapped not only in the chamber, but in the slowly tightening noose of her own frustration. To make matters worse, the strong emotions she had been suffering had shifted her body into full estrus. Ylydii females could mate at any time, but in this state she wouldn't be gentle, and she wouldn't care with whom she mated.

In this state, no male was safe around her.

The sensible thing to do would be to request she be removed to the Ylydii ship, or summon one of the Ylydii males and get it over with. Liana was open, having mated with a select number of males from the synchrony in the past, although she had never caught a pup. Some said it was the affliction; others that she was meant for higher things. Liana had never experienced any pleasure while taking one of the little pipsqueaks, but she had done her duty.

Duty had nothing to do with how she felt as the sunslight disappeared and night came over the 'Zangian sea.

Is there anything more I can do for you, my lady? Graleba asked before she left for the night.

No. Liana retreated to a corner, and didn't move again until her attendant had gone. She would stay inside the chamber tonight and meditate; sometimes that helped calm the rush of need.

Her resolution shattered the moment she tasted Burn's dark, delicious scent on the water.

The 'Zangian hovered outside the chamber in the usual place, his back to her, his eyes moving as he scanned the open water beyond the caverns. For a moment Liana simply watched him, admiring the differences between him and a typical Ylydii male. His size, strength, and speed no longer seemed so bizarre to her, although she had more difficulty accepting his dominant personality.

Are you going to sit there boring holes into my back all night, or will you make a run for it? Burn asked.

Neither. She swam over to his side. *I was just thinking what an excellent female you'd make.*

He eyed her. *That's a compliment?*

On my world, it is.

In that case, I thank you.

You know so little of my people. Liana glided away and allowing her petite veils to unfurl. At the same time she released a few slippery notes of luresong—not enough to captivate, only to tease—and waited for him to come to her.

Burn only looked puzzled. *What is that noise you are making?*

Don't you like it? She turned, showing her primary colors. *We sing it to our males back on Ylyd. They like it very much.* She sang a full scale, spinning the wave around him, and braced herself for the impact of his body. Surely he would hurtle himself at her. Any moment now.

Strange sort of song, Burn said, and blew out some bubbles. *There aren't any words. Is it some kind of pulse?*

No male had ever been able to resist Liana's luresong. Burn's hearing must be impaired.

Not really. It makes you feel things . . . differently. She swam around him, making sure not to touch him. *How do you feel?*

It makes me feel itchy, like when I've been topside too many hours.

So she could not tempt him with luresong. It emphasized what an exceptionally strong will he possessed. There were still her secondary veils, the veils that she never unfurled before any male. *Come into my chamber. I want to show you something.*

It was dangerous. The thin space between showing herself and revealing her affliction could be easily crossed, and estrus was one of the strongest catalysts. The last thing Liana wanted to do was hurt him. At the same time, she ached to let go. To be what she was, and not hold back. Surely he could take some, if not all, of her colors.

Once they were inside the chamber, Liana turned and presented herself in the upright position of unveiling. *Watch.* Slowly, carefully, she unfurled her secondary veils.

Burn remained silent and stared as Liana's extended veils surrounded her in a web of color. He went around her, close but not touching, close enough for her to sense the heat of his blood. At last he faced her again.

What do you think? She knew she was the most beautiful creature he had ever seen. No 'Zangian female could give him this.

I think you have more colors than I realized, he said at last. *They are pretty.* He noticed her gape. *Uh, very pretty?*

Liana furled her veils with snapping, jerking movements. *I can't believe this. This is not happening to me.*

What did I do wrong? Burn seemed puzzled.

I am showing myself to you. Displaying all my beautiful colors and singing for you. And it means nothing to you. Liana wanted to bite him for that.

I said they were pretty. He studied her. *I understand now. That's not what an Ylydii male would do.*

No. A proper male would be overcome by my beauty and luresong. He would respond with uncontrollable desire, and beg me to take him. She whirled around, unable to bear the sight of him. *You've succeeded in humiliating me again. Congratulations, Sublieutenant.*

I don't need to see your colors or hear you sing to want you, Liana.

Liana turned. *What?*

You heard me. He inched closer. *I don't even have to see you to feel desire for you. When I sleep, you're in my dreams. When I move through the water, I can taste you. You're always with me.*

But your females do not show themselves to you.

'Zangian females have their ways. They are very playful just before they come into their time, always teasing the males who interest them. When they are ready for a mate, they run away. The males who desire them chase them down.

They are not afflicted like me, Liana said bitterly.

I don't understand what you mean by afflicted. Burn looked all over her. You look normal. Beautiful. There's nothing wrong with you.

Every generation, a female is born with a green stripe below her eyes, and green in her eyes. Liana pointed to the blaze of emerald color beneath her eyelid. *It's a mark of a royal, and no one knows when or to whom she will be born. She just is.*

I already knew you were royalty. He peered at her face. *But your eyes are black.*

They turn green when—it doesn't matter. There was no way Liana could condense ten thousand years of tradition into a few sentences. *What is important is how it affects life. Being of the green, as I am, brings more than status. A royal female develops differently from other Ylydii fe-*

males. *We are stronger and more intelligent. We are born to rule alone, so we are afflicted with the ruler's curse.*

Which is?

I can't. She turned away. *I've only used it once, and I didn't mean to. No one told me what it would do. I didn't even know I had it.* She would not think of her father. She would not. *Accidents happen, and things that are done cannot be undone. I will not harm you.*

Burn swam closer. *There are stories about Ylydii females. How they mate and then kill their mates. Is that what it is? How it is, for you?*

She gave him a miserable look. *No. A royal does not harm someone she loves. She reserves her power to destroy evil.*

He had drifted closer, and she could feel the heat of his big body again. *So this showing off and singing is all you do when you mate.*

Our males are small and timid. They have to be courted. On impulse she surged against him, wrapping her veils around him, turning him so they were belly-to-belly. *We Ylydii are very good at courting.*

I can see that. Burn rubbed his cheek against hers before he slipped out of her embrace. *Thank you for telling me about the differences.*

I can show you more.

No, my lady. Burn backed away from her. *If you do, I won't be timid, and I won't be satisfied with courtship. If you do not wish to be mated to a 'Zangian with no royal marks or blood, then you must never do this again.*

CHAPTER 15

"*I* have had enough of this." Jadaira tore open the front of her thermal chest wrap. "My mother is too blind to see what that Terran is doing, and by the time she does it will be too late."

Onkar stopped stripping and regarded his mate. "What is the Terran doing?"

She gave him an incredulous look. "Haven't you seen the way he puts his fins all over her? How he's constantly touching and hovering and nudging at her?"

"Captain Argate has hands, not fins, and he is Teresa's friend." Onkar caught the belly wrap she threw at him. "Jadaira, you know that sort of touching among land dwellers is considered casual and acceptable. He's not attempting to court her."

The Terran male's presence had been very conspicuous during the week they had spent in the outer currents. Noel Argate was an early riser, and occupied the vessel's control tower in the early hours of daylight, but turned the helm over to a crew member as soon as the others came on deck.

Onkar had been a little disturbed at first by the unusual amount of attention Argate had given Jadaira's stepmother. The captain, who otherwise was quite professional in his dealings with the crew and researchers on board, showed a marked inclination to spend much of his work and personal time in the company of the Terran woman. Unlike most 'Zangians, Onkar understood the need for monogamy in an intimate relationship, and in his mind had permanently paired Teresa Selmar with Dairatha mu J'Kane. Seeing Argate with her only made Onkar worry again about the future of his bond with Jadaira.

It soon became obvious that Argate was friendly toward Teresa because they shared a common history. Often Onkar heard the Terrans indulging in what they called reminiscing, which seemed to involve remembering the worst moments of one's adolescence and laughing a great deal. He also saw no overt sign of mutual sexual interest, despite the touching, and suspected that while Argate might be amenable to the idea, Teresa was yet preoccupied with the hunt and thoughts of Dairatha.

Jadaira had observed the same things as he had, but her reaction was completely different. She seemed to resent Argate's affection for Teresa, and her dislike of him deepened with each passing day. Now, after seeing the Terran male take Teresa into a loose embrace up on deck, his mate was seething with rage.

"I won't let him do this to her." Jadaira jerked on her flightsuit. "If he can't keep his fins—hands—to himself, then I'll break his wrists."

Onkar blocked her way out of the cabin. "You can't attack the Terran."

"Oh?" She looked up at him. "Are you forgetting your low success rate with stopping me from doing as I wish, and how hard I can thump you in the head?"

He thought she was adorable when she was angry, which was a good thing, because Jadaira was seldom anything else these days. "This is where I must tactfully remind you that you are pregnant and not responsible for the rapid changes in your emotional state. May I do that without you thumping me in the head?"

Her lips—so like Teresa's now—twitched. "No."

Onkar tugged her into his arms. "May I suggest you allow me to speak with Argate about his behavior?"

"Male to male?"

He pressed her close and stroked her gillets. "Concerned spouse to the primary source of my mate's aggravation."

She sighed. "Will you at least bite him once for me?"

Onkar waited for an opportune moment to speak with Argate, which came later that day, just before the two 'Zangians were to make their usual afternoon dive. Teresa was busy outfitting Jadaira with a special sonar harness, which would help extend the range of the ship's scanners. Argate, who had come down from the control tower, went below, and Onkar followed.

"Something you need, Subcommander?" Argate asked him.

Onkar noted the barely perceptible tremor in the Terran male's voice, and wondered if it was fear. His size often intimidated land-dwellers, but he had not realized the captain was one of them. "I would speak to you privately, if you have a moment."

"Of course." Argate led him into one of the larger, unoccupied re-search cabins.

Onkar waited until the Terran had closed the hatch and settled himself on a chair behind the room console. Since sitting was uncom-fortable for a 'Zangian, he remained standing. "You and Teresa Selmar have been spending much time together since we departed the coast."

Argate nodded. "We're old friends."

"Your friendship does not please my mate, but you are probably aware of that." Onkar knew Jadaira had not bothered to conceal her disgust. "She is very protective of Teresa."

"I'm sorry," Argate said. "I didn't realize that I was upsetting her."

"She expressed a desire to bite you several times this morning." Onkar watched the other man's face. "As you Terrans do not use your teeth the way we do, and considering the thinness of your derma, I persuaded her to abandon the idea."

"Now I'm grateful." The Terran rubbed his arm. "What did I do to upset your mate?"

"You have been touching her stepmother. Rather a great deal, and without concealing it," Onkar said. "We 'Zangians reserve that sort of contact for mates. Jadaira still sees Teresa as being her father's mate, so you can understand her anger."

Argate's facial skin turned pink. "Frankly, I don't. Teresa and I are friends. We're both Terran, both unattached. With all due respect, Subcommander, what we choose to do together is our business, not your mate's."

"There are no secrets among 'Zangians." Onkar had a few of his own, but this was not the time to bring up the reasons for being exiled from his own natal pod. "We dwell together all our lives, so our relationships are perhaps more intense and intimate than those of your species."

"Teresa is not a 'Zangian." This time Argate did not show fear, but resentment. "She belongs among her own kind."

Here was the infamous Terran prejudice of which Onkar had heard so much. It did not surprise or disgust him as much as it concerned him. A person who felt superior to all other species could not be trusted in a position of authority, and on this expedition Argate was shown the same deference as Teresa was.

"Where Dr. Selmar belongs should be a place of her choosing," Onkar suggested.

"Teresa is certainly old enough to make her own choices," Argate told him. "I only want what's best for her, and I'll do what I can to make that happen. Why don't you explain that to your mate?"

"Once I thought I could dictate what I thought was appropriate for my mate," Onkar said carefully. "Strong emotion often makes us feel we have the right to do so, in order to protect the objects of our affections. Fortunately, Jadaira taught me that there can be no true love without absolute trust."

"But she has no problem with biting me for caring about Teresa," Argate snapped.

"She does not know you, Captain." Onkar didn't like the quickness of the Terran's temper, or his defensiveness. "If you intend to make a place for yourself in Teresa's life, you should be aware of the affection she and Jadaira have for each other, and respect it. Teresa may not have whelped Jadaira, but she is still her mother, and she still shares a strong bond with Jadaira's father."

"Yes, I heard about him. He dumped Teresa the moment she refused to let him dictate to her." Argate raised one of his eyebrows. "I guess he's not as enlightened about controlling a mate as you are."

"Dairatha mu J'Kane is an honorable male. He has devoted his life to caring for Jadaira and Teresa."

"His relationship with Teresa is over, and so is this conversation." Argate got to his feet. "If your mate can't accept things the way they are, then maybe you two should go back to the coast and leave us alone."

* * *

There was one good thing about being his size, Dairatha mu J'Kane thought as he paced the expedition vessel. He didn't need thermal wraps to stay warm in the frigid outer currents. He was getting hungry, however, for this far out there was only scant feed available. If Teresa and her band of brainless mouth-breathers didn't soon abandon this hunt, Dairatha might have to.

The only pleasure he had was riding under the vessel's changeable hull, which was a thin, biomalleable alloy that was watertight yet easily permeated by sound. Through it he could overhear every conversation held belowdecks. At first he had only listened for Teresa's voice, and any indication that Jadaira and Onkar were entering the water. He had to make himself scarce when his daughter and her mate swam—he didn't want to explain his presence to anyone—but the water was too cold for Jadaira, and they seldom stayed downside long.

The sound of Onkar's voice had drawn his curiosity, however. The former rogue rarely spoke to anyone except Jadaira, and Dairatha found himself curious to know what had Onkar talking so much. Dairatha had risen beneath the ship and listened carefully, following the conversation between his daughter's mate and Argate, the Terran male whom he'd seen several times with Teresa.

He didn't become enraged until he heard Onkar explain why Jadaira felt angry enough to bite Argate. *You have been touching her stepmother. Rather a great deal, and without concealing it.*

Dairatha had been completely unaware of this. Of course, he had to stay out of sight of the deck most of the time, except at night, so that no one spotted him.

Argate had become angry with Onkar. *We're both Terran, both unattached. With all due respect, Subcommander, what we choose to do together is our business, not your mate's.*

So the Terran male was possessive of Teresa. It was interesting that Argate would feel that way, considering that he had only spent a few weeks in her company. Dairatha wondered how he would feel if he found himself dragged over the side of the deck and plunged three hundred feet below the surface. *Will he bubble, or squeak?*

Yet what had brought on a killing rage was what Argate had next said about Dairatha's former mate. *Teresa is not a 'Zangian. She belongs among her own kind.*

Dairatha didn't care if the Terran male was xenophobic or, like the Skartesh, a separatist. Most Terrans despised off-worlders, from what Teresa had told him over the years. What made his hide go black was the implied intention behind Argate's last statement. *She belongs among her own kind.* Argate was her own kind. With Argate was where she belonged.

Dairatha had endured Teresa's jealousy for a decade. He had tolerated it because he knew it was born out of love for him. Now the dark, possessive feelings were coursing through his mind, twisting and boring into his calm. Who did this male think he was, putting his hands on Teresa, laying claim to Teresa?

If Dairatha had had any doubts, they were dispelled by one of the last things the Terran had said to Onkar. *I only want what's best for her, and I'll do what I can to make that happen.*

Argate said all this very briskly, as though it were decided.

It had been years since Dairatha mu J'Kane had challenged another male over a mate. The last time had been a face-off with several 'Zangian males over the right to chase Kyara, and no one had been able to prevail over him. Terrans evidently did not fight over their females, according to Teresa, and when they did it was with words, not teeth or bodies.

With Argate being the size of a pup, there could be no fight, Dairatha decided. He would simply have to kill him.

Two weeks ago Emily would never have abandoned her console to take a meal interval, but now she didn't feel a qualm about switching the channel relayer to auto-reply. She couldn't work around the clock, as Ana Hansen often did, without feeling as if her brain had turned to sludge. After settling several minor administrative disputes among six different species, most of which had been slimy, spiny, and not in-clined to practice tact, she also felt she had earned a break.

Today she stopped at Lisette's Café long enough to pick up the or-der she had signaled over earlier.

"*Bonjour*, Emily." The tall blond woman inspected her. "Your hair looks pretty, but you still wear the same colors every day. Tell these Ad-ministration people we are not all color-blind. They must use some imagination when designing tunics."

Accustomed now to Lisette's bossiness, Emily simply nodded and paid for the meal order. "Were you able to find those mites I asked about?"

"Bollien mites, *oui*. They are uncooked, but I steam the weffer roots a little; they grew dry in shipment." Lisette handed over the neatly packed food containers. "Your Omorr will enjoy them."

"Thanks." Emily looped the pack strap over her wrist. "He's really not my Omorr. I mean, we're just friends."

Lisette smile turned knowing. "I will remind you of this at your wedding."

Hkyrim had told Emily where Pathology was located, but she stopped by the front reception desk at the FreeClinic to sign in. The Aksellan nurse manning the console turned out to be the large black-and-green spider who had been kind to Emily during her first day on planet, and they immediately recognized each other.

"Zo, Terran, how haz it been with you zince lazt we zaw each other?" the nurse asked after issuing her a visitor's badge.

"It's been a dream come true." Not in the way she'd imagined, but Emily was adjusting and gaining new confidence day by day. "I enjoy my work, my supervisor is terrific, and I've made a great friend."

"You zhould make more. Why don't you vizit the Akzellan cooper-ative zometime?" The nurse showed her on a screen map where it was located. "Azk for me, Ylloh, and I will introduze you to my nezt-zizterz."

Other people had told her that, while they were friendly and benign, Aksellans rarely made overtures of friendship toward anyone. Emily felt flattered and a little flustered. "I will, thank you, Ylloh."

Emily made her way to Pathology, where another pleasant nurse directed her to one of the examination rooms. "I can signal Dr. Hkyrim, if you'd rather wait out here."

Doctor? Emily hadn't realized Hkyrim had a medical degree. "No, I'll just pop in and say hello," she said to the nurse.

The corridor leading to the examination rooms smelled of preservative chemicals and antiseptic, and for a moment Emily wondered if her stomach was up to seeing Hkyrim—Dr. Hkyrim, she corrected herself—performing an autopsy. *I've seen him eat, and I've faced his friends. I can stand a little vivisection.*

She pressed the door chime before enabling the panel, and walked in. The chemical odors were much stronger inside the large, white room. Bleeping, chiming, and buzzing sounds came from the mysterious and important-looking devices and panels that lined the walls. The Omorr was working over some sort of analysis rig; looking through a scope at something small and curled in a round clear dish.

"Hard at work, Doc?" she asked.

"Emily." Hkyrim looked up from the scope eyepiece. "You said nothing about visiting me."

"That's why we call it a surprise." She held up the pack of food containers. "Besides, I owe you a working lunch."

"How kind of you. I completely lost track of time." He removed the round, open-topped dish from the analysis rig. "This is a specimen of wrill, from the Western Sea. Dr. Mayer believes it is infected with an unknown parasite."

"But you don't."

"I am not sure what I am seeing." He placed the dish down and added a little fluid to it before sealing a lid over the specimen. "It is the oddest thing. Judging by the damage to its head, it was killed by enlargement of its brain. It swelled so much it broke open the creature's skull." He glanced at her. "Forgive me. My description was not conducive to enhancing your appetite."

"I don't mind." And she didn't, really, as long as she didn't look in the dish. "Are you hungry? Can you take a few minutes break time?"

"Yes, and yes." Hkyrim turned back to pick up the specimen. "I will just put this . . ." He stopped speaking and stared down at his hand.

"I can come back later." Emily made herself look at the dish. The lid was cracked in half, and some of the clear fluid from the dish had spilled onto Hkyrim's hand.

Hkyrim's hand, the membranes of which had turned a dark purple and were swelling.

The meal pack fell from her hand. "What is that doing to you?"

"I don't know, but it is invading my cells. Please give me that vacuum container there," the Omorr said, and pointed to a nearby container. When Emily did, he took it and moved away. The discoloration was creeping up from his membranes and over the skin of his hand. "Seal the door, and don't touch me."

While Emily secured the panel, Hkyrim placed the dish in the container and withdrew his blackened hand before sealing it. Holding the appendage away from his body, he thrust it under the scope and looked at it.

"Emily, bring a lascalpel here." Pain laced his voice. "Quickly."

She looked around wildly. "Where is it? What does it look like?"

"A silver writing device with an emitter tip, next to the chart on the exam bench." Hkyrim moved from the scope to stand beside a large, transparent tank.

Frantically Emily located the lascalpel and brought it to him, but he didn't take it from her. "Should I signal for help?"

"There is not enough time," Hkyrim said. "You must do this for me. I cannot be sure I will stay conscious long enough."

"Do what?"

"Turn on the lascalpel and amputate my hand."

"*What?*"

"Please, Emily. You must do so now, before it spreads into my bloodstream."

"I can't." She stared at the device in her hand and shook her head. "I'll get a doctor—someone who knows how to—"

"Give it to me, then." He held out another hand. "I do not wish to die like this."

"You are *not* going to die." Emily fumbled with the device until she found the enable switch and the emitter glowed bright white. "Where do I cut?"

"Above the infection site, here." He pointed to a spot above the dark swelling, and then held his arm over the tank.

Emily had to stand close to reach the arm, and for a moment thought she might faint. Something touched her cheek—one of his gildrells—and gave her a gentle caress.

"I know you can do this," he murmured.

There was no time to think, only to act. Emily pointed the lascalpel at Hkyrim's arm and switched on the cutting beam. She felt him jerk as the laser sliced through the top layer of his derma. One of his arms clamped around her waist as she reached the four arm bones. It seemed to take forever, but the instrument was precise and efficient. A few seconds later the infected appendage fell from the cauterized stump and dropped into the tank.

What she had done, and the smell of burning flesh, made Emily gag, but she turned off the lascalpel and turned to him. "What do I do now?"

Hkyrim's face was a pinkish-gray and covered with sweat. "Help me seal the tank and go back to the scope."

She supported his weight as they secured the amputated hand, and then helped him over to the exam bench. Only after Hkyrim had thoroughly examined the stump of his arm under the scope did he straighten. "There are no more of them present. You are an excellent cutter, my friend."

Emily caught him as he staggered back and held him up. "Why did you make me do that to you? What was it?"

"Tell Mayer it was nanites," he said, his voice a whisper now. "Signal the Emergency Room. Don't let them open the containers." His eyes rolled back, and he sagged against her.

* * *

Teresa saw twin plumes of water spout into the air off the port bow—a signal from Dair and Onkar that they had found something—and called up to the control tower. "Cut the engines."

After a week of cruising the empty sea Teresa was glad to suit up and climb into the inflatable. The days and nights of being on board and watching the empty monitors had started wearing on her nerves; she wasn't used to spending this much time dry. Noel refused to let her dive, though, insisting on the 'Zangians doing the scouting under the surface.

"It's for the best, Terri," he had told her. "If something happens, they can both jump out of the water and onto the boat fast. You'd be weighed down by your gear."

Teresa was preparing to activate the winch to lower the inflatable over the side when Argate appeared on deck.

"What are you doing?" He looked angry. "We don't know what they've found yet. Let one of the researchers go."

"I'll find out," she called up to him, and switched on the winch before he could stop her.

Onkar and Jadaira swam up beside the inflatable as soon as Teresa released the lines. Both of them looked unhappy.

Dair cleared the water from her gill vents. "We found a wrill island about a quarter kim east of here," she said. "There's a dead mogshrike on it."

Teresa slipped on her headset and relayed this back to the ship's com officer, then asked, "You're sure it's dead?"

Onkar gave her an ironic look. "Quite sure."

Teresa pressed her lips against a smile. 'Zangians had such an instinctive aversion to the injured or dead that usually they would do anything to avoid them. No wonder both of them looked pale as powder.

"Can you hang in long enough to take me to it?" A dead specimen wasn't what she had hoped for, but given their failure to find any live 'shrikes, it might have to suffice.

Onkar slipped one of the inflatable's lines over his sloped shoulder. "I'll guide you there. Jadaira, go back on board the vessel."

"I'm not getting out of the water until you do," Dair told him.

The big male's bicolored eyes shifted to Teresa. "Have I ever expressed my gratitude to you for raising my mate to be so independent and stubborn that her head might as well be made of rock?"

"No, but I'll take that as a thank-you," Teresa said, and laughed as she started up the inflatable's small propulsion unit.

The wrill island wasn't technically an island, but an enormous pile of discarded carapaces; one of the oddities in the outer currents. In certain areas, wrill blooms in molt would swarm and shed simultaneously. Their old exoskeletons would form hills beneath the surface and, where the bottom was shallow enough, would rise above the surface. Eventually the currents would whittle away the pile until it vanished, but until they did, the shells formed a tiny island.

Although Teresa had seen wrill islands in the past, the size of the one Dair and Onkar brought her to made her gawk.

"Good Lord, that has to be a hundred yards across." She could see the dead 'shrike, too —a huge mound beached on the north side of the island. She leaned over toward Onkar. "Bring me right up alongside the carcass."

The two 'Zangians flanked her up to the artificial shore of the wrill island, and then swam away as soon as she had fired an anchor line into the solidly packed shell surface. Teresa didn't blame them; the stench from the dead mogshrike was already making her own stomach turn. She secured the inflatable and climbed out, careful to find her footing on the slippery surface before approaching the carcass.

"Noel, how is the picture on your end?" she asked over her headset, which also held a small lens above her right ear that was transmitting images of everything she looked at back to the *Briggs*.

"Perfect," Argate said over her earpiece, "but I'm pissed off at you for leaving the boat. This is grunt work, Terri."

"I don't mind being a grunt." Teresa circled around the carcass, getting all angles of it while checking for predators. She wasn't worried about the sterbol or *gnaldorf*, which would feed on whatever was hanging in the water. However, there were a few species of carrion mollusks that had shells covered in poisonous spines, and which could crawl out of the waves, and she didn't fancy stepping on one.

"Big mother," Noel said.

"A twenty-five tonner, I think. Carcass appears to be completely intact." She came around to the front side and saw the massive wound that had sheared off most of the 'shrikes head. "Whoops, spoke too soon. Single head wound; ninety-five percent of the upper cranial case is gone, along with the eyes, snout, mouth, teeth and"—she leaned over to look inside the wound cavity—"brain."

"Another 'shrike?"

"Had to be." Teresa studied the 'shrike's abdomen, which was broad and heavy with feed. "Nothing else with a mouth big enough, or that would shear it off like this." Something twitched under the 'shrike's skin. "Stand by."

She brought out a scanner and ran it over the carcass without touching it. The 'shrike was dead, but escaping gases from the decomposition process—always very rapid in aquatic life-forms—might have caused it to twitch. One of her more gruesome instructors back at BioTech had called the process "death farts."

Teresa was taking a reading for bacterial infestation when the belly twitched a second time. This was more like a stretch than a twitch, however. The skin of the carcass actually rose and then deflated.

Could it be . . . Teresa pulled on a pair of gloves to protect her hands before reaching to touch the surface of the 'shrike's belly. A centimeter before she did, the belly swelled outward and bumped her hand.

Or, rather, the fetus inside did.

Teresa backed away. "Noel, this 'shrike was whelping, and the baby is still alive inside her body." She took the blade out of her harness. "I need a tranq gun and a live specimen containment unit over her, pronto." She also had to film every second of this. No one had ever seen a 'shrike give birth, or knew what the process was.

"I'm bringing over another inflatable with the gear we need. Terri, don't try to take it out until I get there," Noel said with some urgency. "Are you sure you don't have any tranq with you?"

"Sorry, I didn't think to bring any. Hang on." A muffled, gnashing sound made her reach up and switch off the audio so she could hear better. The belly skin of the carcass was moving again, but not in the same way, and not as dramatically. She could see the movements beneath it growing less pronounced. At the same time, the gnashing sound continued, almost like a defective drone grinding internal gears.

No one had ever observed a 'shrike birth.

The gear-grinding sound was growing fainter, the circular undulation beneath the skin almost subsiding. Gears. Gears meshed.

Gears had *teeth*.

Mogshrikes were born with teeth and did not nurse, Teresa knew that much. So the infant 'shrike had no use for the mother after birth. And since mature 'shrikes would eat anything that moved, including other shrikes . . .

"Noel," she said. "You've got to hurry. I think it's trying to eat its way out of the mother's belly."

"We're having problems with the propulsion unit here," Argate transmitted back. "I need ten minutes."

"It'll suffocate by then."

"That's all right," Argate told her. "We'll take both bodies back with us. Stand by, Terri."

Teresa looked at the carcass. The infant's movements were pitiful, and it was clearly tiring. Without tranqs, she could never try to bring it onto the ship, or even get in the water with it. Noel was right; they'd recover both bodies and take them back to the URD for study.

Jadaira's birth had been like this. Kyara had actually died in labor, and Teresa had been forced to cut open her friend's body to get the little white pup out.

Without thinking too much about it, she approached the carcass and dragged her blade along the outer edge of the area that had shown movement.

A puff of gas rose into her face, making her grimace. *God, this thing stinks. If I was stuck in there, I'd eat my way out, too.* She extended the incision as far as she dared, and then heard the grinding sound grow louder and stepped back again.

The slice she had made through the 'shrike's tough hide widened into a gap, through which the end of a small, blunt snout protruded. Blood and fluid sprayed out at her as the infant exhaled and emitted a high, bleating sound. The snout pushed out until it sank glittering, baby-size 'shrike teeth into the edge of the incision and tore it wider.

"Mom, what is it?" Jadaira called from the other side of the island.

Teresa measured the distance to the water. If the 'shrike was able to eat its way out of the mother's body, it was more than ten yards to the edge of the shell pile. It had no means of locomotion on land, and it would suffocate without water.

She couldn't wait until Noel worked out the problem with the other inflatable. "Dair, you and Onkar get up here, right now," she called to them. When she saw them climbing out of the water, she turned to the carcass and plied her blade again, this time creating a lateral incision the length of the abdomen.

For a moment a bloody membrane bulged out of the long gap Teresa had cut, and then it burst, spewing fluid, placenta, and an infant 'shrike the same size as Teresa onto the shells.

"Whoa." Teresa scurried back, but she couldn't stop staring at the newborn. It had the same coloring as its mother, but the body appeared deformed. Its mouth was wider but shallower, and it had no claspers. The domed shape of the upper head and the longer tail and fins were more like those of warm-blooded aquatics.

Teresa forgot about the malformed body parts as the baby 'shrike began snapping and writhing, choking on the air it couldn't breathe.

"Damn it." She looked over her shoulder at the incredulous 'Zangians. "Help me drag it to the edge." Neither of them moved. "*Now.*"

The infant 'shrike went still as soon as Teresa grabbed its tail. Small eyes rolled up as it looked at Jadaira and Onkar, who flanked it and took hold of its pectoral fins.

"Watch the denticles," Teresa told them as they began to haul it toward the water. The 'shrike didn't move or struggle against them, but lay limp, its gill vents straining for water that wasn't there.

"Teresa, why are we doing this?" Onkar demanded, even as he pulled. "We should kill it."

"No." She hated mogshrikes, hated what they did to other aquatics, but she wouldn't be an executioner. "It deserves a chance to live, just like anyone."

"It's not a person, Mom," Dair said, straining against the 'shrike's weight.

"That's what the pod said about you," Teresa said, panting the words. "They wanted me to let you die, and I knew you probably would, but I couldn't do it." She knuckled some sweat out of her eyes. "Why isn't it fighting us?"

"Maybe it knows you want to help it." Dair grimaced. "I hope it smells better in the water."

Onkar sniffed the air. "That isn't the 'shrike."

Between the three of them, they managed to drag the baby down to the water.

"Push it in," Teresa said, "but don't get into the water. I don't want this thing taking a chunk out of you."

The 'shrike's eyes were rolled back into its head now, and its gill vents barely fluttered. Yet the instant water touched its hide, it began writhing, trying to work itself toward the sea.

Dair and Onkar got behind the 'shrike and, with Teresa, shoved it over the last few feet of shells and into the water.

"There it goes," Teresa said, straightening and resting her hands on her hips to watch the 'shrike as it turned to swim off. "We did a good thing, guys. Thanks."

"I'll remind you of this the next time there's an attack on the pod," Dair said.

"I'm sure you will." Teresa shaded her eyes with one hand but didn't see any sign of Noel in the second inflatable. "What's taking them so long?"

"Teresa." Onkar placed one fin edge on her shoulder. "Look at the 'shrike."

The baby wasn't swimming away. It was hovering near the edge of the wrill island, and it was looking up through the water at Teresa.

"Go." She made a forward gesture with both arms. "Shoo."

The 'shrike's eyes narrowed, but it didn't move away. Instead, it seemed to be inspecting them.

Onkar, who was breathing in deeply, turned around and walked a short distance away from the two women. He dropped down and began digging into the wrill shells, then rose. "Dr. Selmar, please come over here."

Teresa could hardly drag herself from the sight of the well-behaved 'shrike, but something in Onkar's tone made her go. She joined him at the hole he had dug in the shells. "What is it?"

Onkar bent and lifted a dark gray piece of dorsal fin out of the hole he had dug. "This belonged to a 'Zangian. It's what I've been smelling since I climbed up here."

Teresa went down on her knees and dug through the top layer of shells with both hands. Under the molt there were more 'Zangian body parts. "Here's another dorsal fin, and a piece of a fluke." She looked up at him. "These might be the two guards who went missing."

"Why would they be so far away from the coast? Who buried them under all these shells?"

Teresa shook her head, then heard the sound of an inflatable approaching and shaded her eyes. "There's Noel. We'll recover the remains and bring them back to the ship, Subcommander."

They walked down to the shore, where Dair and the baby 'shrike were contemplating each other.

"It just sits there as if it *wants* to watch us," Dair told them. "It's not natural."

The 'shrike lifted its head out of the water, opened its mouth, and uttered a sound. Teresa didn't understand it, but the sound had a violent affect on Dair and Onkar, who stumbled back from the edge of the water.

"What?" She looked back at them. "What is it?"

"A pulse." Dair clapped her hands over her ears, as if she meant to block it out. "It pulsed."

Teresa frowned. "Mogshrikes don't produce pulses. They don't have vocal cords."

"That one does," Onkar told her.

CHAPTER 16

*L*iam Mayer finished his examination and checked the scanner display. "Other than missing a hand, and evidently having a spine made of pure arutanium, you are in excellent health, Dr. Hkyrim."

"I am glad to hear it." The Omorr moved to sit on the edge of the medical berth and examined the stump of his arm. "It is odd. I know it is gone, but at times I can still feel it there."

"Phantom pains," Mayer told him. "They'll come and go over time." He looked across the berth at the willowy Terran woman standing on the other side. "That was a very brave thing you did, Ms. Kim."

Emily Kim only went to the view panel to stare outside.

Hkyrim watched his Terran friend. What he had forced her to do was barbaric, and he knew she had been utterly terrified. She was still pale, her eyes haunted, and she had spoken very little since helping the medics bring him to emergency services.

"Your theory proved correct, Doctor," Liam told Hkyrim. "The wrill specimen was infected by nanites. We're keeping the specimens sealed until Enviro can figure out how to neutralize them."

"I believe from what I observed and experienced that the nanites are DNA resequencers," he told Dr. Mayer. "Programmed to alter only aquatic life-forms."

Liam frowned. "Why would they attack you, then?"

"Ancient Omorr were sea-dwellers. We still carry some of our ancestors' aquatic characteristics, such as our gildrells. It likely sampled my DNA and decided I was an aquatic." Hkryim reached for his tunic. "I would like to return to my living quarters, if I may be excused from working the remainder of my shift."

Emily whirled around. "Are you crazy? Get back in that berth. My God, Hkyrim, you just lost a hand."

"I have two others." He glanced at Mayer. "Doctor, would you excuse us for a moment?" Liam nodded and departed. "Emily, I apologize for the discomfort I caused you. It was not my intention and I will always regret having placed you in such a position."

She stared at him. "You're apologizing to me. Hkyrim, I came here to have lunch with you, and ended up cutting *off* your *hand*."

"I would have preferred the meal," he admitted, "but once I realized I was infected with nanites, there was little alternative."

She scrubbed her hands over her face. "You are completely nuts, do you know that?"

He dropped his tunic and went to her, using his two uninjured arms to encircle her waist. "You saved my life, and very possibly the lives of many others."

"Hooray."

He pulled her close. "I was afraid, too, Emily."

"Oh, God, I never want to feel that scared again," she whispered, resting her cheek against his chest.

From the wetness Hkyrim felt, and the sounds he heard, he knew Emily was crying. He held her for a long time, stroking her hair with one hand, until the sounds and the wetness tapered off.

She lifted her face. "Don't you ever ask me to amputate your hand again, do you hear me?"

"I will do my best, Emily," he promised.

She looked at his stump. "I guess there's no way they can clean it and sew it back on."

"Not safely."

"What were those things?"

"Nanites. A bioorganic mechanism that measures only a billionth of a meter in size. Nanites are a type of drone that functions at the atomic and subatomic level. They can be programmed to do many things, such as duplicate, construct, deconstruct, and resequence atoms."

"Microscopic drones?" She appeared astonished. "Why would someone build them that small?"

"Medical application of nanotechnology is still in its infancy in many parts of the galaxy, but we have begun using them as probes and to treat certain diseases. We design viruses now that attack and destroy other viruses and diseased cells, as well as build healthy replacement organs from diseased organ cells." Absently he used a gildrell to wipe the last tears from her cheeks. "These are not medical nanites, however. I believe they are DNA resequencers—nanites programmed to alter a life-form through direct manipulation of its DNA. It is a type of nanotech that is illegal to create or use."

"Is that what they did to the wrill? They altered it?"

"No; that is why I didn't know what they were when I examined the specimen. The nanites were lodged in the wrill's brain, but they had not altered its cells or DNA." He recalled the wrill's burst skull and wondered if the nanites had been responsible for the damage. "It was only when they attacked me did I make the connection."

Emily frowned. "But if the nanites didn't reprogram the wrill or whatever they do, why was it infected with them?"

"It is probably being used as a carrier, to deliver the nanites to the intended victims." Hkyrim looked out through the view panel and saw a group of 'Zangian pilots crossing the FreeClinic commons. "Highly evolved aquatics."

I would like to wish you well, Administrator Hansen, Carada said after Ana had delivered the standard opening greeting for the summit meeting. *I am told that you are to be, what is it called again, Miglan?* The Ylydii bent to hear her assistant's mutter. *Ah, yes. Married. To whom is this commitment being made?*

Ana politely gave the ambassador the name of her fiancé, Dr. William Mayer.

A healer? And you are in Administration. Carada seemed amused. *Well, you may have little in common, but if you can be satisfied with one male for the remainder of your existence, I suppose it is an acceptable prac-tice. You certainly won't ever have to wonder who sired your pups.*

Shon saw Ana's brief, startled reaction disappear as she graciously accepted the ambassador's congratulations and continued on to the schedule of discussion topics planned for the session.

I am not finished speaking, Carada said, interrupting the Terran woman. *I found this concept of monogamous commitment quite interest-ing. It has definite applications in other areas that concern us.*

Now Shon was startled, but not for long.

We have been at an impasse since coming to this planet, Carada con-tinued, apparently oblivious to the three-way alliance that the other members of the summit had been gradually forming. *I did not come here to waste my time arguing over issues; I intend to solve them. I see now that the application of fresh ideas and a new direction are the only sensible ways to proceed and to accomplish anything while we are here.*

Nathaka, the 'Zangian delegate, gave the other aquatic a puzzled look. *What do you mean?*

"I think that is very generous of you, Lady Ambassador, to bring such an open mind to the negotiations," Ana said. "I'm very flattered that my engagement inspired you as well. Now, if you would introduce these new ideas of yours as we bring up each topic—"

There is no need to wait, the Ylydii assured her. *My proposal is a sim-ple one, very easy to understand.* She turned to face Urloy-ka. *The Nin-rana need water, and the Ylydii will provide the technology to replenish the planetary water tables, along with enough water stores to enable your sur-vival until your world recovers.*

"What do you wish in return?" the obviously suspicious Ninrana delegate asked.

A symbol of your commitment to lasting peace between Ninra and Ylyd, Carada told him. *You are the leader of your world, are you not?*

"I am the chief over all the Red Basin tribes," Urloy-ka acknowl-edged. "That is the majority of the population on Ninra."

Excellent. Then you will marry my daughter, Liana.

Before Urloy-ka or any of the delegates could react to Carada's proposal, one of the Ylydii males darted to the front. *You cannot give her to him! He will* eat *her!*

Shon had never noticed the little male before, but there was no mistaking the ferocity of his response. *One of the Lady Liana's admirers, no doubt.*

Silence, Carada said, shoving back the smaller male. To the Ninrana, she said, *This will be a political union between our worlds, with equality of position for both partners. As spouse to the ruler of Ylyd, you would have involvement in our government. As spouse to you, Liana would have involvement in yours.*

"And this is all you want in return for the tech and the water?" the Ninrana demanded. "A marriage?"

I prefer to think of it as a permanent and lasting alliance, Ambassador Urloy-ka. I will be quite happy to sign a contractual agreement as to the specific terms. However, be aware that I do not offer my child lightly, nor do I intend to languish about for another week while you argue with the others over it. Accept or refuse, and do it now.

Ana gave Shon a stricken look. She knew, as he did, that it was just the sort of solution that would appeal to the desperate Ninrana.

"What about the Skartesh?" Shon asked. "Are those I represent to be cast aside and ignored while such preferential treatment is shown to the Ninrana?"

Carada made a dismissive gesture. *You have already negotiated having your colony established on the moon belonging to the 'Zangian delegate. We will leave you to work out this matter with them.*

She is mine! The small Ylydii male surged forward. *I won't let you throw her away on a mouth-breather!*

Carada's expression became long-suffering as she turned to two of the Ylydii female guards. *Remove the noisemaker at once.*

Shon had no choice but to do what he could to derail Carada before Urloy-ka responded. "The Skartesh object to the prejudiced nature of this proposal, which will not benefit two of the species involved in this summit. We strongly insist that it be retracted at once."

"No need of that, Major," Urloy-ka said. "She is right, your species has already found their place on the 'Zangians' moon." He looked at the Ylydii. "Very well, Ambassador Carada. As long as the contracted terms are acceptable to me, I will marry your daughter, and you will give my people what we need to restore our world."

When Fokrej appeared at the opening to Liana's cavern, Graleba tried to send him away. *My lady is resting now, male. You may come back later.*

Later she will not be here, the male said. Two of his gillets were torn, and his snout was swollen, as if he had been beaten. *Later he will come for her, and she will be taken away.*

Liana came out into the light. *What are you babbling about, Fokrej?*

Carada has struck a bargain. The smaller Ylydii male could not seem to keep still. He darted back and forth in the center of the cavern. *After all I have done for her, she defers to that dirt-dweller.* His stunted veils thrashed the water. *Marriage. To an alien mouth-breather. Is she insane?*

Liana looked at Graleba, who only finned confusion. *Fokrej, what has Carada done?*

Your mother has formed a political alliance with the Ninrana. She is giving you to him. He went to Graleba and shoved her toward the opening of the cavern. *Get out. Get out!*

Frightened by the uncharacteristic behavior, the attendant fled.

Fokrej turned back to Liana. *I will help you, but you must come with me.*

Come with you?

I have a ship. I will take you back to Ylyd, to the synchrony. I will protect you from her and that filthy mouth-breather. He advanced toward her. *You know it is what you want. You are of the green. I am the only one who can satisfy you now.*

Liana braced herself for a blow. *No.*

You know she will make you do it, and you would spend the rest of your life on a desert planet, Fokrej told her. *A planet where they have been eating off-worlders for centuries. If they didn't dine on you, you would have to live in a tank. Like an animal on display. Forever, my lady. Forever.*

But you would take care of me, I suppose, she said. *When you are not torturing me.*

I would give you what you want. I am fertile. I understand your needs. I would give you time to whelp, and then we would go back to our play. He displayed his barbs for her. *I am the only one with a heart as dark as yours is, Liana. Only I can please you. We will go back to Ylyd and take refuge among the synchrony. They will never permit her to come near you again.*

Liana felt sick, and backed slowly toward the opening. *No.*

You will come with me now. Fokrej whipped his fins across her face.

Something inside her snapped. Something that had been held rigid and unbending for too long. *NO!*

Liana hurtled at the smaller male and drove him into the cavern's rough rock wall. His body bounced off the hard surface, but before he could swim away she barreled into him again. And again, and again. When he hung limp and motionless, she fled the cavern.

She would not allow him to touch her again. She would never go to Ninra. It was decided, finished, over. She could not do this anymore.

Liana swam as fast as she could, streaming over the caverns and turning until she was on a direct course for the shore. There she would beach herself, on some remote stretch of sand where no one would find her body until it was too late. If it was not a fair exchange in the eyes of the goddess, or the creator, or whoever had chosen to give her this existence, it was too bad. She was through with all of it.

Two 'Zangian males came up on either side of her. They were pacing her and trying to say something to hear. Liana abruptly changed direction and darted away from them. She nearly collided with a third male, who had been following her from behind.

Get away from me, she said.

Incredibly, the male gave her a look of blatant interest. *You are on the small side. Are you fully grown for your kind?*

Liana flipped around him and swam toward clear water. The water on either side of her soon filled with other 'Zangians, all males who seemed to be trying to catch her eye. A few fell off pursuing her to tussle with each other, which was even more confusing. Soon Liana couldn't find a way out of the mass of eager males crowding around her.

Why doesn't she run?

I don't know. She's not 'Zangian.

Beautiful, isn't she? I will have her.

No, I want this one. Our pup will be unique.

A huge, dark form knocked aside several males and came up on Liana's side. It was Burn, and he was furious.

What are you doing?

Trying to get away from them, she snapped. *Why won't they leave me alone?*

They smell you. Everyone can. And you're swimming too fast. Burn closed his eyes for a moment before turning to look at the other males. *She is mine. You will not chase her anymore.*

One of the bigger males came toward him. *I don't believe you. I challenge you.*

Burn swam at him so swiftly that the other male was flipped head over flukes before he could blink. The big 'Zangian used his tail to knock into the male a second time before he backed away. He then turned and looked at the others. *If you think I won't kill for her, think again.*

His flat warning wiped the excitement from the faces of the other males, whose circle around Liana gradually widened.

Burn came back to her. *You have to leave now. Don't swim fast, and don't go back to the caverns. Go anywhere but the caverns.*

I'm not leaving you to fight them alone.

They won't challenge me. He gave the other males a contemptuous look. *You'll be safe. I'll be right behind you.*

She didn't want to be safe. *What happens if I go back to the caverns?*

You can't go there, not until we both calm down. The wildness in his eyes matched how she felt. *The caverns are where we mate. If you go there, and I catch you, I'll take you.*

Liana glided against him. *That's what you want, isn't it? Just like them.*

Yes. No. Don't touch me. He looked angry now. *I can't help it. Swim somewhere else. Anywhere else.*

I don't want to swim anywhere else. Liana backed away from him. *Let's see how fast you are, 'Zangian.* She turned and shot off with the current toward the breeding caverns.

Burn knew there was trouble as soon as he came back from the feeding grounds with his dam, and males started streaking past them without even bothering to acknowledge them.

You see how they treat us, Znora said. She had been complaining, as usual, about everything the other 'Zangians did or didn't do. *We could be exiled rogues for all the attention we are given. Byorn, if I am ever to recover our proper positions within the pod, you must abandon this military nonsense and stay home.*

I've been staying home. Burn turned around and tracked the 'Zangians, who were all swimming in one direction. The odd thing was, they were all male. *Why are they doing that?*

Znora looked and immediately blocked his view with her body. *Never mind. Let us go down the coast. I feel in need of a long swim.*

You hate going on long swims. He moved around her to have another look. *Where is everyone going?*

You are too young to see males making fools of themselves like this. Znora gave him an annoyed, maternal nip. *Come along now.*

Burn had never hurt his mother in his life, but he was seriously tempted to return the favor. *Tell me what they're doing or I'll go find out for myself.*

It is a breeding frenzy. Males do that when a female flaunts herself too much. Znora finned her contempt. *Now that off-worlder female will take a 'Zangian pup with her back to her world.*

Off-worlder?

Burn shot around his mother and followed the stream of males. He ignored her command to return and searched the seascape until he saw something like a black-streaked rainbow darting through the throng of males.

Liana.

Burn had never seen 'Zangian males behave in such a strange way, but he knew immediately why they were swarming around Liana. The way she swam was unbearably erotic, as was the scent she was spilling into the water.

Seeing the other males pursuing her as if she were nothing but food infuriated him. It took every ounce of his already shaky self-control not to ram through the pod and knock away every male in his path.

He tried to be patient as he dealt with the other males and Liana. He held them off as he told the young Ylydii how to extricate herself from the situation, and warned her of what not to do. He was forced to admit how close he was to losing control over her, so that she would understand how precarious her situation was. After all, she was Ylydii, she didn't understand how dangerous the situation was.

Now the brainless female was swimming straight for the breeding caverns. Swimming fast and sure, arrogant in her confidence, as if he were nothing more than one of her cringing Ylydii males, waiting for her to issue orders for him to scratch her hide or lick her flukes.

I don't cringe, and I don't take orders.

He fought the instinctive urges long enough to keep the other males from chasing her, but they had mostly dispersed now. There was nothing to keep him here, nothing to prevent him from going after her. *I warned her. She knows full well what will happen if she swims that way.*

His muscles knotted as he fought against turning, tried not to fill his head with her scent. She was halfway to the caverns now, but not far enough away. If she disappeared from his sight, the terrible urges would ease. He could go back to guarding her, and there would be nothing between them, and she would be safe.

I don't want to swim anywhere else.

That had been one of her taunts, hadn't it? If the Lady Liana wanted a chase, he'd give her one.

Burn surged into the current. Going after her didn't make his blood cool or his head clear; if anything, the clenching need inside him grew worse. Logical thought was impossible; his mind was too busy sorting out her scent from the others in the current and telling him how to adjust to match her direction. His body was cutting through the water and throbbing with heavy need. Then nothing else mattered but getting to her and having her, filling her with his seed and planting his pup in her body.

Liana glanced back over her shoulder, spotted him, and switched currents, riding a faster, heavier water stream to the caverns. Burn made the same jump and cut the distance between them in half, then in half again.

Three hundred more meters and he would have her.

Liana didn't enter the part of the breeding caverns the Ylydii had been occupying. She didn't enter the caverns at all, but swam above them only a scant few inches above the sharp rock domes. It confused Burn at first—when he caught her, he needed privacy and a rock shelf—but then he remembered that she couldn't breathe out of water as he did.

That's fine with me. He increased his speed.

Burn caught up with her at the far end of the caverns, and swam over her before he clamped his teeth on the back of her neck and tried to wrap his fins around her to turn her to face him.

Liana reversed direction, sliding out from under him and slashing at him with her veiled fins. They prickled his skin, but the stinging sensation sizzled through him with a peculiar intensity.

Burn hovered, watching her, waiting for her to lower her fins and her guard. *That's how fast I am.*

So you are. She swam down and entered one of the wider caverns.

He followed her in. He wished he could haul her up to the surface and prop her on the rock shelf so that he could penetrate her, but he'd have to find another way to join with her. *Do it again.*

Liana whipped around to face Burn. *What did you say?*

That slapping thing you just did with your fins. He used his bulk and weight to propel her to the side of the cave. *Do it again.*

Anger, and something else, glittered in her eyes, which now had an eerie green cast to them. *I meant to hurt you, you idiot male.*

I know. I liked it. He nuzzled her neck. *Do it again.*

Liana unfurled the veils of her fins and displayed barbs like those the little males had. The only difference was that hers were three times larger. *I won't hold back this time.*

He strummed a harsh laugh. *Who asked you to?*

Liana sank her small barbs into his chest and shoulders. The sting was hotter and deeper this time, but no less arousing. He kept her pinned against the rock so he could properly position their lower bodies. Her slit was as swollen as he was, and her folds had opened to him.

He looked into her eyes. *Again.*

The third time she used her barbs, it excited him so much that he penetrated her, and she released the sound that he had only heard once before, on the Ylydii vessel when he had gone in to rescue her. He didn't know what it was, but it reached down into his bones and pulled something deep and nameless out of him. He moved with it, drawing another, more basic sound from her.

When Burn was sure she was feeling only pleasure, he eased her away from the wall and rolled onto his back.

Liana dug her barbs into his chest before she retracted them. *I'm not hurting you.*

Not in the way you think. He used his fins to guide the movement of her lower body. She fit to him like skin, so tight that he could not flex or curl himself inside her sheath. *I like how it feels. And that sound you make. Make it again.*

This? She filled the water with her song, and then wrapped her veils around him.

The song made Burn's flukes curl, and the permeating fire of her barbs drove him out of his head. He was rolling with her, driving his body into hers, and nothing could feel this good, this satisfying. She was trembling, her barbs locked in his hide now, and he could feel her pleasure squeezing his shaft in the same rhythm as her song.

Yet beyond the pleasure was something else—a primal need to fill her and know that her belly would swell and that they would create something beautiful together. That need was as fierce as her barbs and as inflexible as their joining, but it could not be his alone. This child would be of two hearts, but also of two species and two worlds.

Liana. He repeated her name until she lifted her face from his chest. *Will we make a child together?*

I think . . . yes, we will.

Will you stay with me? Will you love our child? Will you live for our child?

Her eyes darkened, the green glow fading a little. *I will try, Burn.*

Burn buried himself inside her and felt the rush of his seed, eager to pour into her womb. He held back somehow, instinctively waiting to hear her song peak and fragment over her pleasure. Her womb contracted, drawing him in deeper, and then release slammed into him and took him to the place only they could find together.

While Onkar wandered around the wrill island, Dair watched with Teresa at the water's edge, where the infant 'shrike swam in a circle. "It's not possible. They can't communicate. Why should they? They eat everything they could ever talk to."

As if to prove her wrong, the 'shrike breached the surface and pulsed again before dropping back down.

"I think you've got an argument on your hands here, honey." Teresa dropped down on the shells and rested her head against her knees. "So do I."

"Mom?"

"I'm all right. It's a lot to take in all at once." She stared blindly at the mogshrike, who was hovering just below the surface and watching her. "You used to look at me like that, you know? Through the walls of the treatment tank, when you were at the FreeClinic."

"Jadaira." Onkar drew her away from her stepmother and across the shell island until they were out of Teresa's hearing. "There are some very serious matters to contend with here."

"Yeah, I know." She glanced back at Teresa. "I think I'm about to get an adopted baby brother 'shrike."

"It is not just the 'shrike. It is the island itself." He nodded toward the hole he had dug. "There are not only 'Zangian bodies buried beneath the shells."

"What else is there?"

"From the smell, larger aquatics and more 'shrikes. I've uncovered parts from at least fifty individuals and I've barely begun digging."

"What killed them? The mother 'shrike?"

"No." Her mate glanced at Teresa before he resorted to balaenea. "The body parts are cut up, not torn, and they were skillfully dismembered and skinned with a bladed weapon. It is possible that is how they were killed, as well."

"Who would chop them up? Why?"

"Judging by the decomposition, they were all killed within the last five to seven rotations. There is another thing. The parts of them that are left are those that would be considered inedible by humanoids who consume flesh."

Dair felt sick. "The Ninrana."

"Urloy-ka and his entourage may have killed them. This would be a logical place to hide bodies one did not wish recovered," Onkar said. "Wrill moltings attract many carrion eaters. In another week or two, the body parts would have been completely devoured."

And the evidence of the crime equally obliterated. Dair loved the sea, but for once the quick way it cleaned up after predators seemed ghastly. "Why would they kill so many?"

"I do not know." The sound of a launch approaching made Onkar look out at the sea. "Say nothing of this to Captain Argate."

Noel Argate was standing in the inflatable and waving an arm toward Teresa, who was still sitting and watching the infant 'shrike. Dair's gaze shifted to one side of the launch, and a very familiar dark silhouette beneath the surface streaking directly at the launch.

"Onkar, that's my father out there. *Duo*, he's going to ram the boat." She began to run for the water's edge.

"Jadaira, no! The 'shrike!"

Dair skidded to a halt at the end of the shells. The baby 'shrike seemed enthralled with Teresa, but it was a born killer, nearly as long as Dair in the water and with five times as many teeth. In a fight, she would lose, and she had to think of the pup in her belly.

"Argate!" She shouted. "Incoming!"

The captain was too far away to hear her, and then it was too late. Dairatha plowed into the launch, knocking the Terran over and into the water.

Teresa jumped to her feet and shrieked. "Dairatha, no!"

Dair's blood froze as the baby 'shrike casually swung around to look in the direction of the splash. Her heart nearly stopped when Onkar dove into the water in a smooth, dark blur of motion.

It all happened so fast there was hardly any time to think. Onkar went first to the Terran, who was struggling to tread water, and flipped him onto his back. Argate clutched at his dorsal fin while the big male turned and headed off Dairatha, who had been moving at high speed toward Teresa on the wrill island. The males bumped heads and shoulders, until Onkar's rapid orders seemed to galvanize Dairatha into action.

Dair's father didn't run away from the 'shrike, however. He headed straight for it, his body tense and ready to attack.

Dair saw Teresa's expression and caught her breath as she guessed her thoughts. "No, please, Mom. Don't do it."

Teresa dove into the water and resurfaced, and then calmly swam into a position that placed her between the baby 'shrike and her mate.

Dairatha came to an abrupt stop and breached the surface. "Get out of the water, you stupid woman!" he roared.

"I delivered this baby, and I'm not letting you kill it," Teresa said. "Go away from here, Dairatha. You've done enough harm for one day." She turned back to look at Dair. "You stay right there and protect my grandchild."

Everyone, including Teresa, froze as the baby 'shrike moved slowly forward in the water. It didn't swim with the silent grace of its species, but with the slightly jerky hesitation of a 'Zangian newborn. When it was close enough to touch Teresa, who was treading water as quietly as she could, it lifted its head toward her belly.

Dair expected to see her stepmother's insides spill out and color the water scarlet. She did not expect to see an infant mogshrike nuzzle her with its snout like an affection-hungry pup.

"It's all right," Teresa breathed. Carefully she lifted a hand and stroked the top of the 'shrike's head. "This is like petting sandpaper. Spiny sandpaper." It rolled in the water and presented her with its smoother belly. "Do I scratch the belly of a mogshrike? Well, I petted it on the head and I still have a hand." She used her fingernails to scratch between the shorter belly spines.

"Get away from that thing," Dairatha hissed, but even his recessed eyes were wide with disbelief.

The baby 'shrike rolled back over, turned toward the big 'Zangian, and released a louder, deeper pulse than it had before.

Dair blinked. "Did that thing just tell my father to back off?"

"I think we should give it a name. Now what do you call something that turns your life upside down and makes you do things you never thought you'd have to?" Teresa was back to petting its head. "Charley. Frances. Ivan. Jeanne. Or maybe I should wait until I find out what gender it is."

Another hissing sound startled Dair, but this time the 'shrike breached and screamed out a pulse, splashing and terrorizing Teresa before it sank below the surface and went limp in the water. Dair squinted to see the red tag of a tranquilizer dart sticking up by its dorsal fin. She followed the direction of the sound and saw the corresponding dart gun in Noel Argate's hand.

"Would you warn me the next time you do that?" Teresa shouted, putting her arms around the baby 'shrike to keep it from sinking to the bottom. She pulled her arms back with a grimace, and the unconscious 'shrike floated up to the surface. "What do you know. It can float, which means it has an air bladder."

"'Shrikes can't float." Yet there it was, drifting as if being rocked to sleep by the surface waves.

"If your mate will stop trying to kill me," Argate said, his voice strained, "we should get this thing back to the *Briggs* and contained before it regains consciousness."

Dair looked out to where her father had been, but the big 'Zangian had vanished.

CHAPTER 17

"I promise you, I know what I am doing," Paal told Moleon as they approached the quarantined area of the barax hive. His excitement was making it hard to stay on two legs. "You see, when I approached them before, I gave tones of command, as always. If our barax have evolved through contact with the Core, as Chemist T'Kaf and Dr. Mayer believe, then I must converse with them. It is a completely different tone, one I use when I sculpt with them."

The Skartesh hunter adjusted his quiver. "As you say. I say, if they begin to swarm and bite us as they did before, we are leaving."

The Hlagg sculptor grinned up at his taciturn friend. He had learned that such gruff threats were Moleon's manner of expressing care, and they always delighted and amused him. "You will see that I am right about this."

The barax hive had taken on new dimensions since the last time Paal and Moleon had paid a visit to it. Large and complex silvery-white mound structures rose from what appeared to be a sinkhole in the ground. Thousands of dark green barax clung to the mounds, which they were actively sculpting into stranger and more bizarre shapes as they built them up.

Moleon came to a halt and stared, transfixed by the sight of them. "They are like the ice hills of Skart."

"You must visit my homeworld sometime," Paal chided. "These are tiny compared to the sculptures I have created with my little friends." Confidently he walked within a few feet of the mounds and stopped, holding his hands out and open. The tones he released were gentle and beguiling, a call from his artistic nature to that of the barax.

The insects all over the mounds ceased working and looked down at the two intruders.

"You may wish to be more polite now," Moleon warned.

Paal smiled before he launched into his tonal invitation. It was a very polite request for those members of the hive who wished to share to join him in an exchange of information. Once he had finished, he placed the N-jui translation pad on the ground and slowly backed away, still showing no aggression or fear.

"The chemist truly believes they will be able to communicate with us through this device?" Moleon sounded skeptical.

"It is used extensively among her species, and they have communicated with every life-form on their planet." What a place the N-jui homeworld must be, he thought, and how difficult would it be to obtain a temporary visitor's visa? He would have to inquire about it as soon as he talked his barax out of killing the colonists.

The two males waited, and watched. The barax seemed to be communicating with each other, and went on with their private conversations for some minutes before two trundled over to the pad. They inspected the device thoroughly before climbing up onto the pad, which would read and translate their chemical messages into spoken language, and spoken language into chemicals they could taste.

YOU WANT WHAT

Paal was startled by the brevity of the barax's first message, and the effort it took to speak to the insects instead of using tones. "I am Paal, a Hlagg sculptor. I have worked with many of your ancestors to sculpt and build great art. I request peace between our kind and some information."

BUILD YES PEACE YES INFORMATION YES

"Is that an agreement?" Moleon asked.

Paal nodded. "Insect syntax is a little hard to comprehend if you're not used to it. We can translate the sounds they make, which express brief concepts just like that." He turned to the barax. "We wish to know why you are building toward the colony of humanoids. We wish to know if you mean to do harm to us."

BUILD WONDER HARM NO BUILD WATER PIPE HARM YES

"Water pipe."

"Irrigation and wastewater pipes. The recycling plant cleans and sterilizes the water before it pumps it out here, to irrigate the botanicals." Moleon pointed to one of the nearby outlet pipes.

"The barax aren't building toward the colony at all. They'd going to seal off the pipe." Paal turned to the waiting insects. "Why do you wish to harm the water pipes?"

INFECTED HARM WATER PIPE STOP HARM CORE

"The water isn't hurting them, it's harming the Core." Paal looked out at the gnorra trees before asking the barax, "How is the water infected?"

SMALLER ONES SLEEP PIPE WATER HARM CORE

"Smaller ones would be something not as big as they are," Paal reasoned out loud. "The smaller ones sleep—hibernate, perhaps?—in the pipe water. The smaller ones harm the Core. But who are the smaller ones?"

Moleon eyed the outlet pipe. "I think we should take a sample of the water back for analysis."

"Good idea." Paal turned to the insects. "Thank you for speaking with me and my friend. We will leave you in peace, and ask that you do the same for us." He went to collect the translator device, but the barax weren't finished speaking just yet.

PEACE YES COME SEE SPEAK BUILD WONDER PAAL YES

The sculptor grinned down at the pair. "Then I shall return and we will talk of building wonders together again, my friends."

Paal and Moleon took the water sample directly to the FreeClinic, where Liam Mayer sent it down to Pathology for a complete analysis. Hkyrim brought up the results to Mayer's office personally.

"You are supposed to be on medical leave, Doctor," Liam said as he took the data pad from the Omorr.

"I dislike being idle," Hkyrim said. "Also, I asked my lab technicians to inform me if there were any substances brought in for pathogenic analysis. The water is contaminated with the same nanites present in the wrill specimen."

Liam consulted the pad. "We'll have to put an alert to the entire colony. Luckily this isn't being used as drinking water."

"No, but it is possible that the nanites may have been programmed to replicate and infect every source of water on the planet."

Liam nodded. "How did they get into the wastewater from the sea?"

"Seawater is used to make the liquid atmosphere for the 'Zangian pilots' ships," Hkyrim said. "Once it has been used, it is drained from the strafers and piped through the recycling plant. It's also possible that the 'Zangians are carrying nanites in their bloodstream." He removed a photoscan from his jacket and held it out. "The nanites did not stop resequencing the DNA of my amputated hand."

Liam looked at the image, which showed a 'Zangian pectoral flipper inside a sealed tank. "That's not your hand, Doctor."

"Not anymore." Hkyrim glanced down at his bandaged stump. "I have more photoscans that show the transformation process from hand to flipper as it happened. Naturally the nanites wouldn't resequence DNA that is already identical to that of their program, so it is likely that the 'Zangians will suffer no physical harm from their exposure."

Liam tossed down the datapad in disgust. "But why do this? Why infect a planet with nanites programmed to make everyone into duplicates of the native aquatics?"

"Not complete duplicates, and not everyone," T'Kaf said from the open doorway. "Only one aquatic species, with which Dr. Hkyrim unfortunately shares some DNA, an insignificant amount but just enough to fool the nanite program. I recommended that all the Omorr be evacuated from the planet, that is, if they wish to remain Omorr."

"Which species were these nanites created to change?" Liam asked.

"The mogshrike, of course. I don't understand how they migrated. The nanites were supposed to stay in the sea."

Hkyrim frowned. "You know who released the nanites into the seawater?"

"Yes." The chemist turned her calm countenance toward the Omorr. "I did."

"I've checked and rechecked the entire inlet," Teresa assured Noel Argate. "Everything is up and running. Let's release it."

"Maybe in the morning," Noel said. He was at his desk and studying the results of the preliminary scans one of his men had made on the 'shrike. "I've got a ton of datawork to plow through." He looked up. "Why don't you go get some rest? You look wiped out."

Teresa started to tell him where he could shove his data, and then nodded and went off to her cabin.

The *Briggs* had made it back to the coast in less than a day after capturing the baby 'shrike, but ever since they had docked, Noel Argate had adamantly refused to release their reluctant passenger. First he wanted to allow it to recover from the tranquilizer he had given it, and then he thought it prudent to scan and observe the creature for several hours. After that, all the containment equipment being used for it had to be checked and double-checked.

"I'm just being thorough, Teresa," Noel would say whenever she questioned him about it. "As you demanded I be."

Several times Teresa thought her old lover was stalling. Everything he said reminded her of how he had spoken to her when they were students: always with that upper-hand tinge of patronization she despised.

Still, why would Noel go to all this trouble to capture a live 'shrike to observe its behavior, and then keep it penned up like a goldfish? She was just being paranoid.

Jadaira and Onkar had left the inlet after seeing the *Briggs* safely to dock. Dair had muttered something about going to see Shon Valtas, but Teresa had been too distracted over the 'shrike to pay much attention. Now all she wanted to do was get her baby out of the containment tank belowdecks and back into the sea, where it could feed and swim freely.

Noel's dragging things out was pissing her off, but he was also right. They couldn't rush the process.

"Dr. Selmar," Ballie called from the corridor outside her cabin. "There are some people from the colony up on deck to see you."

Teresa had signaled Ana Hansen and her lab chief, T'Kaf, about their triumphant capture of the 'shrike, and was delighted to see the N-jui waiting for her up on deck. She knew Ana was tied up at the Peace Summit, but seeing Liam Mayer and an Omorr physician with T'Kaf made her frown.

"T'Kaf, we did it! William, what are you doing away from the hospital?" She smiled at the Omorr as Mayer introduced him. "Did Ana tell you about our adventures on the high seas?"

The Terran surgeon looked grim. "Teresa, is there somewhere we can talk?"

"Here is fine." She glanced at T'Kaf. "What, is the council having a snit fit already? Am I in trouble?"

"The trouble started six months ago, Dr. Selmar," the N-jui told her, "when I impregnated some of your bioengineered wrill with nanites."

Teresa must not have heard her correctly. "I beg your pardon?"

"She said, she spiked your wrill." Noel Argate came up on deck. Twenty of his MRD officers, each carrying sidearms, circled around the outside of the group. "T'Kaf, I'm very disappointed in you. You could have kept this quiet for one more day, and then no one would have ever known how naughty you were."

"This male," T'Kaf told Teresa, "forced me to repeatedly give him aid. He has records pertaining to an unfortunate accident in which I was involved on N-jui."

"She blew up a laboratory," Noel told Teresa. "Killed several people, and had her chemistry certifications and licensing stripped. Terrible thing, got her permanently barred from ever returning to her homeworld. Of course, a girl's got to eat, so T'Kaf forged a new identity for herself. That's the problem with counterfeiting IDs," he told the N-Jui. "You never know who is going to be checking into them."

"You blackmailed her," Terri said.

Noel shrugged. "I couldn't find anything on anyone else. Your crew members are remarkably well-behaved people."

"Captain Argate threatened to expose me," T'Kaf said, "unless I followed his instructions. He brought the nanites here two cycles back and told me to release them into the sea. They were only supposed to infect the mogshrikes, and resequence their DNA."

"Which they did."

Hkyrim extended one of his arms, which Terri saw ended in a stump. "Just for your information, Captain, they have the same effect on Omorr."

"The nanites may also have affected Commander mu T'Resa's physiology, as well as hormonal production and growth rates among some of the younger 'Zangian males," the N-jui said to Teresa.

"Oh, dear." Noel grimaced. "Well, nothing's perfect."

Teresa was struggling to grasp everything. "You released nanites into the open ocean to change the 'shrikes, and it did all this, too? Christ, Noel, why?"

"We are invading the Hsktskt homeworld, which is going to be a water world when we're done bombarding its polar caps," Argate told her. "We know the lizards can live comfortably in water for extended periods of time, and suspect they're clever enough to build temporary floating cities. We need aquatic soldiers who can fight them. Soldiers who can be trained to do what's necessary."

"You mean, terrorize them and then eat them. Like the legend of the rogur."

Noel smiled happily. "We've tried it with a dozen other species, but none of them were large enough, or aggressive enough, to scare Hsktskt, much less eat them. The 'shrikes will do both." He pointed to the deck. "Down there is my first foot soldier. Hey, I've thought of a name for your new baby, Terri. Adam."

Teresa turned to William Mayer, desperate now. "How many nanites? Were they self-replicating? Will they hurt the 'Zangians?"

"I released several billion, Doctor," T'Kaf said. "They are self-replicating and there is no way to count them now. They have no effect on 'Zangians."

"What about the 'Zangians Onkar found buried on the wrill island?" she demanded of Noel. "Did you butcher them, too?"

"I don't know what you're talking about." He yawned. "I never killed any aquatics. I just redesign them from the inside out."

She drew back to keep herself from lunging at his throat. "You're more of a monster than the 'shrikes are."

"What's done is done, Terri." Argate patted her shoulder. "The 'shrike goes back to MRD with me tomorrow on a shuttle. We'll train it and bring it back to gather others like it; take them and train them. Within one year they'll form our first aquatic infantry division. Within two years they'll wipe out the Hsktskt and end this war." He spread his hands. "Voila, the League worlds will be safe again, and I'll be a general."

That she could ever have loved this man staggered her. Teresa shook her head as if to deny it.

"Use of this type of nanotechnology is illegal, Captain," Hkyrim said. "The League will be informed of your actions."

"Who do you think gave me the nanites, Doctor?" Noel asked the Omorr. He laughed at their expressions. "Come on, people, wake up. Wars are dirty. Do you know that the Hsktskt raided one of our SEAL facilities a year ago, and killed our best biologists? They took everything we had developed on alterforming, too. Now we're finding Hsktskt agents who look just as sweet and innocent as Terri, here, blowing up intelligence compounds and assassinating generals. That's why we don't fight fair. We can't. We only let you civilians think that we do."

"William?" Teresa gave the surgeon a desperate look.

"We'll petition the council to block Captain Argate's departure, first thing in the morning," Mayer promised her. He was watching Noel's men, none of whom had drawn a weapon yet.

"That's it, then." She felt almost as numb as she had when she lost Dairatha.

"Be a good sport, Terri," Noel advised her. "It's something you should be used to by now, anyway, don't you think?"

T'Kaf came to Teresa. "I apologize for my part in this. It was wrong of me to conceal my past and deceive you into thinking I was suitable for employment. I have no defense for what I did; only to say that I was once young and careless."

Teresa looked at Noel. "So was I."

"I feel that I have done some good here. It pains me to think that this one mistake will again destroy my reputation." She touched Teresa's hand. "I hope you will speak well of me when I am gone. For now, there are things that must be done, no matter how unpleasant we find them."

Teresa did feel terribly betrayed, but she also understood that Noel was the reason the N-jui had become involved in this monstrosity. *Another life in ruins, on top of ruins.* "I'm sorry he used you like this."

"I have learned something here. I hope, with the exception of my actions on Captain Argate's behalf, that I contributed something, too. If not before, then perhaps with what I do now." The N-jui walked across the deck and seized Noel Argate, lifting him off his feet.

"Put me down!" The Terran struggled wildly.

The MRD officers took out their weapons and pointed them at T'Kaf.

"Captain Argate, you once expressed curiosity and disgust about how some N-Jui females devour males after mating." She cocked her head and stretched out her large, curved mandibles. "I must inform you that in fact all females are capable of devouring males, and that we do not necessarily have to mate with them first."

Noel Argate had just enough time to scream before the N-jui bit off his head and swallowed it. At almost the exact same moment, the MRD officers opened fire.

"T'Kaf!" Teresa screamed.

"No, Teresa." Mayer caught her by the arms and held her back, out of firing range.

The N-jui's mandibles did not stop chewing until pulse fire riddled her entire body and all twenty officers had drained their sidearms' power cells. Then, with the inherent dignified grace of her kind, she put down Argate's body, spat out what remained of his head, curled up on the deck, and died in the echoing silence.

Terri stared at T'Kaf, and then grabbed Mayer's sleeve. "William, I have to talk to Jadaira. Right away."

Burn didn't want to leave Liana alone with only an attendant, but their mating had left her exhausted, and he had promised Shon he would sit in on the latest security briefing at the URD.

I won't be long, just an hour or two.

She curled against him, rubbing her cheek against his chest. *Come inside when you return. I'll feel safer if you sleep in here with me. Tomorrow we can tell them . . .* She drifted off.

The attendant, an older female named Graleba, gave him a silent if somewhat disgruntled nod as he left the cavern.

She's Ylydii, I'm not, Burn thought as he swam over to the URD. *It will probably take everyone some time to adjust to the idea.*

Shon wasn't at the security briefing, which had ended early so that he could meet with Jadaira and Onkar about some emergency issue. Burn left the water and wandered through the URD until he found the three closeted in one of the conference rooms.

"I come all the way over here to be briefed, and here you are, telling war stories." He looked from Dair to Onkar to Shon. "All right, maybe not war stories."

"Someone has been killing and eating aquatics in large quantities," Shon informed him. "Dair and Onkar found what was left of them buried on a wrill island. Among the victims are your two missing guards."

Burn closed the door panel and secured it. "How did they die?" He sounded harsh, but he didn't care. The two guards had been his friends from childhood.

"They were dismembered by a blade. All their bones were removed."

"That's how Ninrana do it." He turned to Dair. "You remember all the bones they have saved on that bleeding rock of a world they inhabit?"

"I don't think it was Urloy-ka and his people," Shon said. "They've been complaining that they miss fresh meat ever since they joined the summit. They don't know this planet or the ocean well enough to hide the bodies so cleverly. And there has been little opportunity for them to slip away from the URD to kill so many."

"But Ninrana use blades, and they debone everything."

"They are quite infamous for their death feasts, Burn. That's why I think this was staged, to make it appear as if the Ninrana killed these people," Shon said.

"Dair and I may have uncovered the remains earlier than the killers expected," Onkar added. "The delegates are scheduled to go on an outing tomorrow. Administrator Hansen thought it would be good for them to get away from the negotiation table until the Ninrana-Ylydii alliance could be absorbed. The wrill island is located on the route they were going to follow."

"The delegates would think the Ninrana killed them." Burn put a fin to his head. "It would bring back the horror over their practices before the Skartesh invasion."

"It would have far more damaging effect than that," Shon said. "The Ninrana pledged to give up death feasts and ritual sacrifice in exchange for a place at this summit. This would automatically disqualify them from participating further. The Skartesh are only permitted at the summit because the Ninrana agreed not to take revenge for their invasion. A promise Urloy-ka would undoubtedly revoke the moment he was kicked out of the summit. The Ylydii only agreed to come to the summit if the Ninrana and Skartesh issues were at the table, so they will leave, and the 'Zangians would not agree to participate unless every species was represented."

"The peace process would not only be disrupted," Onkar said. "It would be permanently damaged. None of the delegates would ever trust the others again."

"It's like finding a bomb just before it detonates." Burn looked at Dair helplessly. "Can't I go out and shoot whoever is responsible?"

She shook her head. "We have to find out who did this first. Tonight." The wall panel chimed, and she went over to answer it. "It's my mom," she told the men. "Probably about my dad. I'll take it over in the office next door."

Burn listened as the other two males discussed ways to deal with the wrill island, but Dair came back almost immediately. "Shon, you were testing DNA a few weeks ago. Why?"

The oKiaf looked slightly uncomfortable. "It's an Intelligence issue."

"It's a Hsktskt SEAL, you mean." She made a frustrated sound. "Major, I really hate hearing stuff like this from my mother."

"How did Teresa know . . . ?"

"Noel Argate—who is now missing a head—told my mother about it right before he was killed. She says she'll explain all that later. What occurred to her was that there could be a Hsktskt SEAL at the peace summit causing all our trouble." Dair gave Shon a hard look. "If you had evidence that an enemy alterform is on this planet, we should have been made aware of it."

"We don't know that there is," Shon admitted. "We only suspect there might be. Some alterformed cells were found on one of the mercenary derelicts. The cells were in preform condition."

Burn scowled. "What?"

"It's the radical stuff, cousin. Preform is the stage a SEAL goes through before a complete physical transformation," Dair told him. "Like what Shon went through to look like Rushan Amariah."

"Whoever this spy is—if there is one—had a complete genetic makeover," Shon said. "The cells aren't that old, so it was fairly recent. Maybe within the last three cycles. The only way to tell is to check DNA. Alterforming leaves certain flaws that can't be erased." He gave them an ironic look. "Mine are registered at the FreeClinic, in case you think it's me."

One of the 'Zangian guards overrode the door panel lock and strode in. "Sorry, sir," he said to Shon, "but you said if anything happened—"

The major was already on his feet. "What is it?"

"Ambassador Carada and two members of her delegation were abducted by the Ninrana delegate, and have been taken off-planet," he said. "The ambassador's daughter was found shot in the head."

While Dair and Onkar scrambled the pilots' pod, Shon went with Burn to the URD infirmary pool, where Liana had been brought from the breeding caverns. The sight of her lifeless body in the water, now stained with blood from a massive head wound, made Burn tear off his flightsuit and dive in. He wrenched her away from the attending 'Zangian medic and held her in his arms, calling her name softly.

"Liana?" He was careful to hold her under the surface so she could keep breathing. "Open your eyes, come on now. I need to see them again."

Shon watched as Burn's voice made the young Ylydii female stir. The two parallel marks on his chest burned as he felt the brush of her soul.

Burn looked up at him, bewildered and aghast. "She can't die. We're mated. She's carrying my child. She can't die."

The medic looked at Shon, shook her head, and then silently retreated from the pool out to the sea.

Shon lowered himself into the water and swam over to the tragic pair. "If it is her time, Byorn, you have to let her go."

"It is not *her* time," Burn shouted. "Someone shot her in the head. Someone who I'm going to find and tear apart as soon as . . . as soon . . ." He choked on the words and looked down at her. "Can't you do something?"

Shon studied Liana's young, thin face. She was black all over, with veiled fins of more colors than he had names for. She was like nothing on his world, just as Burn was. It was not her time; life had been stolen from her. Just as it had been stolen from Jadaira.

I can't do this again. If I do, they'll know. I'll never be free.

But what was freedom, if he had to deny what he was, and hide it, and hide from it?

"Give her to me," he said to Burn.

The 'Zangian wouldn't let go of her. "She'll wake up now. Any minute." Burn was no longer seeing Shon or anything else. "She has these eyes, Shon. Black, but they glow green. That's how you know she's special. A royal."

Shon knew then that he wasn't going to be able to pry the Ylydii away from Burn. He took a deep breath and put one hand in the water and rested it over her wound.

"Don't be afraid," he told the 'Zangian. "This gets pretty intense."

Burn stared at him. "What does?"

On oKia, all males had some measure of the touch. It was usually only enough for them to heal their own minor wounds quickly and cleanly. In a few, it was enough to heal the wounds of others, as long as they weren't serious. Only one or two males in every tribe had the ability to heal serious wounds, and usually became their tribe's healer.

Among all the tribes, there were only two other males like Shon, who were born with a touch so powerful it could literally bring the dead back to life. One was Shon's father, who had refused to use his touch after it had failed to bring back Shon's brother, who had been dead too long to revive. His father had never told anyone of Shon's gift, and Horvon Jala had promised to keep it secret as well.

There was no conscious act to the touch. Shon put his hands on the wounded, and poured whatever was inside him down through his hands and into the wound. The marks on his chest, which had been removed with alterforming but had reappeared almost immediately, burned with the energy he flooded into Liana. From between his hand and Liana's wound a brilliant white light glowed.

Shon had no idea where it came from, or what it was, but he knew instinctively that the light was the true power. He was only the conduit it used.

Liana stirred, and then cried out. So did Burn, who had turned his head away to protect his eyes but still held Liana in a fierce grip.

Knowing she was near death, Shon gave everything he had to the touch, and then felt it ebb as Liana grew stronger. He watched through the light and saw the wound close and the blood disappear. Finally the Ylydii was whole again, and he removed his hand.

Burn blinked several times, and then stared at him. "You did that to Dair. You're the mysterious force."

Too drained to speak, Shon nodded, and moved away from the young lovers to hold on to the side of the pool. Using the touch took something out of him each time, although this wasn't quite as bad as when he had revived Jadaira. That time he had thought that he might have pushed past the limits of his tremendous gift.

Shon looked over his shoulder and saw the two aquatics swimming together under water. He wasn't sorry he had exposed himself in front of Burn. To return stolen life was never wrong. It simply caused more complications in his life than he wanted.

Burn surfaced and looked at Shon. "I owe you, Major."

"Yeah, you do." Shon smiled down at Liana. "How is she?"

"Perfect." The 'Zangian's hide darkened. "Exactly as she was before the Hsktskt SEAL agent shot her in the head."

CHAPTER 18

Liana didn't understand why her life had been spared. She only knew that it had been, through the blinding and terrifying light that Shon Valtas had somehow summoned and poured over her. She no longer needed evidence that a higher power existed. It existed in him, and the exchange had been made.

The life that had been given for hers would not be given in vain.

There was no time to explain to Burn and Shon what had happened in the cavern. *I have to get to the Ylydii ship in orbit,* she told Burn. *That is where they are taking them.*

Shon and I are going after them; you're staying here, she was told. *Just tell me who shot you. Was it that Ninrana?*

Liana looked into his eyes, saw the tiny reflection of herself in them. It gave her the courage to lie to him, this one last time. *I didn't see who it was, but I will never forget the smell.*

Burn look frustrated. *Describe it to me.*

I'm sorry, I can't. I don't have words for it. You have to take me with you.

He left her in the water to speak to Shon, and then returned. *You'll have to share a gunner's seat with me; we're taking a strafer.*

Is it large enough for all three of us?

The one Shon had outfitted with StarFire is. Burn pulled her close. *If anything happens to you now—*

I know. I feel the same about you.

They did not leave the sea to take a transport; the process of transferring Liana via tank would take too long. Instead, Shon left them to retrieve the strafer, which he would land on the surface of the water in order for the aquatics to board.

While they waited for the ship, Burn outfitted Liana in a protective flightsuit. She refused the weapon harness he wanted to strap onto her body, however, as her fins had not been altered like his to manipulate guns and blades.

I don't want you to be defenseless, Burn said as he strapped on his own gear.

I won't be. Burn, what did that male do to me?

Shon? I don't know. He even made one of my scars disappear. He reached up and touched his face, and for the first time Liana realized the blade scar he had received during the mercenary attack was gone. *I've never seen or felt anything like it.*

He healed me with his hands.

That's all I saw him use. Burn looked at her. *We can't tell anyone about Shon. If quadrant knew about his ability, they'd lock him up somewhere.*

Liana understood that better than her mate knew. She looked up through the dome viewer and saw the shadow of the strafer as it landed topside. *He's here.*

Boarding the strafer only took a minute, and Liana slipped into the emergency harness across from the gunner's console, which left her facing Burn. She liked watching him go about his duty, powering up this and checking that. He seemed completely absorbed by the panels and screens and readouts, and yet glanced up when he felt her gaze on him.

Not as glamorous as the front seat, he told her. *One of these days I'll actually be certified and able to fly you somewhere.*

Once it would have terrified her to think of Burn as her mate. Now she saw how foolish she had been, not to trust him, not to tell him. *Why do you want to be a pilot when you're so good with weapons?*

Burn lifted a fin to check something embedded in the console above his head. *My cousin is a pilot, and I've always wanted to be like her.*

You can be like someone without following their path. Liana didn't think of the future. The 'Zangians lived in the now, and here, with him, was where she most wanted to be. *How long will it take to reach our ship in orbit?*

Not long, and it may get very rough up there. His face grew stern. *You keep that harness on and your head down.*

She managed an Ylydii version of a military salute. *Yes, sir, Sublieutenant.*

Burn gave her a headset, which allowed her to listen in on the conversations he had with Shon. The military shorthand they used was like a different language, but as they shot up into space she made out that the other pilots had already launched and were in pursuit of a shuttle on which the Ylydii delegate and two others had been taken by force. She held her tongue as they worked out how best to approach the Ylydii ship and face any attackers.

All Liana needed them to do was to get her on board.

The problems started a few minutes before they caught up with their target.

Major, we've got transmission interference, Burn said. *Looks like some sort of wave jammer. I'm not able to pick up anything from the pod or Flight Control.*

Switch to auxiliary and boost the signal, Shon transmitted from the helm. *You've got to patch us through. I have to coordinate with the pod; we'll need them.*

Acknowledged.

Static crackled over Liana's headset as Burn linked them to the transponder. He was able to reduce the noise, but the signals he sent to the other 'Zangians and the controllers on K-2 went unanswered.

Major, whatever jammer they're using has disrupted all communications around the planet, Burn told Shon. *Nothing's sending or receiving; not even the emergency channels.*

Stand by. The strafer turned as Shon flew through the ring of moons and emerged into clear space. *The Ylydii ship has left orbit and is en route to Ninra. I suppose Urloy-ka will feel safer keeping the captives on his native soil. My track says the pod is flying in escort formation around it.*

Escort? Burn sounded astonished. *Why are they doing that?*

I'd love to ask, but we're relay dead for the moment.

Liana leaned forward to look through the viewer before she said,

Burn, Major Valtas, we can't let the ship reach Ninra. If it does, everyone on board will be killed.

How do you know that? Shon asked.

They're not going to land. They're going to crash the ship on the planet.

Dair had never flown with Onkar as her gunner, and she was becoming impatient with the problems he was having with the transponder. *What do you mean, we can't signal anyone, not even on the emergency channels?*

All transmissions have been jammed, not only ours, her mate said. *I am trying to find a solution.*

Try harder.

She knew she was being more irritable than the situation called for, but this entire fiasco was beginning to get on her nerves. They rushed up to save the Ylydii ambassador, only to discover that Carada and Urloy-ka had decided to withdraw from the peace summit and return to their respective homeworlds.

I don't know where you are getting your information, Commander, the Ylydii ambassador had told her, *but there was no abduction. Delegate Urloy-ka and I decided it was better for us to leave before any more "accidents" occurred. I offered to escort him home on my vessel. You can return to your planet and assure the officials that all is well.*

Lady Ambassador, I request you allow us to board so we can assure you are not in any danger. Dair didn't want to tell her about Liana over an open channel.

Dair and Onkar had boarded the ship, and were greeted by both Carada and Urloy-ka, who showed no signs of being under any coercion. The ship's crew reported that everything was normal and that they were taking orders from Carada. No one was waving around arms or making threats.

Dair stayed long enough for her own peace of mind, and then told Carada that the pod would escort the Ylydii to Ninra. *It will be safest, and you will probably want to return to K-2 as soon as possible.* She then related what little she knew of Liana's injury.

I was told a short time ago that my daughter has mated with a 'Zangian, Carada said. *She is no longer of any use to me.*

Dair's jaw sagged. Ambassador, your daughter could be dead, or dying. Don't you want to see her?

Liana betrayed her people by mating with one of yours. Being shot was what she deserved. I only wish I could have done it myself.

Feeling completely disgusted, Dair and Onkar left the Ylydii ship and signaled the patrol to fly escort for them. Halfway to Ninra the transponders began to fail, and within a thousand kim of the planet they weren't working at all.

Do you think the Ninrana are broadcasting this jammer so they can attack the Ylydii as soon as they're in orbit? Dair asked her mate.

I doubt it. Since the Skartesh invasion, the Ninrana have few ships, and very little advanced technology. If this is indeed a jammer, it would have to be one of the most powerful made. Stand by. Onkar switched to a different channel for a few moments. *Dair, I'm getting a weak signal from the Ylydii ship. It's Carada, and she's received a warning from the planet. Mercenaries have stolen StarFire, hijacked one of our strafers, and are headed this way to attack the ship.*

How is it that her transponder is working and ours isn't? Dair tried to patch through on the channel herself, but the signal faded away.

Her ship could have passed through an opening loop in the jamming field. Onkar's tone changed. *Scanners show a single strafer heading on a direct course for the Ylydii ship.*

Damn it, I need my relay channels open so I can warn the pod and coordinate a defense. She looked out and saw Saree flying past her and assuming point in a standard defense pattern. The other strafers pulled into position around her. *They must have heard Carada's signal, too.*

We have to take out that strafer.

The pod is assuming an attack formation, Shon said over Burn's headgear. *They're defending the ship.*

Against us? Burn tried again to signal his cousin and the other 'Zangian pilots, with no success. *Why are they doing this, Shon? Don't they know the agent is on board?*

Without working transponders we can't know. But if we want to stop the Ylydii ship, we're going to have to fly through the pod.

Everything inside him twisted. *I'm not shooting at my own people. The last time I did that in the simulators, I killed all of them.*

I'm open to suggestions.

Liana reached out and touched his fin. *Burn, you don't have to kill them. You can disable their ships without harming them, the way your cousin did when she saved the Skartesh from mass suicide.*

Those were religion-crazed civilians, Burn told her. *These are trained fighter pilots.*

She held his gaze steadily. *So are you.*

Shon broke in with, *I hate to interrupt, but they're coming for us now.*

Burn checked his panel and saw three strafers on an intercept course. *Shon, I can't do this without wiring up to StarFire. I need you to fly like you're in an asteroid belt. Closed profile, avoidance pattern.*

Acknowledged.

Burn reached out to his mate. *I won't be able to speak when I'm in the bubble.* He had never been good with farewells, but he had always believed in making them. *I love you, Liana. I wish you had stayed on-planet.*

I don't, she told him, nuzzling his fin.

Duo, she was so beautiful. *Wherever we go, I will be with you.*

Shon flew beneath the trio of oncoming ships, avoiding the warning shots they fired and coming up behind them. Ahead, the remainder of the patrol was waiting for them. *Gunner, engage weapons array.*

Acknowledged, Major. Burn gave Liana a final caress before moving back in his harness and engaging the StarFire. The targeting/firing sphere swallowed him eagerly, the neuroclamp transmitters taking him into their tight embrace as he went into free spin. The n-trans's delicate leads tickled his haffets as they curled and linked with his brain.

Sublieutenant, we are under attack, Shon said over his com. *Fire at your discretion.*

He had no time to appreciate being hooked up to the weapons array as the first pair of strafers attacked. *Saree and Loknoth,* Burn decided as he locked on to their positions and tracked their fire. He was able to take out the power cells on the male 'Zangian's weapons systems, but the wing leader outflew Shon and streaked away.

Slippery bitch, Shon muttered as he avoided three more strafers coming in on a flanking pattern.

The sphere began to spin faster as Burn countered the pulse fire with his own blasts, taking out weapon cells when he could, and engines when he couldn't. The precision it took not to destroy the other ships was exacting, and he silently swore he would never again complain about gunning the enemy.

With five ships now disabled, the patrol broke formation and regrouped—all but one strafer, which Burn recognized as Dair's ship, the *Wavelight.* Dair moved out of firing range and sat a short distance away, almost as if she were observing the battle.

That's Jadaira, isn't it? Shon asked.

Yes. Watch her; she'll fly right up your nose without a twitch. Burn spun around and prepared to fire on the strafers grouping in a mass attack pattern. *Shon, don't skim around them, weave. They'll hold their fire so that they don't hit each other.*

Good idea. Why aren't you a pilot?

I am. Burn felt the n-trans leads shifting to penetrate his haffets, and winced. *I'm just a better gunner.*

During the weave pass, Burn was able to render two more strafers' weapons systems inoperative, but when Shon tried to advance after the Ylydii ship, the wing leader rolled in front of them in a daring move and took out the *IceBlade's* primary engine cells.

Perceptive and slippery, Shon said, his tone wry and admiring. *I've got secondary engines and thrusters left, Sublieutenant, and then we're dead in the water.*

You're starting to sound like a 'Zangian, Major. Burn assessed the battlefield. Fifteen strafers stood between them and the Ylydii ship, which would soon reach Ninra. *It would be fifteen again.*

If the Ylydii ship reached the planet, it would only take a few minutes for it to cross too far into the atmosphere to be rescued. It would crash, and all of this would be for nothing.

Run that by me again? Shon asked.

Never mind. Fly a straight skim pattern down the line.

Shon understood what he intended to do. *Burn, you can't fire that fast.*

StarFire can, and it's hooked itself directly into my brain. Burn set the sphere spin to maximum. *Do it, Shon. It's the only way we can get at them.*

Shon brought the ship about and flew directly at the line of strafers, turning the *IceBlade* on its side so that it presented only the upper hull to their weapons' fire. Burn began firing at each ship as they passed, so rapidly that the pulse fire appeared as a continuous stream.

Halfway through the strafers, the *Wavelight* came up alongside the *IceBlade* and shadowed Shon's profile. Dair's ship acted like a shield and took the pulse fire intended for the *IceBlade.*

What the hell is that crazy female doing? Shon shouted.

Playing dam, Burn muttered as the sphere slowed. Dair's ship was blocking all of his shots, too. *She'll keep them off our tail, I think.*

Dair did exactly as Burn predicted. Once Shon had flown out of firing range, she took a position between the *IceBlade* and the rest of the patrol and sat like a guard between them, her weapons aimed at the patrol.

Burn disengaged StarFire, wincing again as the leads withdrew from his haffets, and looked around the sphere. The liquid atmosphere tasted faintly of his blood. He rubbed one of his haffets. *Maybe StarFire does need a little more testing in the lab.*

Shon flew on course to dock with the Ylydii vessel. *We're only ten minutes from geostationary orbit,* he warned Burn. *When we board, we have to do this fast.*

Liana was the one who answered him. *It won't take that long, Major.*

* * *

A group of concerned-looking Ylydii crew members were waiting for them inside the ship. Liana waited only long enough to assure that Major Valtas was given the proper breathing rig before she moved past the fussing females and into the corridor.

Burn caught up with her. *Have you picked up the agent's scent?*

You could say that. She swam directly to the ship's helm, where the captain was issuing orders to assume orbit. Carada, Fokrej, and Miglan were also on the helm, and all three reacted violently to Liana's arrival.

My lady, we were told you were dead! Miglan squeaked.

Fokrej hurtled toward her, his barbs ready, only to be knocked aside by Burn. *How dare you touch me!*

Go near her again, Burn told him, *and I'll bite your bloody head off.*

Carada surged forward with her fins unfurled, until she came snout-to-snout with Liana. *How did you do it? A clone?*

An exchange with the Goddess, Liana said. *This female is not my mother, Burn. She kidnapped the real Carada from Ylyd some time ago and took her place.*

Burn whirled to give her a stunned look. *You knew she was the agent, all this time?*

Fokrej uttered a horrible sound and swam directly at the two females. The imposter produced a strange-looking emitter and shot the Ylydii male with a focused beam of energy. The beam punched a hole through Fokrej's skull and killed him instantly.

I never liked him, Carada said to Burn. *But he had his uses.*

Like torturing me to insure my silence and cooperation Liana regarded the SEAL agent. *It wasn't Fokrej who kept me silent. It was knowing you held my mother hostage and would kill her if I did not.* She looked at Burn. *At least, that is what I believed. Just before she shot me in the head, she told me that my mother had never been held hostage. She was killed as soon as she was captured.*

I do regret that, the agent said, *but we needed the body parts. They're down in one of the storage bays, if you would like to wish her a final farewell.*

No, Liana said. *I am finished with taking commands from you.*

You can't stop this, Liana, the imposter told her. *The ship's engines will be failing any moment, and the damage to them cannot be easily fixed. I will have the chance to send off one more frantic message—for which I will turn off our jammer—and tell how the Ninrana have attacked us and are sacrificing us to their Gods, just before we crash. When they search the site, they will find Carada and your remains, along with anyone else who could tell the story differently.*

And Urloy-ka? Burn asked harshly.

The agent looked into Liana's eyes and moved back. *The Ninrana were given a choice: cooperate and live, or fight and watch the Hsktskt bombard their miserable world into dust. They chose to cooperate. What is wrong with your eyes?*

I am a royal female of Ylyd, Liana said as she unfurled her veils, including the two that lay tucked and hidden under twin flaps of hide that ran the length of her spine. She knew her black eyes were turning a bright and glowing green now. *Didn't your research tell you about Ylydii who are born of the green?*

We knew you had the green markings of a queen. Why do you think I was made your mother's twin?

Liana's spine flexed as the multijointed spines of her embracing veils slowly curled out into the liquid atmosphere. It took time, for they were twice as long as her body. *I will be queen, yes, but not because of my colors.* She moved in toward the agent. *It is because of my song, and my embrace.*

The agent scoffed. *Singing does not make a monarch.*

Liana answered with deathsong, and watched the notes paralyze the agent, Burn, everyone on the helm. The agent's emitter weapon fell from her slack grasp and floated down to the deck. Liana's embracing veils lifted, revealing the barbs concealed in the green, flowing membranes. Unlike her other barbs, this pair were a meter long and shaped like swords. Her other veils extended around them, creating a net. She summoned the agent to her with her song, and the imposter swam forward as if in a dream.

Liana's song crested on a high, pure note as her veils wrapped around the agent. With a single contraction, she drove both of her embracing barbs into the agent's body. When she released her victim, the agent's body floated away in three pieces.

It took a moment for the effects of the deathsong to fade, and then Burn came to her. *Is there anything else I should know?*

Yes. Liana touched his cheek. *I love you, and I want to be with you. Always.*

Oh, I'm never saying no to you again. He held her close for a moment. *But let's evacuate the ship first.*

The reception for the Mayer-Hansen wedding was held at the URD, so that Ylydii and older 'Zangian friends of the couple could attend in comfort. Among other refreshments provided were a penned feeding area for the aquatics on the outside of the dome, and a long banquet table inside filled with food from a dozen different worlds. It was there that Ana Hansen found her assistant, Emily, in deep conversation with her Omorr friend, Dr. Hkyrim.

"I don't know, Emily." He was giving one of the dessert dishes a dubious inspection. "Seed pod flesh with ground seed and bark in crushed grain paste?"

"Apple tarts," her assistant told him. "They're delicious, and they don't taste anything like pillow stuffing. Hello, boss."

As Ana greeted the pair, she felt glad that Liam had found a treatment to neutralize the nanites released by Noel Argate on K-2. It made it possible for the Omorr to remain on-planet, and was also helping the Core, who had also had adverse reactions to the nanite contamination.

"Have you tried anything yet?" Ana asked, looking at their empty plates.

"We are still making our choices," the Omorr said.

Ana smiled. "Save some room for cake."

As she walked away, she heard Hkyrim say to Emily, "Do not tell me what the ingredients are this time."

Ana went to William and slipped an arm around her new husband. "You look so handsome in a tux."

"You are beautiful." Once more he admired the traditional ivory wedding tunic gown she wore. "Have you heard from Teresa?"

Her smile dimmed. "Not for weeks. She left the planet right after that 'shrike escaped from the expedition vessel. Dair hasn't had a single signal, either. Teresa charted a private transport; we don't even know where she went."

Onkar walked up and offered a polite wish for prosperity. "There is someone who would like to speak with you both, Administrator, but she cannot leave the water."

"One of the Ylydii." Ana took Liam's hand in hers. "You'll have to act meek and submissive."

She laughed out loud when he leaned over to whisper, "Later."

The newlyweds went to the moon pool, where Ana was surprised to see Dairatha circling around the tank. Another, smaller 'Zangian with a lighter hide was hovering in the center of the pool, and looked up when the two Terrans approached the edge.

"I don't recognize her," Ana murmured, and called to Dairatha. "Is this someone from another pod?"

The big male only strummed a laugh and swam over to the female, who lifted her sleek head from the water and ejected water from her gillets before filling her lungs with air.

Ana nearly fell into the pool when she saw the female's familiar eyes. "Terri?"

"It's me," Teresa Selmar's voice said. "Well, some of the inside things still are, anyway. Everything else is 'Zangian SEAL augmented and still healing, so I can't leave the water yet. By the way, do you know how annoying it is to breathe air when your body is used to breathing water? I feel like apologizing to every 'Zangian I ever made to come up topside."

"I don't believe it," Ana said faintly. "You gave up your body? To become an aquatic?"

"I finally figured out that I was born in the wrong body." Teresa looked down at Dairatha. "We're going away for awhile, Ana. To give me time to learn how to live out here. I'll be back, and seeing you both again. Give my love to Dair." With that Teresa dove under the water and disappeared with Dairatha.

Ana turned to Liam. "How am I going to explain this to Jadaira? A Terran alterforming herself to become 'Zangian?"

"After the honeymoon," Liam said, and kissed her.

Burn saw the two Terrans nuzzling and decided not to disturb them. He returned to the main reception area and went to the panel where his mate was watching from the water. Znora was at her side, and fussing, as she had been doing since discovering Liana was pregnant. Oddly, Liana seemed to enjoy the attention, and even now she gave him an amused look.

He looked at Dair when she joined him. "Well, at least I didn't have to dress up and say all those words with Liana."

"No, you just have to go and rule Ylyd with her," Dair snapped.

Burn strummed out a laugh. "Didn't I tell you? Liana gave up the throne or queenship or whatever it is. There's another female like her who is almost old enough to take her place, and the ruling queen agreed to let Liana stay on K-2."

"Good, you'd make a lousy king." Dair's expression softened. "You also have a new assignment. As your next duty ship, you're flying Rescue Three."

"I thought that was Shon's ship."

"Shon is leaving." She sighed. "I don't know why but he says he has to."

Burn thought of telling her, but remembered his promise to Shon. Also he thought the oKiaf should be the one to tell his cousin about his gift. "He'll be back. In the meantime, give Rescue Three to someone else."

"Someone else?" Dair tapped the side of his head. "Hello, cousin, you've been pestering me for months to fly that ship."

"I know. It's just that someone needs to keep testing Starfire, and Verrig wants to update the strafer weapons array, and . . . I'm a gunner,

Dair. It's what I do best. I know it's not as grand as a pilot, but it's what I am, and what I want to be."

"I'll still need you as a backup pilot," she warned, and then shook her head. "I can't believe it. All those hours training, all those sim sessions, and all it did was teach you that you were fine as you were?"

"Oh, I'll never be the same." Burn looked out at his mate. "But I'm going to try to be better than I was."